Ex Libris

Leslie Bell

A FALCON FOR A QUEEN

A Falcon for a Queen

CATHERINE GASKIN

DOUBLEDAY & COMPANY, INC., GARDEN CITY, NEW YORK

For Terry and Tom with love

THE CLANS
The Mottos

MACDONALD OF CLANRANALD
My hope is constant in thee.

CAMPBELL OF CAWDOR
Be mindful.

SINCLAIR
Commit thy work to God.

MACPHERSON
Touch not the cat bot a glove.

(MAC)LACHLAN
Brave and trusty.

FERGUSON
Sweeter after difficulties.

Prologue

There are places in the valley where I will never go again; there are paths up its glens where I will never direct my pony's steps. The faces, the voices, the names meet me there, and they do not go away. Regularly, of course, I must cross the path through the graveyard to the kirk, where those names are chiseled into the stone. But the spirits do not lie there; for me, they do not lie there. They are the restless ghosts—those who loved—wrongly, wilfully, with passion, without reason. They all wait for me, everywhere in that valley, but especially in some places, to which I do not go. Ballochtorra begins to crumble on its height; the rains and the snows take their toll of the roof, the ice creeps in to break chinks in the walls. The ivy is taking possession; very soon it will need the knowing eye to distinguish what was newly built, in the pride of wealth and ambition, from the very old. The rooks gather in the ivy-grown trees and on the battlements. And forever, ceaselessly, my eyes search the skies for the sight of a falcon.

Chapter 1

I

It is a long way to come from China to the depths of the Scottish Highlands for the sake of a few words splashed in confused Mandarin script down the side of a scroll with a drawing of a bird perched on a bare willow bough. But I had come, unbidden, unexpected, and for all I knew, unwelcome. I had come because my brother, William, lay buried in a churchyard in the heart of the Highlands, and before he had died had scratched those few words. Yes, a long way to come.

I had sent no message, no telegram, perhaps for fear that I could be turned back—from what I knew of Angus Macdonald he was capable of doing that. So I stood with my trunk and my father's leather bag on the tiny station of Ballinaclash, and there was no one to meet me, and, so far as I could judge, no way to get where I wanted to go.

The stationmaster shook his head. "Cluain, is it? Well, that will be a good six miles and more. They are not expecting you . . . they did not send the gig." The curiosity was evident; only an innate kind of courtesy held back the open questions the man longed to ask. "I'm very sorry, mistress, there will be no conveyance for hire about here. As you can see, it is not even a village. Just a halt when there's a passenger, and to collect the post, and such."

"There has to be some way . . ." I shivered; it was chill, and it was going to rain. Who would have expected to be dropped here in the middle of a seeming wilderness, pine and larch lining the steep railway cutting, and the sound of the train already lost in the distance as it had rounded the bend? There were no houses, no smoke curling from chimneys; there was nothing but the promise of rain, and the anxious, bewildered stare of the stationmaster. Clearly, no one came to Ballinaclash unheralded—not even from Inverness, much less from China. Clearly, also, I must be mad to have done it.

But there was something; beside the sigh of the wind through the pines, and the automatic clicking of the railway telegraph in the little office, there was the sound of footsteps behind me, and out in front of the station, tucked into the shelter of the building, was a small, one-horse landau, the horse's head held by a man in a long tweed cape. He too was staring at me, and past me, and at that moment he took off his hat; but the action wasn't for me.

"I see your bags there." I turned; the man who had evidently got off one of the end carriages of the train and walked along the track with his single bag in his hand, had also raised his hat, but he put it back on. A long, quizzical face, under blond-streaked hair; his eyes were an intense, light blue which might have seemed innocent and even childlike if it hadn't been for the lines cut deeply at the corners, lines that almost exactly paralleled those at the corners of his mouth. It was a youngish face, and yet weary—or was it the face of a young man, disenchanted.

He continued, with no trace of shyness. "No one has come to meet you? My name is Campbell."

He was so cool, so matter-of-fact, that he would have flustered me if I hadn't been so tired, and had so much else to think of.

"How do you do," I said automatically. Didn't one say that in polite society, however absurd the place and the meeting? The forms were always observed. "No—no one has come to meet me. I'm not expected. I thought I could perhaps hire . . ."

He was already shaking his head, and I thought I detected a half-shrug of the shoulders, as if in wonderment at the foolishness of some people. "Well, now you see you can't, miss . . . ? Is it miss?"

"Howard," I said.

4

For a second the detachment fell away. "Howard? You're William Howard's sister! Yes—*yes,* I should have known. You look like him."

The sound of the name was comfort. It was so long since anyone had spoken it. No one, since I had left China, had spoken William's name. "You knew William?" I clutched at the thought.

"Yes . . . yes, I knew him. Not well, but then he wasn't here that long."

"No—not long. Just those visits from Edinburgh, and then last summer . . ."

He did not let me dwell on it. Already he had taken my arm, and at the same time was beckoning the man who stood by the horse. "Stevens, give Mr. McBane here a hand with the luggage. All of it. We'll be taking Miss Howard to Cluain."

"Cluain, sir? *Cluain*—" But then he stopped abruptly, as if there had been some authoritative signal from the man who held my arm. I felt I was being rushed, my decisions made for me. And yet, why not? My immediate problem was solved; I was grateful, as well as tired.

"I like to drive," the man said. "Do you mind coming up front with me, or will the wind be too much for you? Stevens can sit with the baggage."

I nodded; what was a little wind? The man had spoken William's name, and seemed to call him back to life. I let myself be helped up on to the seat, and then the man swung himself up beside me, taking the reins from Stevens. Then we waited as the bags were brought, carried by the stationmaster and Stevens, and stowed in the passenger space. Everyone seemed to move swiftly to Campbell's orders, yet there was an odd comradeship between them all; there was no sign of servility cloaking resentment. The stationmaster was relieved to have me off his hands—but yet he had shown a concern for me. He raised his cap as we prepared to move off.

"Well, then now, mistress. You'll be grand now, and like as not there'll be no rain before you reach Cluain . . ."

Campbell made a vague salute of thanks with the whip, and we were off. The vehicle was well sprung, the horse strong and good, even the road between the pines and larches seemed smooth. It didn't even seem cold any longer.

"I hope I'm not—" I began.

"Oh, now," he cut me short. "Please, I beg you, don't start all those politenesses. Would I have left you standing there on Ballinaclash station? If you're silly enough not to have warned them that you were coming, then the least I can do is save you from some of the consequences of your folly. I don't think," he added, without emphasis, "that Angus Macdonald likes surprises."

"Perhaps not. We'll see. All he can do is turn me away."

"He'll not turn you away. The world may think us barbarians here in the Highlands—oh, romantic barbarians, perhaps, but still barbarians. But somehow, in all our poverty, we still have our traditions of hospitality, which we keep. And I suspect that Angus Macdonald is a believer in blood being thicker than water. You're the only grandchild he had left." Then, with devastating candour came the thrust. "It was William he wanted, of course. A girl will hardly be of much use to him."

"No," I answered flatly. "I hardly expect to be of much use."

He glanced at me quickly, and then back to the road, his rather austere face softening a little, as if he regretted his words. "So . . . you decided to come here, after your father died?"

"You knew that my father was killed?"

"The whole kingdom knew it. Perhaps you don't realise how good the British newspapers are at whipping themselves into a frenzy over a tragic and bloody happening far away—most especially when it concerns a bishop of the Established Church. For a couple of days they were in a fever over it. There was talk of sending gunboats. Imperial dignity had been gravely insulted. I wonder if anyone thought of what you must have suffered then—with William so recently dead."

"Perhaps it was merciful that I didn't know William was dead at the time. My grandfather's letter had not reached us. He doesn't seem to believe in telegrams, either."

"Good God!" He looked at me again, for longer this time. "You were quite alone, then, when the news of William came. I'm very sorry, Miss Howard. You've had . . ." Now his voice dropped so

6

that it was hard to hear above the sound of the hooves, the rush of the wind through the trees. "You've had a very bad time."

"My father had many friends . . . they helped very much. Yes, we knew about the talk of gunboats, but no one in England seemed to realise that my father was killed in a local uprising two hundred miles from the point at which the Great River—the Yangtze—is navigable by a gunboat. And what use would it have been? I knew it was the last thing my father would have wished. It was senseless, hysterical talk. These things are dealt with in their own way in China. But people in England seem to have some very odd ideas about China. When I prayed in those days, I prayed that the Foreign Secretary was better informed than the journalists."

They were plain, sensible words, calm words, ones I had long ago reasoned myself into, to try to stop the hurt. But yes, he was right, it had been a bad time. Very bad. But China was often cruel, and violent death was common. The hardest thing to bear had been the thought that it need not have been my father; there were many others he could have sent on that journey. But he never excused himself from what he conceived to be his duties—never sought to, because he loved them. Even when visitation literally meant journeys of a thousand miles, and he would often be cold and hungry, his clothes sodden, or his skin burned with the fierce heat of those summers. No, the progress of a bishop in China had little in common with the stately procession from one parish to another he had described to me, with a kind of a laugh, as being the custom in England. To be fair, the Church paid for a greater dignity than my father ever maintained, he saying that there was so much else to spend the money on in China than keeping up episcopal state. He travelled usually only with one curate, who acted as his secretary. There could have been few bishops who had the frightful distinction of ending their lives with their heads on one of the ever-present bamboo poles of the Chinese. He had been unlucky. He could hardly even have consoled himself in those last horrible moments that he was dying in the cause of bringing the light of the faith to the heathen hordes. He had been unfortunate enough to have been caught unwittingly in a rising against a local war-lord in the remote Szechwan Province—he and the curate

7

and two engineers travelling with him to prospect the route of a future railway into the interior. The forces of the war lord had not come quickly enough to save the foreign devils. It was all the more sport for the faceless mass of peasants that one of their victims had been a high priest serving the foreign god. Some of the leaders of the rising had been punished with the usual refinements of public torture and execution by the war lord. We had all known in Peking that no gunboats or expedition would be necessary. And my father's body had been sent back for burial. They had tried not to let me know how brutally he had died. But I did know; one always knew these things in China.

It had not been enough. Their gods, or my God, had decided it had not been enough. Less than a month after that burial came a letter and a chest which buried the last I had in the world. There was a letter, addressed to my father, in Angus Macdonald's formal script and phrases: "Your son, my grandson, William Howard, has died as the result of a hunting accident in the lands above Cluain. He is buried among his forebears in the kirkyard of St. Andrew in the parish of Ballochtorra, according to the rites of the Established Church of Scotland. Should you wish . . ." My father had no more wishes; he too was buried, according to the rites of the Anglican Church, in the British Legation compound in Peking. And I was in possession of William's personal effects, dispatched to Peking along with the letter. And they included the scroll, the line drawing of the bird on the bare branch, with the confused, inaccurate characters in Mandarin splashed down its edge.

And to what, and for what, had I journeyed? From Peking to Tientsin, by river to the coast, by larger boat to Hong Kong, then by British steamer through the Red Sea and Suez Canal to the smoke and soot of London. Then by train on to Scotland, heading towards the heart of the Highlands, to Inverness, and then, by branch line to Ballinaclash, and from there . . . well, this man, Campbell, was taking me where I had decided to go—to Cluain.

How little I knew of it. How little I had cared to ask. Of course, all the English-speaking world had some fanciful notion of the Highlands. Hadn't we all seen those formalised sketches of the Queen and her Consort, and the castle they had built at Balmoral?

—and from a later date there were those sad daguerreotypes of the dumpy little Queen in her widow's weeds seated on a pony held by her gillie in his Highland dress. Pictures of stags and misty glens, tales of feuds and rebellions, and brave, hardy men—the novels of Walter Scott. But the Diamond Jubilee had been celebrated the year before, and Victoria was now very old, and had to be in the last years of her reign; Edward, the Prince of Wales, had waited almost beyond a man's patience to assume the responsibilities for which he had been a figurehead so long. The century was dying, as the old Queen was; and I knew very well that the reality of the Highlands must be quite different from those misty pictures. There had to be winter here, and people who did not live in castles. Why hadn't I asked more about Cluain? In the letters written in answer to William's I had hardly mentioned it, must less questioned him about it. Had I resented his inexplicable attachment to it, the place he had not even wanted to visit? He had gone to Edinburgh University to study engineering, and he had been expecting, in time, that he too would be planning and building China's railways, competing, as all the foreign interests did, for the concessions of its rich trade. But Angus Macdonald had known he was in Edinburgh, and letters had passed between them. William had at first gone to Cluain unwillingly. "I suspect this old man is possessive," he had written to me before the first visit, "and I have to be free to do what I have always dreamed of doing. I have to belong to myself." There had not been any more written about being free. He had returned to Cluain at Christmas, and at Easter, and then the whole of the following summer. But it had been the onset of winter at Cluain again when he had died, and now it was the early days of June.

My father had died in the middle of a Chinese winter without knowing his son was already dead, and his belongings and Angus Macdonald's letter already on the way. It had been the frozen earth for both of them, so far apart. I wondered now why, since I had not asked William, I had not thought to ask my father about Cluain: Was it because I sensed that he felt a guilt about it, and it was cruel to probe it? I knew it was a breach that had never mended. He had married the only child of Cluain, and had taken her far away; she too lay in the Legation compound in Peking. He had known Cluain only for one summer—one summer's idyll in the Highlands, and he had been deeply in love. So I asked nothing, did not care to remind him, and he did not speak of it. I had let myself be absorbed in the life of China—the life that foreigners knew, that is, because no outsider could truthfully claim to know it fully. I had thought I would probably marry there—and yet I had fixed my thoughts on none of the young men who came and went at the Legation. I had wanted someone who would stay in China. Unconsciously, perhaps, I had waited for William's return. I would have wanted his good opinion of any man I would marry. I had thought to make China my life, as it was my father's and would be William's. But now it was all behind me, the silken luxuries and savage cruelties, and I was headed towards Cluain, forearmed with so little knowledge, open to the wind. Perhaps, then, I shivered.

"You're cold," the man said. "I'm sorry. It was thoughtless of me to have put you up here on the box. I could have ridden down there with you. But I've been a week in Edinburgh and when I've been away from here I have a terrible longing to be back. And when I'm back I have to sit up high, and see it all again. I know I'm home then."

"I'm not cold," I answered. "Perhaps just tired. And I know what you mean—about seeing it all . . ." There was so much to see, and try to know. It was beautiful; even my tired, bewildered gaze could appreciate that. Beautiful, but not soft. We passed from clumps of trees to vistas of open meadows, and beyond them boggy moorland. The wind raced through the young green crops; we seemed to climb and descend endlessly—sometimes through open expanses of moor, sometimes the road wound down and up a glen so narrow that the very light seemed to be shut out. As the clouds scudded before the wind, from time to time, I saw the mountains —I knew they had to be part of the Cairngorm Range. I had studied the map of Scotland so many times since Angus Macdonald's letter. We passed little cottages huddled where they could find a vestige of shelter—I knew the snows would come here, as they did in China. It was strange and wild, and it exhilarated me in a way I

10

had not expected. My mother's blood was in me also, I thought. Suddenly I began to understand the feeling of recognition which must have stirred in William.

Then I saw it—a great place perched on a craggy outcrop above a river, a river whose white water tumbled and sparkled even on this grey afternoon. The place itself was high and old, turreted and battlemented; the centre building was of a great age, and had once been a fortress dominating the narrow pass through the glen. But obviously when times had grown more peaceful, portions had been added to it, and gardens laid out in broad terraces that descended to the river. Despite the gardens, its splendour had still a kind of grimness about it.

"What is that?"

"Ballochtorra."

It was a name already in my heart; William would lie buried somewhere near.

"Who lives there?"

"A Campbell." Then he added, turning and half-smiling at me—the first time I had seen a smile. "I do."

"Then why did you say it like that—a Campbell?"

"Because you, Miss Howard, are a Macdonald, whether you're called that or not. In Scottish history, ever since the massacre at Glencoe—oh, and before that, even—the Macdonalds and the Campbells are thought to be implacable enemies. It wasn't always true, of course. Often they had fought on the same side—just as often they've faced each other with drawn swords. As have most clans in Scotland. They've raided each other's cattle and castles. They've taken each other's women. Sometimes they've even arranged peaceful marriages. But you and I—we're supposed by outsiders to be hereditary enemies, but in fact it was different septs of our clans who were involved at Glencoe. You are a Macdonald of Clanranald, and I'm a Campbell of Cawdor. But still it was Campbells who were quartered on Macdonalds at Glencoe, and who took their hospitality, and who slew them that morning in the February snow—all from seven to seventy years old. Five o'clock in the morning, and many of them tumbling out of their beds, and

11

ending lying naked and dead in the snow. It isn't forgiven or forgotten—even if the Macdonalds were rebels against King William of Orange—and the Campbells were said merely to be carrying out orders. That it was done by stealth by men living in the houses of their victims is what is not forgiven. It happened more than two hundred years ago, but we're still supposed to hate each other. Scotland's been peaceful for a long time now, and it's only fanatics who keep bringing up the Stuarts and Bonnie Prince Charlie. We have our old Hanoverian queen living here among us, and none would think of harming her, or her son. But it's a romantic, foolish game we Scots play that all the clans still share ties of brotherhood and blood. We've been as cruel to each other as men could be—Ballochtorra there would tell its tales, and its dungeons were there for other reasons than storing wines. But your name is Macdonald and my name is Campbell, and we're supposed never to let the memory of Glencoe die. Even though you and I are distant cousins."

I sat upright. "Cousins? How?"

He shrugged. "It does happen. Oh, it's an old story, and your grandfather would like to keep its memory bright, because he won himself a great personal victory from it. He won the best that Ballochtorra owned. He won the dower house of Ballochtorra, which is Cluain. With it he won the best lands in the strath, the lands that in the old days gave Ballochtorra its grain and cattle—gave it the lands to rent out to tenant farmers, who, in turn, gave service to the Campbells in times of trouble, so that the chief of the Campbells would protect *their* lands and houses, their women and children. Most would take the name of Campbell—or Macdonald or Frazer or Grant—whatever was the name of the chief they served. That's how the clan system worked then, when it was a real need, not a decoration. They clung together for mutual protection, as families do. And as families do, they often quarrelled. It was a system. It worked in its time. But that time is over now. On the order of the English, after the Stuarts' last hope vanished with Prince Charlie at Culloden Moor, the clan system was broken. For many years no Highlander could wear the tartan, or bear arms. But we would do better to forget it, or at least understand where it

12

belongs. It would be better if you and I were not expected to mistrust and dislike each other just because of our names."

"Montague and Capulet . . ."

He sighed, a sound I heard even above the wind. "Yes, Montague and Capulet, if you like. Forgive me for indulging in all this lecturing on something you perhaps already know—but you will perhaps be happier here if you remember a few of these things." We were crossing a graceful arched stone bridge, and he glanced up at the heights of Ballochtorra. "That was one of the things so attractive about William—he had many qualities we all liked. He was like a clean wind blowing through all this nonsense. He hadn't come with any preconceived ideas. He didn't hate Campbells because of their name. And he went against everything your grandfather believed in when he came to visit at Ballochtorra."

"He always said he would be his own man."

"He was. I never believed he would do anything he didn't want to do. You were very fond of William." It was said in the same matter-of-fact tone.

"I had only one brother. In China one is isolated. There are fewer of one's own kind. I hardly know how other brothers and sisters feel about each other—if they are as close as we were. He was the elder—he led me everywhere. For a long time I didn't know what to think before asking William. He was like Father—but so much nearer my age."

"And he led you here?"

"Perhaps."

We had started on the steep ascent again, the road winding up around the castle to take the bend along the shelf of the crag. We came to a gatehouse, stone-built, but quite new, I thought—turreted in the fashion of the castle; splendid iron gates were embellished with a gold-tipped shield, the armorial bearings a bird of some sort, with long arched neck, like a hissing swan. The gold leaf was so fresh I could read the motto above the bird: *BE MINDFUL.* I wondered if it were meant as advice or warning.

I could not help the touch of acid. "For those who have lost their best lands to another clan, you appear to be very prosperous."

13

He nodded. "Oh, yes—our good farming lands are gone. What we still have are the moors for rich men to shoot on."

"Then you are rich."

"Let us say my wife is rich."

I was too tired; I couldn't take in any more of it. So I let the remark slide past me. I knew that soon I would face Cluain, and whatever waited for me there. I felt my shoulders sag, and it was then I truly began to feel the cold. The trees that had been cleared to give the castle its prominence were appearing again, an ancient planting of oak and beech. We were rounding the bend and coming out into a broad meadowland beside the river when I saw him. It would have been easy to miss him. He stood within the shadow of a beech, and the leaves above him were the only things that moved; the dog at his side was just as motionless. The man was dark—I could barely see his face in the shadow; he wore a kilt, some faded red pattern it was, and a ragged sheepskin jerkin above it. He looked at us steadily; his hand was raised, but not in greeting. We were almost past before I saw the bird perched on that raised gloved hand. A large bird, what kind I didn't know, but with intensely dark eyes, as still and unblinking as the man and the dog. Perhaps they all moved their eyes to watch us, but none turned a head. Oddly, though, Campbell, beside me, raised his whip in brief, rather curt salute; the man did not respond. Then they were behind us, that strange trio, and somehow I managed not to turn my own head to look back at them.

"What will you do at Cluain?"

"Who knows. Perhaps I won't stay."

We went on in silence for some time. Then he said: "Angus Macdonald was bitterly grieved by William's death. William must have seemed an answer to all his hopes. I have only glimpsed him once in the months since then. He seemed to me very aged. Perhaps it would be a kindness if you made yourself stay, whatever happens."

"Does that mean you believe I will not be welcome? I told you I was not expected."

"Who's to say? Cluain is not an ordinary household. If you should

14

need a friend . . . if you should need somewhere to come, Balloch-torra is close by."

"And your wife—will she welcome me?"

"She will welcome whomever I do. She welcomes a lot that I don't. That is no reflection on her, but on me. I'm not . . . very sociable."

"You have done *me* a service for which I'm sure my grandfather would wish to thank you. I'm sure Cluain will not fail in the Highland hospitality you were speaking of. After all—as you said—I am his only grandchild." And then quickly added, to cover myself: "Most likely I will not stay long."

"Not stay? A pity . . ." A pity for whom, I wondered. But now he was gesturing again with his whip, and the reins urged the horse to a quicker gait. "There it is now—Cluain."

It stood there alone in the broad meadows that rose gently from the river; the wind riffled through the young green grain; the cattle grazed the early summer grasses on the higher pastures, and those down towards the river. The cloud had lifted, and the mountains were clear and sharp, the wind blowing straight off them. I could not easily pick out the dwelling house of Cluain, because the other buildings dominated it. There were not just the usual outbuildings of a good farm, but a long series of identical stone sheds, adjoining one another, which must be used for warehousing, I thought. Then there was the odd stone pile with the chimneys that ended in pagoda-like domes that might have come there straight from China. It was a strange sight—the grouping of buildings in the midst of a rural scene, like some factory pile lifted from the industrial North through which the train had taken me, but with these stones cleansed of soot and grime by the slashing rain from the mountains. I had not known what to expect a whisky distillery to look like, but this had not been in my mind.

"Angus Macdonald claims," Campbell said, "that he makes the finest malt whisky in the whole Highlands, and I've never heard anyone seriously dispute that claim. Now he is old, and William had become his great hope. I'm afraid he is a very sad and angry man . . ."

The road down from Ballochtorra's crag had taken such a wide curve to bring it to the level of the river meadows that now it had to wind back on itself to approach Cluain; the whole group of buildings faced us on a diagonal, so that we looked into the very centre of it. The house I could now identify—the first building we would reach, the smallest and oldest. There was a stable block, and a cobbled yard that served stables and house and distillery. Across the road, beginning in a line with the distillery, began the long row of warehouse buildings. These were low—one storey only, but with roofs of dark slate. Although the pagoda chimneys of the distillery dominated the scene, the brooding bulk of the warehouses—stretching along the road like a great gabled terrace—had a compelling quality about them, a sense of permanence. From the height of Ballochtorra I had seen the roofs of farm buildings behind the distillery, and strung out along the road past the warehouses, some cottages with garden plots. A town all to itself, it seemed, and yet strangely quiet, as if everyone had gone and left it.

But it did not remain quiet. A dog barked, and as the landau drew near to the house a great flock of geese came at a wild run from the direction of the warehouses, hissing and shrieking. Behind me I heard Stevens's half-stifled oath, and Campbell had to hold the horse in tighter to prevent it shying. Stevens slipped out of his seat and went to the horse's head; we moved on at a slow walk, and Campbell tossed the whip to Stevens, who used it to gesture the geese away. Finally, even the big gander in charge of the flock began reluctantly to accept our presence; he gave a honking signal, and the whole white stream of birds turned and waddled back to the warehouses, delighted, I guessed, with the fuss they had caused.

"Damned animals," Stevens grumbled. "They should not be allowed. This is a public highway."

Campbell did not answer him. The flurry of geese seemed to have brought no one to mark our arrival. The landau now stood before the house. In the confusion, I had not had time to look at it closely, but now it took on its overwhelming importance, as the very heart of Cluain. It was not, as we stood beside it, after all, so small. It was simply that the other buildings were bigger. They all shared the same, almost painful, neatness. The house was much the oldest of the group—the dower house of Ballochtorra, it would have stood for perhaps two centuries before the distillery. It was L-shaped, built about two sides of a courtyard. The high stone wall of this courtyard was flush to the wall of the house itself, and an ancient studded door, like the door of the house, faced directly on to the road. Despite the noise of our arrival, both remained unyieldingly closed. The whole structure was built of massive, irregularly cut stone, two-storeyed, with gabled windows in the steep-pitched roof. What lifted it from the mere dignity of its age and good lines was a piece of sheer fantasy. Where the two wings of the building joined, a tower rose, its slightly inward-inclining walls reaching well above the rest of the house, and capped with a perfect rondel of slate, and a magnificently ornate weather vane. Its total proportions were so perfect that it seemed almost like a child's toy piece. My eye had long been educated to the studied delicacy of the Chinese houses, their walls and courtyards, the exquisite sense of detail that was not absent from anything they fashioned, so I responded to this place as if I had been born to it—as William must also have done. He had written that Cluain was beautiful; how beautiful, and in what way, he had not said.

Stevens went and banged the knocker on the door; it seemed to be minutes before we caught a glimpse of a figure near the window of one of the front rooms, and almost as long before the door at last opened. The woman who stood there wasted no effort on taking in the details of the scene; her gaze went at once to me, and eyes—brilliant, dark, deeply set, and shadowed with black brows and lashes—seemed to scour me with their examination. She was dressed in servant's dress, completely black, even to the apron, severe, unadorned. Black hair, streaked with silver, was drawn sharply to the back of her head; it was a handsome face. Tall, slender, she had an unassailable dignity, standing there, just looking at me.

Even the man beside me, so cool and self-assured until now,

17

seemed struck with the same feeling as I. I could feel my throat dry. So, in the end, it was the woman who spoke first.

"If you had sent a telegram, we would have sent the trap. You are William Howard's sister."

How had she known? I was not so much like him. But she gave the impression that she knew things most people did not.

I struggled for composure; I was not going to be put out by a servant. But she was like no servant I had ever encountered. I made a movement, and Campbell came to life, leaping down off the seat, and hurrying round to help me down. Stevens had returned to hold the horse. I advanced towards the woman. "Mr. Macdonald is at home?"

"And why would Mr. Macdonald be at home at this time of day? We work at Cluain."

The insult was deliberate, telling me that if I expected to put her in her place I must know that I first had to find it. As I came closer I saw that she was older than she had seemed. There were fine lines in her pale skin, many lines; and then I saw her hands. They were shockingly red and worn with work, the skin broken at the knuckles as if caustic soap had bitten into it. But she held them before her like a badge of virtue, despising all who could not boast of gainful toil.

"I may wait then?"

She held the door a little wider. "Aye, certainly you may. I see you have brought your bags . . ." She did not pause to see the effect of the remark, but turned and called over her shoulder, as if she knew someone would be close by. "Morag . . . you are needed."

From the back of the hall a girl came at once, and indeed she had been waiting and listening. She rushed forward, like a sudden flaring of light beside that dark figure; red curling hair spilled without discipline from her cap; she had red, soft full lips and golden amber eyes. It was a perfect little heart-shaped face with white skin that flushed to apricot with excitement. No more than the woman beside her did she look like a servant, but she wore a white apron, and she bobbed me a slight curtsey.

"Welcome to Cluain, Mistress Howard. Och, it will do your

grandfather's heart good to set eyes on you." And she lifted her own glowing eyes to mine, and smiled.

There was a bustle as she ran forward to get the bags; Campbell helped her with them, for the woman in black would not step across the threshold. Silently she indicated where they might be placed inside the hall, as if Campbell were her servant also. I felt the hot blood of embarrassment rush to my face. I turned to the woman directly.

"You have the advantage of me, since you know my name. May I know yours?"

"I am Mairi Sinclair, housekeeper at Cluain."

"Then, Mistress Sinclair, may I, on my grandfather's behalf, offer this gentleman, Mr. Campbell, a cup of tea? He has been kind enough to bring me—"

But she was looking past me, and her wintery lips twitched.

"Sir Gavin, perhaps you will accept the hospitality of Cluain?" She knew he would not.

He didn't even look at her, knowing better than to play her game, it seemed. He returned to the doorway, and raised his hat to me. "I hope all goes well. If I can be of assistance . . . You saw I live not far away."

"Thank you—"

But the words were cut short by Mairi Sinclair. "We all know it's but a short step to Ballochtorra, Sir Gavin. Master William was not long in finding that out."

And then to my horror she closed the door in his face, and I was left there in the sudden dimness of the hall, for a moment helpless between this dark wraith of a figure, and this radiant sprite of a girl. Then a sentence from one of William's letters flashed into my brain, yet one other thing I had passed over, not wanting to question, perhaps jealous again. *There is a dragon-lady here whom I believe the Chinese would respect and admire —and there is also an enchantress.*

*   *   *

My eyes grew used to the dimmer light. What the stationmaster had predicted had come true; the rain, now it had come, slashed fiercely against the panes. There seemed a sudden massing of cloud across the valley—the strath, Gavin Campbell had called it. I repressed the shiver that rose, and cursed myself for an impetuous fool. Why had I not sent at least a telegram from London? Even more, why had I ever left those many friends in China who had offered homes to me, certain, as we all were, that young English-women always found husbands among the superfluity of men who came to reap the pickings of the rich trade. I had been a bishop's daughter, and there had been many who had loved my father. There had been little money—even bishops do not grow rich on missionary work. But we had been rich in friends and good-will; where servants and food are cheap, guests are a pleasure, not a burden. I could have made a slow progression from Peking to Shanghai, and even to Hong Kong, and I would have been welcome in a dozen houses. But I had chosen to come here, with no certain knowledge that I would stay, that I would even be asked to stay. And I had come all because of those nightmarish Mandarin characters scrawled down the length of William's scroll.

Remembering them, I lifted my head and looked carefully about me.

Approaching in the landau, the house had seemed miniature; inside it had space and depth, and a kind of grandeur, possibly the grandeur of antiquity. It was spare and high and severe; the thought came that it was a little like the woman who ruled over it. There was a great stone fireplace here in the hall, and two carved oak chairs set stiffly before it. There was a dark refectory table with silver candlesticks upon it. The hall ran the whole length of this front wing of the building; I could see where the staircase curved outward around the tower. It was a stone staircase, floating, seeming without support except for the massive slabs set into the wall of the tower. It had no bannister, only a rope handrail attached to the wall. Narrow windows gave light fitfully. But there was other light; everything that hand could polish gave back the outside light—the planked oak floors, the candlesticks, the dark carved furniture. There were no flowers, no rugs, no pictures. Even in the beautiful severity of the Chinese houses I had come to admire, there would have been a single

20

flower or a dried reed in a vase. Here there were no concessions
to human delight, or pleasure—nothing. But no denying hand could
take away this beauty. It had been shaped by unknown masters
of their craft hundreds of years ago. Having stripped it down to its
bare bones, it was only the more beautiful.

Then something brushed against me, and in the silence I almost
shrieked.

It was a cat. With difficulty I stood still as it investigated the
unfamiliar smell of my skirt and boots. I had known cats before—
the house in Peking had 'ways had cats, plump, striped creatures,
or black and white, on or o' r always sitting on my father's
desk, or on a chair or e veranda, stalking among the bamboo
brakes in the garden. But there had been no cats like this one.
It was all white, immaculately white, as if it often walked in the
rain, and preened itself daily. Finding no comfort from my skirts
it went to Mairi Sinclair, as to someone well trusted, and from the
shelter of her skirt, it raised its eyes to me. They were without
colour; no green or a blue in them, a pinkish tinge in that grey—
an albino cat staring up at me, an elegant slim white shape
against the black folds. It occurred to me that here also was a
thing without colour or adornment, and Mairi Sinclair's creature
as much as a cat will ever be. She did not put a hand down
to pat or fondle it. I began to feel that for both such an action
would have been unnecessary.

"I take it you will be staying the night?"

"Possibly." We both knew there was no place else to go, and
that obviously I had come with the thought to stay for many
nights. "That is," I thrust at her, "if you have room for me."

"Room, aye—and beds aplenty. All dry and well-aired. We have
few guests at Cluain, but you'll find nothing amiss in the arrangements. Come, Morag."

With a quick, jerking movement she seized the trunk by one
handle, and indicated to Morag to take the other. They set off
along the hall. I was left standing beside the leather bag, and
there was nothing to do but grasp it and hurry after them. It
was a large bag, and almost too long for me to carry, so that it
bumped against each step as I climbed. I found myself panting;

21

the two women ahead of me were so quick, and I had a sudden awful fear of plunging sideways over that unprotected stair. I was too tired. I longed for hot water, and food, and a warm bed. I longed not to have to face my grandfather this night.

When I reached the hall upstairs the two women seemed to have vanished; the stairs ended there, and two passages opened to follow the L-shape of the house. I stopped, bewildered. I could hear the quick words that passed between them, but they were nowhere in sight. Then I looked and saw that the tower itself had an arched opening—and a further spiral of stairs led on upwards within the walls themselves. It was still wide; the steps were broad wedges. They ended at the top of the tower in the most extraordinary room I had ever seen. It was suprisingly large, following the curve of its outer walls, with three windows that gave a view of the valley—past the distillery and along the river, across the gradually rising lands to the mountains, and up to the crag on which Ballochtorra was perched. There was a stone floor, and the centre of the room contained a raised platform piled with split logs, a long copper hood reached up to form a chimney flue, ending where the sloping curved ceiling came to its point. The ornate weather vane I had noticed must have capped the chimney pot. There was a fourposter bed, just fitted within two windows, hung with tartan curtains and covered with a wool spread of the same pattern. There was a tall hanging-cupboard with a drawer at the bottom set against the next space between the windows; beside it was a washstand. The third space was given to a desk that could only have been made especially for this room—it took the curve of the wall, and its ends were cut on the slant. The dark carved oak chair set before it was its match. There was an oak bench before the fire, and a standing sconce with two candles. Tartan curtains hung on wooden poles at each window, straight, without fringe or tie; they were a great splotch of colour against the white walls. The last space left between the windows was the door-way in which I stood.

The room was austere and plain—and quite magnificent.

"Was this—? Did my brother use this room?"

Mairi Sinclair turned from her task of stowing the chest as

22

neatly as it would fit beneath one of the windows; she was frowning, and I thought for a moment that it irked her because the curved walls must forever defeat the straight lines of most objects. "This room?—yes, the Master directed it."

Morag took the bag from my hand. " 'Tis high and lonely up here, and when the wind blows and the snow falls, you could feel you were lost on a mountain."

And high and mighty, I thought. Whoever lived in this room and saw Cluain's treasures spread before him would be tempted. Who would not feel the lonely splendour of this place, who might not ache to possess it? My grandfather had wanted William.

"Fanciful thoughts, Morag," Mairi Sinclair said. "The tower room is the pride of Cluain." Her tone almost suggested that she thought me not worthy of it, but at the same time she had sought to isolate me here. Whoever lived in this room must also be able to live with their own company.

I went close to one of the windows now and looked down on Cluain's two wings, and into the courtyard that was screened from the road by its high wall. Even from this height I could tell it was a garden that the Chinese might have delighted in—filled with the herbs of their wonderful cooking, and their healing medicines. The straight paths that met precisely in the middle at the sundial were encroached by the sprawl of lavender and thyme, sage and chamomile, fennel and parsley. The pervading neatness of Cluain was here defeated. The plants went their own wild, sweet way. I hoped I saw the hand of my grandfather here.

"The garden . . ." I began. There had to be some way to make contact with Mairi Sinclair.

"The garden is mine."

I repressed a sigh, and turned back to face her; for a moment her expression seemed unguarded, and she was not so much fierce, as pitiful, defending what she thought of as her own. But I could have been mistaken. Her tone was absolutely unrelenting as she spoke again.

"I'll be getting down, then. Morag shall bring you some water to wash. The Master will be here directly."

"You'll send for him?"

She shook her head. "No one sends for Angus Macdonald. It is almost time for him to be in for his supper. He is very punctual. You will oblige him by not keeping him waiting, Miss Howard."

Then they were both gone, with a backward look that contained a nod of encouragement from Morag. The rain came more strongly now, beginning to blot out Cluain's world, the mountains disappearing in the cloud, the mist boiling up until it almost veiled Ballochtorra. I was left alone, to make what I would of it—alone, except for the cat, which had settled itself upon the bed, paws folded in against its chest, staring at me with its wide colourless eyes. I tried to stare it down, but it was I, of course, who lost that contest.

*　　*　　*

Morag was back; I had heard the murmur of some song as she mounted the tower stairs, and she swept into the room with her blazing hair like some cheerful light. "There now, it's nice and hot," she announced as she set down the jug and a pile of snowy towels on the washstand. "And I'll just be giving you a wee bit of a fire. It's a little comfort you're needing now." As I watched, she rearranged the kindling with deft fingers, and put a match to a screw of paper. The dry wood caught at once; it was impossible not to know that Morag was one of those creatures for whom things always went right—quick, neat, clever in her movements, wasting no effort. She was as superior to her tasks as her face and hair were to her plain servant's dress.

"Do you live here, Morag?"

"Aye. I have my own room down there along the passage from Mistress Sinclair. The Master sleeps in the other wing. I have my own fire, and 'tis nice and cosy. The wages are fair, and the food is good—everyone eats well at Cluain."

"Is that why you came?"

She laughed. "I had not much choice, had I? I was born at Cluain. Mistress Sinclair delivered me. My father worked in the distillery, and we had our own house then. But he was killed when I was a wee thing—one of the drays overturned on the ice on that steep bit beyond the bridge at Ballochtorra, taking the whisky to the railhead. So then my mother came here to help Mistress Sinclair in the house. She stayed until I was eight, and then she was away to her sister in Inverness. She could not stick the loneliness any more—or Mistress Sinclair, she said—and I was welcome to come with her if I wanted."

"But you stayed . . ."

"I did. I had been to Inverness, and seen it, and the place where my aunt has her dressmaking business, and I did not like it—not one bit. Besides, the Master's wife was alive then, and she favoured me—her wee girl, she used to call me. My mother knew what she was about, leaving me at Cluain. I had my tasks to do, of course, but I had a better time of it than my mother could hope to give me. Lessons I had from Mistress Macdonald, and advantages that were beyond my mother. And Mistress Sinclair is not so bad when you know her ways—we rub along, and I am not such a fool that I have not learned from her, too. Where else would it be like this?—me with my own room, and the right to be private when I please. I've seen those skivvys in those town places, and I have no wish to be like them. No one even knows their names . . . No, 'tis not for Morag Macpherson. And Mistress Sinclair, she knows it. You think she's fierce? Well, she's proud, but what's wrong with that? Terrible skilful she is, at everything she sets her hand to. And a wonder with her herbs and remedies. People around here would far rather have her than a doctor—they come for miles to have her treat their ailments, and never a penny does she take. She says that the herbs and wild plants of the hedgerows grow free, and God put them there, and gave her the knowledge to use them, so she has no right to charge. A great Bible-reading woman she is. The doctor would like to see her stopped, of course, but she makes no claims, and takes no money. If people come to her, that's their business. Besides, the doctor's a great one for his dram, and none too clean . . ."

She rose from her crouching position before the fire, the flames now leaping high towards the metal hood. "There now, it's chattering I am again. Mistress Sinclair says my tongue is my great fault.

I'll leave you, mistress. The Master will be in directly—" She paused. "I think he will be glad to see you. This past winter he has not had an easy time of it. Ill, he's been, with a cough— and at times he seems very tired. He will not have the doctor near him. Since Master William died . . . ah, well, perhaps the sight of you will lighten that sorrow, mistress." She dusted her hands together. "You'll find him in the dining room. 'Tis the only room he ever uses at Cluain. 'Tis the door on the right of the hall as you go down . . ."

She was turning to go, and then her gaze fell on the cat. Suddenly her voice took a strange edge, almost ugly. "Devil take that thing! Isn't he always where he should not be, and never a finger to be laid on him, because he's Mistress Sinclair's!" She made a threatening motion towards the cat, but I saw that she did not attempt to touch it.

"Leave him, Morag." I don't know why I said it. The cat had made me uncomfortable before, but now I sensed that it had often taken that place on the bed. "He seems to like it here."

"Och, he likes it fine. He knows he's not supposed to be up here—does a body ever know what damage a cat will be doing? But he took to coming here when Master William was here— and you're the first that used this room since then. I do not care to touch him, myself."

Backing towards the door, her eyes were less friendly as she looked at the cat. "I must be away. Mistress Sinclair will know I've been gossiping. She knows everything, that one. But a body has a right to a little information about a strange place—and it's precious little you'll get from Mairi Sinclair . . ."

She was gone, and now I approached the cat; I put my hand tentatively on his head. He did not stir. "Were you William's friend, Cat? Did you know him well?" He answered nothing, of course, and no welcoming purr rewarded my gesture. He merely stared at the fire. I shrugged, and turned away. He had not come here for my company, that was certain. Perhaps he liked the lonely grandeur of this room. He seemed hardly a cat to sit cosily by a kitchen fire.

I took my toilet articles from the leather bag, my fingers stiff with a chill and tension that the hot water did nothing to help. When I picked up my brush I was suddenly aware of staring at the blank white wall before me where one would have expected a mirror. Then I became conscious of something odd about this room—something that I recognised now as being common to the other parts of the house I had seen. The furniture was old and rich, and it shone with the polishing of careful hands. The curtains were in good repair, but apart from their tartan pattern, utterly plain. I searched for something here that was not essential, and there was nothing, no ornament, no vase, no picture. One book only lay on the desk, and I knew without looking at it that it was the Bible. Surely William would not have suffered this—the clutter of his possessions must have disturbed this austere order. Angrily I turned back to where my reflection should have met me in a mirror, and there was nothing. It was as if in this room Mairi Sinclair strove to make the occupant feel as if he or she did not exist.

Anger drove out the sense of desolation that had been creeping upon me. Feverishly I brushed at my hair, and my fingers arranged the knot without aid of a mirror. I did remember what I looked like—I *would* remember. I did exist.

Defiantly I tied a red ribbon about the knot of hair, and found the red kid fur-lined slippers that I wore in the Peking winters. I found the cashmere shawl that William had brought me back from a visit to Canton, riotously glowing with the rich embroideries that the Chinese loved, and touched here and there with a thread of gold. I, at least, would not be forced into Mairi Sinclair's mould.

"Come, Cat," I said, as I went toward the door. Surprisingly, he obeyed. He was out of the door before me, a swift white streak, and then, quicker than I, he was off down the broad spiral. When I reached the floor below, he had disappeared.

I went on then, unaccompanied, to my meeting with the Master of Cluain.

Chapter 2

He stood there—a powerfully built man in whom the strength seemed too suddenly to have wasted. He was not so tall, but the breadth of the shoulders was great, only now they appeared bent forward unnaturally, hunched. His distinguishing feature was massive eyebrows hooked over deep-set eyes. There was a strong thrust of jawline, but most of the face was lost in the gathering furrows of age, and the dim light of the room. He stood, legs apart, facing out from the fireplace, and he half-turned at my entrance.

"So—you have come. William's sister."

"My mother's child."

Why did I always have to make the tart rejoinder? Could I not have greeted him without provocation in these first words? "Learn to curb your tongue, Little Sister," William had once said to me, using the name the Chinese had bestowed upon me, "and you'll have the men at your feet—that is, if you want those kinds of men!" I looked at this big, aging man, and I knew that he would never be at my feet. I hoped I would never be at his.

He gestured irritably. "Well, come in, come in! And close the door. There's draught enough with this wind."

I did as he bade me, and then went and stood near the fireplace. His voice was deep and strongly accented. "You've come a long way. Are you staying?"

"A while. If you'll have me."

He shrugged. "If it pleases you. You've a right to the roof of Cluain." It wasn't much of a welcome, but then he hadn't asked me to come in the first place. A silence fell between us, which I left him to break.

"Why *did* you come? You could not find anyone to marry you out there?"

I flushed. "There were some. That's unimportant. My father was killed and—"

"Aye—I read of it. I was going to write . . ." The tone softened a little. "But I never got to it. In any case, the letter would have missed you, as it happens." It was said with some relief, as if this absolved him of any fault. "I never did like him—your father. I'll not pretend any different. He came here just for one summer, and took away my only child—and she still so young. He was English, and a minister of a different church. And he took her not just to England where I might have seen her from time to time, and might have come to know my grandson. Och, no—he must carry her all the way to China, that miserable cesspool of pagans, where she died of one of their stinking fevers. No, there was no love lost, and I cannot deny it."

"*I* loved him." I had to say it.

Surprisingly, he nodded. "That's as well. I like to see respect in a child—"

"*Love,*" I insisted. "I loved him—and William too."

Perhaps the outright declaration of love was too much for this taciturn Scot; his tongue would not come easily to such a word, nor hear it too readily from others. He half-turned away from me, as if in embarrassment. "*That's* why I came." Then I stopped. I could not tell him about the scroll. Some time, but not now. "I had to see where William . . . Well, I knew he was growing attached to Cluain."

As if I had wounded him and he could bear no more of it, he left the fire abruptly, and went to the sideboard. For a moment he bent over it, both hands placed there as if to steady himself. The voice was muffled and choked when he spoke again.

"Aye—and well I knew it. He would have been grand for

30

Cluain, and Cluain for him. But he's dead now—and there's an end to it." He cleared his throat thunderously, and his body straightened; the big head with its brush of white hair came up. "Sit down, then, and welcome." But still he did not look at me. "You'll take a dram with me?"

"A dram?"

Now he turned back. "Are you stupid, Gurrl? Have they taught you nothing of your heritage? A dram—*whisky!* Cluain's whisky!"

"I—I've never drunk whisky."

"Then you are sadly ill-educated. Or perhaps you drank only brandy or champagne out there in the bishop's palace."

"It was no palace. We were quite poor."

This seemed to irritate him also. "He didn't only take my child, but he could not even leave his own children decently provided for. Well, we'll not fret it. Doubtless you'll find someone to marry you. But if it's to be a Scot, then you'd better learn fine soon what his national drink is. Some women drink it— some don't. But here at Cluain at least you'll know what it is."

He was unlocking a cupboard in the sideboard with a key he selected from a ring he carried. Glasses stood waiting ready on a silver tray. He poured from an engraved decanter into two glasses and came back and placed one in my hand. I had not sat down, as he had bidden me, so we faced each other, standing, across the breadth of the fireplace. The firelight caught the glow of the amber liquid in the good crystal glass. He raised his slightly towards me.

"Well, there it is, miss. *Uisge beatha* we call it in the old Gaelic tongue. Aqua vita, the Latin scholars say. Water of life. Cluain's distilling—and your heritage. Well, miss, here's to us!"

He tossed his own glass back, and incautiously, I was too hasty in following his example. It was in my throat before I felt the fire of it, an aged smoke that seemed to pour into my lungs; I gasped for breath, and struggled not to choke. I was certain he could see the tears that came to my eyes, but I would not allow the cough and the splutter to come. He had been expecting that, I thought, and with a certain malicious pleasure.

I had to wait until my breath was even enough to speak. The whisky had an extraordinary aftertaste on my tongue, and although I knew the alcohol couldn't have affected my legs so quickly, I sat down without ceremony on one of the broad oak settles placed at each end of the fireplace. I knew he was waiting for a verdict, and I had my own satisfaction in withholding it.

"I'm not miss, you know—nor Gurrl. My name is Kirsty." But I had the feeling the name "Gurrl" had come to stay.

The words disturbed him. His big features twisted with a look of bitterness. He sat down opposite me, and the movement was that of an old man.

"Kirsty—Christina. Well, my daughter gave you *that* name but she could not give you the spirit and great heart of the woman she called you for. You'd have to be bred here in the Highlands to be her kind. But then my grandson came, and it was as if he had been to the place born. Now he's dead, and there's no one for Cluain but an ignorant girl, God help us! No one for Cluain . . ."

And then he drained the last of his glass. In desperation, with no words of comfort to offer him, I took another sip from my own. This time it wasn't so bad. At least it was warm; I could feel its glow move subtly through my veins. *Uisge beatha*—whisky —water of life. Cluain . . .

II

The hot dishes were brought in wordlessly by Mairi Sinclair, and left on the sideboard. My grandfather cut the meat, and we helped ourselves from the other dishes. As Morag had said, the food was good—it was excellent. I had been hungry, but the whisky had made me ravenous. I noted the plates we ate off, the silver utensils one would not have expected in what I had thought of as a farmhouse. But it was also the dower house of Ballochtorra, and judging from the furniture, must have shared some of Bal-

32

lochtorra's riches. But here, also, while we ate off fine china, there was no single thing what was superfluous. The windows of the dining room looked onto the enclosed garden, and there the plants waved and nodded in their own cheerful disorder. But no rose such as climbed those old walls perfumed this room; instead, there was the smell of beeswax, and the peat and wood burning in the fire. Everything shone, and was set with mathematical precision. The great sideboard and the long table with stretchers joining its magnificently carved legs, were precisely parallel. The two settles were at exact right angles to the fireplace, with no cushion or footstool to ease the sitter. Under the window opposite them was a smaller table—still of the same carved dark oak— it must all be about the Jacobean period, I thought, though I was hazy about such things. On the table was set a huge book bound in faded, though polished, brown leather, with brass trimmings on the corners, and an ornately fashioned brass hinged clasp which fastened and held the pages together. There were such ones on display in the richer homes of the residents of the British Legation in Peking, though it was characteristic that my father, a bishop, had never thought of declaring his faith in any such obvious manner; the small, thin-paged book he carried in his pocket had been sufficient. Beside the Bible, and more interesting to me, was the one note of individuality that the room contained. A chess set was there, the board and pieces polished, as everything was, but with the look of use about them. But no unfinished game was set up. The pieces waited, their four solid ranks opposing. Whoever dusted and polished them had learned in what order to replace them. But by now I was beginning to believe that the two women of this house, the older and the young, between them were capable of learning all they put their minds to. It could not be true that all Scots were as intelligent as the engineers and scientists they exported to the rest of the world; but quite certainly the stupid would not have lasted long at Cluain.

My grandfather ate in silence. I thought there might have been a prayer, but there was none. All, apparently, were not like Mairi Sinclair. Then, after a while, my grandfather laid down his knife and fork, and stared at me, as if he had suddenly, once again, become aware of my presence. I realised that he was totally unused to eating at this table with anyone else—he had forgotten that one could talk at meals. William, I thought, would have changed that. No one had ever been able to stop William talking.

The words came in fits and starts. "You know what Cluain means in the old tongue, lass? Did your mother talk to you of things like that?—about Cluain, and such?"

"She died when I was four," I reminded him.

"Aye, she did. So she did. Killed by the foulness of that savage place he took her to. Well, it's done now. But Cluain—Cluain means a broad, green meadow—a pasture. Och, we use a fancy name to call the whisky by, because the old words aren't understood. Royal Spey, we call it—because of the river. But Cluain's it is, and made from Cluain's own barley, and dried over peat cut from Cluain's bog, up there on the mountain, and, most of all, brewed with the water from Cluain's own well—not river water, mind you, but from our own well. The water's a great part of it— Christina's Well, it is called, and it is the most precious thing on Cluain."

He forgot who I was. He had a new listener—a new pupil. So he must have talked to William on that first night, seeing the one who could carry on Cluain for him, seeing the longed-for grandson.

"It must age, you know. And it must age *here*. Whisky that's new-distilled can boil your eyeballs out—send you daft. But here the climate is right. Don't ask me why. As soon ask how a good whisky is made, and you'll get a hundred answers, and a hundred different distillings. Some think the climate here is damnable, though it suits me, you see. It suits the whisky, too. Aye, it lies there in its oak cask—best if you can get casks that have been used for storing sherry—gives it colour, in time. Three years is the youngest whisky you can sell by law. But those who buy for blending know Cluain. They come up here from Glasgow and Edinburgh and they bargain and they buy just as the new spirit is distilled. They are content to leave it to age here, untasted, because they know they are buying the finest malt whisky the Highlands make. They ask no questions of Cluain any more. Some leave it only the legal three years, and then take it away to blend with their grain spirits—that's blended whisky, Gurrl, and if it weren't for the malt in it, it would not be even as good as your rotgut gin. And then some—those who can afford to wait—they wait, and they leave it here, and it grows better with the years. Och, mind you, most of it ends up in a blend, but we all know that without the pure malt distilling, there would be no such thing as the Scotch whisky they sell all over the world these days. There's few that will pay the price, and wait the years to drink a pure malt brew. Perhaps there's few that have the head for it, except those that are brought up to it, here in the Highlands. But never mistake it. Malt is the heart and essence of it. It gives it the flavour and warmth. No whisky without malt, Gurrl—no whisky at all . . ."

Almost without noticing it, we were back at the fire again, seated on those opposite settles. Mairi Sinclair had come to clear the dishes silently, and I noticed that my grandfather was silent also while she was in the room. But we were alone again, and he held another glass in his hand, and again he seemed to have forgotten my real identity. He had taken out a pipe without troubling to ask me if I minded him smoking it. But I could not stand in William's shadow forever, and finally his eyes snapped alive. He seemed to come out of a dream.

"Och, why do I bother? What's it to you? 'Tis God's will, but 'tis hard when a man's worked all his life and there's no one to pass on his knowledge to—no one to care how a good malt whisky is made."

"Cluain is a farm as well as a distillery." Why did I seem to bargain for a place here, when I didn't even know that I wanted to stay? It was not the reason I had come.

"The farm is all right. It is a very good farm. But the glory is the whisky. Cluain is famous for it. What can a wee gurrl be taught about it? There's no woman I know who could run a distillery."

"I'm useless to you, then?"

His words were brutal. "Useless—yes. Just about useless. Unless you can find and wed a man that's fit to take over from Angus Macdonald. And that man will not be easy to find."

"You place a high value on yourself, Grandfather."

"I do that! Any man that's fought and worked as I have *must* place a high value on himself. He has proved that value."

In the dim light that came from the fire, and the gathering twilight, I knew he would not see my faint, rueful smile. And I didn't much care if he did. I had come rashly, on impulse, fleeing from a China that no longer held anything I loved, coming here because of that scroll, and the scarlet characters splashed on it. What could I prove?—what could I do? I could stand beside William's grave, but that would not bring him back, nor answer my questioning. And then what? Cling on here at Cluain, knowing my grandfather would hardly turn me away; but stay on unwanted —useless, as he put it. William had been fond of the Chinese philosophy that observed the bamboo bending before the wind and surviving, while the great oak was uprooted. "It is easier, Little Sister, to go where the wind blows at one's back, than lean against it." But he had never really practised that himself, nor could I. So in time I would leave Cluain, I thought. I would then take that road that so many of my kind did. A bishop's daughter, I would have references enough from his friends in the Church; but what waited would be no better than the position occupied by so many other women of small education, and less money. I would make a wretched governess, I knew. I did not know my place well enough; my quick impulses and sharp tongue would be no asset. And yet, that was all there was—that, and Cluain. If only, I thought, this old man sitting here had once held out a hand to me. But I would not beg, nor would he. We both were lonely, and alone. But what gigantic pride stood between that fact, and neither of us admitting it.

I rose. "I'll go up now."

He nodded above his pipe, as if he didn't care. "Aye. As you wish. You'll find a candle in the hall."

There was no good night, as there had been no words of welcome. I took the candle, as he had said, placed ready in its pewter holder. But I didn't need it. In this far latitude the light still lingered. The narrow slits of windows gave little aid on the staircase, but when I reached the tower room it was still washed with

36

the grey light of the evening. But the heart of the room was alive with the fire; Morag, I supposed, had laid turf on the glowing wood, and a bed of coals was forming a powdery ash. I crouched for a moment before it. William must often have assumed this posture here, and now I followed him. But suddenly the image of William receded, and unbidden, the thought came to me that this was not a room for a young woman alone. It invited another presence—a young man, not one's brother. It was a room to be alone in with a lover. How large that bed looked, and how large the world beyond the three windows. How wonderful to be here with a man one loved, lost, as Morag had said, as if in the snows of the mountains. How, then, the fire would glow; how warm the bed. I felt the heat rush to my cheeks. I was alone, I reminded myself. There was no man—no man I loved. There was only the fire and the rain slashing against the windows. I got up quickly. Useless to dream.

On the washstand something new had appeared. It was a small swivel mirror with a drawer beneath, such as a man used. It would only let me see my face, not the back of my hair, or the hang of my dress—but it would do. And beside it a half-page torn from a notebook, a well-formed but somewhat laboured handwriting, and with correct spelling. *I thought you would need the mirror. I have set a hot water jar in the bed. Be careful lest you burn your toes. Morag Macpherson.*

I smiled, grateful, wondering what I would have done in these first hours at Cluain without Morag. And smiling, I caught sight of my own face in the mirror. Did I look so much like William that the man Mairi Sinclair had called Sir Gavin had recognised me?—or had he simply made the association afterwards? We both were dark-haired and white-skinned; we both had eyes that were more grey than blue. Were mine as deep-set as William's?—as heavily lashed in black? I suddenly thought of my grandfather's eyes; had both William and I inherited from him that smudged darkness? It was strange, but I had never really thought until now about how I looked; I had somehow taken it for granted that I would do quite well. In Peking, every young European girl was paid compliments, called pretty, even if she were just passably so. I had been called pretty, but I knew it wasn't quite true. Not *pretty*. But William had been almost formidably handsome —and now I was said to look like William. I sighed, and turned away from my image in the glass. What did it matter? If I left Cluain to go South in search of a position the fact that I might be called pretty, or handsome, or whatever else, was a positive disadvantage. Who wanted a good-looking governess who wore red ribbons and slippers?

I went to the window and through the gathering twilight I saw the lights of Ballochtorra. It looked strangely far away now, and far beyond my reach. Lights burned at many windows—they had not yet drawn the curtains against the coming night, but they were prodigal of their lamps. There even seemed to be a few windows on the lower level which glowed with the brighter light of electricity. It was exciting and extravagant in this remote place —like the gold leaf on the crested gate. Now I grew hungry for the lights and the voices, the sense of company, and a place shared. Was there a large family at Ballochtorra? I wondered. Did they sit together, and talk and laugh? Cluain was so silent, except for the rain. One of the turf logs burned through then, and quickly folded into the bed of coals. The gentle sound came like a crash.

But there was someone else as alone as I was. On the road beyond the walled garden I heard, very faintly, the sound of the pony's hooves. At first the rider was indistinguishable in the grey light; he came out of the mist on the road leading from Ballochtorra, and I thought then that I recognised him. His long legs were thrust forward on a big, tough-looking Highland pony. He rode bareheaded in the rain, without the traditional Highland bonnet to match the kilt. He had been in the rain a long time; even his sheepskin jerkin seemed to be sodden. The dog followed closely at the pony's flanks. The man held the pony with one hand; on the other, gloved, was perched the bird. Now the bird was not so still as it had been in the beech wood. It turned its head from side to side; but it made no attempt to fly up from its master's hand, hardly seeming to need the bright red streamers that attached it. I pressed closer to the glass, straining to see the strange procession. The bird danced a little on the

38

glove, and I had the sensation that its bright hawk's eyes noted me; but the man did not look up. They moved on past the house and the distillery building, along the road that led up the valley. I followed their progress for as long as I could, longer than it took for the pony's light tread to fade into silence. Then the mist shut them off. I was alone again.

Now, to close out the mist and the emptiness, I drew the curtains and lighted my candle. Then I turned to the task of unpacking. But even with the opening of the trunk I gave up the idea. Fatigue had been fought too long, and the whisky was almost druglike in its effect. I fumbled among my clothes and found my night shift. I washed, and gave my hair a perfunctory brush: Would I ever be convinced that it was worth the hundred strokes at night? A strong sense of depression was settling on me, in the way the mist had crept down from the heights of Ballochtorra. I laid more turf on the fire just for the comfort of seeing the flames leap up, and was ready to climb into bed when the notion came suddenly to me. I think it was born of the loneliness engulfing me—the frightening conviction that I had come all this way for nothing—without real purpose. I needed now urgently to touch someone or something that was familiar and loved, to drive away the sense of loss. I went back to the trunk and felt about in its depths until I found the box laid so carefully among the layers of my clothes. It came out, and in the candlelight the rich polish of the inlaid wood seemed more beautiful than ever before. I took the contents out tenderly; the figures lay securely each in their carved and padded niches within the box. When they were all out I turned the box over and opened the hinges wide; the chessboard was not flat, the hinges sunk so that they were out of sight, and the box itself was the playing surface. Then I laid the pieces on their squares—lining up the Queens and Knights, the Castles and the Kings, the Pawns forming their protective ranks before them. There was comfort just to hold these things, a feeling of order restored. It brought back to me sharply the thought that whatever happened, the game of life was still there, and the strongest game was always played by the attacker.

It was a chess set of great beauty and rarity—certainly, I believed, the most valuable thing I owned. It had been given to me by William, who had received it in thanks for a favour done by him for one of the Mandarin class. Neither of us could have put a price on it, and I had never asked William what he had done to have such a reward. It was one of the rarities of China—the "rat" chess set, carved of Indian ivory, with all of the pieces having the bodies and faces of rats, but clothed in the costume of medieval China, the long gowns, the fans, the knights mounted on richly caparisoned horses. Amber and ruby eyes gave them an astonishingly lifelike appearance. It had been made, William said, more than a hundred years ago. "Take it, Little Sister," he had said lightly. "It may be the only dowry you ever have." We made jokes about being poor; clearly William did not believe he would remain poor. He was clever and quick; he would come back to China with an engineering degree and help build her railways; we had seen too many fortunes made in the China trade not to be infected with the belief that William might do it also. We were children of a clergyman, but we were realists.

With the pieces set up in their ranks, my hands grew restless. I began taking them off and setting them aside. It was madness what I was doing, but I couldn't help it. My fingers traced the moves of that last game with William—for some reason they seemed burned into my memory. Piece by piece, as the game progressed, my forces had fallen to William's. And then we reached the last move—it had been bold, and I had not seen it coming. Swiftly, William's hand with the knight, and a little, triumphant laugh. "Check to the Queen, Kirsty! Now puzzle that one out, Little Sister." And he had gone off, chuckling, to some appointment. This had been shortly before he left Peking to begin the long journey to Edinburgh. There never had been time for another game, and in the weeks after he had gone I had not disturbed the pieces, and I had known there was no way out of the check. With the Queen taken, the King must fall. The check was complete.

The time had passed, and I had played with my father, or practised moves by myself, solved chess problems from books, determined to show William how I had improved when he returned. And it had all been wiped out. First my father's death, and then the letter from Cluain. The sympathetic voices of friends had murmured, "Stay here, Kirsty. China is all you have ever known. In time you'll marry here . . . Stay, Kirsty . . ."

But I knew I would go. With the letter about William's death had come the scroll. I saw the crimson characters scrawled along its length—not much like William's careful rendering. And yet they could only have been made by William. I had translated them in my own rough fashion, and then, not believeing my senses, had carried the scroll to my father's translator, a scholar of both Chinese and Manchu. He had shaken his head. "It does not make true sense—your brother's thoughts were not concentrated." Truth, or imagination, once the doubt had been aroused, I knew I must go. The wind was blowing away from China. My time there was over. I bent, as he said I should, before the wind. "Check to the Queen, Kirsty." The game was done.

I was tired almost beyond thinking, but rest would not come. I went to the window that overlooked the garden, and drew back the curtain. The light from a candle in the dining room cast the faintest glow beyond the window. My grandfather was still there. Perhaps tonight, in the desperation of fatigue, was the only time I would have the courage to ask what I had come to know. I let the curtain fall, and then I went back to the chest. For a moment my fingers closed over the box that held the scroll, and other things of William's which had been sent back to me—papers belonging to him, draftsman's instruments in their velvet-lined case, a silver watch, a collar stud. Not much else. William had still been poor. And then I released my hold. Time enough—the characters on the scroll would mean nothing to Angus Macdonald. First I would hear his own account of how William had died.

I pulled out my robe. It struck me again that it also was red— that favourite Chinese colour. A red silk robe, padded with layers of cotton against the Peking winters, high-necked, in the Chinese style with bands of embroidery at the neck and wide sleeves. Such garments had been cheap for Westerners to buy in China; in this setting it seemed outlandishly rich and foreign. I could not help it. This was all I had. My grandfather would have to accept it, as I must accept so much about Cluain I did not yet understand.

41

The soft-soled slippers made no sound upon the stairs. When I lifted the latch of the dining-room door his head was still bent over what absorbed him at the table. His eyebrows came together in a frown of enquiry—almost annoyance.

"Well?" Again there was no welcome in his tone. I was an intruder into the solitude of his years, the thousands of nights he had sat here alone.

Slowly now I advanced towards him. He had only a single candle beside him, and it flickered subtly over the polish of the chessboard which he had moved here to the centre of the big table. Here was no reflection of the richness of the one I had left upstairs; it was a plain board, and the pieces upon it were plain, with no decoration but the shape needed to identify each one; I recognised the classic Staunton set, the sturdy, weighted pieces of boxwood and ebony that the fingers could grip firmly, and the player could hear the decisive, satisfying rap of wood upon wood as he moved his piece. It was on such a set as this that William had taught me to play.

I laid my candle on the other side of the board and the shadows cast by the chessmen raced together and joined. The fierce old eyes looked at me across them. Unbidden, I drew out a chair and seated myself opposite him.

"You played with William?"

"I did."

"Did he win?"

"Aye—he had a head on him, my grandson. A head I could have used for Cluain."

"I would like to know how William died. I came here to learn that—to hear it from you."

"I told in my letter how he died. What does it matter—since he is dead? All men must, in their time. His was before his time—when I had need of him."

That, almost more than anything, was what made him bitter. He could not forgive William for dying because he had needed him; he had begun to believe that William was seduced away from China, away from my father and myself, and it might have been true. And then William had died and had cheated him. Had he ever loved William, or merely needed him?

42

The silence between us was heavy. The true darkness had come now, and the light of our separate candles and the glow of the dying fire was the only thing that warmed Cluain. And then, as my eyes dropped from the old man's, lest he should see my yearning for William, and for some comfort and companionship, I looked closely at the chessboard, taking in for the first time the disposition of the pieces—those that were set to the side of the board, and those that still remained. The familiarity I had sought asserted itself, the pattern I knew too well. Only one move remained.

I reached out and took up the knight and placed it swiftly. "Check to the Queen."

Now our eyes met again in a look of dawning wonderment, of recognition.

"He played that game with you?" I said.

He nodded.

It was as if a wind had stirred in that quiet room, a cold draught had swirled about us. Somewhere, from back in time and beyond death, William had reached to us. He had played this game with us both, and both had reached the impasse which must acknowledge his victory.

"Was it the last game he played with you?"

"Aye."

"With me, also."

And now the silence was more than before; in it we knew we shared a bond, and for the first time we felt we shared our blood. William was there between us, strong, living. Who could believe he was dead when he was so forcibly with us? It was as if he himself had drawn me here, to be his instrument, his tool, to play the game as he had taught it to me, to attack, to dare, to seize and use what came in life. What he had not said, but what his life implied, was that when one went before the wind, one also used the wind. I was here because of him. His life was over, but mine was not.

"I would like a dram, Grandfather."

For a moment I saw the lids close on those faded, but still burning eyes. I thought a shudder racked that strong body, and then the shoulders seemed to sag even more. It was as if he were touched

43

by a force he did not fully comprehend, but could not now withstand. Wordlessly he rose from his chair and went to the sideboard. He poured a good measure into two glasses and returned and set them each beside the candles. Then he raised his glass to me in slight salute.

"You were sent. I did not perceive it, but now I know. William has sent you. Welcome to Cluain."

I returned his gesture, and we both drank. This time it was not strange, or burning; the peaty taste was only the essence of the smell of the peat fire burning here and in my room. The comfort I had sought was in his words, spoken at last, and in the warmth that slid through me with the liquid. I allowed it to carry away my fatigue and my loneliness. I thought of how many times William must have sat where I sat now, the candles burning, the chessmen set out before them both, and the glass of whisky to each hand. Was it right to believe that someone could reach from beyond death to bring two people together like this?—was it tampering with forces that neither of us understood to try to invoke his name and his spirit? Was it an evil or a benign contact that we made? Were not such things forbidden? Forbidden or not, we both believed it was William who had drawn me here—inexplicably drawn together this old man with hunger in his eyes, and myself, hungry in my own fashion. The instrument of the contact had been the chessmen. William's hand had lain on these pieces, as it had done on those upstairs. He seemed to move them at his will—as he had surely brought me to this meeting. Strangely, I did not feel afraid. If William, though dead, was our bond, then let it be. There could be no evil where there had been love.

I looked at the old man and knew that the veil of indifference had been removed. He seemed to see me for the first time, and yet he was also looking at something, or someone, beyond me.

"Aye—you have the look of him, even. And I did not see it. It was as though I were blind. All I saw was a wee lass. I did not look . . . I did not see."

"Then tell me how he died."

"Died?—he died. I wrote that in the letter."

"You did not say *how.*"

44

"A hunting accident. I wrote it . . ."

"You did *not* write it. William had never been hunting in his life."

"Och, I did not mean the English kind of hunting. Did you imagine this is country to set a horse at a gallop after a fox? No, he went with a gun after birds, or rabbits, or some such thing. A young man out for a walk with a gun."

"We do not carry guns in China—no one who is not military. We are careful to try not to give offence—we are the Foreign Devils, and William had the peculiar position of being a bishop's son. I doubt that he had handled a gun in his life . . ."

"Here it is different. Every man will snare or trap or shoot to add to his family larder. Most will poach when they can. They must. Life is hard. And if you are rich you do it for sport. The Prince of Wales comes here to shoot . . ."

"William was not the Prince of Wales. Who was with him?"

The big head sagged as if with the weight of guilt. "That was it. There was no one with him. He did not know it was a foolish thing to do. He did not tell anyone that he was going with a gun. He used often to take long walks. But only the most experienced here go with a gun. There was no time for him to learn."

"You didn't warn him?" I accused.

His reply was submissive, as though in accepting me, he would deny me nothing now, not even the price of his own conscience. "Perhaps not enough. It is hard, when you are old, to remember that a young man does not know all the terrain, cannot find his way in mist and rain. He was foolhardy to go so much alone, but could I hold back a young man of spirit? Would I question him as to his comings and goings?"

"No—you could not. Not William. Then how did he die?"

He sighed. "That visit he intended only staying a few days—it was all the time he could spare from the university. On the second evening he was missing. He did not return when he usually came. It was early November, and the evenings were very short then. But I did not worry too much—he had made himself welcome in a number of places up and down the strath, and he often tarried in one or the other. But by the time supper was finished I knew something was amiss. And then I checked the guns. He had taken one.

45

I was not sure he even knew how to use it. We could not set out to search in the dark, but by dawn—and dawn comes late in November—every man on the place, every household along the strath—and, aye, even every servant at Ballochtorra who had the sense to keep upright on the moor had turned out to search for him."

"How long?" I could dispense with the details of the search.

"Two nights he was out. For one not bred to wrap himself in a plaid, and make a bed from the heather and bracken, it was bitter suffering. It was cold, lass. Even for us, it was cold. The second night there was some snow. And he had the gunshot wound in his knee. He could never have walked."

"You found him—where?"

"Close by. That was what near killed me. He had somehow crawled into a rock opening in the crag up there by Ballochtorra. Only a slight shelter from the cold and snow—and he had gone unconscious. Not able to cry for help. We had believed he had gone farther afield, and were searching up on the mountain. Indeed, it was a wee bit of kitchen boy from Ballochtorra that found him, trying to help with the search, but not daring to be away from his post too long—not strong enough to go with the men sent out by Campbell. We brought him back and I got a surgeon from Inverness to remove the bullet—I did not trust the man here not to bungle it. But we could all see that the fever did not go down. I sent for a man from Edinburgh. By the time he came, William was dead."

I was relentless, even though I could see that each word seemed to scar him as it came. "How long?"

"Three-four days. He was nursed devotedly. Mistress Sinclair did not sleep in all that time—as I did not, even though I went to my bed. But the wound, and the exposure . . . Stronger men than William have gone down before such things."

"But the wounding? How did it happen?"

"He could not talk when we found him. His gun had been fired. He did not know about guns—how to treat them, how to handle them when walking in rough places. He shot himself."

"He shot himself!"

He sighed. " 'Tis too easy to do when a man walks with a loaded

46

gun in rough places. Those who should know better have done it. Could I blame him too much? But I did blame him. Folly, it was! A life wasted . . . my grandson's life."

I held tightly to the glass. "Did he recover consciousness at all? Did he never speak of how it happened?"

"There were periods when he talked—but they were wild words, not to be understood. And Mistress Sinclair told us not to encourage him to talk, for it took his strength. What was the use to question him, or blame him—then? It was better to leave him in peace."

In peace. The words on the scroll gave no impression of peace. "It was up there he died? In the tower room?"

"Aye. I had had him put there when he first came to Cluain. I wanted him to know the feeling of being master of it—to be able to look over lands that he could call his own. And when Mistress Sinclair suggested preparing another room on the lower floor while the search was going on, so that it should be easier to nurse him, I would not permit it. I did not want him to wake to some strange place. He had his few things there—I would not let her touch or tidy them. All the time the search was on she kept a fire high, and the bed warm and ready. She had her medicines ready, and she is better than any doctor in that way. But it was not to be. He came, and he was gone, so quickly. I had come to believe that the dearest desire of my heart was to be given to me. Vengeance is mine, sayeth the Lord. I knew then that I would have no joy in my old age."

"Why vengeance?"

He rubbed his hand wearily over his eyes. "Do not ask, Gurrl. Is there any man who has not done that on which judgement will be passed? Who shall not pay in the end?"

"God is merciful. He is a God of love as well as vengeance. My father always taught us that."

His lips twisted in a bitter disclaimer. "A comfortable philosophy for those who can let themselves believe it. For those who think they are without sin. The past is not undone. It is forever."

My hand went forward and I let my fingers play over the figure of the Queen on the board, held frozen, it seemed, by that perpetual check from the Knight, held forever.

47

"There is the future, too," I said quietly. "The future is not yet written. It lies with us."

"When William went I knew there would be no future. I did not care."

"*I* care. I am William's sister, and a part of him still lives with me," I cried. "He would never have let me believe that there is no future."

"There, Gurrl, do not take on so. Perhaps you're right—perhaps so. But finish up your dram with me, and take yourself off to bed. It's rest you need. And do not be afraid of your room and your bed because it was the place where William died. I would not have put you there myself, but Mistress Sinclair had made the arrangements . . ."

I finished the last of the whisky in a quick, angry swallow, and did not choke on it. "I will never be afraid of any place where William was. And if he died there, then I am that much closer to him. My father also taught us that. Love is stronger than fear." I thrust my chair back from the table, and reached for the candle. He almost let me go, but as I lifted the latch, the commanding words came.

"Wait, Gurrl!"

"What is it?"

"Do not be in such a hurry. Perhaps you are right. Perhaps there is a future, though I cannot see it myself. It is not in my ken." Now his tone altered to a persuasive pitch it had never possessed before. "Kirsty . . ." My name for the first time. "Kirsty, find and wed a man that I can feel would have been William's equal. Find that man, Kirsty, and Cluain shall be yours."

My hand trembled violently; the shadows darted all over the room. "That is an impossible bargain! You are asking something of me I have no way of knowing that I can fulfil. A man!—*what* man? And why should the man I marry have to be measured against William? Every man has a right to be himself, not another man's shadow. No—there can be no such bargain, Grandfather."

But he did not believe me. "Go to your bed. In the morning you will see. In the morning you will see that Cluain is worth the having."

"In the morning—in the morning I may leave!"

He merely shrugged. "Please yourself."

In the quiet of the house the sound was very loud as I pulled the door closed, and let the latch fall.

*　　*　　*

She was waiting for me. She stood on the first step of the spiral stair within the tower. She had probably been watching through the slit window the pale light that had come from our candles into the garden. She held her own lighted candle, and she must have stood there for a long time, for it was burned nearly to its end, as mine was. I went towards her, and she did not step down, so that I was forced to raise my face to hers.

"Mistress Sinclair . . . ?"

She did not wear her black to bed. A plain white shift, severely buttoned to the throat, was partly covered by a long red plaid. Her hair was unbound, the black streaked with shining silver; it softened the stark good looks, made her seem younger—no, not younger, but without age. The roughened hand clenched and unclenched the plaid across her breast.

"You have been speaking together for a long time," she said at last. And then, as if she could not hold the words back: "What about?—*what about?*"

"My business, Mistress Sinclair."

"*What* business?" Her eyes were wild, anguished.

"Please step aside, Mistress Sinclair. I wish to go to my room."

Her hand let go the plaid, and reached out and clutched my wrist with fierce strength. "*Tell me*—what business?" The candle jerked with her pull, and the hot grease splattered down on my hand. I smothered the exclamation of pain.

"Step aside!"

She had not anticipated my own strength. Now my hand reached up and caught her shoulder, and pulled her down off that first step. The way ahead was clear, and I went quickly, gathering my robe so I would not trip. Still she would not leave me. When she recovered I could hear her coming after me, a few steps behind, but at least the twist of one spiral away. The candlelight pursued me, and told me how close she was. I reached the door of my room and flung it open. But she was there before I could close it properly. I put the weight of my shoulder against it as she grasped at the latch.

The haunted, staring face was almost witchlike now, the beauty gone in a look of madness. For a moment longer she pushed against the door, and the insane, silent struggle continued. Then at last she seemed to crumble, as if some force had deserted her. She stepped back; the pressure came off my shoulder, and the door crashed against its frame. It was held open just by the thickness of the massive iron latch. Through the tiny space I heard her whisper, a plaintive, almost pleading sigh.

"It is not yours . . ."

I should have slammed the door shut and found safety. But I needed answers. "What?—what is not mine?"

"Cluain. Cluain is not yours!" It was a wailing, sobbing protest.

She was mad—quite mad. I lifted the latch and it fell into place. Then I slid the bolt home with trembling fingers. I turned and leaned against the door, and breathed a sign of thankfulness that for the moment I was beyond her reach. My body sagged as I waited for my heart to cease its pounding. Then, when I did not hear her steps retreating, I listened more intently. The whisper reached me through the stout planks of the door, and the words were accompanied by an eerie scratching, as if her nails clawed at the wood.

"Cluain is not yours."

The intensity of the words struck me with terror. I gasped, and my body slid down the door until I was crouched on the floor. I laid down the shrunken stub of the candle, and rubbed my hand where the grease had burned, and her terrible, plucking fingers had dug into my flesh. But she heard me, and she must have bent also. The whisper came again, close to my ear. *"It is not yours!"*

I stayed there, unable to move. I did not know how long. I watched the candle begin to drown in the pool of its own grease . . . slowly, slowly. The wild hammering of my heart would not shut out that horrible whisper. *"It is not yours!"*

Then the flame flickered erratically, and died. At last I heard the soft footsteps in retreat down the stairs. But the words would not leave me.

*   *   *

I was stiff and cramped before I had the strength to gather myself up and find my way by the light of the last embers of the fire to the desk where a new candle stood ready. When it flared up and steadied, I went back to the chest and once more sought the box in which I had brought William's few things. I carried the scroll and the candle and went to the bench before the fire; I took time to lay a few sticks of kindling on the embers, and I huddled there for some time, listening—listening and hearing nothing. The smell of peat was the smell of Cluain, its fires and the essence of its golden, smokey whisky. I held my hand before that small blaze, but it seemed to have no warmth.

At last I made myself turn and take up the scroll. It had a slender bamboo rod at each end, and a red silk ribbon with which to hang it. Every knot of the bamboo, every fine line of the drawing was now more familiar to me than any other thing I had ever owned. How many hundreds—perhaps thousands—of times had I searched and examined and studied it. Its message had always been unclear, but now I thought I knew the terrible, desperate urgency with which William had sought to communicate.

His mind had been clouded with fever and drugs. How had he managed to escape her surveillance long enough to stroke these characters with his brush? How had he managed, on that injured leg, even to drag himself as far as the desk? In a moment of lucidity—or in a fevered return to the lessons of his childhood, he had gone back to the language he had struggled to master in preparation for a lifetime in China. What William did, I also had always to follow, and I had tried to learn it as well. Had his wits been sharper than they had supposed, his strength greater, so that he had written it deliberately in a language that no one in this household could read? But he had known, when he dipped the brush in the vermilion ink—and the pain of this seared me as if I had thrust my hand into the fire—he had known by then that this

51

would be his last message. And he had written it with the hope that my father and I would read it. It was a message he had never been able to complete.

I had puzzled over it so long, convinced that it was my own lack of scholarship that defeated me. But the translator had done nothing to help my bewilderment. He had shaken his head. "Young Master has forgotten his lessons. He does not take trouble any more. The characters are untidy—mean little." I had known my first frustration all over again. There are thousands of characters in the Mandarin language—and a thousand implications contained within each character. Chinese etiquette demands that nothing shall be said directly. How impossible to set down a simple, urgent message. We puzzled over it, the translator and I—he so much more expert, and yet so much more inhibited because of that. He had hardly dared say the words that had been my first reading of the characters.

"Your esteemed brother—he can hardly have been well."

"How do you know?"

He shrugged. "Untidy—not like him. Confused. The reading is not clear."

"Tell me—tell me what you think he says!"

His elegant scholar's finger followed down the characters splashed on the edge of the stiff parchment; his anxious eyes had looked sideways at me.

"I think he says . . ."

"He says *what?*"

"I think he says . . . *'She has killed—'*"

Chapter 3

I

The morning had an overwhelming normality about it. Morag woke
me bringing the jug of hot water. Impossible, except for the splatter
of candle grease around the door, to believe what had happened
the night before. I came up from sleep as if it had been a comfortable womb—slowly, with reluctance. Only the fact that I had to get
out of bed to slide back the bolt brought Mairi Sinclair to mind.

"Och," Morag greeted me, "there's no need to be bolting doors
around here. Who's to come in?"

She must consider me foolish and silly. "I—I didn't think."

"It's that heathen place you've come from. Well, let me tell you,
there's nothing at Cluain to be afraid of. Well, now, there's your
water. Mistress Sinclair said to let you sleep a mite longer this
morning, because you would be tired after your journey. But she
doesn't like to be kept waiting too long with washing the dishes, so
I'd hurry if I were you . . ."

The cheerful patter continued while she stripped back the bed-
clothes with quick, competent movements; obviously everything was
performed with great thoroughness at Cluain. Morag was well
trained, but her chores didn't interfere with her talk. She talked of
everything that came to mind—the red Chinese robe, exclaiming at
its beauty, and how strangely it was fashioned; the fineness of the
day, the sun already high and beginning to have warmth; the sky

53

was washed a clear blue. "A great growing day, it is, mistress . . ." And then she added, with a touch of wistfulness as if with memories of a summer childhood when household duties had not pressed so urgently, "A day to be running in the meadows. Mistress Sinclair will be out in the hedgerows gathering her wild flowers . . ." With her words I heard the soft sigh of the breeze, the cries of the birds, the river in full spate after last night's rain. The world of Cluain about me was fair and beautiful; it was as my grandfather had said it would be. There was no mist and no mystery. As I washed, even the sight of Ballochtorra perched on its crag seemed a part of memory, a sort of drawing of a fairy-tale castle in a child's picture book . . . there would be a princess with golden hair. I dressed, and kept telling myself that last night had been a dream, the confusion of fatigue and whisky. But as I went again to the door, the spots of grease declared quite plainly that it had been no dream. On the spiral stair, though, they had been removed. There was no evidence now of that insane struggle.

The dining room was empty, but my place was laid. There was hot porridge in a tureen, fish cakes, rashers of bacon, fried eggs— all kept hot over spirit lamps. Angus Macdonald ate a hearty breakfast, if this was his usual fare, and for a lone man he lived in some style. But I was not hungry; I took some fresh brown bread and a pot of honey, and tea. As I ate, I thought about Mairi Sinclair. What gifts the woman had, and how perversely she displayed them. The bread would be of her baking; she must supervise the dairy which provided the sweet, rich goodness of the butter. The honey was the best I had ever tasted—I thought of the bees droning lazily over the herb garden, giving the honey its wild, aromatic flavour. I thought of the lean herds of China, and the sleek cattle I had seen yesterday; I thought of the spiced, exotic dishes the Chinese ate, and the plain goodness of the food here. It should have come from the hands of a plump, comfortable, house-proud woman, gossiping as Morag did. And I kept remembering the haunted, anguished face of the woman the night before, afraid of something much more than the invasion of her kingdom by another female. She did not fear just for her place here, but for Cluain itself.

But whatever graces and gifts she had, she had another side, and I must both face it and ignore it. I would have to go in to her in the kitchen now, and wait to see how she reacted to me. Was last night some aberration she would prefer forgotten?—or would we continue as we had left off? And between us, forever, stood those unforgettable words on William's scroll. One day I would charge her with them—with them, and nothing else. And she might shrug her shoulders, indifferent and calm, and claim it was the ramblings of a fevered brain. And what did they mean, after all, and who was accused? I sighed, now more puzzled than at any time since I had first deciphered the characters. Knowing Cluain and the woman had made nothing easier or more clear.

For a while after I had eaten I wandered uncertainly about the room, lingering over the small task of loading the breakfast dishes on the tray, trying to spin out the time before I dared to face her in the kitchen—her own, indisputable domain. But there was so little in this room—so bare, so stark. The last century and a half might not have been, if one could believe one's eyes. No picture of my grandmother, or my mother; no sewing basket, no writing table, no animal by the hearth. Outside the birds sang and the herbs waved; inside it was static, a set piece. I paused before the table which held the chess set. Last night's game, and its moment of revelation, might never have been. I fingered the White Queen in a moment of disbelief; but it had happened—it had. Then my hands moved on to the Bible. It probably was very old; the leather was drying out, even with the polishing. The brass corners and clasp shone. Then I tried to open it. It was, as I should have known, locked.

It was then I took up the big silver tray and started for the kitchen.

The dining room opened into a passage, and the kitchen door was opposite. Close by was a door that led to the garden, and on the other side the passage twisted out of sight around the curve of the tower. A door back there would lead down to the river, and the path I had seen from my window going around to the stables and the distillery. On the stone floor, beside a bench, was ranged a neat row of boots. Tweed coats and capes hung in a line above them. As in all farms, few of the household entered by the front door and crossed that shining wood surface. I steadied the tray on one hand, and reached for the latch of the kitchen door. Instinctively I had drawn in my breath, making myself ready to look into Mairi Sinclair's face.

But it was her voice I heard. And it was raised to a pitch of intensity I knew too well—not a tone she would have used to Morag in giving her instructions, or chiding her about the day's tasks. This was something deeply felt, and important.

"Och, it sickens me to see you hang about like this! Here it is gone late in the day, and the Master's been at work since early. Don't you *care*—now more than ever?"

The answer was slow, heavy with scorn. A man's voice, deep, hardly concerned with the answer he gave her. "Och, hush, you. Everything's in good order, and will be when we start distilling again. What's there to do at this time? God Almighty, we've only just finished after a long winter's work. You know right well we'll not be distilling again until the barley's harvested and the weather settles colder. From now on, my time's my own."

Her furious voice cut him short. "And what kind of farmer are you that there's nothing to be attended to? The cattle are up in the shielings to look to, the tackroom's full of harness to be mended, the fences to be inspected. Does a farmer ever have time to call his own? You and your roaming ways—will you never have done with them? Never showing yourself near the farmyard. What does the Master think of you . . . ?"

His exasperation was plain. "Och, enough! *You* go and gather your eggs or make your butter or whatever else it is that you must next do for Cluain. *I've* earned my days to myself, and earned them right well, and he knows it. If I've a mind, on a day like this, to take some bread and ale and time to myself to walk where I want, then I'll do it, and no man will tell me else. He knows what I do for Cluain—well he knows it, and he doesn't dare question what I choose to do when there's no need for me about the place. He has other men who can mend the fences, and herd the cattle on the shielings—and plenty of that I've done in my time. Let him whistle to the wind for me, and I'll come when I'm right and ready."

"It is not wise. Only a fool neglects his opportunities . . ."

"Wisdom, is it? Oh, God, your head's stuffed full of knowledge, and not an ounce of wisdom in it. When you walk along the roads and watch for your herbs and flowers, do you ever think to raise your eyes to see what's above you? Do you ever stop to listen to the birds, to watch their flight? Or do you only look to see where they've left their eggs? Well, if that's so, I'm sorry for you. I've no intention in the world of spending my life serving one man. I'll serve myself first, and then see what comes—"

" 'Tis Cluain will suffer . . ."

"Let it." The words were final, and measured.

"Have you lost your senses?"

"Perhaps, but no great loss."

The silence fell between them, as if she had heard more than she could answer. I listened to the banging of iron pans, a mark of speechless fury. I used the noise as a chance to rattle the china a little on the tray, and fumble at the latch. Mairi Sinclair was there in an instant; the door was flung open as she confronted me. She made a swift movement to take the tray from my hand, but I swept past her as if I had not seen the gesture.

"You have some magic with the bees, Mistress Sinclair. It is the best honey I have ever tasted."

"I was coming to take the dishes—"

"No need, surely. Are you so grand at Cluain that I may not come into the kitchen? After all, you have the right to *my* room."

She met my thrust in silence. I went on past her, to the big scrubbed table in the middle of the flagstoned room, putting down the tray with exaggerated gentleness. It was only then that I allowed myself to look around.

He stood leaning against the mantel, but his shoulders came higher than the shelf; it was not the face I recognised, because it had been nearly lost to me in the dimness under the beeches, and last evening he had bent his head before the rain. But the figure was unmistakable; even in the heat of the dispute with Mairi Sinclair his body had yet retained its quality of stillness, of being contained within itself—the same as when he had stood with the dog and the bird on his gloved hand, the self-containment of the man alone in the rain. He wore the faded red kilt—or perhaps another one, for

57

this seemed dry—a shabby, almost ragged garment, and long socks knitted in the same pattern; I was startled to see a dagger—I would later learn to call it a dirk—thrust into the band of the sock by his right hand. The sheepskin jerkin was slung across a chair, the shoulders still dark with moisture. He was holding a tankard with both hands, which he lowered slowly from his lips. It was the same kind of prideful indifference I had seen displayed in so many small ways since I had come. Clearly this man was not in the habit of springing to attention.

I returned his stare without letting my eyelids flicker. If he thought he could stare me down, let him try. He was more than ordinarily handsome; he must have known it—but from his attitude and his dress he didn't seem to care if anyone else should be impressed with the fact. He seemed too rigourously bent on telling all the world that he was free of its opinion. Was there some lingering thought in his mind that anyone would doubt it? His skin was oddly white for a man who was used to the outdoors—a natural whiteness, not a pallor. Everything else was black—the tumble of rough hair, the straight hard black line of his brows—from this distance it seemed that even his eyes were black. The line of his mouth matched his brows, a face cut deeply by the horizontals of brows and eyes and mouth. There was no softness to be discovered in body or face.

And then, with great deliberation, with me looking at him, he set the tankard on the mantel shelf, and picked up the sheepskin. He nodded, not to me, but to Mairi Sinclair.

"I'll be away, then."

I watched in a kind of stunned disbelief at the studied rudeness of the gesture as he went to the kitchen door, opened it, and closed it, not with a bang, but not gently, either. He must have known who I was; obviously he was an intimate of Cluain. This was not just an absence of welcome, but a complete rejection.

I had to ask her, though my lips were stiff with fury and outraged pride.

"Who—who was that?"

I thought she took some pleasure in the insult he had offered, and her own pride came thrusting up. I knew from that moment

I would likely never speak of what had happened last night. In the broad light of day, this woman was not weak, and would not be intimidated.

"Who? That was Callum Sinclair. My son."

And then, with no more concern than her son had displayed, she went to the door and took down a black shawl from its hook. She went out, as he had done, without a further sign to me, but she was not hurrying after him. A moment later, from the windows of the kitchen, I saw her in a leisurely but purposeful stroll along the flagged path of the garden. She walked a few paces, paused, bent to touch or smell; for a moment I thought I saw her lips move as if she spoke to those plants, and their nodding in the breeze was their answer. In those minutes she seemed to me to become a different creature. Her body lost its rigidness; her waist and neck and head seemed to bend and sway with the grace of a beautiful woman; she moved as the plants did. And, it seemed natural, the cat was there also, running before her, the white body disappearing into the grey of the lavender, the colourless eyes peering from the tall thyme. She paid no attention to the cat, nor he to her, but they were a pair, a company. They were supreme in a kind of splendid isolation.

"Well, then—that's Callum Sinclair for you."

Morag stood in a doorway that led, I guessed, to a scullery beyond. She was wiping her hands in her apron.

"And his mother," I added. How easily I had slipped into the role of friend with this girl, her manner so easy, frank, without servility, but without presumption. Did this natural dignity belong here to this people, to this country?

"Och, aye—his mother. 'Tis his father they'll never be knowing."

"Dead?"

She shrugged. "Who knows? They do tell me that when Callum Sinclair was born here at Cluain—here, in this kitchen, I think—his mother seemed near to death, and Mistress Macdonald, who had taken her in at Cluain out of charity when no one close would, urged her to say who was the father, so that her child could have a name, and a claim on some kin. But she never spoke, and she lived, and no one has ever known, or dared guess—before her face, that is—who is the father of Callum Sinclair. And it is my own opinion that whoever they might have guessed and riddled then, none of them ever did know the answer. It was near thirty years ago, and since then Mairi Sinclair had become a much respected woman in these parts. No one ever talks about it any more. For sure, there has been no other man, for all have observed her like hawks. Let once a woman fall, and she is never free of the eyes and the tongues again."

"Did she have no family, then—at that time?"

"Mistress Howard, I was not born then, and by the time I had grown into curiosity, people were already forgetting—save the odd old woman who will be forever talking about things past. I have not much time for those kind of people myself, but my mother was a great one for collecting stories, and since she did not care for Mistress Sinclair, she made it her business to know all that could be known of this one."

"So . . . ?"

Morag lifted her shoulders. "Well, they do say that she lived alone with her father, the only child still left to him. A terrible hard man, they said, very close with his money, and never giving company or a dram to anyone. They were poor—or so he made out to be. Mairi Sinclair worked very hard, but he sent her to the little school down here in the strath. A long trudge it was—and work to do on the croft in the evenings, and a cow to milk before setting out in the mornings. Very prideful, her father was, and he could not abide the disgrace of his daughter being with child and unwed. They say he beat her until she was like to have died. The wonder is that she did not miscarry of the child—perhaps that's what he intended. That's the way some men are, mistress—too many of them. He put her from his door, and for a time she stayed with neighbours until she got her strength again. But they were a big poor family, sending children off to Canada and Australia, and it was no place for her to stay. She was bound for Inverness herself when Mistress Macdonald invited her to stay at Cluain. She was a very kind woman, your grandmother. There was something said at the time that the Master did not want her here, but your grandmother overruled him. I suppose Mistress Sinclair

60

was a strange woman, even then, and her father was not liked. But she came, having no place else to go, and she stayed, and Callum Sinclair was born at Cluain. Och, she kept herself to herself after that, and tended her child, and gave herself to Cluain as if she could never do enough for it. There were never any complaints about Mairi Sinclair. She read her Bible and soon there was Mistress Macdonald sending off to Edinburgh for books about herbs for her, because she seemed to have a natural skill with them. The mistress encouraged Mairi Sinclair to write down her own records—how much of this and that she used in brews. They say she had a grandmother who was gifted in that way, but she was an unlettered woman, so the recipes were never set down. The boy—Callum— was clever too, and Mistress Macdonald could not be stopped from sending off for special books for him also, as he grew. Remember, it would not have been long after Mairi Sinclair came to Cluain that your own mother was up and off to China, and perhaps your grandmother was lonely. And as the mistress was poorly in health, in time she began to pass more and more of the running of Cluain into Mairi Sinclair's hands. At the time the mistress died, there was no change at Cluain—it went on as it had done before. There never was a better run household in the whole of Speyside, and the people were coming for years past to Mairi Sinclair for her skill with the herbs. They would even send for her when there was difficulty with a cow in calf, and the like. Stronger than a man, they said, and more gentle. She can soothe beasts with her very words—a soft tongue she has with anything that is dumb. No one ever questioned her staying on here after your grandmother died. Angus Macdonald would have been mad to let her go. People had long ago been saying that Andrew Sinclair had done himself a great disservice by sending her from his house. He had lost a rare woman."

"Were they never reconciled?"

"Never, mistress, never. He could never bring himself to speak to her again, and, indeed, in time, I thought she would not have wanted it. So bitter he was—probably more bitter because she had turned out so well—that he did not even leave his wee bit of land to her or his grandson. It was left to some far cousin off in London, or some such place, who never bothered even to come and see it. 'Twas only a poor bit of land, after all, with the gorse growing in on it, and fit only for a few sheep. But poor as it was, Mairi Sinclair was not to have it. The wee house on it fell into ruin, and the land was left go wild. They do say the cousin wanted to sell it, but none about here would buy—out of respect for Mistress Sinclair. They do say, also—though I can't tell if it is true—that to this day Mairi Sinclair has never set foot on her father's land again. And could you wonder at it?"

Absently, Morag moved to the range, and took a teapot off the hob. "Will you be having more tea, mistress? Och, no"—as I held my cup from the tray towards her—"I'll bring you a fresh one. Mistress Sinclair is a great one for doing things right. No sloppy ways in her kitchen . . ." Her eyes widened as I refused milk and sugar. "That's a very strange way to drink tea."

"Most people in China drink it that way," I replied, as absently as she had begun her own action. She stood by the range with her thick kitchen cup stirring the sugar vigorously, and I had my fresh cup of fine china, but there hardly seemed to be any difference between us. I was finding a kind of democracy of independent spirits at Cluain.

"They say," Morag continued, nodding towards the dark figure pacing the garden, "that the Master offered to pay for Callum Sinclair's schooling, when he had outgrown what the local dominie could offer, for he was a very bright lad. But Mistress Sinclair would take nothing she had not earned herself, and it was she who paid when he went to school in Inverness, and even to Edinburgh for a year. I can tell you none ever expected to see him back here again. Who would suppose he would come back to a place where all knew his story, and none knew his father's name? At nineteen he went into the distillery full-time, and when he had reached twenty-four, or thereabouts, he was running the place, almost. Och, not the business side, though he knows enough about that. He is not present when the buyers come to make their price. But he knows it right enough. He knows all there is to know about the business. He has some uncanny knack with the whisky—he has the nose and the eye for it, and he seems to know just exactly the moment when the foreshots become true whisky, and when the spirit itself runs into the feints. It is a gift as well as an art, mistress, and he has it."

"Then my grandfather values him highly?"

Morag shrugged. "He does—and he doesn't. Callum is fierce independent. He demands his rights—and mostly gets them. There's no great closeness between the two, though the Master has taught Callum all he knows. Callum comes and goes as he pleases— never neglecting the distillery, mind, but never letting it have all his life or his interest. Anything less than that of course, does not please the Master. I suspect that was what the trouble was about. Four years ago there was a great quarrel between them—Callum went back to Edinburgh and took some work there. But it was not long before the Master was sending for him to come back. And when Callum did, they struck their bargain. Callum lives now in a wee house up off the road, that he repaired and put in order himself. Not very often will he come and eat at his mother's kitchen table, and he has never spent a night under Cluain's roof since he came back. Before that—I remember when I was a wee thing—he moved himself out of the house and had a room over the stables. Always independent, he was—and nearly always getting his own way. In the silent season when they can't distill, then he's off and away, and no man owns his time. He has his mother's gifts in a way . . . he knows every fowl and creature that moves. He walks the moors in all weathers, and no harm ever comes to him. He has never had an ill day in his life, Mistress Sinclair says. 'Tis my own opinion . . . well, who am I to say what is what with Callum Sinclair? There's not many he would be giving any in- formation to about himself."

"What is your opinion, Morag?" I pressed.

She shrugged again. "I think that was why he came back from Edinburgh. He was born here, and he cannot abide the crampiness of the towns. He puts in his time at the distillery, and works like three men, and then is free. He would owe the Master nothing —nor any man, I think."

Morag was nodding, as if she were striving to grasp the meaning of Callum Sinclair's life, her eyes on the figure of Mairi Sinclair as she bent to pinch back a bud, or pull a weed.

"They do fight something terrible at times. But mother and son, they're two of a kind. They walk their own way."

II

I found my own way out by the passage that curved around the tower to the back door of Cluain. On this side of the house it was pasture down to the river bank—again, a parklike planting of oak and beech that told the many years that Cluain had stood upon this land. I noticed the churned-up mud of the path that the cows took to the dairy, but the stone path that skirted the house itself seemed, as everything else at Cluain, freshly swept. I paused for a time looking down at the tumble of the river, but irresistibly the buildings of the distillery drew me. I wondered if I would find my grandfather there, or was he elsewhere about the farm? And what was the "silent season" they talked of, when the distillery did not operate? I was crossing the cobbled yard that was bounded by Cluain's walled garden, the stables and the distillery building when I heard the same terrible shrieking, hissing noise that had greeted my arrival yesterday.

I stopped, and then around the corner of the distillery the flock of geese came in a swirling tide. They came straight at me, their cries raucous, big white wings flapped awkwardly, long necks and beaks thrust forward. I had no time now to consider which door might lead to my grandfather's offices. I ran for the nearest one, the whole horrible tribe following me. It might be locked, and then I would have to go the whole length of the building to the next one. I turned and faced them, waving my arms and shouting, but they retreated just a foot or two, and that only for a moment. Then they were all around me again, and as I struggled with the knob of the door I felt two quick pecks at my leg. Even through the thickness of my skirt it was sharp and painful. As the door opened on oiled catch and hinge, I turned once again and made a vengeful lunging kick at the big gander who led the flock. For a moment he was taken aback; I could nearly have laughed at the almost human surprise he displayed in the way he reared back—laughed, that is, if my leg hadn't hurt so much. But he was coming at me again.

"Go on, devil!—go on," I shouted, and slammed the door.

Outside, the screaming went on for a time, and then gradually died down. I stood with my back to the door rubbing my leg, and trying to get my bearings in the jumble of doors, passageways, and iron staircases. The windows were high-up, round, and gave little light.

"Are you hurt?" It was Callum Sinclair.

I didn't know where he had come from. Perhaps he had been there all along enjoying my discomfort, knowing what must have happened. Then I saw his face more clearly. No, he hadn't been enjoying anything. His face was still clouded and grim, as I had seen it in the kitchen, but it showed concern.

"Not badly . . . I don't think." I pulled up my skirt, not caring what he thought about that, and examined my calf. The stocking was torn, but that angry beak had only pinched me, not broken the flesh.

Callum Sinclair nodded. "You'll do. But you wouldn't have been the first one Big Billy's drawn blood from."

"The gander? Why does my grandfather have such a vicious animal around?"

"It's not his choice. The whole stupid flock belongs to the gauger—the Exciseman—who lives in that cottage by the warehouses. He claims his geese go with him wherever he does, and when he has them, he doesn't need any other watchman. He could almost be right. Of course, since he's been at Cluain more than twenty years, neither he nor his flock is likely to move on."

I noticed while we talked that Callum Sinclair impatiently weighted the spanner he held in his hand; then it wasn't quite true, all that he had said in the kitchen about not caring what went on at the distillery now that his agreed time there was finished. Did he only say such things to worry and anger his mother, to display his independence from Angus Macdonald? It seemed as if he had been occupied with some maintenance task in the building when the geese had alerted him to my presence. It was with such care as this, of course, that he had won his bargain with my grandfather; the indifferent gained no such privileges.

"What is the watchman needed for? In a remote place like this must one guard everything so carefully?"

For a moment he nearly smiled. "Miss Howard—forgive me—you have a great deal to learn about the whisky business. There's a fortune in government excise taxes lying in those casks in the warehouses. If your grandfather had as much money as the government is owed in excise on the whisky he's holding for those he's sold it to, he'd be a rich man."

"Does my grandfather let the gau—" I stumbled over the unfamiliar word, "the exciseman do what he wants at Cluain?"

Sinclair shrugged. "And who's to say him nay? Cluain doesn't pay Neil Smith—Her Majesty's Customs and Excise does. Cluain provides his house, and he takes whatever measures he thinks necessary to guard the warehouses. And Big Billy's about the best there is. At night Smith shuts the whole flock in a pen that's built hard by the warehouse door there—so the foxes won't have a feast. No one could get inside without the whole world knowing it. In theory, a man is supposed to come from Grantown several days a week to relieve Smith—in practice it hardly ever happens. The Excise has long turned a blind eye to it. They know that Neil Smith has nothing else in his life but watching over Cluain. And Cluain is considered very secure. A small, compact distillery—the warehouses a continuous building, only one door that can be opened from the outside. Neil Smith always on duty. And with Big Billy, you hardly need locks. Beside the guard duty Big Billy performs, there's a nice profit at Christmas from the young birds that Neil Smith fattens up. Both ways, Smith does very nicely out of Big Billy."

"Big Billy nearly did very nicely out of me. If this Mr. Smith is such a great guardian of Cluain, why didn't he come out and investigate what I was doing here?"

"Oh, he undoubtedly saw the whole thing from his window, and is laughing his head off, the sour old man. He knows well enough who you are, and if it had been to the warehouses you had gone running, he'd have taken the greatest pleasure in telling you you had no business there. Besides, you couldn't have got in. And he would have let Big Billy torment you a little longer just to bring home the fact."

"But it's all right to come here?"

"We're not distilling now. You couldn't even get a dram of newly distilled spirits drawn off now. So he's no care of who comes and goes here. But of the warehouses, only the exciseman and the owner have the keys. If anything's missing, the owner pays."

"Don't you have a key? I've been told you're the most important man at Cluain."

"Who told you that?"

"Not your mother."

He shrugged again. "It doesn't matter. I am not the Master of Cluain. I do not hold the keys."

I rubbed my leg more fiercely; I had the strange impression if propriety had not forbidden it, Callum Sinclair would have done it for me. It wasn't that he was at all interested in me as a woman, but just that the thought of any wound or hurt aroused his sympathy. I continued to rub.

"Why were you so rude to me?"

"I didn't know I had been."

I waved my hand impatiently. "Oh, I have no time for this game you all play here. You know when. There, in the kitchen."

"How could I have been rude to you? We hadn't been introduced."

"And have we now—except by Big Billy?"

And now his face actually creased in a genuine smile, and was incredibly altered by it. I began from that moment, I think, to wish I could draw it often from him. He laughed, and then his face came to rest again. The horizontals I had noted before were all back there—the straight brows, the eyes, the mouth; but not grim any longer.

"You're quite like your brother, William," he offered.

"I'm pleased you think so. But did you like him?"

He nodded. "William was all right. He had a lot to learn."

I bristled with resentment. *"You* say that! William was always counted very intelligent—clever."

"Clever, yes. That doesn't mean a man has nothing left to learn. William was young—"

"And I suppose you are old?"

He made a slight gesture of acquiescence, waving the spanner. "Very well then. I give you the point. I am not so old. But I have not been protected. I am not the son of a bishop—" And then he stopped, as if the inadvertent words had burned his lips. No one must enquire—no one could—whose son he was.

I gave my leg a final vigorous rub. "Well, then, I am here now. I've run the gauntlet of Neil Smith and Big Billy. Has it been worth it?"

He seemed suddenly at a loss. "I can take you back to the house. Big Billy keeps his distance of me. He will get to know you very soon . . ."

"Never mind Big Billy. Next time I'll flap a shawl at him—or something. But I can't have gone through this for nothing. You will show me the distillery?"

At once all the friendliness, the concern was gone. His face seemed to freeze over, not with deference, but in withdrawal. "You will have to excuse me, Miss Howard. It is not my province. It is your grandfather's privilege—and he is not in the distillery. I am not the Master of Cluain."

I clenched my fists, and for a moment my eyes closed in frustration. When I looked at him again those mud-grey eyes were staring at me in cold concentration. "I," I said, "am tired of hearing of the Master of Cluain. There are other people in the world. Were you my brother's friend? A friend could show me about the distillery."

"Friend?—I don't know that I was a friend. Would he have counted me that?"

"How would I know?"

"He didn't tell you of Cluain in letters—talk about the people here?"

68

"It takes a long time for letters to get to China. He hadn't much time to get used to Cluain. Oh, he talked of it . . . in a general way." Then I stopped pretending, to myself and to this man. "Oh, it's no use! He *didn't* have much to say about Cluain. I think he was afraid of disappointing us. You know, he always intended to come back to China . . ."

"And he changed his mind? He meant to stay on at Cluain after he had finished with the university, didn't he?"

I gestured impatiently. "How am I to know? He never *said* so. It's just what he didn't say. One began to guess." Then I didn't want to talk about it any more. "Well, will you show me the distillery?" I was looking about me, trying to dismiss the subject.

But Callum Sinclair persisted. "So you guessed you were losing William—but he died without you knowing for sure. And then your father was killed. There was a lot written about it in the papers. A lot of talk—gunboat talk. Everyone very upset. And then they said those responsible had been punished, and that was the end of it. We heard nothing more. I knew, of course, that William had a sister. I thought of you . . ."

Two men now had said this to me, in their different ways. They had thought of me, whom they didn't know. But no word had come from my grandfather. The first anger rose again, the sense of being unwanted. More than ever I was determined that Callum Sinclair would show me about the distillery. I would prove to my grandfather I had friends. I would win the same rights as William.

"Talk! Yes, there was a lot of talk! There would have been a lot more talk if one of their precious warehouses had been burned, or an opium shipment taken by bandits. But a man of God—well, there are always more of *them!* That's the way they think."

"You believe there should have been reprisals?"

I sighed, and very slowly shook my head. "No—I didn't want that, even at the very worst moments. I know it was the last thing my father would have prayed for before he died—that there would be no slaughter of innocent or misled people to pay for his life. I think he always expected to die in some such way in China. No, there would have been no wish for vengeance."

He nodded, and looked unblinkingly at me for a long time. "I think I might have respected your father very much if he was really as you say. And you might hope William would have become like him."

"Why?"

"He seems to have had no sense of power. I hate the weight of power and respect—and what is owed to people, and demanded by them because of the position they hold. So many feel the need to possess—and hold on. What is theirs, is theirs. Their pound of flesh!"

I shook my head wonderingly. "What a strange man you are, Callum Sinclair. You should be out organising worker's unions. Do you always talk like this? In the kitchen you wouldn't say a word."

"In the kitchen I would have had to say useless, false words. Did you expect me to touch my forelock, and bid you welcome to Cluain? I leave that to other people. There are enough around to bow and scrape."

Now I laughed. "If you could know that lack of *that* I've had. No one has bid me welcome to Cluain. Will you do it now?"

He shook his head. "No—I couldn't. I don't know that it's right that you've come. Perhaps you'll regret it—perhaps you won't. Your grandfather is one for his pound of flesh . . . remember that. One thing I'll tell you. The first morning your brother was here he wasn't left to find his way to the distillery alone, chased by Big Billy's tribe. No—the prodigal never had a warmer welcome. Hours spent showing him how it all worked. He couldn't possibly have understood a quarter of it that first day. And then the tasting session in the Master's office. Your fine young man was half tipsy by the time dinner hour came around. Angus Macdonald tried so hard he almost ruined it all—trying to pack into William's head in a few hours what it would, in a natural way, take him years to learn. And trying to educate his tongue to the niceties and qualities of Cluain's whisky at all its stages of maturing until William, I believe, could hardly see straight. The old man made it too obvious, and

William almost threw it all away, then and there. For a while I thought it was in the balance, whether or not he would ever come back to Cluain. Your grandfather saw his heart's desire, and he was stretching out his big paws to grab it before it slipped from him. Power—power and greed.

"So now, Miss Howard, after what I've said, are you sure you still want me to show you the distillery?"

I nodded humbly. "Yes—yes, please. I think I trust you, Callum Sinclair. You're outrageously honest—and yet I'll trust you not to laugh at me because I'm a woman, and I'll seem stupid about things most men have some knowledge of."

He rocked back on his heels. "Stupid you're not, or you wouldn't be talking like this. Neither was William stupid. A woman, yes—but women can be the very devil, because they can hide their cleverness so well. They take a man unawares. So, all right then—I'm not the Master of Cluain, but I will try to do what he should be doing now."

* * *

My mind was weary before we were half through with it. I said "Yes—yes . . ." to each thing Callum Sinclair said, and in the first half hour, even tried to ask questions. But in a little while I found I was just accepting, trying desperately to store what I could, and knowing I was making a miserable mess of it. And I suppose that Callum Sinclair knew it also.

But he was patient. He talked slowly, and as he talked, his voice grew more gentle, the words and phrases less clipped. He dropped his stride to my pace as we walked all through those vast soundless spaces of the distillery. I almost could see that this was how he had trained his setter dog to move obediently at his heels, with soft words and easy, patient movements. But he also had trained a wild, fierce hawk, a creature of the skies, and how had he done that?

Almost before we had begun I asked the one question I had prepared, the one that had puzzled me: "Why do they call this 'the silent season?' Why is the place empty?—no one working?"

"You're a little ahead of me. But no matter. Not much of it will make sense, the first time through. Later on, when the weather gets cooler, you'll see the whole thing. We 'go silent' as they say because the weather is too warm and humid now for malting the barley. Visitors to the Highlands think that's something of a joke, because for them the weather here is always cool, if not downright cold. But if we brought the barley in now, supposing we had any left in the stores, after screening it off for impurities, and steeping it in our own water for about two to three days, we would bring it to the malting floors—here, this way. Mind your dress. We keep the place clean, but it's becoming an old building, and not meant for long skirts . . ."

"The malting . . ." I prompted.

"Yes, the malting. After the barley's been steeped it's brought here—" He opened a door, and a huge, completely empty room faced us, the stone floors clean-swept, but the whole place having a smell which seemed almost like a warm mouldiness. "It's stacked about a depth of three feet here, and it begins to germinate. You could almost call it breathing. It takes in oxygen, and gives off carbon dioxide. It starts to give off a fair amount of heat, too, and we have to keep the temperature down at about sixty degrees —and that means the men must keep turning it with these shovels here—" He reached beside me to a row of long wooden shovels stacked along the wall. "We call these 'sheils' and this whole process is called, 'turning the piece.' So you see, in these few months, when the weather's warm and humid, we stop altogether, because the barley will germinate too quickly—it grows little rootlets and these would tangle up, and all you'd get is a matted mess. So, we 'go silent' about this time. For us, here at Cluain, that only happened a few days ago. This is a chance, too, to repair what needs repairing about the distillery, seeing everything's in good order for the next season. Breakdowns cost money. We're very careful with our maintenance. And when you have a farm and your own barley to harvest, then the silent season is a necessary thing. There's talk of some distilleries bringing in barley already malted from outside, but he would never hear of using any but Cluain's barley . . . the product has to be Cluain's from start to finish. But

72

you must know that already." He gave a quick sideways glance at me as he said that.

"But the silent season's a good thing. It gives a man a chance to get the smell of the barley out of his nose—barley in all its stages, dry and dusty, the wet smell of germinating, the reek of the peat when we dry it in the kilns, the smell of beer when it's halfway through its journey, and then that final smell that's spirits. A man needs to forget it. He needs to remember that there's another world outside these walls. I sometimes wondered if William . . . well . . ."

"What about William?"

"We never talked about it. But he took to walking, I noticed. He didn't spend all day here. And those were the times when Angus Macdonald could scarcely contain himself. He didn't want William out of his sight, and William would not have it that way. Well, Angus Macdonald never did have his own son—and he too often made the mistake of treating William like a little boy. So William used to go off without telling him where, or when he would be back . . ." Then he stopped. "And you must be thinking that it would have been so much better if William *had* told him—that last time. If he had, William would not have lain for two nights—"

"Please, no more. I've had enough of death."

"I know. But it's something I blame myself for as well. *I* should have found him. I know every part of this country better than any man around. And I have a dog who lives by his nose. And we failed . . ."

"Please," I said, "could we go on? It is useless to talk of what might have been. My father need never have made that last journey into Szechwan, either. William need never have come to Cluain. For that matter, I need not have come. But I am here. Shall we go on?"

"As you wish."

Had it created a coldness, this refusal to allow him to speak this unfounded guilt he felt? But I could not bear it for him, and for my grandfather as well; they would feel as they must. I had my own thoughts to live with. We went on in silence to the great drying kilns, and his explanations were brisk and precise —that is, if anyone could be precise about what began to appear a very complicated process. How was it, I wondered, that they talked about illegal stills in the mountain country that could be dismantled and carried away, when it seemed that all this great plant was needed to make that warm glowing liquid I had tasted for the first time the night before. I asked Callum Sinclair this.

"What's made in those little illegal stills isn't brewed for the pleasure of tasting it, but to knock a man insensible." He pointed to the drying kiln. "That's what's at the bottom of those odd chimneys you see in every distillery."

"They reminded me of Chinese pagodas . . ."

"We dry it over peat fires to give it its flavour—that, and the barley, makes Scotch different from the American whiskys, their Bourbon and rye. There's no particular mystery about making Scotch. It needs skills—traditional and ancient skills. Perhaps it needs a climate like ours—not just to mature it, but because the climate breeds the *need* for it. Those illegal brews are made, I think, just to help men forget what sort of winter they have to live through here . . ."

As we walked we came on two men bent over the task of re-soldering the joint of a pipe. I guessed Callum Sinclair had been with them when the noise of Big Billy had called him away. He punctiliously introduced both men to me, and both stood up and offered a murmured welcome. "James Macfarlane, Miss Howard. John Murray . . ." As we moved out of earshot he added, "A distillery runs on very few workers—all are skilled—and all are valued. A distillery man is a very special breed. You won't find too much need of worker's unions here. They know their value —and so does Angus Macdonald."

He continued on, and I tried to remember, and most of it went over my head. After drying in the kiln the malt was left for about six weeks, screened for impurities, and separated from the dried-up rootlets. "The rootlets we call malt culms, and feed them to the cattle. After we're rid of all that we grind it up—it's called grist then—and it goes into the mash tuns." He led me on to another room containing four huge circular vessels. "Three thousand gallons," he said laconically. "The grist is extracted four times with hot water—each lot of water higher in temperature until we reach

74

about eighty degrees for the last. Only the first two extractions go on to the fermentation stage—we keep back the third and the fourth to form the extractions of the next batch of grist. All this mashing here is to reactivate the ferments which were stopped during the drying. Have you ever heard of enzymes—?"

"I'm not a chemist."

He nodded. "The old man will be asking you questions. Even if you don't have any answers, at least it helps if you've heard the words. Well . . . let's keep on. The first two extractions from the mash tuns are called worts. Once we have the worts we haven't any more need for the barley, and that goes to the cattle, too. We cool down the worts to about seventy to eighty degrees by passing it through this heat exchanger. Cooled down to this temperature, we run it into the washback, and add the yeast. Through here . . ."

I scrambled after him, ducking under pipes and stepping over some, the ends of my skirts getting damp from the little uneven places in the floor where water—or was it some of the products of the distillations—had collected. No it would be water. Angus Macdonald—and, I thought, Callum Sinclair—would never have tolerated a sloppily cleaned floor. Big wooden circular vessels again "—made of larch," Callum Sinclair said. "Perhaps it's just as well you've come in the silent season. It's a pretty violent affair when the yeast begins to work on the worts—it keeps bubbling all the time, and the men have to keep stirring it with birch sticks to keep it from boiling over. Maybe you wouldn't like the smell, either. It gives off carbon dioxide. The whole business takes about thirty-six hours—which is why I think we all need our time out of the distillery to get our lungs cleaned out. If you were a chemist now . . ." It was growing to be a joke. ". . . I would tell you about the enzymes first producing dextrose from the maltose, and then converting dextrose into alcohol and carbon dioxide. But you're not a chemist."

"When will it be *whisky?*" I demanded.

"Patience. This is where we begin dealing with Neil Smith as an Excise officer. With me, or Angus Macdonald, he's calculated about the amount of spirit that the worts should yield, from the specific gravity of the liquid at the beginning of the fermentation, and at the end. The liquid at the end of the process is a clear mixture of water, yeast and a bit over five percent volume of alcohol —that's about ten percent proof. We call it the wash. This is what the pot stills have been waiting for."

"Whisky," I said faintly. No matter how they scoured and cleaned, the smell would forever be there, locked deep into the wooden containers, the roof beams, the cracks in the stone floors. I wanted to be done.

"Not quite," he said. And he led me through a doorway and out on to a kind of gallery that looked down at two huge copper vessels, pear-shaped, almost, with long necks curved at odd angles. "These are the pot stills," he said. "These are the heart of malt whisky. Let Angus Macdonald tell you about the patent stills— that's the spirit they mix with the pure malt to make a blend. But when someone says a pot distilled whisky, they mean what comes out of these two beauties here. Distilling is just turning liquid into vapour—the wash in this case—and condensing the vapour back into liquid. This is where it's done. The first one, the one with the big neck, is the wash still, and the other is the low-wines still. All distillers have their fantasies about their own pot stills. When Angus Macdonald has to have a part of one of these replaced because the copper is wearing thin, he will personally go and see that every small dent that might have been banged into the first still by accident over the years is reproduced—he does it with his own hands. There are some distilleries where they won't even disturb the cobwebs in case it somehow alters the kind of brew they finally get. We're not quite that daft at Cluain.

"We heat the wash by coals, and there's a copper mesh called a rummager dragged around the bottom of the still to keep the insoluble stuff in the wash from burning. The distillate is driven up the neck of the still, and into a coiled copper pipe—its called a worm—that's buried in a tank of cold water. The alcohol is driven off first because it boils at a lower temperature than water —when it's all driven off what's left in the still is called pot ale or burnt ale, and we just run it to waste. The distillate is called low wines . . ."

76

"No whisky yet?"

He shook his head. "The low wines pass through the spirit safe —the Excise has locks before and after on *that*. We check thermometers and hydrometers to see when all the alcohol has been driven off the wash still. When the distillate leaves the spirit safe it goes into that tank there, the low-wines charger, where it's mixed with that we call the foreshots and the feints—I know, I know . . ." He sought to soothe my bewilderment with a gesture. "It's hard to put this in order, but the foreshots and the feints are the rejects of the second still, the spirits still, so I've jumped ahead of you here—can't help it—whisky is a sort of backwards and forwards thing at this stage. The mix of the low wines, the foreshots and the feints all go into the spirit still—that's always smaller than the wash still. Then it's heated again, and the whole process of the distillate is repeated—up the neck of the still, and down through the worm to cool it. This time we run it off in three sections. The first part, the foreshots, is highly impure whisky—the middle running is what we want, and we send this into the spirits receiver. This comes over at twenty-five overproof, and we keep collecting it until it's down in strength to about five overproof. What's left is the feints, and that's impure whisky, too—so that's how the foreshots and the feints are waiting in the low-wines charger to mix with the next batch from the wash still."

"How can you tell what's the real whisky, and what's the foreshots and the . . . the feints?"

"Over here." He led me along the gallery and down more stairs —what a warren the place was, almost without logic, as if bins and kilns and washback and stills had all been fitted into the building as best they could. We seemed to have doubled back on ourselves several times. How William's engineering mind would have hated the jumble, have longed for a smooth, orderly progression.

"This is the spirit safe, here—and we control what goes into the spirits receiver by using these taps. It comes down to the simple, and difficult fact, that it's here we decide what's acceptable whisky."

It was something like a brass trunk with glass sides and top, fitted

77

with measuring vessels and hydrometers. There were large brass padlocks on each end of it.

"We don't taste it, you see. The Excise doesn't permit that. They know every drop that goes through this safe, and we have to account for it. There's no hard and fast rule for deciding when we turn the distillate into the spirits receiver—when it stops being foreshots and becomes whisky, and then when it turns into feints. It comes out as colourless liquid, of course, and when water is added, the foreshots will become cloudy. When it is clear, we judge it to be true whisky."

"Who judges?"

"Angus Macdonald used to do it. Now I do."

"You're responsible then . . ."

He nodded. "It's something of a nicety to decide when the liquid is a true potable whisky. An error—running the foreshots into the spirits receiver too soon, or letting it run on until some of the feints get into it, isn't anything you find out about immediately. With a good whisky like Cluain's, you'll maybe find out a dozen years later when you compare one batch with another, that it's not quite as it should be. It hasn't maybe got quite the flavour and character and bouquet that Cluain's distilling should give it. But Angus Macdonald doesn't seem to have made mistakes in his time. We've yet to find out how many I have made."

"Why would one whisky be different from another? . . . aren't all malts made the same way?"

"No one has ever answered that. I suppose it starts with the water. The shape and size of the stills have something to do with it—some say the higher the still the better, because fewer impurities will get through. The angle of the lyne arm connecting the head of the still to the condensing unit has a lot to do with it— or so they say. But you'll not find a chemist anywhere who can tell you precisely what makes a good malt. They haven't turned it into a science yet—and I don't think they ever will. The knowledge, the way of doing it all, is passed on. You often get generations of families working in distilleries."

"That was why my grandfather wanted William—"

Then I was sorry I had said it. Callum Sinclair's face hardened;

he had, after all, told me that he was responsible for the judgement of what was good enough to be called Cluain's whisky. I had offended him—in more ways than one. I had to keep reminding myself that no one knew if, in his case, the skill was something he had as an inheritance, or merely learned. Did he ever, I thought, look around the faces at the distillery and wonder if it was from one of them his hand and eye had learned the knack?

"William," he replied, "knew something about chemistry and he was nearly qualified as an engineer. It would have been a whole new career, and many years, before he could be called a distiller. But, yes—your grandfather wanted him. Was it so strange? William was . . ."

He never told me what he believed William had been. Instead he turned abruptly away from the spirit safe. "I don't hold the key to the warehouses, and I won't ask Neil Smith to open up for us. He'll follow you around like Big Billy. Ask Angus Macdonald to show you what's there. Is there anything else you want to know?"

He was back to the man he had been in the kitchen. Deliberately rude, determined to show me how little I mattered.

I put out my hand and plucked angrily at his sleeve. "You haven't finished. I'm sorry if I've said the wrong thing—but you told me I'd never understand it all in the beginning, and it isn't just distilling one needs to understand in a place like this. You know well enough what I'm talking about. And then, you said yourself that my grandfather will be asking questions. Am I to say you stopped short . . . ?"

He sighed, and his shoulders seemed to relax a trifle. He looked at me with faint indulgence, as if I might have been an importunate child. "Very well, Miss Howard. There's hardly anything left, so you might as well have the rest of it, and don't blame me if your head is spinning, and you can't remember any of what I've said. But now—you've got your whisky at last—true Cluain whisky, distilled with care—you could say love—in its traditional manner. What you get into the spirits receiver is about one hundred and twenty proof. It's colourless, extremely pungent, and would lift your head off to drink it. Though it's also a tradition that the Excise

79

turns a blind eye to the men having their dram of unmatured, unbonded whisky every day. It *should* kill them, but it doesn't. They grow to ripe old age in the trade, and you'd never think of laying off a distillery worker just because he's an old man. I think myself they're like herrings in brine. They'd dry up without it."

"Do you drink it like that?" I was thinking of the potent, but marvellously smooth distillate I had tasted the night before.

"Are you asking if I have the tastes of a gentleman? Well, I couldn't answer that. But I don't drink immature whisky."

"Why do you twist things . . . ?"

He gestured. "Oh, let us not go on! You're nearly finished with the distillery—and with me. Let's get to the end of it, and we needn't worry about what my habits or tastes are. Your grandfather wouldn't encourage it."

"I don't care what my grandfather—"

"Miss Howard, you are keeping me. I have other things to do. Now, shall we go on?"

I nodded, clamping my mouth down on words I wanted to spill out. "We add our spring water now before running the spirit into casks, which brings it down to about one hundred and ten proof. The casks are made of oak, and by preference they will have been used for storing sherry. This, over the years, gives a smoothness and a colour to the whisky. The size of the cask is a matter of choice—the smaller the cask, the faster the maturing. But there's a catch to that, though. The smaller the cask, the more whisky you'll lose through absorption by porosity. The oak has to be porous, to a degree, because the whisky has to breathe, without actually leaking. So you will lose something, whether you store it in thirty gallon casks, or hogsheads of fifty-five or sixty-five gallons. You'll mature more quickly in smaller casks, but you'll lose more. You'll not only get a loss of volume during maturing, but you lose strength too. The humidity in the warehouse effects both the volume and the strength. The drier the place the more you lose in volume. That's why the blenders come and buy it here at Cluain and leave it with us. There's nothing quite like the dampness of a Highland warehouse. Then, to bring it down to whatever proof is required, water is added at the bottling stage. But here at the distillery, when you are offered a dram, it will always be of high proof, and our own spring water added to cut it to your taste. Another of the little mystiques of the art."

He half-turned and began to walk away from me. "I think that's all I can tell you. Angus Macdonald will fill in the romance and the tradition of it all. Things he fed to your brother . . . But whisky is business, Miss Howard. Big business. Those who make it had better know what they're about."

I followed him silently through the warren of passages and stairs to the door at which I had entered. It seemed a long time ago; he was right; I would not remember much of what he had told me about the distilling of whisky, but I had learned more than I had come to find out. I had learned about William and my grandfather. I had learned a little about Callum Sinclair.

As if he had made a sudden decision, he almost flung the spanner on to a bench beside the door and took up his sheepskin. He opened the door for me, and at once I heard that familiar hissing sound. But now, when Big Billy and his flock rounded the corner of the warehouses and dashed across the road, the gander seemed suddenly to come to a sliding halt on the cobblestones. With one gesture of his hand Callum silenced them, and Big Billy turned haughtily and drove his way back through the flock, all of them falling in behind him, only little gobbling murmurs coming from their throats.

"Will Big Billy remember me?"

"I think so. He'll try to see how far he can go in frightening you. But he'll learn soon enough that you belong here, and after that it's a matter of facing him down. Neil Smith would probably enjoy seeing you too terrified to step outside the garden—but you must try not to give him and Big Billy that satisfaction. You have to show both of them that you have the right to be here."

"Do you think I have?"

He pulled the door closed with a bang. "I wonder why you bother to ask me? It's none of my business. But since you *have* asked . . . Like William, you have a right here so long as you don't give it away, or have it taken from you. His went by accident —almost by default. I wonder what you will do with your chance?"

The words tumbled out before I could stop them; he seemed the only link to William that was not mired in suspicion and doubt and greed. I had a terrible sense that very soon I might be given my chance, and might fail it.

"What would *you* do—if you were I? *No!*—I didn't mean that! What would you do if Cluain were yours."

He stared at me, his features tightening into something I was beginning to recognise as the shell erected by a man who appeared to want little of anyone, and wanted to be asked for little. "You ask foolish questions, Miss Howard. Indiscreet, childish questions. If Cluain were mine . . . I don't bother my head with such ideas."

"Someone must. My grandfather is old. He says a woman cannot run a distillery. Now—*now* I've seen it, listened to you, I almost believe he is right. You've told me so much. Now tell me what you would do if Cluain were yours."

I seemed to have touched a part of him which even his careful indifference could not hide. His eyes changed oddly, grew thoughtful and questioning. He stepped back and turned and looked over the whole length of the stone building, the two pagoda chimneys, even beyond it to the river, and then across toward the mountains, over all of Cluain's land.

"If it were mine . . . If Cluain were mine I'd mortgage my soul to gut this distillery—use it as another warehouse. I'd build a new one. Build it as it should be. There would be logic and order in it. The distilling would be an even flow from the storage for the barley to the final casking and weighing—not this mad backtracking and overlapping, fitting things in where there is space for them, not where they ought to be. How many times in there did we cross our own path to get to the next stage of the production? That's how wrong it is. It should be a quiet, orderly process, ticking away like a good machine. Instead there is wastage and double effort, and men tripping over each other. They're good workers, these men. They like what they're doing. I would like to see them have a place where they could double the output for no extra work."

"And my grandfather doesn't know these things? Surely he must . . . ?"

"Very likely he does. He doesn't ask my opinion. But I know him. Every stone of Cluain is his work—except the house, of course. He began in a very small way, with no money but what he could borrow, I'm told. He was geared for small production runs—remember, whisky has only fairly recently become a drink of the upper classes. Until the production of cognac was brought almost to a standstill by the phylloxera blight, no English gentleman could be persuaded to drink whisky. Now, of course, its respectable, and sought after. Cluain could sell four times as much as it produces. But your grandfather has his own ways. He has built Cluain and its reputation—and that's no small thing to have done. But he grows timid in his old age, I think—or tired. He could take Cluain's reputation to the bank now and build himself a new distillery with it. But he won't. The old feeling that you must reproduce every dent in the stills, and not dare to sweep away a cobweb hangs on. Cluain has served Angus Macdonald well, and he it."

Then he shrugged. "And who can blame him? At the end of a man's life does he start to build for the next generation when there is none? I know what *I* would do, but I'll not speak for what Angus Macdonald should do."

He turned, and it was finished. "You'll be all right now, going back to the house. I'll see Big Billy doesn't start after you."

"You—you're not coming to the house?"

He shook his head. "I have my own house, and anyway it's too good a day to spend within four walls. I've given Cluain its due for the day—more than that. I hadn't intended to go near the distillery . . . but I knew Macfarlane and Murray would be working and I thought . . ."

"Where will you go?" I couldn't help it; it was an impertinence to ask it of him, but I couldn't help it.

Once again his gaze swept away from the immediate vicinity of Cluain, once again down to the river, over the barley fields to the mountains, up to Ballochtorra's heights. "Where my nose leads me. I have a pony and a dog . . . and a bird."

"Yes, I know." I was giving so much of myself away to him. There seemed no pride in me. But lately pride had begun to seem such a useless, stupid possession, keeping one person from another. There was too much of it at Cluain.

"Then you know enough. A man with a dog, and a bird to fly . . . we will just go, that's all."

I tried to keep him, even for a minute longer. "It's some sort of a hawk, isn't it?"

It was as if I had struck a spark off him; his eagerness spilled out, transforming him. "A peregrine falcon. Giorsal is her name. I found her as an eyass up there on the far side of Ballochtorra's crag, and she has been with me for three years. We hunt these lands together. She is the freest, wildest thing I know, and yet she returns to my glove each time, and seems content. She cares nothing for distilleries or whisky or whatever we do down here. Her element is the sky, faster than any living creature when she stoops in her dive. There's no compliment greater to a man than when such a creature comes back willingly to his hand. Mind you, on the days I cannot fly her, I will happily raid Cluain's meathouse to bring her food, and Angus Macdonald can think what he likes. The time I give to the distillery is time taken from Giorsal. She is demanding—and wonderful. Her name means Grace in the Gaelic."

His face abruptly now took a wry, slightly bitter twist, as if a black humour had come to take the place of his exaltation. "Do you know the ancient rule, Miss Howard, which lays down precisely the social order among falconers of who shall have what, who may fly which among hawks?"

"No—is there one?"

"There is. Precise and definite. It goes so . . . *'An Eagle for an Emperor, a Gyrfalcon for a King; a Peregrine for a Prince, a Saker for a Knight, a Merlin for a Lady; a Goshawk for a Yeoman, a Sparrowhawk for a Priest, a Musket for a Holywater Clerk, a Kestrel for a Knave.'"*

Now he laughed aloud, as if he enjoyed what he had done to such orders and definitions. "So you see, by those rulings I would be flying a humble kestrel. So when I fly a peregrine falcon, I am no less than a prince. Good day, Miss Howard."

I watched him as he walked the length of the building—walked away from me. The shabby kilt was swinging above his knees, and I wondered why I never had seen before how it could become a man, how light and free it made him seem. The sheepskin was slung over one shoulder. Before he rounded the corner of the distillery, I heard him whistle, some lilting, marching melody that belonged to these hills and heaths. The world was wide about him, and he and his falcon would lose themselves in its heart. I looked up at the blue sky of this wondrous, soft summer day, and I seemed already to see the distant speck vanishing into the sun that would be his Giorsal in free flight.

I wanted to be with him—with him and Giorsal, and the dog and the pony. The whisper rose inside me, unrepressed. "Take me —take me with you!"

But he had not asked.

Chapter 4

I

That afternoon I followed Morag's directions and climbed up to the kirk and the graveyard on the hill on the other side of the river. I had to pass Ballochtorra, and cross the bridge below it. As I gained height on the road opposite, the road which forked to go to Ballinaclash, or to the kirk and on to Grantown, I kept looking across at it. Seen from here, viewed straight on, not at the angle I saw it from the tower room, it was a strangely unharmonious building. The central fortress retained its old, rather grim beauty; the rest, the new additions, seemed a tasteless clutter. Too much building had been piled into too little space—the crag had no room for broad sweeps, or matching proportions. Wings were tacked on at different levels, like a lopsided cake. It was strange how ill the mass of it suited the mood of the day. Yesterday, the wind-driven rain, and later the mist that had boiled up about it had lent it dignity. On this blue-golden day that character had been lost, and it lacked the quality of fantasy. Even this early in the day, one side of it was already in shadow, because of the steepness of the glen. By contrast, all of Cluain would bask in the sun until the last of the Northern twilight. Seen close to, the building was massive, overbearing. Its flamboyant style did not seem to fit with the reserve of Gavin Campbell's manner.

Once I was beyond the glen that Ballochtorra dominated, my

eyes swept the sky for a sight of Callum Sinclair's hawk, Giorsal. I had little hope of seeing her—how could I tell one bird among so many, when most of them were unfamiliar? And did not falcons climb so high that they were lost to sight? But I wanted to pretend I had glimpsed her; it brought Callum Sinclair closer to me, drew him back from his independent, self-sufficient journey, the journey on which he had not, and would not, I thought, ask for my company.

I had been late to the midday meal at Cluain. My grandfather had been in, had eaten, and had left again. "The Master is very busy, always," Morag had said when she brought the cold sliced beef, pickles, and the first delicate strawberries from Mairi Sinclair's garden.

"Did he ask for me?"

"He did that, and none of us could say where you were. He did not enquire any further. It is not his way. Were you at the distillery then?"

Something in her tone disturbed me. "Would it have mattered to my grandfather if I had been there?"

"If you had been? Och—there's no saying. It was Callum Sinclair then who showed you about?"

"Yes."

She said nothing more, and finished quickly with the dishes on the sideboard. I had to ring the small brass bell to summon her at the end of the meal. Not again today was I going to enter Mairi Sinclair's kitchen. I asked her then how I would find the kirk. She nodded, knowing my mission. "Should I send word to the Master. He would have the trap harnessed up. He might have a mind to go with you."

"I prefer to go alone."

I had a sense that she, or Mairi Sinclair, watched from one of the upstairs windows as I set off along the road to Ballochtorra and the bridge. And with as much determination as I could summon I shook off the thought of Mairi Sinclair. If I let her obsess me she would become a dark shadow on my life, and her insidious power would grow. If I was ever to resist the woman, that anguished haunted animal who had scratched upon the door of the tower room last night, I must hold myself detached from her. But how detached, and for how long? William's words came back to me. ". . . there is a Dragon Lady here . . ." I was glad then, when I was over the bridge, and the road twisted away from the sight of Ballochtorra and Cluain. The land opened out, and the sun seemed warmer. I began then to raise my eyes to look for the birds, with only the faint, but persistent hope that I would see Giorsal. Giorsal meant Callum Sinclair. But how did one pick a hawk from the sky? I felt depressed suddenly. The land and the people seemed more foreign than China. I would know only as much as I was permitted to know. I would never see the hawk in flight, stooping for her prey. I would only see the tamed, acquiescent creature on the glove—as if that was all there was to reveal.

The outline of the kirk was obscured by the ridge of a hill, but I recognised the dark shapes of the yews that Morag had described. It was not so far from Ballochtorra, but out of sight. It stood alone, a tiny church with a square tower, without a village, or even a single cottage near it. It seemed so forsaken, as if no one ever came there, or had ever been there. And yet, it was in good repair, the stone work well mortared, the plain windows intact, the latch of the gate lifted silently and easily under my hand. A good stone wall kept at bay the cattle that grazed the hillside; only one or two bothered to lift a head. They were sleek with summer grass. Farther down were fields of barley and oats; somewhere, a meadowlark sang. There was utter peace here. Suddenly I was reminded of my father's grave within the British Legation wall in Peking. Someday, I thought, those alien feet would trample it in some new rising against the Foreign Devils. It was far better that William lay here.

I found his grave easily enough—there were not so many of recent years, few whose headstones were not weathered beyond reading, or toppled and half-buried in earth and grass. There were several rows, though, whose headstones looked newly placed; they were polished marble slabs, but some of them bearing dates that went back several hundred years. The names were the same: Campbell . . . Campbell . . . Sir Andrew Campbell, his wife, Catriona . . . Mary Campbell . . . Sir Robert; three rows of Campbells, all lying in long-tenanted graves, with newly placed markers. Then, directly across the gravel path, I found William. It pleased me that here was no polished marble slab; the headstone was a piece of granite, barely cut to fit its place, the words chiselled deeply in it, WILLIAM MACDONALD HOWARD, and the dates his life had spanned. I was glad that no Bible text followed it; I was grateful to my grandfather that he had sought to give William the dignity of this simple memorial, the very roughness of the stone almost signifying that his life had not been finished, nor worn by time. There was no flowery text to extol his virtue —young people have not had time to establish that. The granite, by contrast, to the polished marble told another tale—my grandfather's belief in work and toil and simplicity decrying the formal splendour of the establishment at Ballochtorra. There was more than a hint of scorn for the polished niceties of the gentry.

The grass grew long on William's grave already, though this was its first summer. I wondered if I should bring tools one day to cut it; the Chinese every spring made a ceremony, called Ching Ming, of the cleaning of the ancestral graves. The siting of the graves was important to them; a well-placed grave could bring good fortune on the surviving family. "William . . ." I whispered. I wondered if I would be here next spring to perform the ceremony of Ching Ming. Why did one come to talk to the dead where they lay buried? William was more present in the tower room of Cluain than he ever would be in this grave. But he lay in a fair place, and the free winds blew over him, and the clean winter snows would blanket him. The Chinese would probably have considered this a good siting. I was more than ever glad that it was not the British Legation compound in Peking, bitterly cold, stiflingly hot, dirty, always. I sat down in the long grass still wet from yesterday's rain, and leaned against the granite stone. "William . . . why did you tell me so little? What does it *mean?*—what did you expect me to do?" No answer came, of course. No answer. There was nothing but the words scrawled with fevered hand on the scroll. William could tell me nothing more.

Then came the music. It was a great burst of sound, the sudden releasing of spirit in the mighty first notes of the Bach fugue. I stood up, electrified, frightened almost, by the great, unexpected thunder of it, and at the same time a sense of passion that a highly skilled musician was holding in tight discipline. It went on, the wonderful, remembered cadences of it. The chances of hearing such music in China were few, but I remembered this. In Hong Kong there was a church with an organ good enough to permit its great harmonies to come through. One did not forget such sounds. Now here again, in this tiny church in the Highlands, too small, I would have thought, for a pipe organ, with too small a congregation to warrant such an instrument, or such an organist. The music simply did not belong here. This was no doleful tune of sin and repentance, not the austerity I had expected in the Church of Scotland. It was a great song of praise and exaltation and joy. I stood in awe, my hand resting on William's stone; I hardly dared to draw my breath.

It ended, and I did not move, hoping, perhaps, for more of it. But nothing came. I waited, and finally there was the sound of the side door opening, and the lock being turned. The man stood on the step for a moment, accustoming his eyes, I guessed, to the stronger light, pausing to lift his face to the sky, and possibly to listen to the high, thin song of the lark. I knew him, and without thinking, I raised my hand. He caught the movement, and looked towards me. Then he began to make his way among the long grass and the graves.

"Miss Howard—you're here alone!" His brow was wrinkled, but I thought he was glad enough to see me.

"Yes, Mr. Campbell—I'm sorry, it's Sir Gavin Campbell, isn't it?"

"I seem to make a habit of finding you alone in places no one would expect a young lady to be."

"Why not?" I glanced down at William's grave.

He shook his head, the brusqueness of yesterday's meeting gone. "I'm sorry. Of course you would come. But somehow—well, one always expects nicely brought-up young ladies to do the expected things. But you—you don't wear black crepe and lament in public. You merely come all the way from China alone, without so much as a telegram. I suppose I was so amazed yesterday it didn't really strike me until afterwards. Standing there at Ballinaclash halt with your bags, no mourning veil, no tears, no one to meet you . . .

If I hadn't been there, I almost think you would have *walked* to Cluain."

"I would have had to," I said. "Without the bags, of course." Then I added, "I'm really not all that different. I think I was just so frightened of coming, I simply came. If I had told my grandfather—if I had waited to be invited—I probably wouldn't have had the courage. As it turns out—I don't think he would ever have asked me. I think he had just not registered the fact that I existed. You see . . . I am not another grandson. It didn't actually shock me. I'm used to it, I suppose. The Chinese think that way about girls. No one wants them. China teaches one a lot of things, Sir Gavin. To survive, for one thing. To hold onto life— and all I have left is here. So I don't wear mourning, or a veil. All that seems rather useless to me. My father believed in life, and to him death was nothing. William believed in life too— though he didn't say it the way a clergyman does. And you—*you* believe, don't you?"

"How do you know?"

"The music. That was you at the organ, wasn't it?"

"Yes."

I looked at him directly. "It was the best thing that had happened to me since the news came about William. It was life . . . and joy. No one plays like that—*that* music—unless the belief in life is in his very soul. You could even tell me now that you don't believe in God, and I *know* you believe in life. My father often said it was the same thing."

"Are you a musician, Miss Howard?" He was not affirming or denying what I had said.

"No—not at all. One hears little but drawing-room ballads in China. Not very well sung or played. It was the merest chance I had heard the Bach before, and remembered it. It was Bach, wasn't it?"

"Yes—"

"But why was that all? I would have stayed here all afternoon if only you had gone on. Why did you stop?"

"It was the end, really. I'd finished, and I was just sorting through some music, getting hymns ready for next Sunday. But

92

before I left I suddenly felt like flexing . . . well, perhaps your father might have said flexing my soul. No one in this place is supposed to hear that sort of thing—hardly anyone ever does. It would be a trifle suspect. This is a very stern God they worship here. But I play the organ for the few hymns they sing on Sundays —I find that duty easier and less hypocritical than reading the Lesson. The laird is expected to do something. If it weren't for the fact that people around here know I can manage a horse and a gun about as well as the next man, they might think that playing the organ was a rather odd occupation. The hymns are elementary. The village schoolmistress could do very well with them. I sometimes think I cheat her of a pleasurable task."

"But the organ—that wasn't built just for simple hymns. Even I know that."

He leaned against one of the Campbell stones and looked back at the church. "No—the organ is far better than a church of this size should have. It's an absurity, really, to have it here. It's too big for the space, for one thing. But it was paid for by my father-in-law, and he doesn't know how to deal on a small scale—with anything. The whole church was restored by him. The roof leaked, the tower was tottering, the choir loft was about to crash down. The congregation is so small the minister only comes over to hold a service every third Sunday. It could have been left to its final ruin, and hardly any one would have noticed. But now you see what it is—with an organ far better than it warrants, and large brass plate to make sure the Almighty knows who paid for it all."

"You're rather unkind to your father-in-law."

He shrugged. "It would be difficult to be unkind to him. He wouldn't notice. You see, when the restoration was carried out he thought that his daughter would be buried here with all the other Campbells of this branch of the family. Now he couldn't have her lying beside a ruined church with the sheep and cattle grazing her grave, could he?"

"You're asking my opinion? I think you talk entirely too much, Sir Gavin. I'm a stranger—I don't know your father-in-law. You may play the organ like an angel, but your tongue is sharpened with more than a little malice."

He looked back at me, and actually laughed. "Bless you, girl. Do I hear your father talking? Don't worry, I beg you. You'll hear at least that much of my father-in-law and far more, probably, before you've been here very long. My father-in-law is James Ferguson."

"Who?"

"Oh yes—I'd forgotten the name wouldn't mean anything to you. You haven't been in whisky long enough. He is one of the whisky magnates—*blended* whisky, which I'm sure is never permitted near Cluain. He has as many blends as there are letters to his name, and if the way he spends money is anything to go by, he has a fortune made from all of them. He has—like all shrewd merchants —all qualities, all prices. All things to all tastes. I imagine your grandfather would disapprove of him utterly, and yet he sells to him. *All* the malt distillers sell to Ferguson. He needs the leavening of a whisky as fine as Cluain's to give *something* to some of the rubbish he buys elsewhere, or distills himself. A good malt can be cut very thin, you know, and made to go very far in blending. Ferguson was one of the first to invest heavily in patent-still grain whisky. He let the others make the expensive stuff, and merely bought their product. But whatever he touches, whatever he does, everything turns to gold, and the public have come to know it. They rush to invest with him, and he's in a great hurry to spend the profits. Witness the church and the organ—and Ballochtorra itself."

"He couldn't have *built* Ballochtorra!"

"No—he restored the old tower, and added the rest. A suitable home for his only child. Mind you, if he had been quite so famous eleven years ago, or had known he was going to be quite so rich, he might have looked higher than a mere baronet for her. But still . . . I believe she wanted to marry me, and that's always a help."

"And you?" I asked coldly. It was outrageous, what he was saying, and yet I couldn't bring myself to break away from him, as I should have done.

"Me? Good God! I was madly in love. She was eighteen, and so beautiful I could hardly believe that she would even look in

94

my direction. Now, eleven years later, and a mother, she is matured, and London society is beginning to say she is the most beautiful woman in the kingdom. Myself, I'm not much accustomed to London society, so I'm no arbiter—but to me she is beautiful. You will see, though—you will meet her very soon."

I felt ashamed; he had loved her, he most probably still loved her. If a man chose to deride his father-in-law, then it might be just that this place—this lonely graveyard and playing an organ that is a gift from such a man—had brought out more than he meant to say.

"It was even a good laugh in those days. I could still make a joke of being poor." He seemed determined to go on. "You see, I had fallen into the baronetcy simply because my father was a distant cousin unexpectedly next in line. I hadn't grown up with that in prospect. My father had scraped to send me to Cambridge, and from there I had thought I might be lucky enough to get an organist's post in some cathedral. I loved horses, as well as the organ. I couldn't afford either, really—except that the organ could be made to pay my way in life. And then, my father was suddenly Sir Bruce Campbell, because a young, unmarried second cousin had tumbled into the river—dead drunk, they say—and two months later my father died, and I was Sir Gavin. I'd visited Ballochtorra once in my life, and I didn't want either it or the title. It was almost in ruins even when I was a child. All at once I had a title, a castle, and no money. And a position as an organist was going to be much harder to find. Deans usually don't engage young men whom they think the congregation might suspect of looking down on them. I went back to Edinburgh, where my father had his law practice, hoping for some recommendation for a post—and almost at once I met Margaret—my wife."

"The meeting turned out well." I wished my tone hadn't been so tart.

He looked back at the church. "Yes, you could say it turned out well. I hardly remember those days clearly. When you are so much in love, nothing has any sequence. I can hardly sort out what happened. I just know Margaret's father was suddenly present—and

95

in charge. I suppose I was young for my age—we were both very young. And we were married."

"And went to Ballochtorra and rebuilt it?"

"Before any of the rebuilding could begin we had our time there—just Margaret and I. The architects and James Ferguson were planning, and we were enjoying ourselves. We had one wonderful summer almost camping under open roofs. When you are young, and the fire is warm, and the wine is good, you barely notice such things. I suppose I should have thought about who was paying for the fire and the wine, but I didn't. It didn't seem to matter, then. It matters, though. In the end, it matters.

"You haven't met James Ferguson, but you undoubtedly will. He is a man who makes it his business to meet people. That you are a bishop's daughter will recommend you as much as the fact that you are Angus Macdonald's granddaughter. Though a Chinese bishopric doesn't count in the House of Lords."

"You're very bitter."

"Am I? Perhaps it's simply that I am no longer so young. I know now who pays for the fire and the wine."

"Should you be saying this to me?"

"Why not? You came from China all alone. You don't act like a miss just out of school—you're William's sister, and if I'm not mistaken, you're just as knowing as he was. You'll see it for yourself. Is it so terrible that I should speak it? I don't run about crying it to the earth."

"You play the organ—when you think no one hears. It speaks for itself."

"Only to those who know already. So I'm talking to you. I'm giving the words to what you will guess—and perhaps come to understand. Without James Ferguson there would be no Ballochtorra now—just a vine-covered ruin. There would be no church, no organ, nor horses in the stables. There would be no gamekeepers, and no game perserved on the moors. Gavin Campbell would be scratching for a living somewhere, and the sheep would be clipping the graveyard now."

"You said Mr. Ferguson had expected his daughter to be buried here. Why wouldn't she?"

He looked at me with a sideways glance, and then at the neat row of graves. "You don't miss much. Yes, we had thought that we both would lie here—and hence the restoration. But since then —I hope I haven't some dark genius for bringing such things on my relations—two cousins have died. One with his regiment in India, the other of typhoid in the Congo—*that* one was a mercenary of Leopold of the Belgians. It happens that they both in turn were next in line to the Marquis of Rossmuir. The solicitors have had to scramble about to find the heir, and it seems I am the one." He made a gesture of dismissal. "Oh, there's no riches with it. Rossmuir is an ancient title, but there's nothing left of the family lands but a few hundred acres of overgrazed grass up in Ross, and a much smaller castle than Ballochtorra was, even in the beginning, and which no one has lived in for more than a hundred years. The present Marquis is nearly ninety, bedridden, living in a few rooms in Edinburgh on the small income the land brings in. There doesn't seem any possibility that he will beget an heir to prevent my assuming the title. So you see, my father-in-law is torn between leaving things as they are here—or taking on the really challenging task of restoring an ancient ruin, and the traditional burial place of the Marquises of Rossmuir. What prevents him beginning now is that it's not in good taste until I have actually inherited the title—and the old man could stop him. And then, it's so far away in the wilderness up North, who would ever see it? No use splashing money about if it's only to be seen by a few crofters and sheep, now is it?"

I turned on him angrily. "I think you're despicable! Why do you take this man's money when you so despise him? And if you do, haven't *you* the good taste to keep quiet about it!"

He sighed. "You're right. I'm behaving like a vulgarian. And a smug one, into the bargain. I can't stop a father spending money on his daughter and grandson—it does give him pleasure. But for myself—as you say, the least I might do is accept it with grace. But what is it about you?—have you inherited a gift from your father of making people spill out their souls? I've said things that should decently be left unsaid. And yet I know if I don't say them, they'll be said to you by others—your grandfather for one.

Perhaps I care that you hear my version of it—though why I should I don't know. Perhaps it's just that a man has a need to talk, sometimes—and I have the conviction that you don't repeat gossip."

"The children of clergymen are brought up not to. We learn very early on never to notice who comes to our father's study for council or advice, and never to repeat any little piece of information a tired man lets slip. No—I don't think I gossip very much. And I'll be interested to meet Mr. James Ferguson. We weren't wrapped in a silkworm's cocoon in China, you know. After all, the great powers were in there for trade—and the biggest part of it was to sell opium. Whisky seems infinitely preferable. If a man makes a fortune out of whisky—well, it's only what my grandfather would *like* to do."

"Your grandfather's a different breed. He's a stubborn, prejudiced, rather narrow-minded old man, but his heart and soul is in making the best whisky this country can produce. He cares more for the quality of his product than for money—and always has. If you could choose your ancestors, then Angus Macdonald might not be a bad choice. Nor is the ancestor we have in common."

"You said we were cousins—distant cousins. Who was the ancestor?" But I was still thinking of what he had said about my grandfather. It pleased me that he did not appear to begrudge the respect that Angus Macdonald himself had claimed as his due. It made up for some of the things he had said about James Ferguson.

"She was Angus Macdonald's mother, and a Campbell of Ballochtorra. She lies there." He was nodding to the ground beyond me.

It was an overgrown grave beside William's with the same rough granite marker, though smaller and worn with the weather of the years. I thought it significant that my grandfather had buried William in the plot where one would have expected he himself would lie. The ground beside William was empty, and unmarked, as though waiting. Beyond that was another similar marker, probably Angus Macdonald's wife, my grandmother. The long grass waved about the stones obscuring the names. I swept aside the grass near the marker Gavin Campbell had indicated and read the name lettered there: CHRISTINA CAMPBELL MACDONALD. My eyes went back to him, questioning.

"Why not over there—with all the other Campbells?"

"Her father forbade her to marry John Macdonald, Angus's father. He had other ambitions for his daughter and Ballochtorra than the son of the laird of a small, poor island in the Hebrides —and a Macdonald into the bargain. Ballochtorra had fallen on hard times even then, and it needed a good marriage to restore it. She met her Macdonald in Glasgow, I believe, and came back to Ballochtorra for permission to marry him. When it was refused, she simply took off for that far island with her man, and never came back. Not that she was welcome at Ballochtorra. She was all that her father had left, the youngest child, his only hope. Both sons had been killed in the Napoleonic wars. His other daughter married a Grant, and went to Canada; there were no male children of that marriage. Christina's father had inherited a place in debt, and he got it further into debt. Gambling was his vice, not drink. He never forgave Christina for not saving him. That, at least, is how they tell me the story."

"But she is here—buried at the church of Ballochtorra. So she did return."

"She returned because Angus Macdonald insisted on it. They say that mother and son were very close—she lost her other sons in infancy. So her pride and ambition rested in Angus. We're an unlucky family, on both sides, when it comes to offspring. To lose one's children is not such an unfamiliar thing to the Scots— it's a poor country, and made poorer by bad landlords, and the breaking of the clans. Sons leave—go into the British Army to earn their keep, emigrate because they've been driven from their ancient clans homes to make room for sheep. But usually there are enough of them—the women have been strong and prolific breeders—for a father to have sons and daughters about him in his old age. But Ballochtorra has not been lucky. There have been too few sons. For the Macdonalds it has been the same. Angus was Christina's only surviving child. He brought her to Ballochtorra when she died—it must have been a fearful journey for a young man to arrange in those days, with no help and no money. He

99

came to Ballochtorra, and he insisted that this was where his mother would be buried. He had some notion, they say, that she had been homesick all her life for these glens and burns—that the Western Isles had never been her home, although she gave her husband and family and her new kinsmen her whole devotion. Her father, as laird of Ballochtorra, tried to refuse the right of burial here, and just as strongly Angus Macdonald insisted, pointing to the fact that she had been a member of the kirk when she was a girl. In the end even Sir Graeme Campbell's tame minister had to agree. But still Sir Graeme refused her a place in the family plots. In the kirkyard she might lie, but not beside her family. That is why she is there—with the path between them. But at least she had been spared the fate of being nicely cleaned and polished up like all the other Campbells. I sometimes wonder if some of these shiny headstones mightn't hide a darker reputation."

"Then how does my grandfather come to be on Ballochtorra's land—at Cluain? If Sir Graeme would not forgive his daughter, how does the grandson come to be here?"

"He hasn't told you that part yet? I would have imagined his old triumph would have been one of the first subjects he would have talked of."

"We had other things . . ."

"Yes—I expect so. As they tell it, Sir Graeme was old at the time, and sick. He had quarrelled with every member of his family, distant as they were. There were none who would have anything to do with him. Angus asked nothing of him but that his mother should be buried there, and insisted over his objections. Somehow, it got into the old man's head, after Angus had gone back to his island, that the young man had shown a proper filial respect, and a sense of duty, even if he was a Macdonald. This was something Sir Graeme hadn't experienced from his own family. He couldn't break the entail on the title or on Ballochtorra's lands, but Cluain had been split from it by some legal quirk a hundred years before. He had let the farm run down, but he held off enough of his creditors to save it from them. Cluain was still in his gift. In a fit of what the Campbells called sheer perversity, but what I like

100

to think of as a late attempt at making amends to his daughter and to a grandson he should have been proud of, he left Cluain to Angus Macdonald. And he lived only six months longer than his daughter. So Angus Macdonald left his island, from which his own people had already dispersed, mostly to emigrate, and he came to Cluain to claim it. There was a fierce legal fight. The Campbells claimed undue influence over a man they said was senile— and yet, of course, the row that everyone knew about over Christina's burial proved there could have been no influence from Angus—quite the opposite. Angus had no money for lawyers— just the merit of his case. The story goes that he marched into Samuel Lachlan's office in Inverness one day, told him why he had come, asked him to take the case, and if he won he would be paid from the profits of Cluain, and if he lost—well, Samuel Lachlan might wait a long time for that debt to be settled. You'll be meeting Samuel Lachlan—he's a part of Cluain's history now. Even in those days when he was still quite a young man, he was becoming known as one of the cleverest solicitors in Scotland, and very near with money—not the kind to take a case with so little prospect of payment at the end. And yet he did take it— who knows why? Perhaps he was tired of ordinary sorts of law suits. They say he came down to inspect Cluain before he would agree. Well, for whatever reason, he took it, and he won. It took almost a year before the appeals were through. In that time Angus Macdonald lived in a crofter's cottage on Cluain's property —the Campbells claimed he was in illegal possession, but no one cared to face Angus and his gun. In the end Samuel Lachlan persuaded the Campbells it was useless to carry the claim to the High Court in Edinburgh. They gave in. There is a famous local story of the day the top-hatted Campbell solicitor came down from Inverness in his carriage—the railway wasn't there in those days—followed closely by Samuel Lachlan in a dirty hackney cab, wearing the shiny black suit which was the only one he possessed— myself, I think he's still wearing the same suit. The deeds and keys to Cluain were handed over to Angus Macdonald. Cluain, in quite good repair, and fully furnished, with the best lands in the strath, was his. Ballochtorra, with the roof starting to fall in, and only grouse moors and mountain bog to its name, belonged to the Campbells. It must have been a bitter sight for the new baronet in those days—he was the one my father inherited from—to look down from Ballochtorra at Cluain. Most especially when Angus Macdonald began to build his distillery. The story has it that the very day the deeds were handed over, Angus mortgaged Cluain, house and lands, to Samuel Lachlan for the capital to build his distillery. And even the distillery was almost an inheritance from Christina."

"How so?"

"When she was widowed out there on her island, she grew desperate for something to employ the people. The land was very poor, and the salt-spray from the Atlantic would hardly let a seed stay in the ground, much less grow and flourish. Sheep had been introduced in a last attempt to make the land pay. And of course, where you have sheep, the people must make way for them. But the sheep were in too small numbers to pay, and a few crofters still survived—her tenants, her family, now her clan. She thought of what had gone on here as she grew up, and she built herself a small distillery. But it was the sea that defeated her. She couldn't grow the right quality of barley, so it had to be brought from the mainland, and then the finished product had to be shipped back—all at much more cost than those closer to the cities and the new railways that were just starting to come. It was a very small distillery, mind you, and her output was tiny. And then one year the entire product of her warehouses—that is, all that was legally old enough to be sold as whisky—went down when a vessel foundered. It was the end of the distillery. She couldn't borrow any more, she couldn't hold out any longer. It was then, they say, that she sent Angus to Islay to work in a distillery. She couldn't give him the life of a gentleman, nor could she pay for a commission in a regiment—and she must have seen too many leave the Highlands to go off and die in England's wars. So she sent him to learn a craft and a trade, one that she believed in. When Angus Macdonald inherited Cluain, he inherited the perfect place to make malt whisky. There were his barley fields, his streams,

102

the peat, the climate. There were literally dozens of distilleries within a very few miles of his door. He was not an innovator—just carrying on with an ancient skill that had always been carried on in these glens. He believed, like Christina Campbell, that there was money in whisky, and he wasn't too much of a gentleman to soil his hands in the trade. Those men of the Western Isles are a tough lot—they have had to be to survive over the centuries. There's no softness in the living there. What poor soil and sheep haven't taken, the sea has. So Angus Macdonald came here afraid of nothing—least of all hard work. When he was secure in the title to Cluain, he went back and married one of his kinswomen, and he gathered together a few distillery workers and their families from Islay. He was making his own island race here among us. The farm was run on a shoestring, and the distillery built on money borrowed from Samuel Lachlan. It was a huge gamble that paid off. Angus Macdonald has taken in about forty harvests at Cluain, but his golden harvest is maturing now in those warehouses." He looked down at the granite marker. "I don't know if he's ever come to admitting to himself that he loved William. But one thing I'm certain of—he wanted him."

"You know a lot about my grandfather."

"I've made it my business to find out. I've pieced together the story of Christina and her father, and Angus Macdonald bringing her home here. No doubt your grandfather would tell it much better, and I would have liked to have heard it in his words. But he and I have never been on those kind of terms. The barest civility passes between us. I'm sorry for it, but he's not to be moved. He can't forget that the Campbells tried to dispossess him of Cluain, and every time I look down on that place I know why they tried so hard. I've seen what he's built, and I admire him. But he's a man like that granite there—hard and enduring. You'll find very few chinks in that face he turns to the world.

"It was William who began to build a bridge between Cluain and Ballochtorra. He came quite often—and why not? It is the only place around here to visit, and he wasn't much occupied at Cluain. Angus Macdonald didn't approve, but William kept coming." Then his voice dropped until it was almost a whisper, words forcing their way out that he may have tried too long to keep buried in his own mind, words like the swift rush of the wind past my ears. "And again—why would he stay away? He was more than half in love with my wife."

I wasn't really aware of when he left me. I suppose I stood there for a long time, staring down at the grass waving on the graves of William and Christina, side by side. When I looked up, Gavin Campbell was gone, as I hoped he would be. There was only the gentle tugging sound of the cattle grazing near the kirk-yard wall, and far above, the same lark. I lifted my face and scanned the whole wide sky; there was no far, high-flying speck that I could see. If Giorsal, the falcon, hovered up there somewhere, she was beyond my gaze and reach.

My eyes went back to the grave, to the freshly chiselled name in the granite. "Did you love her, William? Did you love her—and not tell me of it? Was *she* the enchantress you found here?"

The breeze that blew through the small plantation of larches in the corner of the kirkyard was my answer.

II

My grandfather was waiting, and terse. He had his stance, as before, in front of the fire in the dining room, but this evening a long shaft of sunlight struck across his face, and he seemed older than in the greyer light of last evening.

"I hear you've been through the distillery with Callum Sinclair." The words greeted me as I came through the door; I jerked around to face him, and the door slammed.

"Yes. Have you some objection, Grandfather?"

"I do. I'll not have you being familiar with the distillery workers."

"Familiar!" I came towards him, feeling my face flush with

anger. "Familiar! That is the last thing I can imagine anyone being with Callum Sinclair. It was hardly my choice, though. He simply doesn't permit familiarity."

"He kept his place, then?"

"What *is* his place, Grandfather? He seemed to be everything—to know everything. And if he hasn't a place at Cluain—a real place—then I don't know who could."

"He's too independent—and he does not know everything, in spite of what he may claim. He's bad for discipline among the other men. He goes off on his own while they work . . ."

"But he works for Cluain as no other man does, isn't that so? And they all know it—and accept it? So what might be a privilege for them is right for him. After all, you keep him on at Cluain."

I seemed to have won my small argument, and rather wished I had not. My grandfather moved with irritated haste to the sideboard. Would it always be like this between us, I wondered? But then he turned back, and the two glasses were in his hands; he held one towards me. "There—there's your dram. Health to you." And he tipped back his glass without another look at me, as if we had been doing this for a long time, and there was no need for ceremony. Perhaps the arguing and the confrontation was to be part of our life together, a signal of acceptance. I sipped slowly, and now the whisky was familiar, and rather pleasing.

I sat down on the settle. "Well, then, if you had given me time I would have told you that I was looking for you to take me through the distillery—I'd just heard Callum Sinclair telling his mother he wasn't going near the place today. And as I was crossing the yard that gander, Big Billy, came chasing me. I have his bite to prove it. I just ran in the nearest door, and Callum Sinclair was there. Perhaps he spends more time working than you think."

"Perhaps. So you've met Big Billy, have you?" His face creased in a near-smile. "Well, he's the real boss of Cluain. Once you know Big Billy you can fairly claim to be on your way at Cluain. I suppose you know all about distilling now?"

105

"No. I don't think I ever will. Callum Sinclair told me it takes years—it was all the chemical things I didn't understand. I'll never remember which part of the process follows the next."

"Perhaps you shouldn't bother. William was more confused than he pretended to be. You don't become a distiller overnight by studying the textbooks."

I sighed. "That was rather heavily impressed on me. Perhaps I *won't* bother."

The big eyebrows lowered. "Please yourself." I watched his body sag into his chair. What a cross-grained pair we were. And I should be for his comfort, not his irritation.

So I said, in a softer tone. "I went to William's grave."

He nodded. "So they told me."

"They tell you everything."

"The Master expects to be told. Morag knows most things that happen here, and she is a good wee gurrl. A level head on her for all her chatter. It would have been well for us all if she had known where William was bound that day . . ." His voice trailed off, the regret and pain blurring to silence.

"I liked the granite stone," I said. "I was glad you gave William the same kind as your mother's—and laid him beside her."

"How did you know it is my mother's grave?" The words were sharp again, suspicious.

"I read the headstone—Sir Gavin Campbell pointed it out to me. He was there at the kirk—practising the organ," I finished lamely. Perhaps I should not be telling this part of it. Gavin Campbell might cherish the privacy of those organ sessions, not wanting them talked of through the countryside.

"Campbell was there, was he? And fine well he knows where Christina Campbell is buried. It was she who brought Cluain to me."

"He told me so. He told me as much as he knew about the story." I suddenly burst out, wishing for once I could cut through this man's prejudice and layers of remembered enmities. "He admires you, Grandfather."

"Let him admire," he answered, as if admiration was his right.

106

"Let him envy, too. The Campbells lost Cluain, and they've never forgiven that. Justice was done."

"Oh," I gestured wearily with my glass. "How does it effect *him?* He was only a second cousin, or something of the sort. He never expected to inherit Ballochtorra. Cluain had been in your hands for a long time before he ever laid eyes on the place."

"The Campbells always were greedy."

"What need does he have to be greedy? Ballochtorra doesn't appear to need money."

"No. His lady wife has enough of it. Or rather her slum-bred father. Out of the Glasgow slums James Ferguson came, and made a fortune on cheap whisky. He spends like a madman. And Campbell lets him spend. But Ferguson hangs onto his daughter's skirts, and is a noose around Campbell's neck. Where's the sense in being a gentleman, and having fine horses, and playing the organ, when your father-in-law can scarcely speak the Queen's English?"

"Is that Gavin Campbell's fault . . . he seems to love his wife."

"Seems to!" He tossed his huge head back. "Och, once they were young fools together, and it appeared the genuine thing. But tell me how a man can stand by and watch his wife change from a nice, simple, well-enough educated young gurrl—aye, James Ferguson is aware of his own deficiencies in that direction, and he bought the best teachers for his daughter. And she changed from being the simple wife of a local baronet into a London social butterfly. There's been a house rented for them in London these past five years, and I hear now that Ferguson has bought a grand big affair there, and is refurbishing it from top to bottom. There is always a room ready for James Ferguson wherever his daughter is. She knows who has the purse strings."

"You seem to know a lot about James Ferguson's doings, Grand-father."

"Och, Morag chatters . . ." He seemed not to realise what he revealed of himself. "They say he is getting the London house ready in time for the Coronation. And that can't be too far off."

"The Queen is not dead yet."

"She hasn't many more years . . . But before she is dead, Ferguson is hoping that the old Marquis of Rossmuir will be dead, and Campbell will have the title. It would be his greatest dream realised if his daughter were to sit with all the other peeresses in the Abbey wearing a marchioness's coronet when the new King is crowned. I think he would like it almost as much as a knighthood for himself. Who knows—he might even get that. Whisky has created more than one baron . . . Money talks.

"But still and all," he added as he went again to the sideboard to refill his glass, "Ferguson has yet only one grandson. She has given him only one grandchild."

*   *   *

After supper he brought out the chessboard. "A game?" he said, and I knew it was not a game, but a challenge. I nodded, and we sat opposite each other, as we had the night before. Mairi Sinclair came in to ask if there was anything else needed. Her features worked strangely as she took in the scene, but when she met my eyes, her own at once became blank, as if she had determined that never again should I glimpse what had been uncovered by that wild, unrecognisable creature on the stairs. That woman, she seemed to be telling me, did not exist. I had imagined her.

But this day, like yesterday, had contained too much, had had too many encounters. Angus Macdonald's eyes were on me sharply, and each move I made on the board scrutinised for what it told him. Did I play an attacking game, or a defensive one? Would I attempt to lure him into a gambit, sacrificing a Pawn or even a more important piece to trap him? Had I got the nerve for it? That night, I had not. I played badly, weakly, not anticipating even the ordinary moves I knew by heart, letting myself fall into too obvious traps he set for me. But there was too much else in my head, and emotions do not make good pieces on a chessboard. The old man won too easily; I thought I saw a dawning contempt in his eyes, disappointment, too. He was not even suspicious that I might have allowed him to win in order to flatter him. If I had, I would have been more skilful about it.

After he won the second game I didn't wait for him to dismiss me. "I'll go up now, Grandfather. I'm tired." If it sounded like an excuse, I didn't care.

It was not chill as it had been the night before, but I set a match to the fire laid ready in my room, just for the pleasure of seeing that room glow with its light as the light outside began to fade. I sat for a while beside it, slumped on the bench, unwilling to begin the effort of washing and making ready for bed. My thoughts flickered erratically like the flames; the names I spoke to myself were William's, and Gavin Campbell's—and Callum Sinclair's.

Then I heard it, clearer this night because it was unmuffled by rain or mist. I went to the window at once, and they were there again, that odd quartet—the pony too short for the man's long legs, the dog, sleek today, his coat free of mud, the unblinking falcon on the raised gloved hand. The man must have seen the smoke rise from this tower chimney, but not by the slightest movement that I could detect did he acknowledge my presence at the window. Pride could not keep me from standing there, hoping, waiting for a turn of his head, the faintest nod. Callum Sinclair gave none. I watched him out of sight. Tonight there was a difference. I had believed, yesterday, that he shared my sense of loneliness, and I had experienced a kindred feeling with him. Now I knew that Callum Sinclair would admit to no such thing. If he were lonely he would not recognise such an emotion. If he were lonely it was a state he had dwelt in so long that he would not be aware of its existence. He seemed to want nothing—and no one.

I went then, back to look at the scroll again. I would not forget it, must not. I would not let them lull me here into forgetting why I had come. That strange woman, Mairi Sinclair, was the mother of a strange son, and the fevered words on William's scroll might well have truth in them. The slow fire of my anger and grief was kindled again, and now there was a kind of jealousy as well—of Gavin Campbell's wife. William had not told me. Of all the omissions of his letters, it was this I found hardest to accept.

109

When Morag came to tell me that she had come, I could see the curiosity alive in the girl's face, the faint apricot blush staining her cheeks, and the shining red curls almost crackling with excitement at the uniqueness of the happening.

"It's herself! Lady Campbell has come to call!"

I rose from the desk in the tower room where I had been trying to write a letter to Peking. It was a morning of discontent—the sun strong and golden, but in this whole lovely world I surveyed from these windows there seemed no place I could say was my own to venture. The distillery was my grandfather's and Callum Sinclair's, the garden belonged to his mother—beyond was Ballochtorra and the kirkyard, but that was where I did not want to go again so soon. The fields and the pastures were beautiful in the morning light, but a kind of tiredness of spirit was on me. They would all wait.

But I did give the stray ends of my hair a little attention, and put on more elegant shoes before I followed Morag down the stairs. In the hall I automatically turned to go to the dining room, but an agonised whisper from Morag halted me. "No—no, the parlour! She's in the parlour! I've lighted the fire, and Mistress Sinclair is brewing tea . . ." She was pointing to a door opposite the dining room.

The parlour. How strange I had not been tempted to try this door, to look inside—for all I knew it might have opened on an empty room. Why did I suppose that at Cluain all the doors must be locked? Was it Mairi Sinclair's hovering presence that deterred me; had I already so much given way to her possessiveness that I did not dare to open a door, or go and sit on a garden bench? If that was true, then I had come from China for nothing, and she would succeed in driving me from Cluain.

So I lifted my head and straightened my shoulders, assuming the air of the mistress of the establishment, as I opened the parlour door.

I had expected to dislike her on sight, but that was impossible. She had been staring towards the window, and as I entered she turned her head slowly with a movement of supreme grace, and rose to her feet.

Her voice was gentle, soft, almost childlike. "Miss Howard—I hope I have not come at an inappropriate time. I wanted to welcome you among us. And, of course, to offer my sympathy on your father's death. And William—dear William. Gavin and I were both so fond of him. It is so sad for you . . ."

They were ordinary enough words, but when she said them, no one could have believed she did not mean them. I went forward to offer my hand, and she came to meet me. Yes, it could be true—it was just possibly true, what Gavin Campbell had said; she might have been considered the most beautiful woman in the kingdom. She was a golden creature—golden hair swept up under her hard riding hat, golden eyes with darker flecks in them, and a fringe of dark lashes, incredibly white skin. I couldn't help thinking, in those first moments, that she reminded me of a kitten not quite grown into a cat, a golden striped kitten, with a kitten's delicate grace, a kitten's velvet paws in little white gloves, a kitten's unconscious ability to charm and delight, no matter what she did. Her tan riding habit, accentuating her tiny waist, and the creamy lace at her throat were all part of a superbly organised design. Only a very beautiful woman in this age of overdressing could have worn clothes so simple—simplicity that must also have been outrageously expensive.

"And may I present my son, James—Jamie, we call him. I hope he does not bother you, but he was very anxious to come. He and William were friends."

I had not noticed the child. He had been standing over near a high-backed chair, waiting with still solemnity until his mother had finished speaking. Now he came forward and shook hands. A fair-haired, beautiful child, but he had the intense blue eyes of his father. One day he would be very much like Gavin Campbell.

111

And one day soon, when that old man died in Edinburgh, he would be the earl of somewhere. For some reason the thought made me want to laugh, and so when I took his hand my smile was broad, and it was answered by a flashing smile from him, which utterly changed and irradiated that solemn little face.

"How do you do, Miss Howard," he said, bowing. And then, quickly: "You look very like William."

"It was kind of you both to call," I said. "Won't you please sit down."

"Thank you," Lady Campbell said. "Jamie and I have just been admiring this room. It *is* very splendid, isn't it? One doesn't see much like it these days. Now it is all frills and bows and sashes, like a little girl's dress. This furniture must be *very* old." She said it with a kind of breathless reverence, as if she had not the means herself to command such things. I found later it was a habit of hers to admire other people's possessions extravagantly, as if she had none of her own.

I looked around the room, and did not say I had never been in it before. The furniture was the dark, carved oak that was in the other rooms, as sparse, as devotedly polished. There was a long table, a tall press, stiff chairs softened only by faded red silk cushions. This room was grander than the others with its linenfold panelling and carvings on the mantel. There was a central brass chandelier, and wrought-iron fire dogs. It also had the only carpet I had seen in the house—a silken, worn, fragile thing, in fading reds and golds. Instead of the inevitable Clanranald tartan at the windows there was red brocade, very old, and fraying at its long folds.

"Perhaps it should be *your* furniture, Lady Campbell. It probably came from Ballochtorra in the first place and was brought here to furnish Cluain, as the dower house."

"Do you think so?" Her red lips twisted in a smile. "I'm rather glad it's not mine. I don't think I could live up to it—and I do so like to curl up on a sofa. Perhaps I *do* like the frills and bows, after all."

"Those are ours," Jamie said suddenly, pointing at the fire dogs. "They have our crest. The Campbells of Cawdor."

112

I leaned forward and looked closely, and saw the shields embossed with the swan with the arched neck. They reminded me uncomfortably of Big Billy. "So they are," I said. "But my great-grandmother was a Campbell of Cawdor—and, in any case, I don't think my grandfather would give them back." I heard myself with amazement. Was this the same person, two days in the Highlands, and already falling into the romantic notions Gavin Campbell had warned me of?

"I *know* he wouldn't," Jamie replied. "He wouldn't sell *my* grandfather a part of Cluain—even though he offered a great deal of money for it."

"Oh, hush, Jamie!" his mother said. "You talk too much. We all know Mr. Macdonald would never sell Cluain."

"Grandfather didn't. He still thinks it should be part of Ballochtorra—as it once was."

"Greedy little boy. You can't have everything."

For once I was thankful for the appearance of Mairi Sinclair. She opened the door for Morag, who now wore an even more stiffly starched apron and cap than before, her hair severely tucked in, but her high colour and excitement unquenched. She bore a large silver tray set with cups and a silver tea service. In silence, as Mairi Sinclair stood by the door, she laid it gently on the table, and then went to the hall and brought a second tray, this one set with plates of scones and bread and butter, tiny griddle cakes, two kinds of jam, thinly sliced ham, little golden cup cakes. All this at eleven o'clock in the morning, and all presented as if Lady Campbell's visit had been expected for a week. I looked with respect at Mairi Sinclair; she had even brought the scents of her herb garden in the fresh parsley and watercress. She did not acknowledge my glance with a look of her own; just stood with the rough hands folded before her, seeing that Morag did each thing correctly, and then both withdrew, the door closing soundlessly.

"So!" Lady Campbell said. "That's the wonder woman of Cluain! I've never had a chance to study her before. Oh, she's in the kirk every Sunday there's a service, but always in the back pew, and always the first out the door when the service is ended. Before the last of the gossipers are off the steps, you can see her striding down the road towards home. They say . . . they say that in any weather she refuses to ride in the trap to kirk when Angus Macdonald attends. How many times has Gavin stopped to offer to take her even as far on her way as Ballochtorra, and all we've had is a shake of that head, half-hidden in the folds of a plaid? She will keep that plaid when every other woman in Scotland is wearing a hat. And yet . . . if only I had her for Ballochtorra. *My* lazy lot couldn't produce this"—she indicated the splendidly spread trays—"if I'd given them a month's warning. And how she keeps this place! Do you suppose . . ." She gave a little, childish laugh as she accepted a cup of tea from my hands. "Do you suppose a speck of dust is ever *allowed* into this house?—or is it all frightened away by the sight of her? No—perhaps I don't want her for Ballochtorra, after all. She rather frightens me. She would think me a silly, useless thing—which I am. But one doesn't like to *know* that servants know it too well."

"You are a fairy, Mama . . . and she is a witch! A witch all dressed in black."

"That's wicked of you to say such a thing, Jamie! Mistress Sinclair does nothing but good. She is a good woman."

"Some people say she is a witch," the boy insisted.

"What a baby you are! There's no such thing as a witch."

"She must be a witch, or she would have saved William. But William died."

I thought that white skin turned whiter. She shot an anguished look at me, and then turned to her son. "Never let me hear you talk such nonsense again, Jamie. Wicked nonsense. It is cruel, and unkind—and untrue! You know what your father says, it would be better to have Mistress Sinclair nurse one than half the doctors in Edinburgh. Now hush, child, and remember that Mistress Sinclair is a good woman . . . Here, Jamie, have a griddle cake. They are much lighter than the ones at home."

She distracted the child, and he munched happily. The dark presence of Mairi Sinclair seemed altered by the good things she presented. We talked for a few minutes of nothing of consequence. The weather—what I might expect of a Highland summer. "You will need your woollens *all* the time," Lady Campbell warned.

"Thank heaven Papa will have the London house ready this winter. But it will take a lot of persuasion to get Gavin there. I almost think he loves it best here when the snow is thick. Oh, but the wind from the mountains . . ." The fresh scone crumbled between those delicate fingers, and she left it unfinished on the plate.

She rose to go. "You will come to Ballochtorra, won't you? It's so dull here—no company. Of course, when the shooting opens we will have almost more company than we want. The Prince of Wales has consented to pay us a visit . . ." She tried to say it as if it were nothing, but a look of pleased triumph lighted her face. It was the supreme accolade for such a young hostess. Again the little laugh. "Of course it is most kind of His Royal Highness, but it still frightens me a little. So much to prepare. Papa is sending lots of extra servants from London, but still so much can go wrong. All the guests bring their own personal servants, of course, but I must fit them all in somewhere. And all according to the rank of the master. I expect there will be anarchy in the servants' hall. It will be a simple affair, but we must give *one* entertainment apart from the shooting. A small dinner, with dancing afterwards—just the local people who would expect to be invited to meet the Prince. *You* will come, won't you? The Prince likes pretty women . . ."

I murmured something, a little awestruck, and already wondering as women always do, what I would wear.

"Do you ride, Miss Howard?"

"Not very well. There were some tough little ponies in Peking, and one just learned to hold on."

"I'm sure Gavin will be pleased to mount you from the stables if there is nothing suitable here. William used to use our horses." The light little laugh again. "I don't think Mr. Macdonald liked that, but William always did what he wanted." She took a last look around the room. "I'm glad I've been here at last. Cluain has always fascinated me. How strange your coming here has given me the first chance to pay a visit. One could hardly pay a call on William. You *will* come to Ballochtorra, won't you?" she pressed again. "I am at home every day, except when I ride.

It would be nice to have a friend close by. You *will* call me Margaret, won't you . . . ?" It spilled on, the needless, almost guileless generosity, as if she must make an enormous effort to please, she who pleased with no effort but just looking as she did. It was as if a great uncertainty possessed her, as if she must gather everyone into her fold, so that there could be no enemies, only friends.

We went to the front door. Mairi Sinclair was there before us, waiting by the open door; a man, probably summoned from the stables, was standing holding a fine bay mare and an almost cream-coloured pony. Morag stood beside the mare, and she was feeding her from a bunch of young carrots. She offered a shy smile to Margaret Campbell, and the answering smile was radiant. I noted the carrots and thought that Mairi Sinclair was oddly indulgent of Morag at times—or was it that she simply liked animals, but could not unbend to feed the mare herself?

Margaret Campbell's light, graceful form swung up to the side-saddle with only the semblance of assistance from the stableman. Jamie managed to mount by himself, proud of the fact. The woman's beautiful young face looked down at me. For the first time I saw the faintest hint of shadow upon it. "Thank you for receiving me. I've enjoyed myself. It's lonely here. William and I used to ride together . . ."

And then she wheeled the mare, and the child followed eagerly. They headed down the strath away from Ballochtorra. Big Billy and his flock came towards the pair, but somehow were halted by the faintly imperious wave from Lady Campbell's riding crop. Could she charm even that surly brute, I wondered? I was conscious of Mairi Sinclair staring after them, just as I was, that lovely couple, graced by beauty and wealth.

But it was Morag's voice that came from the doorway. "Hardly a thing did she eat—and all that fuss! Well, a body can't stay a slip of a thing and eat your fill and do no work. True enough that Master William rode with her . . . I'm thinking she's looking for other company now."

Mairi Sinclair turned on her fiercely. "Hold your tongue, girl! Hold it, I say! We'll not have evil gossip here—"

116

I could not face them. I let them go back into the house, and I stood there watching as the riders continued on down the road. I was hearing again Gavin Campbell's words. "He was more than half in love with my wife." His voice so toneless, as if it were something he had come to expect. *"An enchantress . . ."* But somehow my jealousy was dissipated. Even I could not help falling under her spell; if she beguiled and bewitched, it seemed hardly more fair to blame her than if she had been a child, innocent, unknowing. I stood there until they were out of sight.

When I went back into the house the door to the drawing room was closed. I opened it and looked inside. It was as still, as silent and waiting as if no one had entered here. There was not a crumb of the many Jamie had shed to betray his presence, the rug he had rumpled was straightened, the faded silk cushions plumped up. Only the fire spoke of people having been here. I was sure that Mairi Sinclair was only waiting for it to die, and Morag would be here clearing out the still-warm ashes, and laying a fresh one. A beautiful, sad, unused room, that should have been full of life. Had one of my ancestors stitched the tapestry fire screen—yes, that also bore the Campbell arms. Christina Campbell had locked us together—Cluain and Ballochtorra.

*　　*　　*

That afternoon, after a mostly silent and hurried lunch with my grandfather, I took out the old serge skirt and the boots I had worn when I rode those Peking ponies. Without permission, I borrowed the Inverness tweed cape I found hanging with the various plaids and walking sticks in the kitchen passage. I took a stick that seemed to fit my height. And then I walked all afternoon. I walked along the way Margaret Campbell had ridden, past the distillery and the warehouses, over the small humpback bridge that crossed a burn which had been diverted and channelled around the warehouses, past the small houses that must be tenanted by the distillery workers, the houses with their neat garden plots. Children played there, young children, sometimes tended by older children, hardy, barefoot, rosy children, with shy, engaging smiles.

The women did not seem to be about—except for one old woman sitting in the sun by her doorway, who waved her pipe cheerfully at me. Did the women work in the summer on the farm? I supposed it was so. Work was part of these people's lives, inescapable, unless you were Angus Macdonald's granddaughter, or as free of toil or worry as Margaret Campbell. I turned off on a track that led upwards through Cluain's pastures, and bent to follow roughly the twists of a small, fiercely running burn, whose water was icily cold. The track threaded away from the pasture and into a shadowed glen. A little farther on, steppingstones led across the burn to a neat stone cottage, with a stout paling fence about it, and a well-thatched stable. But its door was shut, and no smoke came from the chimney. Did my senses tell me right that this was where Callum Sinclair lived? It would not be among the other workers —and there seemed no other place this side of the river. It somehow resembled him, this place—the clear-running burn separating him from the rest of the world, the closed door, the air of aloofness and self-sufficiency. This was his manner, and this could well be his place.

Beyond here, the track grew rougher and the glen steeper; I turned back to the high pastures of Cluain. All the time as I walked I kept scanning the sky for the sight of the falcon. If she were in flight would she note and mark me with her hawk's eye, not something to interest her, and pass on overhead, unseen, unheard, as aloof as her master? I walked until I was tired, until the pasture gave way to heather. I flung muself down on its rough cushion, listening to the bees drone about me. William had described to me how these heather moors of Scotland turned a mauvish haze in the autumn, how the long shafts of sun would suddenly light a spot and turn it to royal purple. But he had not told me how Cluain's world looked from up here. I could still see the distillery buildings—not handsome, but no longer ugly to my eyes. I could see the far glint of the river, and the rich green meadows. Ballochtorra was out of sight—from here one saw only the back of the massive crag. This was wholly Cluain's world. It was no wonder my grandfather loved and possessed it with such fierce passion.

118

I returned with a muddy skirt and a raging hunger. I was waiting, changed, with brushed hair, before the fire when my grandfather came in. "You've been walking, I hear."

"Yes."

"Then have a care. We'll not want to send men to be pulling you from a bog."

"Will you trust me not to go into a bog? I do not carry a gun, Grandfather, and I cannot be kept on a rein."

"I thought women had other things . . ."

I held out my empty hands. "What does Mairi Sinclair leave to me? Would you have me disturb—"

"No—no," he said quickly. "Do not disturb anything. Go—but go safely."

He handed me my dram of whisky without question. How good it tasted as it was meant to be drunk, with my stomach rumbling with hunger, and my cheeks flushed from the sharp air and the long walk. I looked up from the fire and found Angus Macdonald's gaze on me, as if he also knew that I was beginning to feel Cluain's world. But he said nothing. I knew for a long time it would be something felt, not spoken.

We played chess again. I was tired, and yet stimulated. We played two games, and with the second, I won.

The big eyebrows came closer. "Are you fighting, then?"

"Does one always have to fight?" The tiredness was swamping in. I didn't want to have to fence with him.

"Always," he answered. "Always."

The white cat was on the bench before the fire when I went up to the tower room. He raised his pale eyes to me, and then lay blinking in somnolence. Before I was ready for bed, he went and sat by the door, appealing with nothing but his gesture to be let out. The white shape slipped down the stairs. That night I did not even glance up towards Ballochtorra, nor look down into the garden to see if my grandfather's candle burned. I did not wait for darkness, or the sound of the pony's hooves on the road. I simply slept.

Chapter 5

The life of Cluain flowed about me, and like a stone in its stream I felt myself rubbed and harried by it, soothed and lulled. The rocks were there, bigger than I, immovable, the weights and counterweights of its whole structure were the customs and habits established over my grandfather's lifetime, a part of Cluain as he had fashioned it, and as the years had fashioned him. Against these rocks I was sometimes dashed and bruised, but I was part, then, of the flow of its life, and such things were accepted. But I also accepted, gratefully, the soothing regularity of its ways, the sense that I was becoming part of the established pattern. I, too, was being accepted. Not in all ways, not by all those here, not always without reservation, but I began to see, in the manner and the gestures of those about me that perhaps—just perhaps—the time would come when I too would be one of the rocks of Cluain.

The tower room both held me remote from it, and yet let me learn its world. From there I saw much and learned much, and a kind of humility came to me at times, because, in fact it was all so much more complex than the first superficial glance would have revealed. Slowly, I began to forgive William for what he had not written to me. As I grew more absorbed, the details became more intricate, and how did one write to far-off China of a life like this?—

especially if he had begun, as I did, to experience its fascination, and if he had not wanted to tell a waiting father and sister that he might never return to the dream of his Chinese railways. How could we have been told that the focus could have shifted from that huge, still mechanically unconquered land, to this green strath, to these lonely glens, to this seemingly narrow world, where all was already settled in its seasonally rhythmical pattern? No, we would not have understood. We would have thought his vision had shrunk, and been disappointed. And then, perhaps, he had never meant it to be so. Perhaps he had not cared even to speak to himself of capitulation, lest it make it too irrevocable. It could not have been easy for a young man to allow his dreams to change shape, to alter, and to admit the dominance of Angus Macdonald. And the predominance of Angus Macdonald was the biggest rock of Cluain's world.

So I looked from the tower room, and I saw the ways of Cluain. I saw the passage of the days, the times, and the events. I saw the milking herd brought in in the early morning, and again in the evening I saw the changeless, routine work of the farm go on, I saw Mairi Sinclair's lean body at work in her garden, the white cat skipping beside her, or playing its own game of hide and seek with the butterflies among the herbs. I saw, too, and respected, the thin but never-ending procession of people, mostly women, but with a number of men among them, who came along the back path to the kitchen passage door. I saw them come, the women in plaids, often with babies wrapped within the folds, and I saw them leave. It was a silent procession, hardly in evidence if one went downstairs, but almost always, I saw, there was someone about the place patiently waiting to consult Mairi Sinclair about some ailment, asking for some salve or herbal medicine. There was a special room in which she made these things. Often at night I saw the light from her lamp cast out on the path beside the window. At times I would pass people seated on the bench in the kitchen passage, waiting; we would pass words of greeting, but it was understood that I never asked the reason for the visit. I saw some of them leave, faces lighted a little with relief, or at least a sense of hope imparted. And then I would look at that black-clad figure with new respect, but looking was as far as it went. Never again was there a repetition of that first night's encounter on the stairs; never again did she unveil the emotions that had distorted her features, nor give that anguished cry. We were acutely aware of each other, and yet our lives hardly seemed to touch. I left her domain entirely to her, did not question or interfere with her routine; I behaved, in that way, entirely as if I were a guest with the freedom of the house, and still respecting the fact that there were places to which I would not presume. And she—she left me strictly alone. We passed no words that were not necessary. I never went to her kitchen; the room where she prepared and stored her herbs was kept locked. I rarely even went to sit in the garden—"her garden"—I thought of it as being. Certainly, the few times I was there, she never ventured out. A line of neutrality had been drawn. Some day, if I stayed at Cluain, I knew it must be crossed, but the time was not now.

Morag was our messenger between the two territories. It was she who brought the hot water, the clean towels, my freshly laundered clothes, she who turned down the bed at night, and warmed it with a hot jar; she who fussed over me a little, and asked me questions about China, insatiable to learn of a world she did not know. She had no inhibitions, like Mairi Sinclair, no bitternesses, like my grandfather. She wanted both to learn and to tell. Her tongue rattled on regardless of what her hands did. Without Morag, there was so much of Cluain I might never have known, or which would have come to me more slowly. Once as we made my bed together, I commented on the lack of pictures in the house, the absence of ornaments, the little touches that a woman might leave on a house. My mother had grown up here, my grandmother was not so many years dead. Had they lived with this starkness all their lives? And where had the mirror come from that Morag had produced so swiftly that first evening? So far, it was the only one I had seen at Cluain.

"Och, mistress, come now—I'll show you. Mistress Sinclair is in the dairy, and will be busy there this next hour. She does not leave it to the woman who comes to help to see that the churns are properly scalded, ready for the new milk . . ." And I was following her down the tower steps, unable to resist her beckoning voice.

123

"Wait there, mistress—first I must get the keys." She was gone before I could stop her, and back again in half a minute. "Quickly, now, mistress—I'll just unlock, and then I must put the keys back. I will lock up again later. Keys have always to be in their place at Cluain." She unlocked the door of a room I had never before entered, and rushed down again to replace the keys on the board outside the kitchen door. It was a strange part of the simplicity of the ways of this country. Everything was locked, and yet all keys were displayed where any of those passing could have them to hand. The order was in locking; the trust was in leaving the keys on full view. It was the same with my grandfather, who made a ritual of unlocking the cupboard which contained the whisky each evening with the key from his chain, and yet he had shown me where the second key lay in an unlocked drawer directly above.

While Morag was gone I opened the door, and it revealed the most unexpected room of all at Cluain. Here was all that I had missed. Here were the pictures, many of them stacked against the walls, here were the little ornaments, some of them valuable, that might have graced the mantels of the rooms below, here were the family portraits, and the little painted miniatures of years ago.

"It was your grandmother's bedroom," Morag said, coming close behind me. "I almost grew up here. She was often ailing—always delicate. She needed things brought to her, and a child is good at fetching and carrying. Och—not that I minded. She was so good to me. Always sweets for me, and explaining whatever it was she was doing. She gave me most of my lessons here. She was a book reader, your grandmother. The long winter days, when it was too harsh for her to be about, she would be here in bed, with a big fire going, and her books about her, and always an hour or two to spare of teaching me something from them. See, mistress, even the bookcases were brought up here because she did not, in the last years, very often go downstairs."

Unspeaking, I wandered about. It was a confusion such as no other room at Cluain displayed. The books, yes—the pictures upon the walls. These I understood. But what of this indiscriminate jumbling of ornaments—Meissen bowls and plates, a Prunus vase my mother must have sent from China, silver vases, Delft pitchers, engraved glass goblets. So much of this must have been part of the furnishings of Cluain the day Angus Macdonald took title to it. Laid face-down on the writing table were some framed daguerreotypes; when I turned them over I saw faces more familiar than my own was now. These same likenesses had been the only adornments of my father's study in Peking—the likeness of my mother, with myself as an infant on her knee, William standing by her side; my father as he held his first-born child after the christening, the four of us together after I had been able to stand on my own feet to face the camera. My grandmother must have looked at them often. They had not always lain face-downwards on the table.

I moved along, stopping to lift away from the walls some of the pictures stacked against them. Nothing distinguished, that I could judge, but the ordinary rural scenes that might once have hung on the walls of the rooms below—a portrait or two—which ancestor I didn't know. There were rolled-up carpets and rugs. There were four mirrors, of various sizes, one of them exquisitely framed in silver-gilt, valuable, and I guessed, rare.

I went to one of the two big gable windows. The room was on the south-facing wing of the house, overlooking the herb garden, and giving a lower, not so awesome view of the Cairngorms as the tower room. It was large and lofty—with the fourposter bed it was quite a grand room, but without the intimidating quality that the tower room could sometimes possess. From here, the sight of Ballochtorra was blotted out.

I turned back from the window. "Why this, Morag? Why are all these things here?"

"It is not so easy to understand, mistress. When Mistress Macdonald died, gradually the things were brought here—the ornaments and pictures and such. Mistress Sinclair said it was for safekeeping. She did not want them broken, or worn out. And the Master, he did not seem to notice, or care. He never comes in here. Mistress Sinclair seems to think it is sinful to have ornaments about—though I think myself there cannot be much sin in a picture or a carpet. But she thinks life should not be too easy. She has her ways, mistress, and a body gets used to them. I tell you, though, I missed your grandmother sorely when she was gone. More than my own mother she was to me. I was ten then—almost eight years ago, it was. But Mistress Sinclair has not been unkind, you understand. She let me have a few little things for my room—a small mirror, some flower pictures. She lets me take one book at a time from the bookcases. But I have read them all now, and I am going through a second time. I have to come here to dust every week, and I think of your grandmother very often . . . a good lady, she was, Mistress Kirsty, and sad that she never saw Master William or yourself . . ."

So Morag's voice ran on, as constant a sound of Cluain as the river, explaining and telling. I stood before the window again, thinking of a different Cluain that my grandmother had presided over, a softer, gentler house. Yes, Morag must miss her, as I would have done. I turned back, and Morag was gone, leaving me alone to look once again at the pictures, to read the titles of the books—the Brontës, Jane Austen, Sir Walter Scott, Wordsworth, Tennyson, Coleridge. The idealised porcelain figurines of the shepherdesses on the mantel did not represent the real world as Mairi Sinclair had experienced it. And Morag, with her innate sense of tact and discretion, was leaving me to discover this other side of Cluain for myself. After that, I went back to the tower room and unpacked the pictures I had taken from my father's study—the same ones that lay in my grandmother's room, and I set them up on the desk. I knew I was staking my first claim on Cluain with that action, and Mairi Sinclair could make what she liked of it.

I continued to walk Cluain's world, and beyond it. I would follow the tracks wherever they led, sometimes through the gently sloping barley fields, sometimes to the higher meadows where the cattle cropped the summer grass, sometimes going farther into difficult country, rough and steep, where the tracks led to the moors on the slopes of the mountains, and would end in the peat diggings. The rich brown sediment was cut to the depth of several spades, and the water ran from the bog into the channels left by the cuttings; at intervals the peat was stacked to dry, piled neatly on end, waiting to be carted down to Cluain—or to whomever owned the bog. I was not always sure when I went beyond Cluain's land. Much of the moors, I knew, belonged to Ballochtorra, and so did the belts of forest. I wandered there, and sat on the film of pine needles, listening to the wind in the high branches; occasionally, then, I would catch sight of the red deer which roamed the moors and forests, some of them with their fawn, peacefully grazing, living through the days of their respite, their growing days, before the guns of the autumn would come. And finally I found the courage to explore the craggy area beyond Ballochtorra, the place where my grandfather said William had lain. There were massive outcroppings of granite, and some tall trees clinging precariously to the thin soil, oaks and beeches that had survived the felling of poorer times when fuel had been short; but mostly here it was slender, dense, second growth, birch and larch and fir which must have seeded themselves, the cover lavish and beautiful in the summer months. And there were places where the rock was so sheer that no cover at all could find a hold there, and birds were its only inhabitants. It would have been from some such ledge that Callum Sinclair had brought down the eyass peregrine he had called Giorsal. There were many places among these rocks where William might have fallen, many places where he might have dragged himself to find a little shelter. I thought of these places whipped by wind and flying snow, as they had been at that time. I did not ask my grandfather the precise place where William had been found; that much I did not want to know.

But Angus Macdonald himself was not unknowledgeable of my wanderings. Sometimes I was back to the midday meal after he himself had come in. He never waited the meal for me, nor got up to serve me if I were late.

"I'm sorry," I would apologise. "I went farther than I intended."

"One day you'll go too far." He nodded towards the sideboard. "Your meal is there."

And the day came when Morag brought the summons from him to come to the stableyard. I found him there, and a man I had never seen before—not one of the farm or distillery workers—who jerked his bonnet towards me. He was holding the bridle of a Highland pony, a grey, plump creature, who looked at me with sure, calm eyes.

"Think you can ride her, Gurrl?" my grandfather asked.

"I can try."

"Try her about the yard. See how you suit her." It was obvious that he intended the pony to be suited by me, not me by the pony. She was short, and I swung myself up to the sidesaddle before either man could extend a hand. My legs seemed to trail, but she had such a broad back, I felt as if I couldn't be shaken off my perch. And that awkward-seeming animal had a surprisingly even gait, and a good mouth. She was not nervous, not tense, just knowing. I felt, as I rode about the stableyard, that she would tolerate me, and do her duty by me as long as I treated her with equal respect.

"She'll carry you well, mistress," the man said. "She's not young, but she's stronger than many I've known, and sure-footed as a goat. She'll not lead you into any mischief."

"What do you call her?"

"She is called Ailis. But if you—if Mr. Macdonald—well, you may call her what you please. She'll not mind."

"She should be called what she's always been called—Ailis." I stroked the grey mane; she stood, quiet and patient, tolerating my long legs, my stranger's hand. "Are you selling her, then?"

"I must, mistress. My wife and I, we're bound to Canada—to relatives. Ailis has been with us these thirteen years. We would leave her with a good master in a place she's used to."

"Used to it, she is," my grandfather said. "She must know every road and track and path in this country, eh, Mr. Ross."

"All of it, Mr. Macdonald. The pony of an Exciseman goes everywhere. She's carried me safe and sound since she was a three-year-old, over every kind of country, and never put a foot wrong. You'll get no speed from her, mind, but she's the stamina of a dray horse, and six times the sense."

"Well, then, it's settled. You'll take her to the end box, Kirsty, and rub her down, and water and feed her. She'll be yours to take care of, mind, and I'll tolerate no neglect . . . Now, Mr. Ross, if you'll kindly come to the office we'll finish our business, and you'll take a dram with me. Duty paid, of course," he added, a rare attempt at a joke. The Exciseman paused for a moment, laid a hand lingeringly on Ailis, and then moved off.

128

I slid down off the saddle, and looked at my gift horse. She returned my look, and then she slowly turned her head towards the stable, as if she knew exactly where she would be housed, and how plentiful the oats would be—a broad, inelegant-looking creature, whose presence here spoke for him what my grandfather would not say. She would carry me well and safely, knowing this whole countryside; there would be no repetition of what had befallen William. Ailis was to be my companion and my guide.

So I led her to her box, and the stableman, John Farquharson, came to help me unsaddle, and showed me which pegs in the tackroom would be for Ailis's harness. He helped me rub her down, and water and feed her, and he evidently enjoyed working with that comfortable, plump little creature. "Aye, she's a fine wee lass," he said. "A nice change, mistress, from the big lads I'm dealing with all the time." He nodded towards the stalls of the huge Clydesdales that pulled the distillery drays loaded with the whisky casks to the railhead at Ballinaclash—and to the empty boxes of the farm work horses, those that pulled the plough and the grain wagons at the harvest. There was only one other animal in the stable at Cluain—the "Sunday Lad" he was jokingly called, an undistinguished-looking horse which drew the hooded trap when Angus Macdonald left his farm. The stable and smithy's shop reflected the house. Everything that was necessary was there, all clean, oiled, painted, well-fed, well cared-for. The Clydesdales were magnificent in their strength; the Sunday Lad would never be given a second glance, nor would the trap he pulled. They were decent, and more than adequate for their purpose, but they would rouse no envy in anyone's heart. It was precisely that effect that my grandfather sought. "It's a fool," he once said to me, "who shows the world all he's got. There's just that much more they will want to take from him." So in this age of display, my grandfather drove a modest horse and trap, and there was no way of telling if he could have afforded more.

The Sunday Lad did not so often come out on Sunday. The first Sunday I was there Angus Macdonald made his gesture to the curiosity of the community, and he drove me to the kirk. "Och, they'll want to have their look at you, but they know fine well that your father was an Anglican bishop, and they'll not be expecting his daughter to be a prop of the Presbyterian establishment. They hold no brief for bishops in Scotland, you know. It's for the sake of your mother, and for your bother lying there in the kirkyard that you must occasionally show yourself. Myself, I've little time for the kirk. I would not say I was not a God-fearing man, but I'm not in agreement with the kind of God I get served up by this minister, and his sermons are too long, by a long way. And then, I've reason to remember that the ministers of the church were often on the side of the lairds during the years of the Highland clearances, when the landlords wanted the people out, and the whole country turned into a sheep-walk. Too few of them stood by their human flock, and too many instructed them that it was God's will that they obey their lairds, and remove themselves from the straths where their families and clans had lived for hundreds of years. They sent those poor bewildered creatures off on those rotten hulks to die of cholera and typhoid on the way to Canada, and they sent them with a sermon, saying it was God's will. And the people were meek, and obeyed, because it had always been the clan system to obey the chieftain. But I cannot forgive the men who helped make it easy for the lairds."

"Your father was a laird."

"Aye, he was that. The laird of a poor, small little island and *he* owed allegiance to the Clanranald chief. The people left Inishfare because the land could not support their numbers. It was not the sheep that drove them out, but the potato famines, and the poor-ness of the soil. It needed no minister to tell them to go. We were so small we had no minister of our own—just one who was rowed to us a few times a year for marryings, and christenings, and churchings, and such. Our dead we buried ourselves, and said the prayers over them, and the minister added his bit when he chose to come. But we mostly lived without him, and were not the less godly for it."

"So you have one more reason not to care for my father?"

"Aye—you might say that," he admitted calmly, as if his judge-ment could not be questioned. "They're all cut from the same cloth, whatever kind of God they say they represent. I never saw a starving clergyman yet."

And I would hotly deny that, and tell him of my father's labour in China—the burning heat of summer, the bitter cold of the winters when he worked among the poor, and was ill among them, and often received no respect or thanks for his pains. But my grandfather took no notice. "More fool he, then. If they laughed at his Christian God, then he would have done better to expend his labours elsewhere. There's enough lying in ignorance and want in the slums of Glasgow without wasting men among the heathen and 'rice Christians.'" And I never found an answer to that.

So I was presented for all to look at in the kirk of Balloch-torra. Mairi Sinclair, as Lady Campbell had predicted, declined to ride with us in the trap, nor had my grandfather even invited her. "She's already more than halfway there," he said, when the trap was brought to the front door, and I murmured her name. "In the winter snows, and the hot summer mornings, she's the first in kirk, and the first to leave, and no thank you to man nor beast for carrying her there. Leave it alone, Gurrl."

We did, and I was embarrassed to find myself in the front pew, opposite Margaret Campbell and Jamie. Jamie waved, and smiled at me, and the minister frowned at him; Margaret Campbell turned at Jamie's nudging and bowed her head, more, I thought, towards Angus Macdonald than myself. My grandfather did not appear to see her. It might have been one of the few times in her life that Margaret Campbell had had the experience of not being seen.

And Gavin Campbell was in the organ loft, playing the simple hymn tunes on the organ far too powerful for them. As I listened to the homily, I understood better why he preferred to be there, and not in the front pew. But it was over at last, and the congregation had their chance to examine me in detail. There was a rather frigid handshake from the minister, and a moment's conversation with Margaret Campbell and Jamie as they waited for Gavin to come down from the organ loft. It seemed to me that he made an unnecessary delay. My grandfather did nothing more than remove his hat while Margaret Campbell spoke. He nodded to her, and made his way down the path to where he had tied the Sunday Lad, and I was up on the seat beside him before Gavin Campbell made his appearance.

About half a mile along the road we came abreast of Mairi Sinclair. My grandfather did not even check the pace of the Sunday Lad as he went by! by the barest tip of his fingers to his hat he acknowledged her presence, the tall slender black figure wrapped in the red Sinclair plaid. "Nay, Gurrl," he said to me, as I laid my hand upon his arm. "Leave it . . . leave it be."

I ventured then one of my few questions. "Does Callum Sinclair come to kirk?"

"Callum Sinclair?" My grandfather flicked the reins lightly over the Sunday Lad. "What should I know of what Callum Sinclair does or does not do? It is not my business—nor yours, either."

* * *

It was my grandfather's gift of Ailis which made me much freer in the world of Cluain. The sturdy little creature carried me over the miles of ground my own legs could never have walked; she would follow without direction trails at which I had hesitated before; with her I reached mountain slopes that seemed impossibly distant, and she was sure-footed as a mule in the steep places of the glens. I cut no very fine figure on her, I knew; I wore the old serge skirt with the Clanranald plaid about my shoulders, or to cover my head when the showers passed over. But I was free—wonderfully free, and the pony seemed to understand my joy in it, and even to share it. She was not quick, but she never seemed to tire, and when I went to her box in the morning she accepted my gift of sugar calmly, and showed no resentment at the sight of the saddle. Perhaps she also enjoyed the lack of routine of our days. When we set out we took whatever direction seemed to offer itself that morning; sometimes I even let her do the choosing, and I think her pride was flattered by this. We became a pair, the garron and I, and it was she who led me to Callum Sinclair.

I saw him very seldom about the distillery yard, and he would pass me with a murmured greeting, tossed to me, I sometimes thought, as if I were a child; he never stopped to talk, and I never had an excuse to detain him. I would see him often on the pony, with Giorsal and the dog on the road that led past Cluain and Ballochtorra. Since I did not go to Mairi Sinclair's kitchen, I never again encountered him there, but occasionally the pony would be tied up in the stableyard, and I would know he was inside. It was hard to imagine that Giorsal accompanied him there, and the dog, but harder to imagine him without them. Did Giorsal perch on the kitchen mantel, and the dog lie before the range? Did he come as a duty to see his mother—or to eat, as so many seemed to do, at that table? He would not be the only one to leave Cluain's kitchen with fresh-baked bread, and slices of ham. My grandfather must have known that no one of the many who came to consult Mairi Sinclair went away empty-handed, and he did nothing to prevent it. All that would have been settled between them long ago. Mairi Sinclair scorned to hide the giving, perhaps taking quite literally the biblical injunction to heal the sick and feed the hungry. But her son did not linger very long in the kitchen of Cluain; he was like his falcon, bound by the long red streamers, but impatient to be free.

After a time I had to acknowledge to myself that I was indeed searching for Callum Sinclair on those journeys with Ailis. I knew now that it was his small house, set off by itself, that I had discovered on one of my first walks. Shamelessly now, I turned Ailis's head in that direction. For almost two weeks I went that way, and always the door of the cottage stood closed, and I heard no movement of the pony in the stable; when I was early enough the chimney still smoked from the morning's fire, but the silence over the place was absolute.

And then the morning came when I rode that way early enough to hear the ring of the axe right across the strath. He was engrossed enough at the work that he didn't even hear our approach —only the dog set up a fierce barking, and he turned and looked towards us as we came up the track by the burn. He stood, then, resting on the axe beside the pile of timber he was splitting, breathing heavily, and with a gesture motioning the dog to silence. I faced him across the rushing water.

"Well—aren't you going to ask me in?"

For a moment he didn't move. Then with a slight shrug he

came and opened the gate, and Ailis moved through the water on her own accord. "If it amuses you."

"Amuses me? Why should it amuse me?"

"Well—aren't you paying a call on the tenantry? I expect you any moment to commend my honest toil. Or have you come with a message from Angus Macdonald telling me I've been away from the distillery too long?"

Avoiding his outstretched hand, I slid down off the pony. "You know very well I don't carry messages for my grandfather. Nor would he send me."

"You're right about that—he wouldn't. Why have you come then —curiosity?"

"Probably," I admitted. "You keep to yourself, Callum Sinclair."

"And how else could it be? I'm hardly welcome in the front parlour of Cluain."

"Have you tried?" I tossed the words over my shoulder, not giving him time to reply. "Well, do you invite me into *your* parlour? I *am* curious."

"And I'm expected to satisfy your curiosity? A man's home is his own, you know, and he's a right to keep to himself if he fancies it." Then he shrugged again. "Well, why not? You're here now. And I was just finishing up the wood. It's time for a cup of tea. You can make it for us while I stack this lot."

So I entered Callum Sinclair's house alone. He went back to his log pile, and I was left, again like an inquisitive child, to do as I liked. On the outside it was not like the houses of other distillery workers, which were built of stone and slate, like the warehouses. This was much older. It had probably been here as long as Cluain itself. The thatch was new, and the windows seemed bigger than most—I guessed that Callum had enlarged them. Also missing were the inevitable hens that scratched about the doors of other households. There was a tidy, almost painfully constrained look about the place, as if no one really lived here.

But when I opened the door the kitchen-living room was more comfortable than I had expected. Callum Sinclair's hard-boned austerity did not extend too far; I was surprised at the sight of the shabby but still good leather sofa before the fire, the big roll-top desk

134

over against the opposite wall near the window, the bright red curtains and cushions, a fairly new Turkish carpet that covered most of the wooden floor. I didn't know what I had been expecting; not the bare-earthen poverty of many Highland cottages, but, unconsciously, perhaps, a repetition of Mairi Sinclair's painfully ordered environment. It was a relief to see an open book flung across the broad arm of the sofa, to see the untidy jumble of them that spilled from the deal shelves running along one wall. There was another open book beside the unwashed breakfast dishes on the big table, and a scatter of crumbs over its surface. I lifted the kettle and put it in place on the range.

"I didn't really mean it." I turned at the sound of his voice. "I am not so inhospitable as you think. I was coming to make it."

"You think I don't know how to?"

He went over to the sink and pumped water to wash his hands. "I don't know what to expect. One doesn't know about a bishop's daughter. Here in Scotland we don't know much about bishops— we think of them living in palaces, and their families . . ."

"Their families have no more money than the diocese can afford. My father's diocese was thousands of square miles, and his converts so poor he had to try to feed *them*—with money subscribed in England. There wasn't much left for himself. The only luxury William ever got was the promise of an education—and he didn't even have time to finish that."

"And you—what were your luxuries?" He had dried his hands, and was putting on a tweed jacket. Somehow, here in his own house, he seemed suddenly less withdrawn, less on the defensive —the tweed jacket instead of the sheepskin, the buttoning of his shirt collar, the way he carried the used dishes from the table and swept off the crumbs with a flick of a cloth. He brought fresh cups on a wooden tray to a table near the range, and made the tea with swift, efficient movements. His movements were part of the attraction of the man—nothing wasted, everything quite sure and unhesitant. And when there was no more to do, he was still.

"Luxuries? I had my father and William. That is more than most have. We were a close family. We had books, and good Chinese food. We had servants—but in China it is impossible not to

135

have servants. I was probably the least fashionably dressed female among the Europeans, but it hardly mattered. My father was often shabby, but no one seemed to mind that."

He rose and poured the tea. "It doesn't matter with you, either." And his eyes took in the old skirt and the muddied boots, the plaid that I was coming to wear as Highland women did, serving as a garment for every purpose. His gaze was quiet and steady; I could take his words to mean what I pleased.

"Have a scone. They come from Cluain, so I suppose they're yours."

I shook my head, and looked at him over the cup. "Can't we stop this nonsense? You're an educated man, Callum Sinclair. All this game about being subservient at Cluain is unbecoming—worse than that, it's foolish. Cluain isn't mine—and you are not a servant . . . Can we have that settled?"

He actually smiled—a faint motion, like light breaking grudgingly through winter clouds, and then being covered too quickly. Like my grandfather, he didn't seem to have had much practice in smiling. "And you're no fool. Well, all right—it's settled. I'll try to remember. Or at least I'll try to forget that you're Angus Macdonald's granddaughter."

"If you feel that way about him, why did you come back to Cluain? There must have been other positions open to you—places where you wouldn't have had to . . ."

He raised his eyebrows. "Wouldn't have had to work with my hands? Well, I suppose I could have found something. But that's just it. I *like* working with my hands. Most of all, I like being in the country—*this* country. I've known it all my life, and if there's any place I've loved, it's here. The only way I could have this and my independence as well was to work for Angus Macdonald. I could have worked for another distillery, but Cluain is . . . different. I thought about Canada or Australia, as so many of we Highlanders are forced to do. I probably would have herded sheep in Australia, or hunted for fur in Canada. Oh, I might have escaped some of the master and servant tradition. But I would not have been in the place I wanted to be. And no man is a servant who does not feel himself to be one. So I have stayed . . . for one reason or another I have stayed."

"You didn't just stay," I pointed out. "You came back."

"I came back only when Angus Macdonald asked me to. The head stillman was killed when a cask fell off a dray and crushed him. There were others here—but none Angus Macdonald thought would do as well for Cluain as I. Whatever it is that whisky needs—the nose, the eye, the sense—apparently, in your grandfather's opinion, I have it. If he could have done without me, he would have. We have no great liking for each other. But he sent for me, and we struck our bargain. I would work whatever hours the distillery required as long as it was required. In the summer I would be free of farm work—I would not harvest his barley, or herd his cattle. As long as the distillery was served, I was my own man. If I choose to work past midnight when we are in production, then it is because I am needed. And I will wade through any snow to get down there by six the next morning. But here, in this house, in the hours and the months that are mine, he has no rights. I do as I please. That is what we agreed. That is how it has been for the past three years."

"But can't be forever."

"Why not?"

"Most men marry. They take wives. They have children . . ."

He made a gesture of impatience. "When the time is right. I have not yet found the woman worth giving up what I have—"

"They marry," I repeated. "They give their hostages to fortune."

"Marry!" It was as if I had let loose a storm. He rose abruptly, the fluid body suddenly now tensed. "Marry—and put fetters on myself." The cup crashed down against the hob. "With a mother like mine who never needed to clothe herself in the respectability of marriage, how would you expect me to feel? If she could stand her solitary state, and bear her son alone, and nameless, what need do I have to rush into those kinds of bonds . . . ?"

I was strangely touched that he should in this way refer to his birth. He was sensitive and irascible, and I knew that every minute he was acting as the son of Mairi Sinclair would act. I liked it that he felt no need to make apologies for her, and was proud of her courage. They might quarrel, those two, but they were the same breed, as Morag had said.

"And yet—most women give themselves into the bondage of marriage. They do as they are told. They bear children and nurse sick husbands. They accept—"

"What else can they do?" he said, with the maddening complacency of a man. "What else is open to them?"

"Some choose to give themselves. Freely." Was I mad? Would he think I was referring to his mother.

But his expression changed to a thoughtful regard. "Yes—there are those who choose. Those who give freely. And they are the only ones worth having. Come—I'll show you something."

Completely unself-consciously he seized my hand and jerked me to my feet. My cup was banged down on the tray, and I was being pulled after him. The door was opened and slammed after us. Then I was thrust up against the end wall of the cottage.

"Stay there, and be still. She is accustomed to strangers, and will not bate off, but very few ever come here, and she may not like it in the beginning. Just be still. She will see you, and grow used to you."

And then he went on, quietly now, into the shed that adjoined the stable. I waited, flattening myself against the wall, trying to keep in the shadow cast by the overhang of the thatch. I was very still, as he had commanded, but I couldn't still the endless hammer of my pulse, the dryness of my throat against which I couldn't even swallow.

He came finally, and the falcon was on his gloved hand, the bird wearing a red, plumed hood, as I had not seen her before. He stood in the open space, the red streamers wound through his fingers, and gently, with his right hand, loosened the leather thongs that held the hood in place, and slipped it off. The hawk saw me at once, and for a moment I thought she would start up; but she simply moved a little on the glove, and flexed those fierce hind talons. Then her head turned, scanning the whole horizon, taking in any new facts of her world. And then, sure that all was as it had been, the huge dark eyes focused on me. I instantly knew, not from any foreknowledge of hawks, but from the sensation those eyes

138

produced in me, that this was truly a bird of prey. She lived by killing. She did not kill, except to eat, and even knowing that it was wrong to let her sense my fear, still I felt fear. I longed to twist and turn as her prey must do to escape those terrible sharp eyes, those great, powerful hind talons.

And now Callum's hand was upon her, stroking her with his forefinger, preening that shining, healthy plumage. And still I was transfixed by those dark encircled eyes—the darkness that would permit no light to refract into them, that made the hawk's eye as great a weapon as those talons.

She seemed a big bird, almost as long as Callum's arm from elbow to fingers, feathers blue-black above, whitish below, barred cross-wise with grey. There was a look of great power to her, power known and understood, power in control to be used as it was needed.

"She is very beautiful." My voice was a whisper. "Giorsal . . ." I took my tone from the way Callum spoke to her, and he talked constantly to her.

She turned her eyes upon me again as I spoke her name, moved again a little on Callum's glove, accustoming herself to the strange voice.

"Yes," he said quietly. "She is more than beautiful." And then, gently, he released the red streamers from his fist. For a moment longer the bird remained there, moving slightly, so that the little bells attached to her legs jingled above the sound of the burn. Then with one great spreading of her wings—effortless to her, but which rocked Callum's arm—she rose. It was a swift climb but not too high; for a time she circled the cottage and its surrounding area, hovered, as if undecided about what she would do. Then she used all the power of the long wings to make her climb, up . . . up. I strained to see her, but finally she was beyond my gaze, a speck that vanished into the sun.

"See now—the strath," Callum said. He was tense with excite-ment. "See the birds rise. If they are wise they are going for cover—the partridge and the grouse, the jays and the rooks. You know what she is to them—she is the shadow of death. They must try to evade her—they can't outfly her, any of them. She is the swiftest

thing that lives on this earth. When she stoops to her prey—dives—
some say she reaches nearly two hundred miles an hour. How they
pretend to measure it, I wouldn't know. It doesn't matter what the
speed is—she is the swiftest thing that lives."

"And you have let her go!"

He looked at me, wonderingly, and then remembered that I had
everything to learn. "That is the joy of it. She will come back. She
is tame. This is her home—as this whole wide strath is her home.
In the winter when the days are short and game is scarce, she
would sometimes go hungry if she were in the wild. But here she
knows she will be fed. You see, that is the true freedom. Now
she is free, she could choose never to return. She could go south when
the winter comes, as her kind have always done, down to the
estuaries in England where the ice does not form, and other birds
winter. In the summer she could go much farther north—to Sweden
and Finland, the tundra country. But she was born here, and like
me, this place is in her heart and her consciousness. She returns,
always—freely!

"She is an eyass falcon—one taken from the nest. I found her, the
first summer I was back here, three years ago. One of the gamekeepers from Ballochtorra shot her mother—I know, because I was
watching the peregrine fly the strath, hunting for food, and I knew
she had nestlings she had to feed. Where the male was I don't
know—shot also, I suppose. Gamekeepers don't like them because
they take the grouse. I watched the mother for weeks and I saw
how often she flew to the crag beyond Ballochtorra, and knew the
nest must be somewhere there. They like to nest on cliffs or mountain sides where they are safe under an overhang. When I knew the
mother was shot I went to find the nest. There's some fierce
climbing about Ballochtorra, and I couldn't see the nest. But finally
I heard the shrieks—the cries of hunger and alarm. When I reached
the nest her two brothers were dead—the male falcon, the tiercel, is
smaller and lighter than the peregrine by about a third. Giorsal had
eaten what meat was on them, and she was near to dying also. She
was still unable to fly, unable to hunt, even lowly things like mice,
the sort of thing they would despise when they are grown. So I
carried her down, this weak little thing, in a satchel, wrapping her

140

in cloth so that she couldn't spread her wings and damage them. She would need them all perfect if she were to fly as she should. But she was so weak she hardly struggled at all. I had meat for her, and she needed food and warmth. I brought her here, and it was days before she got enough strength to even try to challenge me. Then the great trial came. Before that she didn't care how she got the food, so long as she got it, but with strength, her confidence came. She would be tamed then, or not at all. I put her on the gloved hand, and I had to teach her to eat what came from my hand. That means staying awake as long as she does, until she eats what's offered from the hand, and falls asleep herself. Two nights and three days it was. I was half dead. I carried her everywhere, within the house. I spent those two nights with her on the glove, resting my arm along the arm of the sofa, reading aloud—both to keep myself awake, and to get her used to the sound of my voice. She gave in, in the end, and our comradeship was begun. When you have fought out a battle like that, you prize nothing that comes easily.

"I was lucky. Giorsal was a good bird. Often an eyass will be no good—screamers all their lives. Like some women. I had so much to learn. I made her a perch there in the shed at the back of the stable, her own room, which I could darken, so she could be quiet and happy. I had the jesses ready when I went to get her, but the rest had to come piece by piece. I had to learn myself. I stayed up more nights learning to tie a falconer's knot, learning to tie the hood on with my right hand and my teeth. But after that first struggle, she took to it all as if she had been born to it. From the beginning, then, I represented food and shelter to her. She became so tame that I knew the problem would be to give her the confidence and the need to go and make her kill as she should. A peregrine is a . . . a noble bird. It would do her—or me—no good to have her live her life as a tame bird on a perch. She had to experience the other side of her nature. I wanted to see her in her own element, ranging this whole country, hovering and stooping, making her own killing. Even if I lost her, once she did experience that freedom, I had to take the chance.

"I was glad of the long evenings, that summer. I knew she must be trained to make her killing before the summer was ended, as she would have in the wild state, or she would be ruined. She had taken to the jesses and swivel and leash so well—the jesses are the leather straps, and the brass swivel links the jesses to the leash. The swivel lets her move freely on her block, or the perch, without getting tangled up. I had her out on her block in the yard here every day that it was fair. You see how it has a hook in it to tie the leash into. There's another block out there beside the burn, so that she can bathe and preen and dry off in her natural place, which is a stony, running stream." He grimaced faintly. "Naturally, she loved it. To her it was the best of all worlds. She had companionship, food, protection, shelter. She took to the hood well. When you put a hood on a hawk she is calmed. She ceases to see—and I suppose, to care—about the world around her. She learned to be carried on the glove, hooded, when she was quite young. I used to take her down to the distillery to get her used to the noises and the different voices, and finally I could take her there even without the hood, and she would not bate off unless something very unusual happened. She was very well-mannered, as trained hawks are expected to be. But still she did not seem to want to fly on her own. She was growing fat and lazy. So I had to let her go hungry, and when she was hungry enough I would swing the lure, baited with fresh meat, so that she had to come to me for it— always on the leash of course. When the leash is long enough to let the bird fly to the lure, falconers call it a creance. I made the leash longer and longer. She grew angry at me when I left her hungry, and then she began to understand that she must fly for her food, must learn to take it as it whirled in the air before her. I had her coming a long distance to the lure, and then the final day arrived— by now I was praying because the bird and I, we seemed like one. I had given her life, and she had given me—well, I don't think I could name quite what she had given to me. There was a richness of experience I had never known before. But I knew we had to come to this climax, or it all would be worthless. That day I took off the leash and the swivel and she flew to that far tree there. I could hardly see her among the foliage. All I could see was the red jesses —and hear the bells. She might be gone forever. I swung the lure, and I prayed. I don't often pray. She came to the lure, and snatched the meat, and went to her tree to eat it. And then I held the meat in the glove. It was a long way to see such a scrap, but hawks can see anything. Once they have fixed their object, their eyes focus like the lens of a telescope. She knew the meat was there, but she also knew that she was free. She came then, swooping. I will never forget the sight of her wings, nor the sound of them. She came and ate on the glove, and she stayed. I have never known a moment like it in my whole life."

His pale skin was flushed; the dark eyes seemed to shine like his falcon's. *"That* is what I mean by something given freely." Triumph and exaltation flooded into him in that memory. He was recounting the story of a love. Of a creature sought and won, like a woman wooed. Perhaps it was at that moment that I began to love him, to wish myself that creature.

*   *   *

There was more he told me that day, but I do not remember all of it. What I was hearing about the hawk was mixed with what I was feeling about the man. I witnessed in that recounting the pride and power of a lover, and my thoughts and emotions were mixed wildly between the two. I was glad when the falcon had returned, because now his attention was all on her, and he did not look into my face as he talked.

The peregrine roamed the sky above us—not so high now that we could not see the great gliding grace of the wing spread, the feinted stoops, the playful dives. The whole strath was stilled. The falcon roamed her territory, and all now had taken cover. All knew that she was there—the beautiful, deadly shadow of death.

"She is playing," Callum said. "She has killed this morning, and eaten well. She has no need for food. Now she is flying for the love of it. She learned her own element, you see. But still she comes back to me."

And she did come back. She tired of her games, and came down near the cottage. She hovered for long minutes, watching the new outline of my shape against the cottage wall. But I had not moved, nor had Callum. Then for a longer time she perched in a tree near by. But the bond between them seemed complete, and she knew that Callum would have warned her if I had been a threat. So then, with a final glide, she came back to Callum's gauntlet, outstretched to receive her. Now she stood very quietly as he gathered in the jesses, and gently drew the hood over her head. I saw how he had to use his teeth as well as his free hand to draw the thongs of the hood tight enough to stay in place. Blinded now, Giorsal was at rest. He carried her back to the outbuilding of the stable.

Even then I did not move. I was as transfixed by these thoughts of Callum, as I had been by the brooding stare of the hawk. When at last he reappeared I felt drained and weary. I did not want to go back into the cottage. I had to be alone with this new thought, alone where my face and voice would not betray my weakness. Callum brought Ailis from the hitching ring beside the stable, and before I was even aware of his gesture he was swinging me up into the saddle as if I were the weight of a child.

"Is it possible . . . ?" My voice faded into a whisper. I felt my hands shake as I took up the reins.

"Is what possible?"

"Do you think—could I—could I ever see her kill? So free and wild, as you said she was—and still coming back to your hand. I would like to see . . ."

"You want to see that? It means quite a ride. We have to go up on the moors, where it's very open, or you'll see nothing. But if you like . . ."

"I will go anywhere."

"Then I will take you. Good-bye, Kirsty."

I must have crossed the burn, must have made my way down the track to where it joined the road. I returned to Cluain, early for lunch. I do not remember the journey. In my brain was burned the image of the falcon, and of Callum. What was between those two, I wanted for myself.

Chapter 6

———◆———

In much the way that I was drawn into the life of Cluain, so I also drifted towards Ballochtorra. I knew my grandfather did not want me to go there, but I went, following where William had been before me. If I was slightly diffident the first time, it was also the last time I felt that way. Margaret Campbell welcomed me with an almost humble gratitude. As I waited in the grand and formal drawing room into which the butler had shown me, I could hear her voice on the stairs, and the sound of her feet as if she were running. The door opened quickly.

"Oh, you've come! I thought you never would! I hear you've been riding all over the countryside on a fat little garron, and I was beginning to feel hurt that you never stopped at my door."

"It's a little difficult to decide just *which* door one should come to. Ballochtorra is rather formidable—and your butler even more so! And then my fat little garron doesn't cut much of a figure in the stableyard beside your thoroughbreds."

"Oh, you're *not* going to be like your grandfather, are you? Was there ever such a proud, stiff man? I know Ballochtorra is a little intimidating until one knows the way, but you see, you did find it. And *I* am just as much afraid of my butler as you will ever be— and *more,* because I have to do what he tells me. What it is to be mistress of a big house when they all know you weren't born to it!

I'm really not mistress at all. I can only speak to the housekeeper, and the butler and the head gardener, and if they don't like what I am suggesting, I'm told it can't be done. Why, I can't even plant a rose bush where I want it. How William used to laugh at that! Oh, let's not stay in here. This room depresses me if it's not filled with people. Come into my own little sitting room—it's so much cosier. We'll have some tea there."

It wasn't a small room at all, except by comparison to the drawing room. But it was Margaret Campbell's room—full of the charm, the soft colours, the air of restrained elegance which was essentially her own. It was scattered with silver-framed photographs—house-party photographs, shooting-party photographs; in the front row of one I saw the stout, bearded figure of the Queen's heir. Some day there would be the photograph that my grandfather said James Ferguson longed for, Margaret Campbell in the ermine-trimmed robes and coronet of the marchioness. The photos were mostly displayed on a silk-draped grand piano.

"Does—does your husband play here?"

"No—not very often. Gavin doesn't use this room very much. He gives Jamie his lessons at his own piano in his study—that's up in one of the towers. We had to take a window out to get the piano hoisted in. I was terrified it would drop."

"Does it look down on Cluain?"

"No—that's what's strange. It looks straight across the glen at the narrowest part. The dark side of Ballochtorra, I call it. But Gavin likes it."

The tea was brought, and Margaret laughed at how meager it seemed beside what Mairi Sinclair had served. But the silver tray was laid with delicate sandwiches, and a dish of tiny, marzipan-coated cakes; at Ballochtorra the cook strove to tempt the jaded appetites of ladies, not to fill the hungry stomachs of countryfolk.

Margaret ran her finger along the bevelled edge of the table from which she served. A minute trace of dust was revealed. "Oh, I shall have to speak to Mrs. Macgregor again. Not that she can help it, poor thing. How can you hope to keep things clean with building going on? The place is nothing but dust."

"Yes, I heard the hammering."

146

"The whole valley hears the hammering. It is terrible. It should be done when we are away, but my father has taken it into his head that we must convert two rooms which weren't being used into one large billiard room for when the Prince visits. Can you imagine it? Workmen brought from London, even—cabinetmakers for panelling, all that sort of thing. And all in a rush. And Father thought the library was too shabby, and so all the furniture must be reupholstered, and most of the books rebound. Except those that Gavin refused to let him have—he took them all up to his study. The silly thing is, of course, that the Prince never reads a book, even on a wet day. But the new leather bindings are *beautiful* colours . . ."

It sounded silly, and light-minded, and perhaps it was. But whatever she said and did was with such apparent desire to please, that very few could have resisted it. And after all, if there was money to be spent, she would enjoy spending it. Then, too, there was for me the novelty of the change from Cluain. Here there was no austerity, little sign of the earnest drive that sparked my grandfather's life, and the passion for hard work that seemed to be part of Mairi Sinclair's religion. I relaxed against the silken cushions, I listened to the flow of light gossip and easy laughter that came from Margaret Campbell, and I was charmed all over again. In the midst of all this, the enjoyment, the thought struck me that at Cluain I never heard anyone laugh—not even Morag. My grandfather might have replied to that thought that there was little to laugh at.

"Do you play, Kirsty?" Margaret Campbell indicated the piano.

"No." I said it outright, at last escaping from the fact that I played very badly. Here, no one need know that I had tried to play at all, and the childhood nightmare of stumbling through my pieces would be gone forever. It was not even a lie.

"Oh—I'm sorry. I used to have such an amusing time with William. We used to try duets together. He was quite good—not serious, though. Gavin thought we were a pair of fools. Gavin's music is so—so *intense*. He would rather no one heard him play. He spends so much time in that bleak kirk up there, playing for himself. Even in winter, when it's almost too cold to bear. Gavin thinks I'm . . . silly."

"I'm sure he doesn't," I said it gently.

"Perhaps he doesn't consciously think it. But when he goes off to that kirk alone I know he would rather have been what he wanted to be—an organist in some cathedral town. Working all day, training a choir, perhaps, with a good, quiet wife waiting at home. He doesn't really like Ballochtorra. Not the way it is now. And to tell you the truth, neither do I. It was good in the beginning, when we were just married. A ruin of a fortress, really, but it was beautiful in a wild sort of way." Her tone altered, the faint regret changing to a kind of determined optimism. "Well, perhaps one thinks that way when one is young—and it doesn't last for anyone. My father began to build and build, and it has become so big, Gavin seems lost here. He loves the moors and the mountains, but really, I think he would be happier in a cottage. When we are alone here, and I see him down the length of that big dining table, I almost think he wishes I were not here. And then he could just play his music and read his books—and forget about having to find something to say to me."

She was actually smiling as she said it, and those flecked amber eyes were glowing as if she were not tolling the knell of a marriage. Only the slight plucking at the lace of her handkerchief betrayed her. "It isn't his fault. He didn't ask to be saddled with Ballochtorra, and with my father. And now this other title coming, and things will be even more so. He loved me, you know—he *did* love me. But all this has built up like a wall between us—I can feel all the things he loves, his music and books, walking on the moors, on one side of the wall, and on the other side there's my father's money. We can hardly see each other over it all—or speak. The truth is, Gavin would like to *work*—and my father does not think it fitting for his daughter's husband to be involved in business. He must be a gentleman, and wait for his title, and then that little boy from the Glasgow slums that used to be my father will be buried forever. Jamie will probably never see the inside of a distillery, and it is driving Gavin wild that he can teach him nothing about the world that's coming to him. My father says the business will just grow and grow, that whisky will go on expanding, and there will be competent people to manage it. Jamie's name will go on the company director's list, but he will never be in the management of the business. It's money, you see. It has made my father. And me—I love spending it. But it is ruining Gavin. When the house is built in London I doubt that Gavin will come for more than a few weeks a year—only when he must make an appearance. He will stay at Ballochtorra—and I, I will be the gayest, brightest hostess in London, and the Prince of Wales will come to my dinner parties. And my husband will be that awkward Scottish peer that everyone is glad isn't there to spoil the fun."

Her tone wavered. "The odd thing is, I suspect Gavin might be very good at business—if anyone ever gave him the chance.

"Well—I've talked too much—but I've needed to so badly. People misjudge me—or I make them misjudge me. They think I'm such a fool I don't know how Gavin feels. But do they know how I feel? I can't help it about my father. I can't help it that having all the money has made me so lonely here. No wonder I want to escape to London, to fill the house with guests. I must have distraction, or sometimes I think I'll go a little mad. I loved the times William came. He made me laugh, and forget it all. He was so good at so many things—he was so clever . . ."

"Did you talk to him like this—I mean about your husband?"

"You mean William was younger than I, and might have been shocked? But you see, William *knew*. He could see it at once. He was older than he seemed. That's why I'm talking like a fool to you, because it seems almost like having William back again. I don't babble like this to everyone. Oh . . . my father would be furious if he heard me. He knows what goes on in the lives of the people I mix with, all the careful arranging of bedrooms when there's a house party. But he doesn't care just so long as the façade of the marriage is kept up, and the guest list is fashionable, and no divorces ever come of it all. It sounds wicked, doesn't it—and it is! But he is ambitious—so terribly ambitious. He would not approve of that behaviour for himself—and probably not for me, because Gavin would not stand for it. But he wants me to be a great hostess, and so I must know these people. If there are rumours . . . well, that can't be helped. That is part of the game."

Suddenly the long delicate fingers shredded the lace handkerchief with surprising strength and violence. "Oh, you must despise me!"

149

"Why should I despise you? What have I got to feel superior about?"

Her eyes widened. "You're a bishop's daughter!"

"I grew up in China. I've seen too many young girls sold and used to feel surprised that it might happen in other places—in other ways. Didn't William explain any of this to you?"

"He did—in a way. But I never talked like this to William. He was a man. It might have been . . ."

"Misunderstood?"

"Perhaps. I valued William . . . as a friend. He knew I was lonely. It wasn't necessary to say any more. I've said too much now. I've put too much on you. And I don't want you to hate my father. He can't help it. I've seen the sort of place he grew up in." A faint shudder went through her body. "I would do anything—*anything*—to get out of such a place. I can't blame him. He gave me a different sort of education, and I'm supposed to be free of all the need to fight people for what one wants. What he doesn't understand, and never will, is that the world he's pushed me into is just as scheming and full of competition as the one he came out of. And dear God . . . the worst of it . . ."

"What is the worse of it?" She was going to say it, even if I tried to hold her back.

"Gavin doesn't know to this day that my father made very careful enquiries about his whole family before he let me marry him. Of course Gavin was already a baronet, but I doubt seriously if he'd ever more than heard of the Marquis of Rossmuir. My father knew all along that there was a very good chance that Gavin would eventually have the title, even though there were two other men to succeed in between. But he knew one was sick in India, and the other had been mixed up in some gambling scandal here, and was drinking himself to death in the Congo. *That* is why he let me marry Gavin. It was a gamble—and it has paid off. My father loves to gamble. This has been his greatest win yet. Ten years ago my father wasn't so successful or so rich—and there were not titles to be picked up for the asking for his daughter. Titles demanded *solid* money. It sounds so rotten and corrupt, doesn't it? But it wasn't meant to be. I loved Gavin—yes, I did love him."

150

She got up, and the swish of the silk of her gown as she paced was all I heard in the room for a full minute. Then she turned back and faced me. "There—I've said it all. Everything. I've never talked like this in my life. I don't know what has possessed me. Perhaps I've never been willing to admit it before—but my father is visiting us now, and because of the Prince coming, he seems more— oh, how do I say it?—more *pushing* than he's ever been. Gavin is feeling the strain, and so am I. I had to talk . . . do you mind so much? You—I think you like me. You have no reason to like me, but I think you do."

"I do like you. Rather more than that."

"William liked me, too."

"Of course William liked you. Who could help it?"

We both swung to face the door. Gavin Campbell stood there, he was smiling—a smile that told us nothing. There was no way of knowing how much he had heard, and I guessed he was never likely to say. Like William, he knew more than he had to be told. Now he was moving towards us.

"There's some tea left, I hope."

Strangely Margaret Campbell was flustered. "Why—of course! I'll ring for some fresh—"

"No, don't! I don't want the fuss. There must be some left. I don't mind it strong."

"There isn't a cup for you. I never thought—well, you never come in to tea here, Gavin."

"Don't I? I forget to have it, I suppose. Never mind. They told me Miss Howard had come. I thought I'd come to find out what has taken her so long to visit. It isn't very friendly. Has that old man, Angus Macdonald, told you you shouldn't come?"

"Not in so many words. He leaves me much to myself. I expect I was just . . . shy."

"Shy! William's sister shy! The girl who came all the way from China without an invitation is *shy*." He laughed. "You'll never convince me of it—no, Margaret, *don't ring!* I can't stand all the fuss. There'll be six maids as well as Wilson hovering." Still on his feet he took up a sandwich and ate it.

151

"Oh, Gavin, please . . ." Margaret looked at him pleadingly. "You so seldom come in here, and I can't even give you a cup of tea."

He didn't reply to her. "Mairi Sinclair does things rather differently, I should imagine."

"Arrangements are simpler at Cluain," I answered. "It's only a step from the kitchen to the dining room. And there's only Morag . . ."

"Yes—simpler. That's how it should be. Margaret and I are trapped by the people who are paid to wait on us. And there's Jamie, growing up hardly knowing how to tie his own bootlaces."

"Gavin!—that's not fair! He does his best."

"He does more than his best. It's a minor miracle that he hasn't as yet turned into a spoiled little prig. And I know you won't let that happen, Margaret." He looked at me. "You see, Margaret has that rare gift of being able to laugh at herself, and she's passed it on to her son, I think. She never allows him to forget where his grandfather started. And Jamie knows I only tumbled into my position. And I give Margaret credit for that."

Then he walked to the piano, quite abruptly, and sat down. The music that came was not as I expected it to be. The melody was so well known, almost hackneyed, not the sort of thing a serious musician would play.

"I have a feeling Kirsty can sing. William had a good voice." He spoke across the music to me.

I had always been told I had a pretty voice, and I'd never paid any attention to that. But now suddenly I felt that I wanted to sing—and yes, I could sing. I walked across to the piano, and stood slightly behind Gavin, glancing quickly at the music, but having no real need of it.

> "If a body meet a body
> Comin' through the rye . . ."

He was singing also, a strong, good voice, a dark voice, almost, that seemed at odds with his fair hair and light eyes. Across the room from us I could see Margaret Campbell, handkerchief twisting again in her lovely hands. "Why, Gavin . . . I never heard you play anything like this."

152

He shook his head, as if to indicate that she was not to interrupt. I found myself singing alone.

> ". . . all the lads, they smile at me
> Comin' through the rye."

He had turned and was staring at me, that peculiar, straight stare I had first encountered on Ballinaclash station, a stare that seemed to lock out everything else in the world. "Yes, I thought so. You have a voice." The laugh was loud, triumphant. "My God, you *have* a voice!"

I don't know why it should have mattered to him; but in the moments of that stare and those words, even Margaret Campbell was shut out. We might easily have been alone.

*   *   *

Gavin escorted me to the stables that first time, leading me through the back passages of Ballochtorra, the noise of the hammering about us, but the age of the place revealed in these winding, twisting ways. I felt I was back at Cluain. And then Gavin opened the door that led directly onto the stableyard, and here the building was so new that the ivy had not yet had time to take hold. A great over-weighty clock tower dominated a quadrangle of theatrically fashioned horse boxes, and the entrance to the smithy's shop was the traditional shape of a horseshoe. "A bad opera setting," Gavin murmured to me as he slammed the door. "Enough thoroughbreds to satisfy a king's taste, and I keep wondering when the prince-in-disguise-as-stable-lad will appear."

"They are your horses."

"Nominally, they're my horses, and I have to confess that I haven't the strength to say no to any one of the beauties. Why should I?—some other way would be found to spend the money. It pleases Mr. Ferguson. Give him his due, he does know good horse-flesh, and loves it. I just wish horses pleased us both for the same reasons. At least we would have one thing we could talk about together."

153

"It rarely happens that the same things please people for the same reasons."

"William was always making remarks like that. It sometimes gave me the odd feeling that I was talking to someone older than myself."

I laughed, refusing to let him make anything more serious of it. The episode in Margaret Campbell's sitting room had frightened me a little; I wanted to brush aside what both of them seemed to be thrusting upon me. "That's because William and I were brought up on Confucian sayings. The Chinese live by proverbs . . . We used to play games of making up our own, the more ridiculous the better. Like . . . 'the shortest line between two points is the longest way home.'"

"And there's more wisdom in that than perhaps you know, Miss Howard."

We had been standing watching as little Ailis was brought out by a groom, and the voice came to us from the shadow of the smithy's door. We turned and looked, and the rounded, shortish shape of a man in brown tweeds and a matching cap emerged; he was powerfully built for his height, but running to fat, with reddish whiskers and eyebrows over eyes flecked with amber, which was the only way he resembled his daughter.

"Miss Howard, may I present Mr. James Ferguson, my father-in-law."

He swept off the cap. He was expensively dressed, clothes probably from Savile Row, and boots from Lobb, but there was an indefinable air of vulgarity about him, the thrusting red face, the glimmer of the eyes under those sandy brows. He was exaggerated, like the clock tower. He looked what he was, and seemed pleased about it.

"Well—Angus Macdonald's granddaughter. You bear the stamp of the old man, the way your brother did. I wonder if you're his match?"

"Perhaps time will tell that, Mr. Ferguson. Perhaps we'll never know. It isn't a woman's world yet, is it?—and we're really not able to compare."

"Well, you've as sharp a tongue as Macdonald. Your brother, now, he was all charm. All charm and talk."

154

I almost choked on my anger. "Perhaps I'll improve, Mr. Ferguson. At the time you knew William, life was happier for us all."

I saw Gavin's hand as he held the bridle, the fist clenched into a tight ball. It was as well Ailis wasn't nervous.

"Mr. Ferguson—please remember that Miss Howard has lost both William and her father recently. They *were* happier times . . ."

"Och, aye—aye. I know it well, I've a rough tongue on me, Miss Howard. Yes, you've had sorrow, and I can tell you would sorrow for a fine young brother as William was. Bright, he was, and full of promise, and Angus Macdonald was dreaming again of a future. But you can take your knocks, I can tell. You're probably as tough as old boots, and it will stand you in good stead. A pity you're not a boy. Angus Macdonald would have a second chance. But still, a bishop's daughter . . . you'll probably make a good enough match. Someone anxious to have their hands on Cluain—"

"For God's sake!" Gavin burst out. "Will you leave it alone! You may own Ballochtorra, but at least you'll treat its guests with civility."

"Miss Howard will not swoon, Gavin. She knows well enough what I'm talking about. I've never had time in my life to waste on pretty speeches—never learned to make them. She knows—and so do you. I've a call to make on Angus Macdonald before I leave. Perhaps Miss Howard will give me a cup of tea at Cluain. I haven't a doubt we'll talk well enough then. Ballochtorra is a mite overrefined, wouldn't you say, Miss Howard?"

"You're leaving then?" Gavin said.

"Day after tomorrow. I'll be back before the Prince's visit to check that all is in order. Can't be away from Glasgow too long. Things move in a man's absence. Mustn't give them the impressions I've too much time to play up here in the Highlands. People might think I'm slipping . . ."

"Grandpapa, there's nothing slipping." Jamie came running from the box that Ailis had occupied. "McClintoch made me check all the buckles myself, just to make sure. He said we couldn't have Miss Howard falling off . . ."

The face of the man altered quite visibly. There was no subtlety in the expression. The rough vulgarity seemed to fall away in the

155

glow of tender pride that spread upon his face. He didn't care who knew that he doted upon his grandson.

"Och, she'll not fall off that broad back, laddie. She's the heftiest wee pony I ever saw. You'd not compare her, now, would you, to your own Milky?"

"No—but I'd rather have Ailis. Ailis is famous. She carried Mr. Dougal Ross back home one night when the worst blizzard anyone could remember was raging, and he had a fever that nearly killed him. She found her way all alone for near ten miles when you couldn't see your hand in front of you . . . Everyone wanted to have Ailis. But Mr. Ross offered her first to Mr. Macdonald."

Ferguson looked at the pony with real dislike. "There's no breeding in her, Jamie, lad. If you look at her closely now, she's about the ugliest wee pony you'd see in a long day."

"I don't think you should say that in front of her, Grandpapa. She understands, you know."

"To hell with what she understands! Am I surrounded by a lot of fools here! A damned ungainly piece of horseflesh, she is, and I'll see no grandson of mine mounted on such."

"I'd still like her—"

"If you don't mind," I said, "Ailis belongs to Cluain." And while the three stood there, glowering at one another, I swung myself up into the saddle without assistance. Ailis moved willingly, as if she were glad to be free of the place. She moved in her plodding, unconcerned, tranquil gait, not caring in the least for the turmoil she left behind her, nor caring, I thought, for what she must have sensed in me. Without direction she turned on the road to Cluain as we passed through the iron gates embossed with the hissing swan. She was heading for her stable, and I also knew where I belonged.

*   *   *

I went many times to Ballochtorra after that. Margaret was not always there, nor Gavin, nor Jamie. They were out riding, Gavin and Margaret always separately, it seemed, and I did not wait on their return. But Wilson, the butler, had his instructions, and I was

156

always offered tea, and a place to wait in Margaret's sitting room. I never stayed unless she was there; Ballochtorra depressed me. For all the newness of the furniture, the curtains, the upholsteries, the graceful trailing of ferns and plants at the windows, for all the well-kept splendour, it was a place that had lost itself. It had lost the stark beauty of Cluain, which would once have been its own; it had gained nothing by the fussiness of its new additions and decorations. I wondered how the spare elegance of Margaret Campbell's own person had been submerged under this sea of lace and trimmings and heavy velvets. It was, I thought, as if she had long ago given up caring—as if she allowed whatever furnisher her father instructed to come in and have his way with Ballochtorra. She had her presence marked only upon one room that I knew, her own sitting room. Here we sat and talked, and ate those tiny cakes, and she played the piano. There was a kind of desperate gaiety about her at times, as if she were holding off the size and bulk of the house, the retinue of servants who stood ready to answer the bells, the whole ritual of her life. "It is so different here from London," she once said to me. "Here everyone in the whole valley knows who comes and goes, and talks about it if it pleases them. In a city one can be more private. Here I feel I'm . . . watched. I wasn't made for places like Ballochtorra. I don't even sleep very well here—it's the quiet, and then every quarter hour that stable clock that Father put in tolling away. Sometimes I get up just after dawn and saddle up for myself, and ride out, just to feel I can really be by myself. I ride until I'm tired, and then I come back and I can sleep. I wish there were more noise. I like city streets, and bustle, and shops. I like to see carriages stopping next door, or on the other side of the square—better still if they come to one's own door. I like people coming and going . . . friends, acquaintances . . . even strangers."

And Jamie would sometimes come bursting in. "Mother, today Father and I rode up beyond Ben Carden. You can't think how tiny Ballochtorra looks from there." And again, "Today we had to shelter from the rain under that crag over by Drumnoch . . . Father gave me his coat." And another day, his face petulant with disappointment, he would report that his father had gone by himself. "He rode off . . . I don't know where he's gone . . ."

But never again did Gavin come and join us in Margaret's sitting room; he never again came to drink tea with us, demand sandwiches, never played the light, easy melodies for me to sing the words to.

And Ballochtorra continued to depress me, and especially I disliked the stableyard, where I had to go to get Ailis. This was wholly the creation of James Ferguson, heavy, overdone, the horses too pampered, the grooms too much their servants. And often as I left I found myself giving a swift, upward glance to the room where Gavin Campbell might have been, his own tower room. But his figure was never at the window where I could see him; I never heard the sound of the piano; I never was really sure which one of the towers and turrets of Ballochtorra, spanning the five centuries of its building, was the one he inhabited.

* * *

Riding, in those weeks, I came on Gavin only once away from the kirk, though Margaret said he was often on the moors. It had been a dry day, though overcast, the mountains lost in the clouds. Not a day to venture too far. I turned Ailis across the bridge at Ballochtorra, and instead of going towards the kirk, she had headed, almost at her own wish, in the other direction, up the steep hill on the road to the station at Ballinaclash. She had as strong a streak for curiosity as I, and I think it was she who first heard the sound from an unaccustomed direction. They were above us still, as we climbed up the glen, sounds that reached us from some place in the plantation of Scots pine and larch that hugged both sides of the slope. We found the track—very rough it was, and soft with leaf mould; we made very little noise, and it was covered by the cries and the sounds that came to us.

It was a clearing where a burn pitched headlong down from some spring above, rushing to join the river below. Over the centuries it had worn its own narrow path, and now the trees pressed about its edges, defining its course, as did the boulders that lined it. A small croft stood there, the usual one of the Highlands, two rooms, thatched, a smoking chimney, a single door, and hens pecking the ground all about it. There was a lean-to stable, and a sty to fatten a pig.

There were two men, a woman, and a boy of about sixteen in the clearing—and Gavin and Jamie. I checked Ailis and held her close, watching the scene. Gavin and Jamie were both wearing the kilt, the green Cawdor kilt, and Gavin was in the stream up to his knees. He had just finished attaching a chain about a boulder that stood squarely in the middle of the burn, forcing the water to flow each side of it, and raising the level almost beyond the banks. The chain was attached to a kind of pole harness I had seen used for dragging felled trees about the Cluain lands, and I thought I recognised one of Cluain's huge Clydesdales in the harness. One of the men stood beside Gavin in the burn, fixing the chain, testing it against slipping; the other man and the boy were at the horse's head, holding him. As I saw the second man in profile, I knew him as one of the farm workers from Cluain, Bruce Bain. Jamie was moving excitedly from one group to the other, until at a word from Gavin he abruptly changed his place so that he was on the uphill side of the horse and harness. Then Gavin signalled Bruce Bain, and he began to urge the Clydesdale forward. At first the big animal could get little grip in the soft ground; I could see the big body straining. The boulder rocked a little on its base, seemed about to move, then slipped back. Bruce Bain rested the Clydesdale a few moments; I could see the coat already beginning to darken with sweat. Gavin shifted one of the chains a little, to get a more secure purchase on the boulder. Then he signalled again. Again Bain began to pull on the halter. "Ho!—come now, lad!—come now!" The Clydesdale managed a step forward, the slack of the chain was taken up. Even from where I was I could see the ripple of the great muscles across the horse's chest. Another step; the boulder rocked, poised. The horse was forward two feet more, and the boulder was now shifted from the hole where it had bedded itself in the burn. Gavin was there, beside it, watching to see that the chains did not slip. I had to suppose he knew the danger he was in, of the chains slipping, or of the horse being dragged back-wards by the weight. He seemed foolhardy, but someone had to

159

check the downhill side of the boulder, and it was Gavin. As I watched I saw him take a heavy iron bar, and use it as a lever to help the boulder out of its position. On the uphill side, the man did the same. The real danger came when Gavin called to Bain to hold the Clydesdale there, and he himself moved forward and plunged his arms down into that icy water, fixing a smaller rock under the boulder to hold its new level. It was an anxious moment, wondering if Gavin would be quick enough, if the horse could hold his position against the weight, if the lever of the other man would give Gavin's hands enough room for his task. Then Gavin stepped back, and called again to Bain. The Clydesdale moved on—a mighty heave this time, as if he were thankful not to be asked to hold any longer. Then the boulder moved up the incline of the burn, teetered there a moment—another use of the bars from Gavin and the other man, another rock to hold the boulder secure, another heave, and the boulder was on firm, almost level ground. From there it was nothing for the Clydesdale to move it a few feet farther into the clearing—the hens dashing screaming away from the monster suddenly in their midst. Gavin scrambled up the bank, his boots and stockings wet, the edge of the kilt, and his shirt sticking to his back with sweat.

His voice reached me. "Right now, Bain. We'll rest the horse, and then we'll move the thing off where it will be out of harm's way."

I slipped off Ailis, and came forward. "Gavin—Jamie!"

"Kirsty! How did you come here?" And from Jamie, "Miss Howard, did you see it? The Clydesdale was wonderful, wasn't he?"

"He was, Jamie. I'm glad I came in time to see it. I was riding on the road below . . ."

The woman made a sketchy, but warm gesture to me. "Och, welcome now, mistress. I'll be giving everyone some tea, now the great part's done. Everyone needs a wee rest." She seemed to know very well who I was. "And that great horse—a marvel, he is. And Sir Gavin so kind . . . We've been plagued with that terrible great thing . . ."

"Thank you, I'd like some tea . . ." I was following Gavin and Jamie to the edge of the burn. "Look, Miss Howard. You see, the boulder crashed down here during a winter storm—it was just held by a tree above." Jamie was skipping about in excitement. "And it bedded itself in the burn, and every time there was a thunderstorm, or the snow thawed, the water would come spilling over, and washing into the McInnes croft. And so Father . . ."

"Jamie, Mrs. McInnes has cake for you, I think," Gavin said. He watched his son run towards the cottage. "An adventure for him, Kirsty," he said. "He would not be left behind when he learned this morning where I was going."

"That's Bruce Bain, from Cluain—and that's a Cluain Clydesdale," I said. We sat on rocks by the burn, and Mrs. McInnes brought us tea in battered pewter mugs, and oatcakes. Gavin began to strip off his boots and stockings. "Will you not come to the fire, Sir Gavin? It's wet through you are . . ."

"I'm all right here, Mrs. McInnes. And make sure, please, that Jamie doesn't eat too much of your good things. I'll be in trouble if he doesn't eat his dinner when he gets home."

"Och, now, Sir Gavin, don't we all know that a wee lad has the appetite of three . . ." And she went off happily to feed Jamie all he would eat.

"Was it as Jamie said—the boulder . . . ?"

"Just about. The tree that was holding it crashed down last winter, and every heavy rain since then has sent the water from the burn lapping past the McInnes threshold. I walked up here one day and saw it myself. God knows, these crofts are damp enough. So I thought that when the burn was low in summer, I would have a try at moving it. Robert McInnes, you know, helps look after the kirk—as does Mrs. McInnes. They kept my secrets well. The minister has yet to hear about the strange, ungodly music the laird sometimes plays in the house of the Lord."

"They're your tenants?"

"No—this is on MacKenzie Grant's land. McInnes just earns a few extra shillings looking after the kirk, and trying to coax some heat out of that stove in winter. Mrs. McInnes cleans the windows and dusts—that kind of thing."

"Grant land?—then why doesn't Mr. Grant take care of the matter himself? You do know, Gavin—well, you must have known

161

that the chains might have slipped. The Clydesdale might not have been able to hold the weight."

"The horse I couldn't help. Perhaps I should have had two, but I didn't really think the boulder was that big—it was deeper in the burn than I thought. And if the chains had slipped, it would have been my own fault for placing them badly. If I'd been killed, it would have been my own carelessness. But I'd no intention of getting myself killed in front of my own son's eyes. I haven't such a taste for bad melodrama as that. It wasn't as dangerous as it might have looked."

"But why do it?—since it's Mr. Grant's estate?"

"Oh—I don't know. The McInneses are such decent people, and old MacKenzie Grant hasn't been on the estate for more than a year—he's sick in England, they say. His bailiff's useless—drunk half the time. The McInneses have asked, but they had no hope of getting anything done until Grant got up here himself, if he ever does again. It could have been years. Robert McInnes doesn't have much to live on—just this place here, on the estate, the right to cut a tree or two for fuel. He helps on the Grant farm, and digs the bog when work is slack. It isn't much of a living, but he's a good man."

"But Bruce Bain, and my grandfather's horse?"

Gavin laughed. "Do you think Ballochtorra's stables could produce anything like that Clydesdale? Oh, I made my arrangements formally with your grandfather. He offered the horse free—he also has a regard for Robert McInnes—but he said I would have to pay for Bain's time. That's your grandfather, Kirsty. He always manages to temper any generosity with a practical bite. I will probably never be given a bill for the services of Bain. But he warned me, did your grandfather, that the horse, if he were hurt or damaged in any way, would cost me a fortune. I believe it." He suddenly lowered the mug from his lips. "Lord, I wish this tea had a drop of Cluain's whisky in it. We make cold water up here in the Highlands, Kirsty. Be sure you never tumble into a burn. You might freeze in the same second."

It was then I saw the blood ooze between his fingers as he held the mug. "Gavin—your hands!"

162

He didn't even look down at them. "Oh, it's good clean water, Kirsty. I won't be poisoned. That rock had a bit of a bite to it—but no fingers crushed, and nothing that won't mend."

"But your *hands*—how can you risk them? The organ . . ."

He shook his head. "You don't really understand, Kirsty. Because you see me at the kirk, you hear me play, you think that's really what I live for. Yes—I'm a musician of sorts. I used to be a much better one. And if I'd never seen this strath, and Ballochtorra and Cluain, I'd be perfectly happy as organist in some quite humble place, as long as it was a living. But these mountains and moors get into one's blood, even if one wasn't born to them, as I wasn't. Playing the organ isn't everything I want to do, Kirsty. It only helps fill the time—the emptiness."

His low, musing tone helped me ask the next question, one I thought I might not have a right to ask. "What else do you want to do, Gavin?"

"You'll not tell him, I know—perhaps he already suspects. But I envy your grandfather. I wish I had my fields of barley, and my fat cattle. I wouldn't even mind hill sheep, difficult though they are. Forget the distillery—I would like to farm the land."

"You can't—isn't there any part of Ballochtorra's land you could use?"

"There's some—around the bend of the river past the crag. But it's boggy, and needs draining. It's subject to flooding, but that can be an advantage, as it leaves you with some good soil, and you'll lose nothing if you're careful to move your cattle in time. I've seen stretches of peat moorland reclaimed to clover pasture. There are places on Ballochtorra where it could be done. A man could make a living from it, Kirsty. Not a fortune—just a living."

"Why don't you . . ." I hesitated. "Why don't you try?"

"I'd need money in the beginning—not a lot of money, but *some*. That would mean James Ferguson again."

"But he would help—surely, for his own son-in-law."

He put down the mug. "That's just it. James Ferguson owns enough of his son-in-law. He can't have my dreams also. He would laugh at such small ambitions—a few acres here, a few acres there. What need does a gentleman have for such petty concerns?

163

His wife's husband worry about grazing for a few cows when he has thousands of acres of grouse moors? No, James Ferguson would never understand, and I've no need to try to explain. He must do things big, or not at all. So I leave it be just what it is—a dream. No more."

I looked at him, his hair clamped to his scalp with sweat, his kilt sodden, his hands gashed and bleeding, and I thought that, yes, it did lie in Gavin Campbell, baronet and soon to be marquis, to turn out in the snow before a March dawn to help with the lambing, to move his cattle to higher ground when the river was in spate, to turn some of his bog acres up there on the mountain into clover grass. It was not a great ambition—but it was a dream.

I got to my feet. "I must go Gavin. I'm glad I was here this morning."

"So am I, Kirsty. So am I."

*　　*　　*

And each evening there was the return to Cluain. Often I had to hurry to be washed and changed before my grandfather came to the dining room. It was very soon after my arrival that I noticed that he minded my absence; I did not know whether it was that he actually wanted my company, or that he demanded my attention. But I tried not to be late—to be waiting with my Chinese shawl and the red slippers, waiting for the invitation "to take a dram with me."

He did not like my going to Ballochtorra, but he never actually tried to prevent it. "Come back from *that* place?" he would say to me, seeming to look at me through his whisky glass. "Well, this must seem humble enough after all the frippery and finery they tell me they have up there."

"Cluain can stand by any, Grandfather, and you know it. Besides," I added, watching my opportunity now, as he always did, to score my point, "I'm surprised you listen to gossip about what goes on at Ballochtorra. I thought such things didn't interest you."

"Och, who can help hearing it? Doesn't everything that Ferguson does cause talk? My own workers, who ought to know better, remembering that they make the best whisky in the Highlands, do pratter on about him like women. Just because he's made a fortune in a few years with the cheap rotgut stuff."

"But you sell Cluain's whisky to him."

"And why not? He needs *something* to make his poison palatable. And believe me, Cluain's whisky is the heart of his most expensive blend. What Cluain distills here is what makes it respectable to have a Ferguson whisky in a gentleman's decanter. That is, for those who think they *must* have the blended stuff."

"I don't understand about blended whiskys. Why can James Ferguson make a fortune in a short time when it takes so long to mature Cluain's whisky? I've never tasted the other sort . . ."

"And may you never. It's hardly fit to be called whisky when it's stood beside Cluain's—and, aye, maybe a few other Highland malts. What a blend is, Kirsty, is the mixing of the product of the pot still, the malt, like Cluain's, if they're lucky enough to have it, with the much cheaper, quicker product of the grain or patent still whisky. Most patent stills are of the type invented by an Irishman called Coffey, and they're known as the Coffey still. They make a spirit, you might say, but it can't stand on its own as a single spirit—you couldn't drink it by itself, as you do a pot still whisky—and that's a fact, not just my prejudice talking. It's simply a *fillings,* something to give volume to the blends of the malts you add to it. You might call grain whisky a silent spirit —without the malts, it simply isn't there, not drinkable.

"The patent still is a continuously working unit, while our pot still whisky is an interrupted process, as I hope our knowledgeable Callum Sinclair made quite clear to you. It costs about half the price to distill as does your malt whisky, and if you set up a big enough production unit, as our fine rich Mr. Ferguson had done, with distilleries all over the Lowlands, and people rushing to invest with him, then you *can* make a fortune. But never forget that he has to come himself, or send his buyers, into these Highlands to find the whisky that will make his silent spirit a palatable drink. He makes a dozen blends at least—a little of this, a little of that —a dash of Cluain with a dash of Glenlivilt with a dash of Glen Grant. Infinite variations, they tell me, with infinite blends, and all priced according to the price he had to pay for the original malts that made the blends. There's no merit to a grain spirit by itself—it's what he adds to it. And the price and reputation of Cluain come high.

"Mind you, though, even the grain distillers can't get away completely from malted barley—they use about twenty percent of it, and the rest can be anything you want, maize, wheat, rye, or oats. But whatever they use, they can't do without the barley—they have to cook their grain until its starch cells are burst open, so that the malt can get into the heart of it. There's many that think malt is brought into grain distilling to give some life and colour and character to the stuff even at that early stage, but the plain fact is that the malt is necessary to bring about the chemical change that will start the fermentation. You cannot do without the malt, Gurrl, no matter what. And you cannot do without the malt whisky. The grain spirit does not need the aging, nor the care in distilling, but it is simply not there without the malt. And never forget it. Malt can stand alone, be drunk alone, as it has been drunk in the Highlands for centuries. Grain spirit by itself is a useless, unsaleable thing. It will bring as little comfort or pleasure to a man's soul as something drunk straight from a chemist's bottle. As long as man needs solace for his grief, but no drunkenness, ease for his tired body, warmth for his blood, he will need the product of Cluain, and its like. Yes, Kirsty—Cluain will go on forever."

"Cluain will go on forever, Grandfather. But you can't—nor I. Will there always be men skilful enough—caring enough—to make sure that it does?"

"They have to care, Kirsty. They have to care—and they are hard to find. That is the whole trouble with James Ferguson. He might as well be making boots or bricks, for all he cares. But we won't worry about him and his like. His day will come and go— and Cluain will still be here. Now let us eat our supper, and then we'll take out the board, and we'll see if the old brain or the young brain will win this night. In chess as well as whisky, experience counts. Experience counts, Kirsty."

And nightly I was battling him over that board, sometimes winning,

166

sometimes losing, but never again did our hands stray into the moves of William's game.

*   *   *

Very slowly, and only by dint of pushing, I was being admitted into the life of Cluain—the life of the distillery and the farm. Every day my grandfather was at his rounds of the farm, checking with the workers, watching the barley stand a little higher, the heads grow a little heavier, scanning the sky and sniffing the wind, like an animal, for rain. He watched for weak places in the fences, lest the cattle and sheep should break through to the precious crop, he gave orders about replacing the missing tiles on the barns and byres, he saw that the sheepfolds and cattle pens were in order and waiting for the snows of the winter, watched the meadows for the moment when he could cut the hay for winter livestock feeding. He would mount a horse who seemed as old and broad as himself, and ride up to the shielings, the small huts built up on the mountain slopes are living quarters for the men and young women who tended the cattle in their summer pasture—they spent their summer watching that the cattle did not stray too far, did not cross into the bog and be lost. There was something that reminded me of the frugal care of the Chinese for their animals in this ancient practice—each animal so precious that it could command this constant vigil. "Ah, well," my grandfather said, "it will not be long we have it so. The people are leaving. There will be few young ones to send up into the shielings. They go to the cities, looking for work, and end crowded into one room in some filthy wynd, with buckets of slop thrown on their heads in the streets. And cattle breeding is becoming more scientific—we will soon have only Aberdeen Angus, and Cluain's herd is becoming famous. We will not risk the necks of the cattle up here in the shielings. We will have only as many sheep as we need for our own eating—pesky things, they are, forever straying, eating the grasses to nothing, eating the crops, breaking into the vegetable plots of the workers. No, soon the farm will become a showplace, the barley and the Angus will

167

be its function. The distillery workers must be well taken care of—well housed. A distillery does not need many men, but good ones we must have. But the young ones that are surplus, the sons who have grown up at Cluain, will be on their way, for I will not have the jobs to offer them, and the agricultural wage is low. But I must stay in business, and I cannot pay more than the going rate—I am no gentleman farmer who breeds his cattle only to have something to point to when his guests come. The barley will provide the whisky, and the cattle bring always higher and higher prices at market—with now and then a blue ribbon for a Cluain breeding bull. And the money will be saved, and another warehouse built. That is how it has always been at Cluain. More than forty years I have been here, and each year something added. The big harvests have provided against the years of the lean ones. We have grown our own food, and we have been beholden to no one. Since the day I paid back the loan that set up the distillery, there has never been a penny borrowed for Cluain. It stands alone—it will stand."

"And the shielings," I said. "What will happen to the land when you no longer pasture animals up here—when there is no one to herd and shepherd them?"

"Och, the land will probably go back to the heather from which I first reclaimed it. The grouse will come in, and I will rent it to some rich Englishman who will come with his fine guns and dogs to shoot it over. Land is money, Kirsty. Never let go of land."

"And yet," I said, as we rode among the livestock, my grandfather's head always twisting and turning, expertly inspecting each animal to watch for signs of sickness, "it will be a pity when that happens. Some more life gone from the Highlands . . . fewer people in the strath."

His old face crumpled in a kind of scowl. "Yes and no—the people have come here for hundreds of years, to the summer shielings. It used to be a good time—a time of release from the harshness of winter. There were special songs they sung at those times, and the lassies would flirt with the young men in the long evenings. There was whisky taken—to keep out the chill. It was beautiful . . . the twilights were long, and the shadows purple on the heather . . . Yes, there were good and bad times, and they are passing. Perhaps it will be no bad thing when it is gone completely. It is a sign of a poor people . . . you took your joys when you could and the summer nights were one of them, with a drop of whisky and a fire, and the stories told in the old tongue. No one speaks that any more, and this is the last generation of lads and lassies who will go to the shielings of Cluain . . ."

All the way back to the house that time he was silent, and his face wore its heavy, brooding look, as he remembered the past, perhaps, when life had been harder, but had held its joys—perhaps not wanting to look to the future when both he and the boys and girls would be gone. I did not dare interrupt his thoughts. It was only after we had dismounted and led the horse and Ailis to their boxes, and carried our own harness to the tackroom, which was the practice at Cluain, since no one could escape the careful and frugal rules laid down by its master, that I attempted to speak to him. We were standing by the pump, and I pumped water for both buckets.

"Grandfather . . ." I panted a little; the pump was well oiled and in good repair, as was everything at Cluain, but a heavy old thing. "Grandfather, is there not some way I could help you a little . . ."

"Help?" He was instantly suspicious, on the defensive. "What kind of help could I need from you?"

I sighed as I picked up my bucket and turned away from him. At times we seemed to go back to our first evening, as if the weeks in between had never been. "I only meant in the office. You work there every afternoon on your papers and letters. I used to help my father with such things. I wondered if I could do anything . . ." I banged down the bucket while I wrestled with the door of Ailis's box, and half the water slopped over. "After all, you keep telling me that everyone works at Cluain."

"Why do you want to come spying into my affairs?"

"*Spying!*—is that what you think?" I picked up the bucket and more water spilled over my boots. It would have been a relief to have hurled the rest at him. "Then you may forget I ever made the suggestion. I thought there might be a few unimportant letters I could take at your dictation. I don't expect to be *trusted* with anything . . . I am not the granddaughter of Cluain, nor its hired help. I am just a guest, left to be idle all day—"

"Hush, Gurrl, you're hasty. You're very hasty. Yes—if I think of it there might be a few letters you might do—a few accounts you might send out, and such. The men's wage packets have to be made up weekly. Samuel Lachlan comes down from Inverness once or twice a month to go over the books—there are some things in between that could be done. Nothing too important, but all of it taking time. And I'm not one to encourage idleness in any . . . Well . . ." grudgingly. "We'll see. We'll see."

I didn't know whether I was supposed to thank him, but I said nothing, just turned away to offer Ailis her water. The energy of my anger and resentment was eased as I rubbed her down. There was something, at least, to be proud of, in the healthy sheen of her coat. "Aren't you a good wee thing," I said to her, standing off to admire the clean legs and hooves, the shining back, and, unconsciously, falling into an imitation of the accent I heard around me. And I gave her an extra measure of oats. She was fat already; let her be happy as well.

Very gradually, then, I was admitted to my grandfather's office, a cold, narrow room, crowded into a corner of the main distillery building, and smelling of the forty years of the malting and the fermentation, an oddly sour smell of old beer, despite the fact that everything was swept and scrubbed meticulously. Even the paper and dockets, particularly the leather-bound ledgers, smelt of it. "It is only fitting," my grandfather answered, when once I remarked on it. "A thing should smell of what supports it. We do not pretend we are a sweet shop."

It was dull enough, the work I did for him, and little enough. *Dear Sirs . . . we beg to draw to your attention . . . Dear Sirs . . . in answer to your esteemed communication of the fifteenth instant . . . We remain, dear sirs, your humble servants . . .* Humble— not at all, I thought, as I carefully penned the words. My grandfather was a proud man, and he made and sold a proud product. I began to think that it eased him to be free of this ritual formula, by which he might seem to lessen himself. Of course, we could not change the wording, which was time-honoured and established, but at least

170

he had only to glance over it, and affix his signature; and it pleased him now that the signature was in a different hand from the letter. His had never been a clerkish script. "You write a fair enough hand," he allowed me. "At least, you cannot tell at a glance that it is a *woman's* hand. Though some would guess it," he added doubtfully. "Perhaps it is not a good thing to let them know that there is a woman—"

"You could have a typewriter, Grandfather. And then no one could tell who had written it."

"A *typewriter!* No good modern thing! Next you'll be suggesting that we distill our own patent grain spirits!—set up blending, perhaps?"

"Oh—I don't know," I answered demurely, looking back to my papers. "It wouldn't do to go *too* far, would it?"

"You'll not laugh at me, miss, I'll tell you! Cluain managed before you came, and can manage after you're gone." And he roared out, the draught from the slammed door lifting the papers on the roll-top desk at which I worked. At first I smiled to myself, and then I stopped smiling. Suddenly I thought of the world beyond Cluain—of the time before I had known it, of the time when I might not be here. It was a cold thought. I applied myself quickly to what needed attention, as much to distract myself from the thought of leaving, as to get through the work itself.

Samuel Lachlan did not at first welcome my presence in my grandfather's office, and on the days he came, I was excluded. Over the years, firstly because he had to protect his investment, and then because Cluain had become an absorbing interest in his life, he had become accountant as well as solicitor; keeping Cluain's books was a kind of relaxation for him, and he resented even the slightest infringement of his domain. The ledgers were his, almost forty years of them. He had grown old with Cluain, and with Angus Macdonald, putting to order the rough notations my grandfather had made of the business transacted since Lachlan's last visit, setting it all out in his neat, eminently legible figures. I was an innovation, and he was too old to care for the new—and besides that, I was a female with no place in an office of business. But I sensed that behind his sallow, thin face, and the perpetually stooped shoulders in the shiny black suit, there lived a passion for the welfare of Cluain almost as great as my grandfather's. This I had to respect, and to try to understand the man who harboured it. When first we had been introduced he had avoided my eyes and muttered. "A pity about your brother—yes, a great pity about William." But the pity was for himself and Cluain, not for me.

The day came when I was careless of the time, and had not left the office before his arrival. My grandfather had been called away to inspect a sick bullock, and I was alone when Samuel Lachlan opened the door of the office. He frowned when he saw the account books open. These were his property.

"Your grandfather lets you do some of this?"

"A very little. I only try to tidy up his notes, really. And just write a few letters about accounts—sending them out—writing to confirm appointments for buyers to come here—helping with the wages. Very simple, really." I felt I had to defend my grandfather.

He came and bent over me; I could smell the age of that black suit. "You understand this sort of thing?"

"Naturally I haven't done exactly this kind of thing before. But I used to help my father with the accounts of the diocese. It released one of his curates for other work."

"Did the Chinese cheat you?"

It was useless to pretend; he would know. "In the beginning they did. And when I found out, and tried to stop it, the system wouldn't work any more. It was like dealing with the Chinese cook—but on a much bigger scale. In a way, it was agreeing to ignore a certain proportion of stealing. It is the way things have always worked in China. If it got above the limit, then there were great rows—discussions, really—and all based on making an allowance for face-saving on both sides. Very important. But I learned —I actually began to enjoy it. I think I saved my father some money—we were always stretched so thin for money. The Chinese thought it was very funny to have a woman sitting in my father's office—but then they laugh at everything the Foreign Devils do. They think we are all very ugly, especially the women—big hands and feet, long sharp faces. It's one of the things you have to get

172

used to in China—whenever you go out, there's always a crowd about you, just pointing and laughing . . ."

He forgot his suspicion for a moment, and seated himself close to me. "Interesting . . . did they sell concessions for the contracts —supplying the mission stations?"

"Oh yes—that had always to be allowed for in the bargaining."

"Did you speak the language?"

"Mandarin—the official language. I spoke it—I wrote it far less well. It is very difficult—complicated. I often had to use my father's chief clerk—it was he who tutored William and me in the language. But I learned to deal with the people who came to ask for the contracts myself—it was a system of agreeing how much cheating there could be. My father was glad not to have to do it. He wasn't . . . well, he wasn't a businessman. I don't think he would have been made a bishop if he had stayed in England. He wasn't good at asking people for money. I don't think he could have built any cathedrals . . ."

"Don't approve of cathedrals," Samuel Lachlan said. "A lot of show, and waste of money . . . And what else did you do in China—what else did you learn?"

I talked, quite forgetting to whom I talked. It was freer talk than I could have with my grandfather. This lonely man soaked it up with an eagerness he did not know he betrayed. "China . . ." he mused. "Well, it's a very long way. They say there are great fortunes made there. I once went to London—when the railway was finished to Inverness. Only stayed two days. Very expensive. China is too far . . ."

We were still talking when Morag came to summon us to the midday meal. I saw Samuel Lachlan's embarrassment, and Morag's disbelief. I was glad my grandfather was late for the meal; there was a weakness discovered in Samuel Lachlan's façade, and it would have been cruel to show that I had seen it.

He was always an honoured guest at Cluain. The meals were always especially lavish when he came, the fire heaped high, as if to try to warm those fragile bones. There were always his favourite dishes—large cuts of roast beef or lamb, fragrant herb gravy, inevitably apple tart and cream. He always carried back to Inverness a basket full of food from Mairi Sinclair's kitchen—"It's shocking what they charge in Inverness for a scone." He said her food relieved his dyspepsia, as did the tonic she gave him. "Samuel's life is very narrow," my grandfather said, seemingly unaware that his own was not much different. "We try to give him some ease when he comes here. There is nothing in his life but work. He has never married. He has only one relation I knew of—a great-nephew who used to live in London, and who has now gone to America. Samuel didn't approve of him . . . Cluain is his child. We have built it together. It is his pride to be associated with the greatest whisky to come out of the Highlands. Money alone could not buy him what he gets from Cluain."

Morag sniffed, and shrugged when I went to help her make up the room Samuel Lachlan always occupied at Cluain, and I suggested that I might put a few flowers on the mantel.

"Och, don't be fussing yourself, mistress. He'd never notice them, that old man. Doesn't he live on the smell of an oil rag there in Inverness? He has a wee house on the quay there by the bridge —three articled clerks he has working in the downstairs rooms, short of space and candles they are. And Mr. Lachlan lives in the rooms above—he's at work by six in the mornings, they say, winter and summer. I've seen the place. The Master once sent me to Inverness with an urgent paper for Mr. Lachlan. I wouldn't care to sleep there, myself—so dirty you can hardly see out of the windows. He has all his meals sent round from a chop house close by. Slops, they are, by comparison with Cluain food. And yet they say he could buy and sell half Inverness, so much money he's made. He underpays and overworks his clerks, and still they tumble over each other to be articled to him. Each will learn the business so thoroughly with him that they will all look to make their own fortunes when they leave him. Och, he has the pick of them. Only the brightest, quickest lads will ever see the inside of Mr. Lachlan's office, you may believe me, mistress. Reminded me of the way Mr. Dickens described that old man—that mister —in one of his books . . ."

I did believe her, and pitied him more. The history of Cluain was there in his neat hand; the first small production figures, the loan and interest paid to build the distillery, the charges for the sherry casks to store the first runs, the price of the fence that was all that had protected Cluain's precious product in those far-off days. "We called it a bonded warehouse," my grandfather said, "but all that guarded it was a pair of dogs and my gun beside my bed. I didn't sleep soundly in those days—the Excise would have had their price on every cask, stolen or not. And when I built my warehouses, one at a time, as they could be paid for, I built them strong and good, with a house for the gauger tight against the wall. I slept more easily the first night my casks were safe behind bars, with good stout walls, and under a roof."

The scraps of Cluain's history came to me fitfully, and I was never allowed the full picture. The post that came daily was left for my grandfather to open, and there were still many letters that were answered by him, and then locked in the drawers of his desk, away from all other eyes except Samuel Lachlan's. The early ledgers, in their faded red leather bindings were available, but the later ones, the last twenty years of Cluain's production and profits, were locked in tall oak cupboards. "Why should I leave my business lying around for the world to see?" my grandfather asked of me when I remarked on the security of locking the cupboards, and then locking the office itself. "Shall I have every man from here to Inverness gossiping about what is in Cluain's warehouses, and what is sold to what blender at what price? The Excise know right well—it is only a fool who would try to hide anything from them, but they are paid because they are men who keep their mouths shut. They would not stay in the service else. Shall I let one blender know what another paid the year before?—not every run of whisky turns out to be of the same quality, though all of Cluain's is good. So they come and they taste, and we make a price, and they pay—the Excise has the revenue fixed, and we cannot afford to give away our product. But I keep my samples locked up, as I am bound by law to do, and I see no reason why I should not keep my information locked up as well. All that is known of Cluain is that it makes a fine whisky and it pays its wages and bills at the right time, not sooner, not later, than the

175

due date. Chatter is for fools like James Ferguson. Cluain has to impress no one."

I had my visit to the bonded warehouses, as Callum Sinclair had predicted I should, and in the company of my grandfather, attended by Neil Smith. Big Billy was there by the door, surrounded by his flock, but we had long ago come to terms; I was accepted by Big Billy in the same way as everyone who belonged to Cluain—we reserved a distance on both sides. My grandfather observed the courtesy of asking Neil Smith if we might go into the warehouses and the little man nodded, and produced his keys, cackling a little with pleasure, as if he were showing off something he owned.

"And I suppose you might say the Excise does own it—or a goodly part of it—until the duty is paid. They'd hardly stand, these days, for the way it was stored in the beginning. But it was hard enough in the early days of this century to stop the smuggling traffic in the Highlands. Just to get a man to take out a license to distill, and then to pay the tax was an accomplishment. In the first years after licenses were issued, the distiller himself often had to ride with his casks strapped on the ponies and guns at his side to bring it to his buyers—so bitter was the feeling here in the Highlands against those who they said had thrown in their lot with the Excise. Ever since the first tax was put on whisky it was considered an honourable thing to distill illicitly, and slip your whisky past the gaugers. It isn't done now, except for the odd bit of rotgut distilled in a hurry up in the mountains—you see smoke in an odd place, and you may know someone is brewing their few gallons. But if an Exciseman goes to investigate, there'll usually be nothing for him to find. No, it's an ordinary, dull enough business now—except that every time the government wants a few more millions, up goes the tax on whisky. All we distillers would be millionaires if we saw anything like the price that whisky fetches when it's sold over the counter."

He didn't seem to care if Neil Smith heard this. Both men might have respected each other, but they had their roles to play. I thought there would be little companionship for the exciseman among the distillery workers. He would have to like his own com-

176

pany, would Neil Smith, given a lonely place like Cluain. Perhaps Big Billy and his dog, a big yellow mongrel called Rover, were enough.

Inside, the warehouses were beamed, earthen-floored caverns, bigger than they seemed from outside. The smell was of sour dampness. The casks were laid in rows, with racks so that they could be stored three or four high, the racks made of huge wooden beams which had been fashioned to take the weight of the filled casks. There were high barred windows in the stone walls. Whatever chemistry or magic was happening to the whisky as it waited out its maturing phase, there was no beauty in the place it waited. We passed by the racks—row upon row of them. One warehouse opened into the other, with great oak double doors, very high— high enough to take horses and a loaded dray. Neil Smith was there at each door with his keys. We hardly spoke—what was there to say? The whisky stood in its kind of sombre, grim majesty, the casks lettered with the names of those who had come and bought, and had left it here in Cluain's climate to reach the age they desired before blending. The dates were there, the names, and Cluain's own burned into the oak of the casks. They would eventually come back to Cluain to be refilled. What stood in those casks, I thought, must have represented a small fortune, and never had a fortune worn such a plain cover.

The silence, as we walked through to the last warehouse, was broken by a dull, tapping sound—a measured tap, deliberate, with a steady pause between each stroke.

"What's that?"

"That will be Andrew Maclay," my grandfather said, nodding towards Neil Smith for confirmation. "Each day he makes his round. He has grown old, Andrew has, listening to that sound. He is tapping the casks, you see. Each day he taps and he looks, lest there be one that leaks—you will tell from the sound of it very soon how much is in it. He gets through a certain number each day. We cannot take them down all the time to keep weighing them, and the Excise allows for two percent evaporation each year. If there is less in volume in the cask as it leaves the warehouses than there should be, calculated on the size of the cask and the

177

amount of evaporation that should have taken place in the number of years it's been stored here, then we must pay the duty. So a leaking cask can cost us dear. No distiller can afford to let his product run into the ground."

I was glad we were through. Cluain's wealth might lie there waiting, but its heart was in the distillery. I did not envy the unknown Andrew Maclay his job.

As we crossed the yard again my grandfather pointed out the pipes that ran from the distillery to the building where the casks were filled, and weighed by the Excise. "Nothing that holds spirits may run underground," he said. "And anywhere it passes through a wall, the wall must be broken into a hole so that the gauger can see that the pipe is whole and untouched on each side. Smuggling has been tried in many ways, and most of them discovered. You'll hear plenty of tales of the distillery with the pipe underground to some other building—even into the home of the distiller himself. But you need not be believing very much of it. Those are tales of a long time ago. We live by the law now, don't we, Mr. Smith?"

"Aye." The wizened little face split into a grin, and the keys jangled loudly in his hand. "Aye—and must. The law is the law."

I wondered why he made the law sound so unattractive. Or was it just the presence of Big Billy, who escorted us triumphantly out of his domain?

Morag was hurrying towards us across the yard, her white apron whipped by the wind, the tendrils of shining hair lighted by the morning sun.

"The gentlemen have arrived, Master. Mistress Sinclair has them in the dining room. The office was locked."

"So—we are late." It seemed to disturb my grandfather. "Ask them kindly to step over to the office now, Morag." He made a little clucking noise. "I have never been late to meet my buyers before. They will say Angus Macdonald is getting old . . ." He turned away towards the distillery, leaving me to linger by the back kitchen walk, watching the procession of three tweed-suited men, who somehow managed still to look as if they were in the city, cross the yard, accompanied by Morag, who flapped her apron to keep Big Billy at bay. A trap stood in the stableyard, and the horse was munching oats. The buyers had arrived, and there would be more entries in my grandfather's ledgers, and more names placed on the casks buried in the warehouses. I went upstairs reflecting on the strangeness of the business—the samples taken from small, plain labeled bottles locked in the cupboards of my grandfather's office, the tasting, the bargaining—though there was little enough of that; the price of Cluain's whisky was almost as fixed as what the Excise would take in its turn. The decisions would probably be made now as to how long they would leave what quantities to mature at Cluain. A strange business, where one bought so far into the future. Some of these men might not live to receive the product they now bought—perhaps my grandfather would not live to see it leave his warehouses. They bought and sold the future. Whisky men were a strange breed.

And then came Morag's quick tread on the stairs to the tower room, the opening of the door without ceremony. "Quickly, mistress —the Master has brought the gentlemen back to the dining room. I've never known him do *that* before, and it almost the dinner hour. They've always taken their dram in the office, and been off. And he says for you to come down at once . . ."

She was flustered; perhaps that accounted for the near-sharpness of her tone. I decided to take no notice of the fact that she had not knocked before coming in; it was not often that the routine of Cluain was disturbed.

I tidied my hair and went down. I never did remember the names of the three men who came that day—they were but the first of a series of buyers and heads of distillers' groups who came to Cluain to sample and taste and leave their order—or, in some cases, to plead with my grandfather for more of Cluain's whisky than he had to sell. "I never have been able, in the last ten years, to distill enough to meet the demand."

"Expand, Mr. Macdonald. Expand. Cluain's name would bring you credit from any bank—"

My grandfather's face crumpled with scorn, but he held back the words that rose immediately. Instead he went and poured more whisky, and took his time about answering.

"We have no need for banks at Cluain. And we have no need for expansion. You may carry the word back to your friends that Angus Macdonald will not wake up in his bed one morning and find that he is owned by another. We make what we want at Cluain, as much as we want—and it will stay that way."

I said I did not remember the names of those men, but I remember the remark of one of them as he took his leave, thanking me, as if I were the lady of the house, for the hospitality.

"My sister's son, Douglas MacAdam, will be touring in the Highlands this summer, Miss Macd— Miss Howard. A walking tour, I believe—he works with us in Glasgow. May I say that he has your permission to call if he should find himself on Speyside?"

The question was addressed to me, but I looked to my grandfather to answer; I could make no assumption about who might and might not call at Cluain. My grandfather nodded. "We shall be pleased to see your nephew if he should come this way, Mr. Hamilton."

And when he had seen them to the trap in the yard, he came back to his belated dinner, and there was a kind of grim triumph about him as he went to the sideboard to carve the meat.

"And *that* word will pass along too. There is a granddaughter at Cluain. The wasps are gathering to the jam . . ."

It was what any girl might have heard, and my grandfather had made the conditions of my staying at Cluain clear enough. But he could not make me like them; I did not like them at all. I could hardly choke down the generous slices of meat placed before me. It was a silent, and on my side, a dispirited meal. I felt as if I were being sampled and sold, like Cluain's whisky.

*   *   *

The little restored kirk across the river from Ballochtorra continued to draw me; so many times on the rides I took with Ailis, when we crossed the bridge, we would go there. Her reins slipped over the post of the kirkyard gate, and I would wander along the path that led me to the two granite stones. I did not think it morbid that I went there so often; I would spread that all-useful plaid on the grass by William's grave, and there was peace and companionship there. I sometimes wondered if I came because the ancient Chinese custom of reporting to the ancestors had unconsciously become part of me also. If I talked to William sometimes, it did not seem strange—I had always talked to William. I expected no answer from the wind that blew through the long grasses in the kirkyard, and swayed the tops of the trees. There were no answers which I would not have to find for myself. But I talked aloud of Cluain, of my grandfather, of the life that flowed about the distillery, the herb garden, of Mairi Sinclair and Margaret Campbell, of Ballochtorra and Gavin Campbell. I talked of Callum Sinclair as my eyes scanned the sky for a sight of Giorsal, the falcon. I dreamed, and I wondered, in the way that I did when I lay wakeful in the big bed in the tower room of Cluain, seeking, searching, the firelight leaping under the copper hood, and William's Chinese scroll an unanswered message. William's presence was in that room, here where he lay; it was also an imagined figure in all the places of that world, on the close-cropped slopes of the shielings, and the rocks of the glen of Ballochtorra, in Margaret Campbell's sitting room, and a third presence when my grandfather and I sat with the candles lighted beside the chessboard at night. The wind played in the long grasses, and there was music in it.

There was other music, and I admitted to myself, by William's grave, that I also came for that. I was not rewarded as many times as I went, but there must have been times Gavin Campbell was there when I was not. Sometimes I could hear the organ as I drew near the kirk, and I would just sit by William's grave and listen, not to the fancied music of the wind, and the birdsongs, but the thunder and the delicacy of the anthems and fugues, the cantatas and chorales which were never heard on a Sunday in that kirk. On occasions I was there some time before I heard the first notes, as if Gavin sat studying and thinking about what he would play. Then once, as I sat in the warm sunshine with my head resting against the rough granite, I must have slept as the soft notes of a piece I had never before heard had drifted into the air. There was a kind of hush that day, no wind, no sound of

181

cattle, hardly a bird anywhere. Gavin's fingers went back, over and over, one gentle little melodic pattern—trying it at different tempos, with different emphasis. I listened, content; I didn't mind the repetition. I could hum the notes myself by then. My eyelids drooped, and I slept.

I woke and he was looking down at me. His face wore an amused expression. "I found Ailis distinctly annoyed because she has cropped all the grass within reach. Do you come here often —like this?"

I wouldn't tell him how often. "Sometimes. I've heard you play before. I like it."

He squatted down beside me. "It puts you to sleep, though."

"Only today. And what's wrong with falling asleep? For all I know, that might have been a rather special lullaby you were playing. I don't know anything about music, you know."

"You don't have to. It's enough that you listen. Next time, come up into the choir loft."

"I like it out here."

"And I would like you there. I could tell you what I was playing, if it interests you. You wouldn't have to guess . . ."

Next time I heard the organ as I approached the church, and I went directly along the path to the side door. I glanced upward to Gavin's figure in the choir loft, but I stayed in the back pew of the kirk where he could not see me. Within the plainness of the Scottish kirk the grandeur of the music was almost over-powering. No wonder they did not want him to play such things when the congregation was present; the God of that music could be felt to be a God of love as well as vengeance. It would go down ill with the sermon. It had nothing to do with cold virtue for its own sake, or the fires of damnation. It was rich and sumptuous and very human. I crept up the stairs of the organ loft, and folded myself into a corner, well behind Gavin's vision. But when he was finished he turned to me at once.

"How did you know I was here?"

"I knew. The sound changes." He laughed. "I always know when I have an audience. Did you like it . . . ?"

"It was wonderful—warm. It didn't sound like kirk music."

"I'm trying to make my own transcription of some of the Verdi *Requiem* . . . to give the organ some of the voice parts. The minister wouldn't approve. An Italian Catholic . . . Come here now, and sing something for me."

"Me? Sing with an organ? With you?"

"Why not? You've been singing hymns and psalms all your life, haven't you?"

"Yes, but not . . . oh, well . . . I can't."

"Come . . . You know it so well . . ." And his fingers moved quickly, adjusting the stops, and the sound that came was soft, like a child's whisper. Yes, I had been singing it all my life, and perhaps he was thinking of William there in the kirkyard, and I absent when he was buried; perhaps he was thinking of my father killed so far away from me, and his body carried back for burial, so that I never saw the face of either of them in death. He repeated the same introduction three times before I was able to open my mouth, but when I did the sound came surprisingly strong, as I had needed the healing grace of it. *"The Lord is my Shepherd; I shall not want . . ."*

When it was finished I turned and looked directly at him, and it was then the tears started down my face. He didn't seem shocked or perturbed; he didn't even say anything. I just took up the plaid, and went back down the stairs, and closed the side door softly behind me. Ailis stood quietly by the gate, lifting her blunt unaristocratic face to greet me. I slipped up on to her back, and she carried me down the strath at her own unhurried pace. I had long ago stopped weeping by the time we began the steep descent to the Ballochtorra bridge. I felt fresh, like the day, but in some way, older. And just before we passed into the steepness of the glen, looking up, I thought, for a few seconds, that I glimpsed Giorsal's soaring, gliding flight far above me, the hovering, the downward swoop on the wind. Was it Giorsal, or a strange falcon coming into her territory? Perhaps, finally, a mate for the peregrine, I thought, and Callum might lose her. And then we were too far into the glen, and she was gone.

I never went to the kirk by arrangement; we left it as it had always been. Sometimes Gavin was there, sometimes not. I would sit in the choir loft, and he would play, explaining a little to me, occasionally coaxing me to sing one of the simple hymn tunes I knew my heart. "Here—can you read these notes?—try it!" I tried more than I meant to, music far above my head. But I enjoyed it. I would leave when I wanted to, and not even say good-bye. But there was one other thing added to the thoughts that flowed through me as I lay waiting for sleep in the tower room, watching the reflections of the firelight on the curving ceiling; it was not so much Gavin himself, but phrases from the music he made, and the feel of it, gentle as the breeze, and then crashing like thunder. When a summer storm swept through the valley, the wind riffling through the ripening barley, I thought of Gavin's music, and sometimes I wakened sleepily to the thought of it when the first sound of the birds began at dawn.

*   *   *

And over all of this, of all the things that made up those weeks of the summer of Cluain, there was the image and the presence of Callum Sinclair. More absent than present. Even after the morning when he had shown me the flight of the falcon, when he had said I might come with him and see her leave his hand and go for her prey, still he eluded me. I still had to ride up from Cluain to seek him out, and often I thought he was not overly pleased to see me—civil enough, but not encouraging. Many times his cottage was as empty as the first time I saw it; I could never arrange a meeting. I always had to take my chances—and luck wasn't always with me. It was not pride that kept me from it—I was beginning to believe that possibly I had no pride where Callum Sinclair was concerned; it was the fact that he seemed to sense that I was on the point of asking to meet him or to ride with him on a specific day, and he would somehow manage to cut me off, a kind of freezing static moment when the words would die on my lips. It was almost as if he was trying to stop me from breaking the bounds of pride, as if he tried to avoid for me the humiliation of a refusal. I encountered him sometimes about the distillery—he would appear there without notice, and some repair

184

or maintenance work would go ahead; my grandfather did not summon him, because that was their agreement, and it seemed that Callum filled his duties, and Angus Macdonald had no legitimate cause for complaint; at these times, crossing the yard, or at the stables, he spoke to me as if I were a virtual stranger, always polite, and apparently quite indifferent. I wondered if he knew the hurt it caused, or was he more concerned to save my face before those that watched us.

I could not reconcile that creature with the man who sometimes consented to take me out riding with him in the hills, letting me follow where he led, Giorsal on his hand, the dog at his heels. I thought wryly at times that I was almost like the dog, happy when he would even look in my direction, and having to accept it when he would not. Like a dog I waited for him, I waited for a nod, a gesture, a word. At times I could not believe it was I, Kirsty, who acted this way; no pride, no independence—no shame, even. All he had to do was lift his hand, and I was there. I had been far more easily tamed than his falcon, and perhaps he valued me that much the less because of it.

He had promised me long treks when he had agreed that I might watch the hawk hunting, and they were long. There were those mornings, too few, when I appeared at the cottage on Ailis, and Callum, looking at the sky, would nod and make a motion towards the stable. "I don't think we'll have much rain, if any—you won't get too wet. And the wind isn't too high. You can ride with us, if you want."

I didn't try to keep the pleasure out of my face; I would never be good at lying to Callum. "Yes . . . please. Does it matter about the wind?"

He shrugged. "I suppose it doesn't. But I get a little nervous when the wind is high. Even after all this time I can still hardly believe that Giorsal will come back to me. If the wind is strong she may not want to turn and beat back against it—she may just feel like flying on and on with it—letting it carry her. A free creature like that— cousin to an eagle. Who can really expect her to come to a lure, to return always to the glove?"

"It is the hand that feeds her."

"Giorsal can feed herself. And do we always love the hand that feeds us?"

"No—not always."

He took food with him on these treks, enough for both of us. Once, recklessly, I followed him so far on to the moors that I knew I could never be back at Cluain in time for the midday meal. I didn't care. I would risk anything my grandfather had to say for the fierce joy of sitting beside Callum in the damp heather, and eating the rough pieces of bread, the cheese and apples and sharing the flask of ale he carried in the pouch he wore at his waist. That morning, dismounted and waiting, we had watched the supreme moment of the peregrine's life; we had watched Callum's setter, Dougal, among the heather, suddenly "on the point," motionless. The hawk, at a great height above, "waiting on," in Callum's phrase. A step foward from Callum, a rush of wings, a shout of *"Hoo . . . hoo!"* Once, recklessly, I followed him so far on to the moors that I knew Girosal did not choose the grouse that was immediately under her, nor the youngest and weakest. The leader of the covey was her prey. She was a swift blue-black cloud across the sky; we had the brief instant glimpse of her turning upside down with the deadly talon stretched—a miss, as the two birds battled for position. Then Giorsal was above, in pursuit for only seconds more. The talon struck from above now, and the spinal cord was severed in that instant. There was a small puff of feathers in the air. The grouse dropped, and on Callum's command, his setter held back.

"It is Giorsal's kill," he said. "I do not often use Dougal to retrieve. Just to flush the game from cover."

I was wild with the excitement of it, and yet an innate caution made me wonder.

"Aren't we on Ballochtorra's land?"

He hardly bothered to look at me. "Of course it's Ballochtorra's land—if that matters. What are you afraid of—gamekeepers? Do you see a gun? Do you see me carrying home a grouse for my supper? It is Giorsal's kill—she will preen and eat it. Show me the gamekeeper on earth who can prevent a bird from taking its natural prey—or fine it, or put it in prison. It might be Gavin Campbell's land, but he doesn't own Giorsal."

"No one owns Giorsal," I said quietly.

Now his gaze had more awareness of me in it. "You are right. No one owns Giorsal."

She brought her prey to Callum as a kind of token signal, but they both understood the game was hers. She withdrew to clean and eat it, and afterward, Callum said, she would be full and sleepy, and readily come back to the glove, and go home to her perch at the cottage. As we ate our bread and cheese we talked. "It's when she's failed to kill that I have to be certain to have something on hand for her to lure her back—a fresh-killed pigeon or rabbit. I cannot leave her hungry, or she may leave me."

"And yet—the hand that feeds us . . ." I reminded him.

"She is gracious enough not to mind my hand when she is hungry. She has all the charm of the wild who have been tamed. No one can ever be quite certain of them. Shakespeare says it through Petruchio as he tames his wife . . . 'My falcon is now sharp and passing empty; till she stoop, she must not be full-gorged, for then she never looks upon her lure.'"

"How well do you know Shakespeare?" I was thinking that of all those I had known, only my father had quoted a writer with such ease.

"Passingly." He shrugged. "They tried to din a bit into our thick heads in that place my mother sent me. We Scots make a fetish of grabbing at any bit of learning that comes our way. In a land so poor, all we've had to live on is our wits. Brain and muscle have been our largest export. So I, like most others, took what I could when it was offered. It was worth it for some things, not for others. They did not teach me, for one thing, to be a distiller—nor a falconer. For that, I had to do for myself."

"You could be so many things, Callum," I said. "It should be you who sits with my grandfather in the room when he talks about the merits of each distilling, each year of the whisky. And yet you choose not to—deliberately, it seems to me. You will not put yourself out to please my grandfather in the least way. And yet you might do so well for yourself if you did." I knew at that moment what I was urging on him, and why.

"Perhaps it is the last freedom a man has left—to be what he wants, and do what he wants."

187

I tried to let it go. "And wear what he wants?" I said lightly. "You are the only man I have seen hereabout who wears the kilt constantly, and that pouch."

He laughed. "Wait until the shooting season starts. You'll see them all out, fancier than a lot of peacocks. So you wonder why I wear this ragged old thing?—and it is called a sporran not a pouch, if you please. Well, let me tell you. The kilt is the best and most comfortable garment ever devised for walking across terrain like this. It does not get wet from brushing the heather, or when you ford a stream, the way trousers do. Until you have felt the friction of the wool swinging against your thighs, you can't know how warm it keeps you when the mist is rising. It is not like a long skirt on a woman—it gives warmth without hampering and dragging. In the old days, when all the Highlander had was his kilt, it was a single long run of cloth, woven by his mother or his wife, and he gathered it about his waist with a belt, and draped the end over his shoulders to keep off the weather. When he lay down at night, in his nakedness, he wrapped himself in it, feet to the fire. He had to be inventive, and thrifty in all things, even the clothes he wore. There were some clans, when they were charging into battle, who even stripped off their shirts for better freedom to swing the claymores. Well that"—he suddenly plucked savagely at the heather—"is all finished. We were beaten—all of us, even those Highlanders who fought on Butcher Cumberland's side, at the Battle of Culloden. That was the end of the Highlander. It was the breaking of the clans. Now we are a picture postcard. If I seem to dress like some sorry remnant from a Walter Scott novel, it's not because I admire the man's books. It's because the kilt is still the most practical and comfortable garment for the kind of life I live."

"And how long will you live this life, Callum? The days are passing at Cluain—my grandfather's days. Will you stay when another man is master here?"

He shrugged. "I don't live for the future. At times I believe I have none, and it doesn't worry me. I let myself see nothing further than this year, this summer—"

"This *day?*"

He was sitting with his weight balanced on one arm, staring

away from me to the place where Giorsal had withdrawn to eat her kill; so he was unprepared, and he fell sideways when I jerked quickly on his arm. He fell against me, as I had intended, and we crashed down into the heather, his body against mine. I put my arms about his neck and my lips found his.

"This day, Callum . . . *this* day!"

For an instant he responded; his body relaxed against mine, and his kiss answered mine. I could feel the communication between us as a living thing. I swear it was there—yes, I swear it. It was not only my longing fancy. For an instant, an unforgotten instant, he was mine. And then it was over. He straightened, and broke from my grasp, his face contorted with a kind of anguished shame.

"Why did you do that?"

I was in no hurry to get up. I felt no shame for myself. I had simply offered and given what I thought his stiff pride would never allow him to take. I wanted Callum Sinclair, and he must be made to know it.

"Why not? Do I have to sit beside you, ride beside you, do anything with you and pretend I don't want to kiss you—don't want you to kiss me. Well, I *do!*" I was getting to my feet now, standing to face him. "And I want more than that. I want you to love me. And if you think that no well-brought up young woman ever says that, then you've still a lot to learn, for all your learning."

I was looking into his face as I spoke, and in those seconds a terrible fear grew in me. There was no way to describe how I felt, or what it was that I sensed. It had no basis in reason. All at once I knew what I could not put words to. There was some kind of darkness between us, that found in me the mirror of what I saw in his features, the horrible, contorted agony of a man which had nothing to do with shame. This was something far more, and I did not know or understand it.

And still my stiff lips went on framing the fatal, stupid words. I felt I was driving him from me forever, and yet I went on. "I want you, Callum. Not to tease—not to play with. I want you for myself, always. I want to see you the Master of Cluain. I want to marry you."

"Woman . . ." His voice was a raging shout. "For God's sake

189

keep away from me! *Keep away*. There is nothing for you and me. Nothing! There never will be."

"You love someone else? *Who?*—who is it?"

"Who? If I love someone, it is not your right to know."

"Perhaps not. But I will know. I will know, and I will wait. I know how to wait. I'm good at it. And I shall have you—"

He cut me off as he turned towards the pony. "Do not wait. Don't waste your days, your years. It will be to no purpose. There will never be anything for you and me. Not now—not ever."

"But you kissed me—I *know* you kissed me."

"Yes, I kissed you, and I liked it. I admit that. But I will never kiss you again."

"Don't you want me, Callum?"

"There's no answer to that. No answer . . ." He was walking away from me, across the heather to where the ponies were tethered. And I was running after him, my skirt dragging and catching, and once I stumbled and fell, and the breath was almost knocked from me. And then I was on my feet again. I was shouting into the wind.

"No answer but pride, is that it? You could not be seen to take anything from Angus Macdonald—even if it is his granddaughter, who loves you. You would not take me and Cluain as a gift . . . Callum, stop! Listen . . . please . . ."

But he had flung himself into the saddle and slipped the glove on his hand. At the sight of that, Giorsal came at once, as if to a command—a swift black shadow across my blurred vision, and then she was back on his fist, and the dog already trotting at the pony's heels.

He turned his head at last. "Forget it, Kirsty. Forget it. For your own soul's sake, forget what you have said. Forget this day . . ." The rest of the words were lost as he kicked the pony into a canter, and they went down that slope at a dangerous speed. The falcon swayed and jerked upon his hand, but clung there, not needing the jesses to restrain her, or the hood to calm her. She clung to Callum as if he were her life.

As he was mine. I never would forget this day. I would push away the kind of blackness that had descended between us; that I would forget. But I would wait, as I had said I would. To love is something; it is something more than most would ever have.

I would love, and I would wait, no matter what. I would outwait him, and time, and whatever other love it was that possessed him. After the darkness that had fallen on me with my father's and William's death, I was now experiencing a rekindling of spirit and life. I told myself then that I would wait forever, if that were necessary.

And then, quite calmly, I went to untether Ailis. I was patient and gentle, and made my way carefully, noting the landmarks, taking care not to be lost—and knowing that Ailis would never let me be lost. What possessed me on the ride back to Cluain was the sense of time to come. I had made a declaration to Callum, and I would wait to see the truth of it proved. In the end he would know that I loved him. In the end he would know that I could wait. Cluain would wait; everything would wait. Despite the awfulness of the way he had rejected me, confidence was there, and it was growing. I came of an enduring race; Christina Campbell, lying in her grave beside my brother, was the proof of that. We knew how to wait, and how to love—to love someone, or something, with a passion. What I could not begin to imagine then was how long the waiting was to be.

* * *

Perhaps my grandfather had seen me ride, late, weary, and wet from one of the Highland's fierce showers, across the stableyard that afternoon; perhaps my absence at the midday meal had angered him. Whatever it was, he barely spoke to me through the meal that evening. After it was cleared off, he did not bring out the chessboard. He waited for a time after the last dishes had been taken away by Morag, then he turned on me with a kind of smouldering fury.

"They say you ride with Callum Sinclair."

"They say . . . who are 'they?' "

"Don't be impertinent, miss. I know what I hear."

"Yes—I ride with Callum Sinclair when I can find him. He's no more readily available to me than to you."

"Then you will do it no more."

"Why not?"

191

"Because it is not fitting, that is why not. Do you think I want to hear tales of my granddaughter running after a distillery worker."

"My grandfather was—still is—a distillery worker. Are you looking to match me the way James Ferguson did *his* daughter? Are you looking for a title—or money—for Cluain? You won't get them through me."

"I'm looking for nothing for Cluain but what it deserves. And Callum Sinclair is not for you."

"But you keep him here—you have need of his services. You grant him privileges no other worker has because of his worth to Cluain."

"What arrangements I have with Callum Sinclair are my own business, and no concern of yours. And Callum Sinclair shall be no concern, either. I forbid you to see him again. I shall speak to him, and if I—"

"No!" I thrust back my chair and stood up, leaning across the table to look into his old face; I could read little there—the eyes had veiled themselves behind squinting folds of flesh. Was it trouble, or fear, or just the obstinate snobbery of a man whose pride would not admit into his future the son of an unknown man, the son of the woman who ruled the kitchen of his home? And yet, that first night he had told me to find a man fit to follow him at Cluain. And there was none more so than Callum. And Callum was the man I wanted. Was it too much for him to face that?

"You will *not* speak to Callum Sinclair about me. You will *not* humiliate him so—"

"I will do whatever is necessary. I will even send him away from here."

"Send him . . ." The thought made me freeze. My voice was deliberately quiet and controlled when I was finally able to utter the words. "That will not be necessary. I assure you that will not be necessary. Callum Sinclair does not want me. Don't ask me how I know that—just believe it! To him, I hardly exist. I swear to you—*he does not want me!*"

The old head nodded. The eyes opened a little wider, and there might have been relief there, or was it just the satisfaction of feeling himself unthreatened once more, unchallenged.

"It is as it should be. He is wise. He knows his place . . ."

"Then you are a fool!" I could hear my tone rising again, and knew it was perilous. "Callum Sinclair's place is nowhere—and everywhere. He is fit for the company of kings, if he chose it. But he does make his choices—they are not forced on him. He is like his falcon. He only stays—he only returns—because he chooses to. And he does not choose *me!*"

I left him then, quickly, so that he could not witness the hurt, and the tears. It was strange; as I had ridden back that day I had known confidence, and I had believed I could wait for as long as was needed. Now I had heard myself speak what Callum Sinclair had tried to tell me, and somewhere now the doubt had begun, the anxiety, creeping in like shadows thrown down on the strath from the crag of Ballochtorra. I had not wept then, but I did now. I wept in a kind of despair before the fire in the tower room. For all its blaze and its glow, there seemed so little warmth in it. I shivered, and held my hands towards it, and there was no comfort in it. All I could see now was Callum's retreat; all I could hear were his shouted words: *"Forget this day, Kirsty . . ."*

*   *   *

Callum tried to elude me, and I pursued him. It was a physical pursuit; it had to be. He never placed himself where I could find him easily, and so it became a matter of my placing myself where I thought he would have to come, of searching and finding the places where he was likely to go. I ceased even to make excuses for lingering around the yard between the distillery and the stables; I rubbed Ailis down so often, groomed and curried her, that she began to be sceptical of the whole game—she would look at me enquiringly, as if to establish that once a day was enough for a little nondescript pony. But she was also good-tempered, and put up with my sudden rush for the saddle when I thought Callum might be leaving the distillery—if I were even certain that he was there. There were so many times we rode out fruitlessly on that road, waiting for the sight of that dark figure with the pony and dog. I even tried, and successfully, to pretend that I was riding sidesaddle, but using an ordinary saddle, and when I was out of sight of the farm buildings and the distillery, I slipped my leg over Ailis's back. It made the going easier, and for that few minutes on leaving I was able to balance sideways on her broad back, and spread my skirt so that the lack of the pommel did not show. She needed only one hand on the reins, and scarcely even that; with the free hand I held up the second dangling stirrup, and covered it partly with my skirt. So long as no one looked closely—and no one did any more—the pretence worked. But once we left the road, and I flung the other foot into the stirrup, I was free to follow the trails that Callum might have taken, to go into the steep and uneven places, and to let Ailis have her head. She led me into parts of the strath I had never seen before, never imagined. She would turn aside from the trail on to a narrow track that followed the run of a plunging burn, and she was like a goat picking her way up and down among the tumbled boulders, deep in the shadows of the overhanging ledges. She had no fear, no uncertainty, and she knew this land, with all its changing faces, as if it were her own pasture. She led me on to the open moorland, and on the pasture slopes, and she knew always where the bog began, and which path would lead us higher and farther in the shortest time. Had she learned all this in the years of searching for the illicit stills with Mr. Ross? If she had not been a dumb animal, supposedly without understanding, I would have sworn that she knew my purpose. I talked to her constantly as we rode. "Shall we find him today, Ailis? Shall we see Giorsal and find him when we watch where she returns after she has stooped?" And there was never the nervous, sensitive snort to answer my words. Ailis was a very matter-of-fact, a very intelligent animal.

And a few times we did find him. He seemed to greet us with no pleasure, but neither did he send us away. But now I always stayed mounted; we would watch the falcon fly, marvel at the grace and speed, then the lazy hovering, the glide on the wind as she surveyed her terrain. Sometimes there was the excitement of the incredibly swift stoop, the burst of feathers in the air, the instant kill. Callum would let me watch, would give Giorsal some time to preen and eat her kill, and then suddenly, without a word of farewell, he would kick the pony into motion, and Dougal would fall in at his heels. Once or twice I tried to follow, but he was faster than Ailis; it was too easy to lose me once he wished it. A slight rise of the moor would take him beyond my sight, the twist of the glen would hide him. When I reached that point, he would be gone, and a half dozen tracks would lead on from there. Unless the ground was very muddy, and the hoofmarks clear, I could never follow, and the few times I did, he still outpaced us. After a time I learned not to hope for too much; then I would let Ailis turn her head towards Cluain and the stable. She seemed to know as well as I did when the quarry was lost. We were never again late for the midday meal. There was never any reason.

"Don't do it, Kirsty," Callum once said to me. "You are wrong to follow me—to come after me this way."

"Has anyone said I have followed you?" It was pitiful, the little effort I made to cloak my longing. "Can I not ride where I please? And if I sight Giorsal . . . ?"

"Those who sight Giorsal are looking for her. They have very keen and watching eyes. Forget about me, Kirsty. Forget Giorsal."

"And what shall I do with my days?" I tried to make it sound mocking, as if I really didn't care. But I was not good at covering myself.

He lost patience with me. "Oh, for God's sake!—do whatever it is that women do with their days. It is no concern of mine. But you must not come where I go. I will not be followed and watched, I will not be . . . hunted."

I knew my mistake. He was right. If he were hunted he would disappear. I would never have him by naked pursuit. He might come only to the lure. And would I ever be lure enough? I watched him ride away that day, and the doubt was growing, large and hard within me, like a stone. What was it Callum Sinclair wanted? What would he take as the lure?

*   *   *

And once, on the return to Cluain, on a trail so little used that the bracken grew high about the pony's flanks, I suddenly came on Mairi Sinclair. It would have been easy to miss her; I was

195

gazing ahead, trusting Ailis as always to watch her own footing, when the pony's head turned abruptly, and she checked. There, watching me, the Sinclair plaid twisted about her head, was the lean, once-beautiful face that I now looked at so seldom. I realised in that moment how many weeks had passed since our gaze had met in this way, how many meals she had served and never once looked fully at me, how many times we had passed in the kitchen passage, and only a nod acknowledged my presence. But now the stare was frank and open. It was one of the times I had managed to find, and snatch a few minutes' conversation with Callum. He could have passed this way; he could have passed his mother and not seen her, though that would be unlikely; Callum had eyes like his hawk. But the bracken was tall, and without Ailis, I would have missed her.

She lifted her face and looked up at me; the plaid slipped back, revealing the streaked black hair. How like Callum she was—and how different. And then there was another recognition. Her eyes looked at mine in the same way they had done on that first night at Cluain—the eyes of a woman desperate, and haunted—but always, except that time, controlled. I knew then for certain that Callum had passed her, and that she knew we had been together, however briefly, however unsatisfactorily for me. For a second her lips moved, as if she would speak, but no words came. She did not need to say them. They were the same as that first night. *"Cluain is not yours—it is not yours."*

I urged Ailis forward into movement. We were a mile nearer Cluain when I realised what Mairi Sinclair had been doing—what had been her reason for being where she was, if indeed she had not followed me deliberately, and not actually watched my meeting with Callum. In her hand she had held a long, roughly woven basket, and the flowers and herbs and berries of the field and wayside were there. I was suddenly aware, as the Chinese always had been, that what lay in that basket could have been for poison as well as for cure. The foxglove—digitalis—dead men's thimbles it was sometimes called, could mean healing as well as death. And among the bracken grew the tall, death-giving hemlock, and the belladonna —deadly nightshade. And who but Mairi Sinclair would know which was the edible mushroom, and which the poisonous toad-stool? She could carry both life and death in that innocent basket.

And William's uncertain characters splashed on the scroll came back, every line traced on my memory. *"She has killed . . ."*

*   *   *

And so many nights of that summer Morag would come, some kindling and turfs in a basket, the hot-water jar in her hand. Often this task was done before I left my grandfather, but just as often as I sat before the fire, or by the window, reading in the long twilight of the Highlands.

"Books, is it?" she would say. "Yes—your father must have been a scholar . . . I remember Master William was forever at his books —that is, when nothing else offered. But then, it is to be expected of a man. He was near to having his degree as an engineer. They make it easier for men, do they not, Mistress Kirsty?" As she talked, she would move about the room, turning down the bed, placing the hot-water jar, taking any pieces of clothing I had left about and folding or hanging them. She always was busy with her hands; her tongue also was busy, but soft. It was hardly necessary to listen to her, except that the words came through. "He spent a deal of time at Ballochtorra, though, did Master William. And yet, I would not have said that he and Sir Gavin were very close friends. The Master did not like it, of course. He likes nothing that brings Cluain and Ballochtorra together." Then a clicking sound from her tongue. "Och, mistress, this skirt of yours is getting to be a disgrace. I mean . . . Well, look you! It is so shiny and worn. You ride so much, and I'm having trouble now sponging the mud off it. Could I not send away to my aunt—the one my mother stays with in Inverness—to have another made? I could take the measurements, and it would come back fitting perfectly—in the finest serge. And a few shirtwaists, while she was about it. These are washed very thin. I'm sure the Master would not mind the expense . . . After all, they are not silks and satins."

"I would be very grateful if you would do it, Morag, but there

197

is no need to speak to my grandfather. I have some money of my own—"

"Och, well, yes. A bishop's daughter. Mr. Lachlan says great fortunes were made in China."

I felt my anger rise. There was too much supposition; all the talk of the opium trade, the barter in railway shares, the great indemnities exacted from the Manchus. Everyone supposed that all in China had had their cut. I thought of the relative poverty in which we had lived, and I choked on the thought of riches. "Morag, that is not so! I can't explain, but it is not so—not for all. And, please, put that back in the trunk—"

She was holding up the long loose coat of monkey fur which I had used during the bitter Peking winters, when the cold dust from the desert had blown hard against one's body. "It should not be hanging, then?"

"The cedar-lined trunk is made to keep the moths out. Please put it back."

"Certainly, mistress." She was respectfully humble again. "It is just that I have never handled a fur piece before. Och, and yes, it will be useful *here* in the winter, make no mistake. You will need more than the old plaid you wear now."

"The plaid serves well enough."

"It's a Highlander you're becoming? Well, you will wear it thin on your days of riding before you've done."

"Done—done what?"

"Do you not go seeking Callum Sinclair?" She turned to me with a gesture of appeal. "Och, mistress—'tis no business of mine, and I ask your pardon. I have no right . . . But Callum Sinclair follows his own way—always has done, and does to this day. And the woman *he* seeks now is as high above him as that bird of his that he flies. High and mighty. Swooping and teasing, she is, and poor fool that he is, he does not see that. Och, a man he is, for all his education—and they all have their times of foolishness. He will come to his senses, perhaps, when the summer is gone, and she is gone."

"Morag—?"

"Och, mistress, I should have a lock on my tongue. Who am I

to be gossiping about my betters?—though it seems to me sometimes that those they say are my betters can do what I would be in trouble for. But Callum Sinclair may seek her in the glens and on the moors, and she may be his for a time, but she will not be his forever. He will have to come down to earth, will Callum Sinclair. And he will crash like a stone, not soft-lighting, like his bird. He will fall heavy and hard. And he will lie there, ready for the hand that picks him up."

"Whose hand?"

She shrugged, her back turned to me. "Who knows? But, mistress, do not wear out your pony and your skirt riding after him. There is a season for everything. All comes right in its time. Those who have waited can wait a little longer." She folded the monkey fur carefully back into the trunk. "Then I will send to Inverness for the skirt and some shirtwaists, shall I, mistress? They will be quite inexpensive. And I see that you have a fine gown that will do excellently when His Royal Highness comes to Ballochtorra. They say it is to be a very grand evening, with all the gentry of the county coming to bow and scrape. Yes, you will look very well in this gown, mistress . . ."

"How do you know I'm invited?"

She laughed. "Does not *everyone* know? There is little enough to talk of in the strath. What is said in the drawing room at Ballochtorra is soon repeated in the servants' hall. From there, it belongs to the winds. We all know you and the Master are invited. We all know that *he* will not attend and we are all waiting to hear what he will have to say about you going."

"He has no say in it! I do as I please."

She turned from the hanging press, and her face, usually pert and confident, was now softened and faintly wistful. "It is well for those who can say it, mistress. May it always be so. But for freedom we must always pay. All of us . . . all that you see ride through this strath on their separate ways . . . some of the ways coming together, and some going apart. Freedom and power are always paid for, mistress . . . Now I'll just take the skirt with me, and make a note of the measurements to send to my aunt. You shall have it back in the morning."

She was gone, and I was left standing by the window, wondering

199

about what she had said, wondering if this was one of the evenings that Callum would pass Cluain without ever raising his eyes to the tower window, without turning his head sideways. Were his thoughts always so much with the woman at Ballochtorra, for that was the only meaning Morag's words could have had? Did he ride out to meet Margaret Campbell?—and did the glens and moors hide their meetings? No—it could not be so. It was not Margaret Campbell's style. And yet fixed in my mind was the imprint of Callum, motionless astride the pony, falcon on the gloved hand, that dark and striking figure. If the imprint was there for me, then why not for her? In her restless, seeking ways, had she also fallen on the image of Callum that I forever carried?—and would it go, as Morag said, when she went to London with the first snows of the autumn? Did she play with him, to ease her boredom, and did he believe that the game was no game at all, but real?

Then the thought came to me for the first time. I went quickly to where I kept the small box in the bottom of the wardrobe which held William's scroll. Once again, my finger traced that shaky brushwork, splashed, I had always thought, by the fingers of a sick man. But in what way had he been sick then? *"She has killed . . ."* Did I read not, as I had believed, the death of the body, but of the heart? And had Margaret Campbell been the cause?

Chapter 7

———◆◆◆———

The Prince was coming. All up and down the strath the knowledge of it was there, heard and felt. It seemed that every hour or so another trap or cart or carriage rumbled over the bridge at Balloch-torra—servants came from Edinburgh, and some special ones, chefs and lady's maids, and extra footmen came from London, hunching their shoulders against the chill of the Highland summer, and scorn-ful of the lack of amenities, the lack of a village or a town where they could spend their spare hours. They viewed the whole terrain with distaste and hostility, and stayed within the confines of Balloch-torra. They thought it shocking, the report came, that the best view from the seat of a baronet—soon to be a marquis—was spoiled by the ugly heap of the distillery. No place for the Prince, they said. No place for them. They would be gone, thankfully, as soon as he was, and well paid by James Ferguson's money.

I did not see Margaret Campbell in those last days before the arrival. I did not want to present myself at Ballochtorra—there would be too much confusion, and no time for talk. And now, I had grown reluctant to talk alone with Margaret, almost for fear of what I would discover. I did not want to believe what I thought I knew. And yet, in those last frantic days before the Prince's coming, I saw her, late one afternoon, pass on the road that cut through Cluain, riding alone, looking straight ahead down the strath; it was as if she hoped I would not be there, would not see her pass, nor expect her to stop. She rode in a way I had not seen her ride before—as if she wished to make herself small and inconspicuous—as if she ever could, mounted on that wonderful horse, dressed as she was, with her back as ramrod straight as ever, and her head high. It was her expression, not her presence, that she seemed to try to hide. How could a creature like Margaret Campbell hide?—she could never be unobtrusive, unnoticed. Women like her had been born to be noticed. But she did not stop at Cluain's door, and from the tower room I watched her progress along the road, until she turned off upon a side track, so rough not even a cart could have gone that way. Even without Morag's voice saying it for me, I was asking myself what a woman, with a household turned upside down to receive the heir to the Sovereign, was doing riding alone in the last hours before his arrival.

The engraved invitation had lain in the drawer of the writing table in my room for several weeks. I had answered formally, although it was known that I would come; it was also known that my grandfather would not accompany me. It had been a courtesy gesture on Margaret's part. I had taken out the dress that Morag had said would do very well for the evening a dozen times—shaken it, tried to push some life into its rather tired ruffles. It would do well enough, I supposed, but it did not excite me. It belonged to the Peking of three years ago, when I had been younger, and had had more taste for ribbons and bows. It was low cut—I had thought at the time my father might have been displeased, but he was not—and it showed off my shoulders and bust, and even I knew they could stand showing. The silver slippers that went with it were a little dulled, but they were all I had. And over it, the monkey fur, of all ridiculous things. But again, there was no choice. And who would see, except the long-nosed servant who took it from me? And Cluain's trap, with the Sunday Lad to carry me, was what I would ride in to Ballochtorra. My grandfather was faintly disgusted when one of the distillery workers, Ross Mackinnon, had come forward and asked if he might drive me, and wait to take me back. His wife would come also, he said. They just wanted to stand about the stableyard and listen to the music, take their share of what was handed out from the servants' hall, perhaps even catch a glimpse of the Prince.

"Have they no pride?" Angus Macdonald demanded of me at the supper table. "Have they turned themselves into servants?—into gaping street fools watching a circus—and if it were even a Stuart prince, not that fat Hanoverian! Who would suppose that they are independent working people, free to come and go at their will, bowing their head to no man?"

"Perhaps they are just kind—and ordinary," I said. "Should I drive the Sunday Lad myself, and enter by the stable door? Perhaps they don't want *that* for Cluain. They are more proud than you think—and life can be a little dull doing the same thing year in year out."

"It has never been dull for me. *I* have never found life in this strath dull."

"You are the Master of Cluain. As long as you can count your barrels of whisky growing year by year, life is never dull. For them it could be just season after season . . . and just growing older."

"Och!" He turned from me in disgust. "You're too soft, Gurrl. They have a good life, and should know it. And no need for frivolity. Waste of time. Waste of money. But then, James Ferguson seemed to have plenty of money to waste."

"Waste—or spend? If he gives happiness . . ."

He looked back at me sharply. "Happiness! What do you know of happiness?"

"Very little, Grandfather. Very little. I am trying to learn."

He grunted, and was silent for a long time, as if he did not care to question in what ways I was trying to learn. Finally he motioned with his hand. "If you can get your mind off the fripperies up there at Ballochtorra, perhaps you'd be good enough to favour me with your attention for a game of chess. Bring the board, please. And try to concentrate your mind. I do not care for too easy a victory."

But I could not concentrate my mind, and that night his victory was a very easy one indeed.

*   *   *

It had not rained all day—not even a passing shower to dampen the road, or wet the heather on the moor where the shooting party had been all day. From Cluain we had heard them set off, and I had sped to the tower room, trying to see which of the distant tweed-clad figures might be the Prince. But there was more than one stout man in the company. They did not pass Cluain, but turned towards the other side of Ballochtorra's lands. It was said that tomorrow they would shoot over the moors above Cluain, and I think the only satisfaction my grandfather had in the Prince's presence in the strath was the fact that he would have to pass by the distillery, would have to see it, and ask about it, and be told that Cluain's was the greatest malt whisky in the Highlands. Whether this would actually be said or not I didn't know—or whether the grander members of the party would merely commiserate with Gavin on the fact that he had such an eyesore on his doorstep. But I guessed that my grandfather firmly believed that the whole story of Cluain would be related to the Prince, and he took a sour pride in it. And I knew he would take care to be well out of the way before the procession of gigs and traps went by, following the earlier ones that carried the food for lunch. It was not in Angus Macdonald's blood to stand, cap in hand, to watch the progress of a prince.

Nor, I thought, would Callum come down to the roadside to see them go by; Giorsal's fierce bright eyes would not look on that famous bearded face—and for the days that the guns roared up on the moors, and the cries of the beaters sounded, she would only be flown in the early hours, and later, when they had departed. Callum would never risk one of the fancier shots in the party trying his skill on matching the flight of a falcon should Giorsal be tempted by the game driven up by the beaters. No, she would stand, safe and calm, hooded, with the jesses and swivel firmly attached to the perch, in her little hut. Perhaps for these days

204

she would eat rabbit that Callum had snared, but she would be no prize for a sportsman to boast of over dinner.

*   *   *

The day passed, and the shadows started slowly down the strath; the pale transparency of a moon rose while the northern sky was still bright as day; my grandfather noted with satisfaction that a few clouds drifted across its surface. "Och, there'll be rain before the night's out."

"Nonsense," Morag said, when I repeated my grandfather's opinion; she was taking away the white dress with the ruffles to see what a hot iron would do for it. "It will be as fine a night as you ever saw, and half the people in the strath will be creeping in by Ballochtorra to see the festivities."

"And will you, Morag?"

In an instant I knew I offended. "I, mistress? No, not I." Her chin had come up sharply. "I have an imagination. I *know* what will go on there tonight. And I've no mind to be of those peeking in at windows. It is not my way."

"But there must be plenty of young men who would want you to go with them . . ."

She handled the latch on the door heavily. "None of my choosing, mistress. I will go and do the dress now."

I ate very lightly with my grandfather; we had supper un-fashionably early at Cluain, at the end of a workingman's day, rather than the hour when the gentry began to feel hungry again. So, for the sake of form, I sat with him at the table, and ate as little as I could. He noticed.

"Better eat while you can, Gurrl. There'll be so many courses, and so many flunkeys to pick up just the second His Royal Highness sets his own fork down, and so much talk—first to the right, then to the left—that you'll scarcely get a bite in. And finish up your dram before you go. It will put heart into you. And don't touch the wines. Spirits and wines have never mixed. Have your dram here at Cluain, and touch nothing else but lemonade all evening. Tonight—although I wish you did not go at all—you are Cluain. It behooves you to do us credit."

I thought of his words as I went back upstairs. "You are Cluain." He was investing his pride in me. I knew, for his sake, for William's sake, for my father's sake, that I could allow no fault, no gaucherie to mar my behaviour. I would have to be all that they might have want of me. And yet, on the way up the stairs, my limbs seemed to drag. I had never learned to dance—it was not the kind of thing we spent much time on in Peking.

It was still early, but the slanting sunlight was casting shadows in the tower room. I wandered first to the fire, a small fire, lighted, I thought, by Morag, to give me cheer; and then I went to the washstand, and looked at myself in the mirror. A lot to do on my hair, yet. A lot to do, everywhere. Then I sensed something amiss, something out of place. I turned and looked around the room, and there was nothing immediately out of order, nothing obviously to see. I looked up, and there, instead of his usual place, when he visited the tower room, on the bench before the fire, or curled on the bed, Mairi Sinclair's white cat was hunched, in an attitude of hostility and defiance, on top of the tall wardrobe. The colourless eyes looked down at me balefully, as if he were blaming me for something. Never before had he looked at me that way.

At once, then, my own eyes went to the bed. It lay in shadow, and at first I had seen nothing except the dress, freshly ironed, that Morag had laid out. I had paid no attention to it when I entered. That dress had begun to bore me long ago. But now I saw what had been done to it.

The disturbance was first evident in the bedcover, the rumpling of it, in that house where everything was forever in order. I moved closer, very slowly, not wanting to see what my senses already told me. The dress lay there, yes, where Morag must have placed it while I sat at table with my grandfather. What had been then a simple thing, a girl's white ball dress of ruffles and ribbons, was now a shredded mess. Fierce claws had raked across its innocent silk and lace, and the fabric had given before the onslaught. The

206

bodice was mutilated beyond repair; the scratch marks even extended halfway down the skirt. A spirit of malevolent, vicious fury had attacked it. I would never, nor would anyone else, wear that dress again.

I walked slowly across the room, stunned, disbelieving, and yet already knowing that the evening had ended for me. I would not be going to Ballochtorra.

I stood beneath the wardrobe, looking up at the cat. "Why did you do it, Cat? Do you hate me so much? Did it disturb you? But you have never touched anything else—ever. You have been so peaceful . . . Why, Cat?"

I sucked in my breath with fear as he leapt. But instead of the digging cruel claws I had expected, only the roughened surfaces of his pads met my shoulder. He clung there, and hesitantly, reluctantly, I made my hand come up to support him. I turned my face to look into his, and what I saw was not the baleful stare I had imagined in the half-light, but a fear, and a frenzy to be comforted. Before I had realised my action, my hand was stroking his head, and then, for the first time, he gave me recognition. He rolled his head against my neck, and I heard his purr. It was like hearing the dumb speak. He had never spoken to me before.

I stroked him for a while longer. There was no hurry now. I would not be sitting at that grand long dinner table at Ballochtorra—one of the favoured ones invited to dine with the Prince instead of merely invited to come and dance and take supper later. I thought absently that I would have to send a message of indisposition; Margaret Campbell would have to alter her table arrangements.

I suddenly thought of it—the last gift of my father's oldest servant, a woman who had taken care of his needs for more than twenty years in China, moving where he did, away from her family, which was a great sacrifice, caring for his children when he had been away on his duties; a woman who had known my mother. She had given me a parting gift—heaven knows what it had cost her of her savings. It was not fashioned on Western lines—her mind could not conceive of why we wore such des-

perately uncomfortable clothes, or why they should be cut so
immodestly. So of a precious, costly roll of white silk, embossed
with prunus blossom whose pink was only to be discerned with
the second, close look, she had had made for me a ceremonial
robe in the Mandarin style—the high collar, the wide sleeves,
the slight indentation to the waist, and the flare to the skirt. She
reported that the Old Empress, Tzu Hsi, wore such a robe, fashioned so, and I had to believe her. How she knew it, I did not
question. Very few people had ever seen the Empress.

And tonight I would wear that Mandarin robe, before the man
who was to be my own King, and it might remind him that others
gave their lives in distant and hard places, for the establishment
of which he would be head.

Still cradling the cat, I went to the door, and halfway down
the spiral stair. "Morag—Morag, quickly!"

I had to call several times before she heard me. She came
running. By that time I had found the robe, hung with my other
clothes, but neglected. I was still holding the cat when she came
into the room.

"Is the range still hot?"

"The range is always hot. But why—" Her gaze fell on the
dress on the bed. "God Almighty!—what has happened? I laid
it here fresh and lovely, mistress—och, that dratted cat! He has
sneaked in here when I was not paying attention. He is forever
sneaking in here, damn him!—get him out of here, mistress! He
was probably taken about because something was lain on the bed,
where he usually sleeps. Och, the lovely dress—the dress! What
shall we do? It cannot be worn. And you have nothing else to
wear. You cannot go . . . Och, the shame . . . You cannot go!"

"I will go. Will you iron this, Morag? Can you heat the iron
and press the skirt and the sleeves? Very gently. The silk is the
finest. It must be handled very gently . . . a warm iron, only."

She took it, held it up, and her face registered her disgust.
"You mean, mistress, that you will wear this heathen garment
before His Royal Highness. It isn't fitting. It is outlandish—
almost an insult."

"I will wear it, Morag. Will you iron it for me, or will I do it myself? Either way, I mean to wear it."

"Very well, then, but it is a disgrace . . ."

"Morag!"

She turned her head away slowly. "Yes, mistress."

As she reached the door I called to her. "Morag, do you want to take the cat. If he has done damage—"

She flung the words over her shoulder. "I would not touch the dratted animal. He is a fiend!"

And she was gone, her heels making an unaccustomed noisy clatter on the stair. I continued to stroke the cat. I knew he had had nothing to do with the dress upon the bed.

*   *   *

I went downstairs when I heard the trap come to the front door. A strange calm had descended upon me; the worst had happened now. After this, the rest of the evening would seem anticlimactic. Here I was, going off to be presented to the Prince in what surely must be the strangest dress he would ever see worn within the whole country. How different my face had looked above the high collar—I had brushed my hair very smooth, and had not bothered with the curling tongs; it was straight and shining, dark, and caught into a low knot at the back. I had done it that way so that my hair would not offend the gown, nor one make the other absurd. An ivory Chinese fan with a red ribbon hung from my wrist; the long white gloves that were meant to cover bare arms were lost in the wide falling sleeves. I thought of the worn old lady who had given this gleaming silk as a present, and wished that she could have known in whose presence it would be worn.

They knew downstairs—all of them. Oddly, the cat had stayed with me all the time I had dressed and had actually sat upon the table while I had done my hair, as if he did not want to leave the comfort of my presence. I set him down now outside the door, and he went before me down the stairs. They were waiting below

209

in the big hall—my grandfather, Mairi Sinclair, and Morag—those two standing by the archway that led to the kitchen passage.

Mairi Sinclair spoke first. "If the cat has done damage he shall be punished. And I shall refund the money for the gown." The words came in a nervous rush, as if she had rehearsed them, and that was all she would say.

"It would be senseless to punish him, Mistress Sinclair. If he did damage, it could only be because he was upset by something, or frightened. He has been many times in the room, and never before touched anything. And as for the dress—I don't care about it. I was almost a child when it was made. I am not a child any longer, and don't care for little girl's dressed-up clothes."

Mairi Sinclair did not answer. In the dimness of the heavy archway I could see no change in her expression—only the clenching red hands before the black gown. The cat rubbed against her legs.

I had come near to my grandfather now; he was scrutinising my face. "No tears?"

"I save my tears for things that matter. I am decently dressed—if strangely. His Royal Highness can be shocked—or amused—as he pleases. He can't possibly know what it cost a peasant woman in China to give me this gown. I am proud to wear it."

His old face creased along its seams. It was impossible to know what his thoughts were, if he cared at all for the destroyed gown, or for the tiny Chinese woman who had given me this one. But he nodded, suddenly, as if he had made a decision.

"There is something else which I hope you will be proud to wear."

He moved to the long hall table. "Come here, lass."

I went to him, and he had taken in his hands a very finely woven long piece of silk tartan of the Macdonalds of Clanranald. He handled it with great care as he hung it about my body, looping it under my right arm, and arranging it so that it was gathered on the left shoulder, and fell in a long swath down my back. "It was woven by your great-grandmother, Christina, and worn by her on a very few occasions. And here—" He was pinning it in place on my left shoulder with a silver brooch which looked as if it

210

had just come from being polished by Morag or Mairi Sinclair. He showed it to me before he thrust it into the cloth. "The Clanranald crest badge, Kirsty." He translated the motto from the Gaelic. *"My Hope is Constant in Thee."* And now he was bringing a second, and this one I recognised. "This was her own, and she brought it to Inishfare with her. The badge of the Campbells of Cawdor—you have the right to wear both. And if the Hanoverian prince has any knowledge of his kingdom, he will know the Clanranald tartan, and he might remember that it was on Clanranald land that Bonnie Prince Charlie first raised his standard in Scotland, and it was on Clanranald land in the Isles he had his last refuge before leaving Scotland forever. I wonder will this foreign prince know so much?—I doubt it. But you may wear these with pride and honour, and know that you are as good as any in that company."

It was then for the first time I felt the prick of tears behind my eyes as he escorted me to the trap where Ross Mackinnon and his wife waited, and handed me into it. But he did not stand by the door of Cluain to watch us go. That was not his way.

* * *

The candles were glowing, and the electric light was putting on its show in the rooms of Ballochtorra when I arrived, although the northern twilight was hours away. The Sunday Lad disgraced himself at the door as I went, unescorted, up the steps. Wilson, the butler, ushered me in, harassed, I thought, by all those strange faces of the footmen behind him, those who had never been at Ballochtorra before. As the Sunday Lad moved off around to the stables, a stable lad rushed out to sweep up his leavings. I gave the monkey fur, sniffed at, into the hands of a woman I had never seen before, and for a moment lingered in front of a mirror in the vastly enlarged and transformed cloakroom. I smoothed my hair automatically, but for the first time I saw myself full length in the pier glass. How absurd it looked—that shining, luxuriant Chinese robe, with the tartan sash woven in its sombre Clanranald colours. But when I moved, the prunus blossom embroidered on

211

the gown caught the light, as did the silver of the two brooches. I could see the shock, near outrage, in the face of the woman who attended the room. Then I realised I had come entirely without money. I would not be able to tip her to redeem the monkey fur. So . . . not for the first time that evening, I shrugged.

In the drawing room there were perhaps thirty people already gathered. My name was announced, and Gavin came hurrying forward. He took my hand. "Pay no attention to it all," he said. "It's all a joke. We'll laugh about it someday." And then, almost as an afterthought, he added quickly, "How lovely you look . . ."

But he had to turn away, as the names of the next arrivals were announced. I was alone, except that a footman was immediately at my side, with a silver tray. It looked like champagne, the pale, straw-coloured liquid that I had never tasted. "Thank you— no . . ." And then the need for experiment went beyond my grandfather's cautionings. "Well, yes . . ." He lowered the tray slightly, so that I might take a glass. Then I looked around, and saw that very few other women held a glass, and those who did were mostly elderly, seated, and heavily surrounded by men. I stood alone, glass in hand, and there was no one to talk to, no one who looked as if they would ever talk to me.

A few more people arrived. I had left it rather late, I thought. "Lord and Lady . . ." They looked at home, familiar, Scottish probably, but already acquainted with the Prince. "Major James McCulloch-Johnstone . . ." Perhaps that was the odd man invited to balance my presence. How Margaret must have searched to find a single man who was acceptable. Still no one came and spoke to me.

Without any words there was a kind of tremble suddenly through the company. The footman disappeared, and the glasses as well— at least for the time being. As if at a command, the company rose to its feet, the elderly ladies helped, but once there, assuming attitudes of such rigidity that I thought they might never be able to let go. There I stood, with the glass still in my hand, no footman in sight, no tray to receive it. People were forming in a line down one side of the long room. I found myself squeezed out, and hurried along behind them searching for a space. And then I remembered the glass in my hand. I left it on a table, that slowly bubbling champagne, still untasted. Then, almost two-thirds down the room I found a space in the line. The doors had not yet opened, but everyone was ready.

"His Royal Highness, the Prince of Wales!"

I was craning forward to see him, perhaps the only one of that whole line, who all seemed frozen. Was it protocol to pretend that he had not yet arrived until he was level with one? The ladies first in the line were curtseying, and the men bowing. There came at that moment into my mind all the thousand forms of Chinese etiquette which I had never mastered. That stout, august figure was moving slowly along the line, nodding to those who were already known to him, and members of the house party, pausing to acknowledge the introduction by Margaret Campbell of those invited to meet him that evening. She moved beside him in a kind of haze of gold, the gown, the skin, the hair—no other colour but the fire of emeralds at her throat and ears; but she could have done without jewels completely—she was a kind of shimmer of beauty herself. They were almost level, Gavin a pace or two behind; and then my legs shaped themselves into the half-remembered complexities of the curtsey, but somehow I couldn't get low enough.

"Sir—may I present Miss Christina Howard."

He had actually paused, and my knees trembled, and I thought I was going to crash over in front of him. Was I supposed to rise?—I didn't know. I stayed as I was. There was a moment of absolute silence, and although I didn't dare lift my eyes, I could feel his gaze fastened on me. But it wasn't me, it was the dress.

"How unusual . . ." My eyelids flicked up, and I met his look fully. I could feel myself flush with something near anger; but this was one place I could make no retort. Then, astonishingly, the soft, plump finger was under my chin, tilting my face upwards, almost causing me to lose that precarious balance. "How charming . . ." The words melted me; I could feel myself begin to smile with gratitude. Did one smile at royalty?

Margaret was saying something in a low tone close to his ear. He was nodding. "Ah, yes . . . our dear bishop's daughter. So tragic . . . he had done so much good for China."

I knew my father had never met the Prince in his life, and the Prince could not know that my father considered that the Christians had done little, if any good, for China, in all the years they had laboured there—and that thought pained him more than any kind of death. But the words were well meant, and to console me. All I could think of was that my knees wouldn't hold me in that position much longer. Was I expected to reply?

Apparently not. The Prince and Margaret moved on, and then Gavin's gaze was on me as I rose stiffly. I had the overwhelming conviction that he knew what I had been thinking. In a flash I was suddenly at one with my grandfather, knowing that I should never have come, angry that this unknown man, however distinguished, should claim some knowledge of my father, should presume to patronise me, even if he had only meant to be kind to this oddly dressed female. The gratitude vanished. I was done with curtseying and posturing; I wished I were back by the fire at Cluain. And somehow Gavin understood all this.

The rest of the evening was a kind of torture. As I suspected, I was taken into dinner by that lone man, Major James McCulloch-Johnstone. He made conversation for the requisite amount of time, all about things that I didn't know anything of—his regiment, his family, which I had to assume was distinguished, his guns. Did I ride?—did I collect anything special?—did I know the Lovets?—had I heard that John Singer Sargent was to paint Lady Campbell's portrait this coming winter? He was making an effort, because for some reason the Prince had chosen to single me out, to call me charming. I heard my tight little replies; remembering Angus Macdonald, I refused all the wines; I was angry and lonely—so terribly lonely. Gavin was far away down the table, and only now at Cluain would the lamps and candles begin to be lighted. There was no waste at Cluain, and here the twisted silver candelabra were placed every three feet along that enormous table, and there was more food placed on the table, and toyed with, than would have fed one of my father's mission houses for a month. I decided then that I must be very like my grandfather; I loved abundance, I loathed waste. The hungry energy of those Macdonald ancestors scratching a living from their bare Western Isle was eating at my bones and heart. I counted this moment, this night of being complimented and flattered by a prince, as the moment when I received my identity. I became a Scot, and a Macdonald. A kind of fierce pride stiffened my backbone then, and when McCulloch-Johnstone finally gave up on such unpromising material, and my left-hand neighbour, an Englishman who seemed to have a title but whose name I couldn't remember, began to talk to me, I gave him little chance. I found myself launched into a kind of mad diatribe on the barley crop, and whisky, and even—how ill-bred he must have thought it—the selling of whisky. I could see the raised eyebrows, the long face grow longer.

"And tell me, Miss . . . er . . . Miss Howard, what did you do with your time in China?"

"In China?—oh, one mostly watches people die. You know—the usual thing—revolutions and beheadings, and people dropping in the streets of starvation. Yes, one sees a lot of people die in China."

He was unutterably shocked. I could see by his face that he thought I was in this company by some terrible mistake. In another minute I might begin to talk about votes for women. He turned away hastily, and I sat in silence for the rest of the meal.

And he was right—it was a terrible mistake that I had come. The interminable meal dragged on, course after course. The flame of the candles swam before my eyes; down the table James Ferguson nodded to me, his face flushed with wine and triumph. Was this, perhaps, his supreme triumph?—had he ever known a moment of victory in business that equalled this social exaltation? *His* daughter —clothed in silk and emeralds and her own beauty, hostess at a table with the Prince of Wales at her side. From this time on he could only wait for the coronet of a marchioness for his daughter, and the courtesy title of an earl for his grandson. Was there anything else he wanted?—would he then be satisfied? From him I looked down the length of the table to Gavin. He sat quite still, talking to neither of the ladies beside him; his face wore that look of weary detachment I had marked the first time I had seen him. He was staring at his wife, and there was no triumph in that gaze. I read a kind of stern sadness, controlled, as if he almost could not bear what he saw. But what did he see?

The dinner was over at last, and the ladies withdrew. If possible this was even worse. Margaret led us upstairs; in passing, she smiled at me. It was that same radiant smile she always had, guileless as a child's. She seemed almost to be trying to say to me that this was no different from any other visit I had made to Ballochtorra, and that we would gossip about it later over the tea cups. But now she had more demanding, difficult guests than I to deal with, and I would understand. I did understand, but it did not make it any easier for me to wait my turn at the pier glass, to see once again the strangeness of the garments I wore. The sheer size of the flounces and ruffles about me, the spilling over of powdered bosoms above the tightly corseted waists, the dazzle of diamonds and emeralds nearly as big as Margaret's, the glow of rubies even more precious, played at my senses. There was a heavy perfume on the air, the tangible scent of money and rank and privilege. It wasn't envy I felt, only a kind of disgust with myself for ever having felt pleased to be invited for this occasion. In the midst of it all I suddenly thought of Callum, and a kind of wholeness came back upon me. I loved, and I loved the right kind of man. I thought of how his lips would have curled in half-laughter at the sight of us all herding about. It made me want to laugh too. I almost did when I overheard, as I was surely meant to, the remark of one woman to another as we passed on our way back to the drawing room to await the gentlemen. "I did not know, did you, my dear Lady Amelia, that it was meant to be a costume ball? How novel!—very droll—a Chinese Scot."

A few of the men joined us later, after the port had gone around. The new billiard room was waiting for the Prince, and in a smaller room adjoining, card tables had been set up. The Prince did not care to dance any longer, they said; no one was impolite enough to add that it was probably because he was too stout. But in the gallery above the máin hall a discreet orchestra was playing, well screened by potted palms. I sat by myself in the drawing room; none of the other ladies spoke to me and I suppose they thought it odd that I was there alone. I didn't care. I would just have to wait out the hours until it was permitted to leave. How did one leave when the guest of honour was staying in the house? What had the invitation cards said—*Carriages at Three A.M.?* The Sunday Lad would have eaten his head off in the stable by then, and the Ross Mackinnons beginning to yawn over the food in the servants' hall. Since the servants were seated in accordance with the rank of the Master, then the Mackinnons would be placed very low indeed. But they would claim, and rightly, that they were not servants at all.

Once James Ferguson strolled near my chair. "Good evening, Miss Howard. I hope you are enjoying yourself."

"Very much," I lied. We both knew it was a lie. "It's a very splendid company."

He could not resist saying it. "Aye, very splendid. My little girl had done very well." Then, looking hard at me, at the Chinese gown, at the tartan sash and the two clan brooches, "And when will Angus Macdonald be ready to sell Cluain, do you think?"

I lifted my head. "My grandfather will never sell Cluain."

"Well then, he will not live forever. I hear he has been poorly this past winter. It will be sold when he is gone."

"Don't be too sure, Mr. Ferguson."

"So then, lass? You think you have it for yourself? Well, it's nothing for an inexperienced girl. Or a man who doesn't know what he's about. Well, you may give Angus Macdonald the message. James Ferguson will meet his price whenever he is ready."

"Give the message yourself, Mr. Ferguson." I got to my feet, almost brushing him aside. "I am no messenger boy!"

I went through the hall quickly. Neither Margaret nor Gavin was in sight. I thought I was at the point when I would damn etiquette, and ask for the Sunday Lad to be brought around; and then I thought again. My grandfather would expect me to bear through whatever the evening held; I would not let him down, nor would I admit my defeat before these people. I would not let the valley know that I had left before the proper time. Because the valley would know everything about this night.

I avoided the rooms where the people strolled, and the cards were played. No one danced; those who had been invited after dinner had arrived, and become part of the company. The large rooms seemed almost crowded. After that huge dinner, supper was already being set up. It was an animated gathering, but curiously joyless. To the people who watched from beyond the windows, it must be a strange sight. Where were the traditional Scottish dances, the men in their dress kilts and ruffled jabots, the women with the tartan sashes —where was the piper? But perhaps His Royal Highness was tired of such ceremonial, and wanted only his cards, with high stakes. It was an English gathering, however many of the company bore lordly Scottish names.

I found the room I sought, the small one almost at the end of the passage that ran the length of the main building. I had only been in it once before—it was a sort of small annex to the main library, which occupied the corner of that wing. I had thought I would find it empty, and it was. No one would miss me, and I would wait until the first carriage came to the door. And then go and get the monkey fur, and home to Cluain. Home.

"Are you tired of it all, too, Kirsty?"

I swung around. "Gavin!" He was seated in a deep armchair, facing the long windows and the very last of the light that silhouetted the opposite heights of the glen. The moon was already there, waiting for the sky to darken.

"Shouldn't you be with your guests?"

"Shouldn't you be out enjoying yourself? No one can have failed to notice that the Prince thought you charming. Other women have made whole careers of less than that."

"Gavin—don't laugh at me—not you!"

He got to his feet slowly. "It's the last thing in the world I would do—laugh at you. You're a proud and courageous woman, Kirsty. If you wanted to, you could have charmed every man in the house, and made all the jewels and finery look silly."

"Oh!—the little country maid? I can't play that role, Gavin. It doesn't suit me. It wouldn't suit my grandfather to have me do it, either."

"No—it wouldn't suit. So you wait it out, as I do. Well, it won't be long."

I was standing by one of the french windows that looked out on to the principal terrace. This was the new part of the house, and down below, nearer the river, the old tower stood, a kind of stern reminder of what this place had first been built for. From here, the music was faint, almost ghostly.

"Take the White. First move to you, Kirsty."

I looked back at Gavin. Between the windows there was a marble chess table, and he was now standing beside it. I took the couple of paces to bring me opposite him, and looked down at the table. I spent some minutes examining the set; I had seen a similar one before—a Cantonese ball-mounted set, carved in Indian ivory of exquisite quality and delicacy. Not really a set to play with, but to look at. I held up one of the pieces against the light from the window, marvelling at the intricacy of balls set within balls—the eternal Chinese enigma.

"How beautiful," I said. "How really beautiful."

"One of the few things I own at Ballochtorra. It belonged to my father." He prompted me again. "Take the White Queen, Kirsty."

"How did you know I played?"

"William's sister? How could you not?"

I acknowledged the fact with a nod, replaced the piece I was holding, and made my first move. His followed rapidly. My next I made almost without thought. The rest was part of the pattern. We followed it through, perhaps both of us knowing, and yet I was unsure. Compelled, I made each move as before, Pawn, Bishop, Knight. Gavin's moves now seemed like an oft-told tale. We reached the point I knew we must reach.

"Check to the Queen, Kirsty."

I looked at him. "Did you play with him?—with William?"

"We played quite often."

"This game—these moves?"

"This game—I don't remember this particular game. No—I don't think we did, ever."

"But you played this game now . . ."

"Why not?"

"Because . . ." Suddenly I shivered. William's presence was too tangible. I looked hard at Gavin, trying to reassure myself that this was a living, independent being, his own man, not an instrument of a dead man, not an old man like my grandfather, not a grieving sister, playing and replaying endlessly the last game.

"Kirsty . . ."

"Yes?"

"Kirsty . . . I'm going. This is a kind of farewell. I could hardly have gone to Cluain . . ."

"You're going—you mean to London? When the house is ready?"

"No, not to London. Never to London. I'm going, Kirsty."

"Going where?"

"God knows. I'm leaving. That's what I mean. Leaving. I have to leave for my soul's sake—for what that's worth."

"Gavin—what are you saying? *Exactly.*"

"Exactly? I'm saying that when this tiny farce is over, when His Royal Highness has set the accolade upon my wife's shoulders as the most beautiful woman, the best hostess—whatever the nonsense is, then I'm leaving. Leaving Ballochtorra, leaving everything. Leaving —God forgive me—leaving my son."

"You *can't!*"

"I must. Even leaving a son is better than appearing a fool in his eyes. In a very little time Jamie will know that my father-in-law pays for everything here. In a little time more he will know what a pretence it is between his mother and father. I can't be here to witness it. I would rather be dead than see his knowing—the contempt—in his eyes."

I knew. At once I knew. There was no need to ask. "Where will you go? What will you do?"

"Who knows? Anywhere—it doesn't matter. What I do doesn't matter. I'll never find an organ to play, but there's always a ditch to dig—a boulder to move—somewhere in the world. Anywhere— away from here. Lost."

"You can't be lost, Gavin. No . . ."

"To them . . . yes. Margaret will miss the convenience of me— for a while. I will never formally take my seat in the House of Lords, and so my father-in-law will lose something. But one day my son will. Perhaps by then he will understand. The only hope I have is that he will somehow understand why I had to go. But you see, *I* matter too, Kirsty. I can't live with myself as things are. Can I expect to live with my son?"

"Can you live without him?"

"I will have to try. Better that than be an object of scorn to him—"

220

"Other men don't mind. Other men marry for money, and make no bones of it. They exchange a title for money, and it seems to men like James Ferguson, and most others, that it's a fair exchange." Why did I argue with him? I knew the truth.

"It was never that sort of exchange. It was a small enough rank, and there wasn't so much money then. We loved each other . . . I'm sure of that. And somehow we lost it. How did we lose it, Kirsty? How could I have let it happen?"

"Could you have helped it?"

"I could, if I'd known. Is one always too young to know these things at the right time. The first acceptance of help from James Ferguson was the beginning of losing what we had—and yet could I have expected a woman like Margaret to go on enjoying poverty? She was not made for it—I should have known that."

"There'll be a scandal . . ."

"Of course there'll be a scandal . . . but it will only dawn on people gradually that I am not coming back from whatever part of the world they'll say I've gone. By then Margaret will be firmly established as a London hostess. I won't even be missed."

"You'll be missed." I looked down at the board. "You're being too extreme, Gavin. There isn't any need . . . you could stay on here alone, if that's what has to be."

"On James Ferguson's money? No, there've been too many years of that. If I stay any longer I won't have the courage to go. I will never be happy away from this place, this strath. Every day I stay the resolution will grow weaker—I will find excuses to delay. Just as I'm delaying now. I tell myself it's for Margaret—just to see her through this. I say I'll have just one more summer of Jamie before they send him off to school and make a stranger of him. And the excuses will go on, and on . . ."

I fingered the elaborately carved figure of the White Queen. "There's no way out of this check, Gavin. I have played the same game too often. William . . ."

"Yes, William . . . I don't forget William."

I looked straight at him. It had grown much darker. There was no light now but the moon.

"Was William her lover, Gavin?"

The sudden clatter of the pieces falling to the parquet as his hand swept them off the board was my answer, the terrible, deliberate crunching of the delicate ivory as they splintered under his feet. It was one of the most awful things he could have done—the destruction, in his despair, of something loved and prized, a part of himself. His hand now partially covered his face, needing to screen it.

"I don't know. That's the worst of it. *I don't know!* That's what will kill me if I stay—never knowing. Or knowing too well. Guessing. Which one?—this one, or another? When? How? Was William one of them? *I don't know . . ."*

I turned away from him, sick. The taste of deceit was in my mouth, and the terrible memory of the letters that had told too little. William—what would he have done? He might have loved, and not counted the cost, not reasoned the error. I suddenly understood much more because I loved Callum Sinclair. Did I stay at Cluain for him—or for the sake of Cluain itself? Had William deceived both my grandfather and himself that he too stayed for the sake of Cluain. The words came back . . . *"there is an enchantress."* Had he been bewitched and enchanted, as I was, sick with longing, lost to reason? Was there a kind of madness here that both William and I had experienced in our separate ways? Was that why his hand had touched me so strongly, why his presence was all about me at every turn, so that he even played over and over this wretched last game of chess? It was almost as if he tried to speak to me. "Not you, too, Little Sister. Here is your check. There is no way out, unless it is to lose . . . unless it is to damnation . . ." But William had never said that. I was being too fanciful, letting myself be carried along on the wave of Gavin's anguish for his own loss. Why should the sense of damnation cross my spirit at this moment? There was nothing wrong in my love for Callum . . . nothing wrong . . . nothing wrong. And yet why did I feel this breath of ice, as if William's cold hand was touching mine across the chessboard, not a warning, but a terrible confirmation that I also must lose. *"Check to the Queen, Kirsty."*

It was not William's hand that touched mine, but Gavin's. "Listen . . . !"

And eerily, upon the stillness of that hour that had crept past midnight, when the moon held its own, came the sound of the pipes. It was below us, and farther over, at the old part of the house. Both of us went to the window, again the crunching sound of ivory under our feet, and Gavin flung open the long window. The rush of chill air met us, and the sound of pipes, stronger.

The moon cast unreality upon the scene; the whole deep glen was in shadow and bold relief. The light blended the old and the new of the buildings into one. In that instant it was a fairy castle, frozen in time and pale golden light. All along that upper terrace, from all the french windows of the new wing, the guests came, the silks and the flash of jewels as brilliant as they had been by candlelight. They drifted, that splendid company, the Prince's figure conspicuous among them, to the balustrade.

It was a sight from the ages that met us. The platform of a tower of the old building was below us, and clearly in our view. The moon struck fire from the shining steel of the two crossed swords, laid at right angles on the ground; it caught the drones of the pipes, and the silver of the clan badges. The piper and the dancer both wore full dress—lace at the throat and sleeves, velvet jacket, jewelled dirk at the garter of the stocking. The kilt and the plaid each wore was different. Even from this distance, though, I knew at once the Sinclair tartan. But no matter what he had been wearing, I would never have mistaken the figure.

My lips formed his name soundlessly. "Callum!"

It was performed with beautiful precision, the sword dance. The pipes skirled, and his slippered feet leapt between the blades; the kilt and the plaid flared about his body, the arms extended outward and bent at the elbows, and so clear was the moonlight that I could even see the grace of the upraised fingers. It was a heart-stopping sight, there upon that ancient battlemented tower, with no room for mistakes, and no forgiveness from his audience either, if one slippered foot should even brush one of the blades. The first murmurs among the watchers had died. Even on that gathering, to whom little was new, he was making his impact. And the word had spread quickly. From the back of the house, from the kitchens and stables, the sound of the pipes had drawn them, those who knew the dance, and those, like myself, who had never seen it before. For most of them, it must have been the first true satisfaction of the evening—an entertainment for a prince, but in the traditional manner, and executed with flawless precision and grace.

But this was not the Callum I knew, the man who would have scorned to dance for a prince. Who was this stranger in finery I would not have expected him ever to put on—the kind of dressed-up travesty of the old sensible Highland garb that now was romanticised beyond recognition? And had I ever thought to see him dance? Perhaps . . . perhaps at a wedding when the whisky had been passed around, and there were other feet to tap the rhythm with the piper, perhaps before the huge fire of an ancient hall like Cluain's. But here, like some hired entertainer, dressed in costume? The grace and skill I might have expected; his presence here, never.

"Is he drunk?" I whispered at last to Gavin. It was the only explanation.

"No—not drunk."

"What then?"

"Mad."

The word was said with conviction, and harsh bitterness. With its saying, the pipes died out on their wailing note, and the dance was done. There were shouts and whistles of appreciation from those who had drifted round from the back of the house; they had carefully separated themselves by a long space from the guests clustered around the Prince. A few urged Callum on to other things. I heard a polite handclapping among the privileged group. The Prince puffed on a half-smoked cigar, and he continued to stand, as if he also waited for more. Perhaps he had been entertained, after all. Certainly, the whole event had had the novelty of the unexpected, and the most supremely appropriate setting. But it should not have been Callum Sinclair there.

But Callum was finished. I was glad to see there was nothing of a bow to acknowledge the applause. I wished that I did not feel a shame for him—one should not feel shame for someone who was loved—but I did. One more thing to be endured on this interminable evening, the evening when I seemed to be losing everything, the night when I was learning the bitterness and price of becoming myself. With a kind of dreadful fascination, wondering how deep

224

the hurt could go, I watched as Callum lightly vaulted the battlements of the tower, and leapt to the balustrade of the lower terrace. He must have leapt the slippery rocks of mountain streams much more dangerous, but that instant when his figure was outlined against the sky was dramatic and slightly theatrical. There were little gasps from the women. And then he was running lightly up the steps to the upper terrace, and heading directly for where the Prince stood. The run slowed to a walk. I couldn't believe it. Was Callum Sinclair, the proud, lonely man, who asked for no favours, going to bow before the Prince and be grateful for a word or two—something to boast of after? I didn't want to look. It was like the shattering of a dream. I stared out across the glen, unwilling to witness the falling of an idol.

But it was the shocked murmur that forced me to look again. The Prince had advanced slightly, graciously willing to accept the bow, perhaps to offer the hoped-for few words. But Callum had simply passed him by as if he did not exist. It was to Margaret, who had been standing by the Prince's side, that he went. The people about her drew back slightly, as if they couldn't believe the scene. She and Callum were isolated in the midst of that circle when he made his low bow to her. And then she, as if she had also entirely lost all sense, instead of gesturing towards the Prince, held out her hand to Callum. I had never thought to see him bow low to kiss a woman's hand, but he did it then, and it was for all the world to see.

Then he was walking quickly along the terrace, his back to the Prince; the same light run down the steps, the same effortless leap from the balustrade. The swords were gathered up quickly, and he and the piper vanished down through the trapdoor that gave access to the tower. They had gone, like two ghosts of the night, leaving behind consternation and scandal, and hurt in me such as I had thought I could never feel. Is there a precise moment when one remembers the wish to die—the first time it comes? I knew it then. But death is not so easy. One has to live the next seconds, and the minutes and the days.

Perhaps it was worse for Gavin, beside me, but I doubted it. He had begun to live with it long ago.

"So she has Sinclair too. Are there none she will leave alone

225

—no one she will not claim for her own. Is she never satisfied? How many more—*how many?*"

Then he took my hand and led me back to the darkened room where the ivory pieces were the final, devastating reminder of William. "I'll help you get your wrap, and send for the Mackinnons. Don't wait for who should leave first. All the etiquette has been smashed. The evening is over."

Chapter 8

————◆◆◆————

I

The late days of August and early September stayed warm, and the barley stood high and golden; then it began to be touched lightly with brown, and was dry when I put my fingers to the heavy sheaves. "It is time to begin," my grandfather said. So they were saying at each farm all over Speyside, and labour was needed everywhere. Everyone on Cluain worked, of course, and the call went out to other straths and as far as Inverness, and the itinerant workers came, bringing women and children with them—the children old and strong enough worked beside their parents, and the young ones tumbled barefooted among the stubble, following the line of workers who moved with sickles through the fields. It was hard work, that endless stooping under the sun, but most seemed to enjoy it—enjoy the warmth of the days, the company, the songs, enjoy the food sent out on the wagons to wherever the workers were in the fields at noon, and the communal eating in the barns where the barley would eventually be stored, and where the itinerants now slept. Mairi Sinclair's kitchen had never been so busy, and she had several extra women to help—my first and only offer to help was shrugged aside, and those days were strangely quiet and dull for me in the midst of all the activity. My grandfather did not come for his evening meal till the last of the workers had left the fields. I watched the Cluain workers on the road home, and the itinerants gather in the barns—

whisky had passed around in the last minutes in the fields, and tired women sang songs to sleeping infants as they carried them back. "The whisky eases an aching back and gives a good night's rest," Angus Macdonald said. "Not too much, or they would not be at their work tomorrow, but enough to warm their hearts." My grandfather made no economies in the food or the whisky. It was always Cluain's best.

It should have been a happy time for me, a time to perceive and enjoy, as these people did, the endless cycle of life in this strath, the celebration of another year's crop. But I felt myself as dry and brittle as the stooks of barley standing in the suddenly arid-looking fields.

My unhappiness was Callum Sinclair, of course. I had not spoken with him since the night when he had taken Margaret Campbell's hand on the terrace of Ballochtorra, and the story had sped up and down the strath, and beyond, of that supreme act of folly, the insult to the Prince—and most talked of, Margaret Campbell's calm acceptance of both. They said afterwards that the Prince had not shown more than momentary surprise, had rather seemed more amused than insulted. But Margaret Campbell had dared much by not rebuffing that gesture from Callum, and it seemed that no one could talk of anything else.

I could not even come face to face with Callum, much less speak to him. He seemed to have no place in the work of gathering the harvest—the only man at Cluain so exempted, and since that was not remarked on, I thought it was probably part of his agreement with my grandfather. He showed no sign of repentance for his act, and would remain independent to the last. He would appear again at Cluain when the harvest was in, and the malting ready to begin, and not before. He rode back and forth on that road that passed through Cluain with no sign that anything had changed, or there was more reason than before to mark his passage—I saw him a number of times—him, the pony, the setter, and sometimes Giorsal. I knew by now that there were many other ways to pass along the strath—the track by the river, paths that bypassed the house. But Callum Sinclair would have scorned to hide from anyone, to avoid the comments—if any dared offer them to his face—and the looks, which could say even more. So he travelled the road as before, and I was more intensely aware of him than ever; I seemed to know his coming long before the familiar shapes appeared, and I was sick with hurt and envy as I watched him pass from sight. It would be Margaret Campbell who knew where he went, and when, and she seemed to care as little for the scandal of it as Callum did. But at least she did not ride that road, or if she did, I never saw her.

Giorsal I did see, though. In those too often wakeful nights that blended to the dawn, and I sat at one of the windows of the tower room watching for the first of the sun, hearing the first stirrings about Cluain as the cattle were brought to be milked, as the ranges were stoked in the kitchen in preparation for the day's cooking—several times I saw Giorsal. Callum was flying her before there was danger from any shooting parties on the moors; it could only have been Giorsal, the great dark lightning streak in the sky, that plummeting stoop to her prey. The strath was her territory; she roamed its sky, wheeled and circled and lazed upon its air currents. But somehow instinct and Callum's training had taught her caution. Her only enemy was the gun, and before there could be danger, she would disappear, off in the direction of Ben Cullen. My whole spirit called after her. Only once did my grandfather speak of what pre-empted everything else in my thoughts. It was two days after the party at Ballochtorra; I sat toying with the food on my plate and saying nothing.

"Well, then . . . can you not hold your head up? Will you let the world see the pining of a love-sick girl for a man that's worth nothing? He has shamed and disgraced himself and his mother, and that woman up there who flaunts—"

"Enough, Grandfather! I will thank you to say nothing more about Callum Sinclair. He has done what he has done—and that takes courage. A mad courage, if you like. He has told the world that he loves a woman. But he never said that he loved *me!* I told you that he would have none of me. What a fool I was to think he would look at me when there was Margaret Campbell."

"Margaret Campbell is a married woman, and should have more

decency and pride. Where does she stand now before the world—before her son? There is shame for them both, but more for her."

"Oh, leave them be," I cried at him. "It is their own affair. Margaret Campbell has not ruined herself. But she has ruined Callum. She will go and leave him here, and then he will be wretched."

"And will you be waiting when he comes down from his dream world? Will you look to take her leavings?"

"There will be no leavings. When Margaret Campbell goes Callum Sinclair will not be free of her. I think he will never be free again. He may go also, but not with her—because of her. He may never see her again, but he will not be free of her. His sort, once they have given themselves, can never be free. I think he will leave Cluain."

"And as well if he did. If it were not for his mother I would—"

"I don't want to hear!" I said. I stabbed the food with my fork. "I don't want to talk about Callum Sinclair. And my head is high—never higher. You will not see me weep. It is a worse kind of feeling than when William and my father died, but no one will see me weep. And I hope he *does* go. If I could, I would make it a little easier for myself. But if he stays, then I will have to bear that, too."

"Have a care, Kirsty. Have a care. No point to ruin *your* life." It was said quite gently, and he was indeed more gentle with me in those next days. I worked in the office, and no words passed between us that did not concern business matters. But even sitting there at the desk with my back to the window I knew the sound of Callum's pony, and I could never stop myself looking around. If my grandfather was not there I would rise and watch him out of sight, as I had always done. I did not weep, ever. There was nothing but a kind of aching silence in my heart. Those were the nights when I played chess with fierce concentration, striving to wipe out the memory of that scene on the terrace. And those were the nights that my grandfather at last began to go down before me. Game after game I won, and he began to struggle, to put out his best efforts. But the terrible hurt had to be assuaged somehow. I could not lose everything.

So it had been a relief when the time of the harvest came. I welcomed the distraction of it, the bustle of the carts leaving with the food. I did not often go into the fields among the workers—just enough so that my presence was seen and felt there, but never dallying in case I might overhear talk—talk about Callum and Margaret. I rode beside my grandfather, and his very appearance was enough to silence even the rowdiest of the children. I began to see him fully in those days as the man he appeared to be in the strath; he was just, not unfeeling, even generous when his help was needed. And yet the jokes fell silent on the lips as he passed, and the children gazed after him in shy awe. I often thought that the minister up in the kirk might have envied the respect that Angus Macdonald seemed able to command without words.

No one saw Gavin Campbell in those days. The Prince had left after the allotted four days, the servants departed from Ballochtorra, and a strange quiet descended on the castle. I heard from Morag that Gavin left Ballochtorra early with Jamie and a gillie, and spent each day on the moors shooting. Occasionally, from down at Cluain, we heard the sound of guns, but it was not always from the Ballochtorra moors. There were other shooting parties in the district, working over rented moors. They would pass along the road, looking curiously at Cluain and the distillery, talking about it. For some reason I resented that. They were strangers to me, as the hired servants had been, when all the faces in the strath were growing familiar. I almost looked forward to the time of the snow, when they would be gone. But when they were gone, I thought, so would Margaret Campbell, and Jamie. Perhaps Callum would be gone, also. And Gavin would be gone, probably forever. It was a time of waiting, these last days of the summer. And I waited to see what my life would become when the summer was finally over.

II

There was something else astir in the strath, something that called my grandfather from the harvest fields, and brought Samuel Lachlan several times down from Inverness—hurried visits without the usual overnight stay. The little man looked grey and fretted, I thought, as I sat and ate a midday meal with him in the dining room of Cluain, and lingered with him over his tea when my grandfather had to hurry back to the fields. Neither of them said anything before me of the reason for the unusual activity—the talk was of the harvest, the weather, an occasional uninterested reference to the shooting season, and Samuel Lachlan's persistent enquiries for details of the Prince's visit; to these I made guarded, agonised replies, and knew that my grandfather's attention was always on me at these moments. But whatever lay behind the visits, and the long sessions of talk in my grandfather's office, the telegrams sent back and forth to summon Samuel Lachlan once again, or announce his coming, I knew who had instigated them. It was James Ferguson.

That burley authoritative figure changed subtly in those days also. He stayed for only one night of the Prince's visit, perhaps not wishing to stress too much his daughter's association with "trade," and lower her standing. Besides that, he did not shoot, and was lost in that company which talked of little else. So he left Ballochtorra on the day after the party, and I wondered what he had made of the scene on the terrace. Margaret had been greatly daring—the risk of offence to the Prince had been great. But Edward did not leave, and the shooting party went on, and perhaps there was faint amusement at Margaret Campbell's strange, rustic lover. The story, embroidered, I was sure would go about the London drawing rooms that winter, but as long as the Prince continued to grant his company, Margaret was safe. In those few hushed moments it must have seemed to James Ferguson that his daughter was about to throw away all that he had so carefully built and planned and paid for. But the Prince had chosen to smile instead of frown—he must have liked his hostess very much. So James Ferguson departed, perhaps not pleased, but at least reassured.

But he was back again a very few days after the Prince's party had left, and it was not for pleasure—and the reason somehow concerned my grandfather. Ferguson waited overnight at Ballochtorra until Samuel Lachlan could be summoned from Inverness, and the three spent the most of the next day closeted in my grandfather's office, though James Ferguson returned to Ballochtorra for his midday meal, and did not sit with us at table at Cluain. He returned for some hours more in the afternoon, and then a carriage from Ballochtorra came to take him to the station. The Sunday Lad was harnessed to take Samuel Lachlan to get the same train, but from the looks on the faces of the two men as James Ferguson departed Cluain, I did not think they would share the same compartment. And, of course, it was Samuel Lachlan's unshakeable rule to travel second class.

And the next week James Ferguson was back again, and so was Samuel Lachlan, this time by appointment; the same sessions of talk took place in the office, the same arrangements over the meals. This time James Ferguson did not even stay overnight at Ballochtorra. He nodded to me absently, rather curtly, when I encountered him in the yard on that occasion, as if he had almost forgotten my identity. He wore then an air I had never expected to see on him —the bluff, expansive look of the successful man of business who now sets out to enjoy his success seemed diminished—though I noticed that when he realised that my eyes lingered on him for a time his rounded figure automatically straightened, and a smile flashed on as if he had touched a switch. He raised his hat elaborately to me as the Ballochtorra carriage drove off; I thought that he had not liked the fact that I had surprised his expression of abstraction.

Samuel Lachlan stayed that night at Cluain. After supper, which was late, since the harvest had now begun, and my grandfather had had to go to the fields after Ferguson had left, I waited for the old man to climb the stairs to his bed before I voiced my question. Angus Macdonald had played one weary, absent-minded game of chess with me, and I had won easily. I rose and took the board away without his saying so.

"Grandfather—is James Ferguson trying to buy Cluain? He said to me—"

He cut me short. "James Ferguson will never buy Cluain. Now mind your own business, Kirsty."

233

I was not offended. I took my time about lighting my own candle. "He once gave me a message for you, and I said I would not deliver it. I gave him an answer—I said Cluain was not for sale."

He gave me a long, concentrated look. "You would be right in that. You had no business to say it, but, by God, Gurrl, you would be right."

The weather held, the last of the barley was cut, and the stooks stood upright, drying in the fields. It would be a matter for the Cluain men to gather them into the barns when the seasonal workers had gone. The evening the last field was cut, a long table was set in the neatly swept yard of Cluain, and the food was brought from the kitchen—such mountains of it as I had never seen before—great sides of beef, and pork and ham, turkey and goose, blackberry and apple tarts, cream and sugar, iced cake laced with brandy. That night every soul who had worked at Cluain during the harvest, and the children who had played around their feet, sat down to eat. And this night Angus Macdonald placed no limit on the whisky and beer.

"They will sleep it off," he said. "They will remember it, and next year those I ask will come again. The idlers I notice and mark, and those are never welcome again at Cluain."

I wondered why he always cloaked his generosities with some other motive. I noticed that even that night he did not sit as a familiar with his men, nor beam with paternal pride on them. No one would ever see his face, flushed and triumphant, as I had seen James Ferguson's face on the night of the party at Ballochtorra. The next day, Angus Macdonald would look about his world with a coldly sober eye, and have no indiscretions to regret.

Nor did Morag join that group. After she had helped with the serving and clearing away, I found her standing a little behind me, her face impassive, the glow of the lantern light and the bonfire in the yard burnishing her hair. She looked beautiful, and rather stern.

"You don't join them, Morag?" The whisky had passed around freely, and there was singing, and a piper, and some couples rose to their feet, and went, a little widly, through the sets of some Highland dances.

"Not I, mistress. Young men make free when there's whisky taken."

"One day you'll have to choose your young man, Morag. You'll not spend your life unwed—not you."

"Aye, that is so. But he shall be *my* choice. The man I want. None other." Then she stepped nearer me in the half-darkness; her voice was barely a whisper above the exultant cries of the dancers. "Do you wait for him still, mistress? Do not. He is not for you and surely you must by now know it."

I should have turned and left her, but I didn't. "I don't wait for anyone, Morag."

"You do, mistress. You do. You still think that when she has gone he will turn to you. It is useless. Have you looked on his face these last weeks?"

"I have not."

"Then if you had, you would know. He is a man gone mad. He is lifted out of himself. He always has been different from every other man, but now the difference is greater, and it comes out of him like a light. He walks and he moves—but he sees and feels nothing. Nothing but her . . . There was a poem your grandmother read to me once. I did not understand it, and it made me frightened. Those last words, I cannot remember them clearly, but I was a wee girl, and they frightened me. Something . . . Och, how did it go?—I repeated them in bed that night, and they made me shiver. Something . . . Do you know it, mistress?—Circle him thrice . . ."

Yes, words to make one shiver.

"I know it.

> 'Weave a circle round him thrice,
> And close your eyes with holy dread,
> For he on honey-dew hath fed,
> And drunk the milk of Paradise.'"

"Aye, that's it. The milk of Paradise . . . exactly so. Once a man has tasted that, it seems to me, he will drink no other. He rides out to meet her. They come and go separately, but they meet. To be sure, he must go without his drink these next few days—a taste of the long thirst that is to come. She has gone with Sir Gavin to a grand party given at Cawdor Castle—the Campbell of Cawdor who is chief of his clan. She is not one to be missing such a thing for some lover here in the strath—and no doubt His Royal Highness will be among the company. Those kind, the gentry, they merely smile at the little things they do among themselves to pass the time. The story of her lover here in the Highlands will not go against her when she is among the London crowd—since he is so handsome, and well-spoken, and could pass, the way they saw him that night, as a Scottish gentleman. He is a distillery worker who flies a falcon—a sport for princes and gentlemen. It will make an amusing tale, I've no doubt, this winter in London. Very original, Lady Campbell will be thought. And he—he will break his heart, and he will not look on another woman. He will be waiting on her now—you see, he is not among *this* company. He will spend his days upon the moors, flying his hawk, until she returns. And she will take her time. There is another shooting party to go to, at some place beyond the Moray Firth. Lady Campbell does not neglect such activities. Is she not bored here?—and that is the only reason that Callum Sinclair is chosen to ease her boredom. And he will be waiting, poor fool!"

I should not have listened, but I let the voice, quiet, calm continue. "They meet in the old bothy of his grandfather—Mairi Sinclair's father. He has a part of it new-roofed, and the track to it is so wild and rough that none do ever go that way. It is the track that goes up beyond his own cottage, away up there towards the slopes of Ben Cullen, towards the top of the glen past the waterfall."

"How do you know this?" I choked on the words, but I had to say them. Everything else receded—the firelight, the pipes, the songs, the cries of the dancers; I heard nothing but the voice near my ear.

"I use my head and my eyes, mistress. I was born at Cluain. I know this strath—its every stream and glen almost as well as Callum Sinclair. *I* am no fool, mistress."

I turned and looked at her. "And you think I am!"

A weird little smile came to her lips. "I would not see you commit folly."

*   *   *

It was clear that Morag had found no one among the young men to linger late with over the whisky and beer that night, because she was up before the herdsman had gone to bring in the cows to milking the next morning. I saw her from where I sat by the tower window; she was wrapped against the chill of the early morning in a plaid, but I knew that quick, light high-stepping walk, and the one glimpse of the red hair that the plaid revealed. I did not think about it very much—Morag was like Mairi Sinclair in her ways. They both did the work that was to hand, and no one would have dreamed of questioning their coming and going. So I marked her crossing the yard, and thought no more of it; after that I did not even notice which way she went. My gaze was searching the valley for a sight of Giorsal; but it was overcast, and the clouds were low. In the mist that tumbled down from Ballochtorra there was the feeling of rain—a change in the weather. My grandfather would be in a great hurry today to get in the stooks of barley. Once more Cluain and Angus Macdonald had been lucky; the barley was cut and would soon be in the barns, and the itinerant workers would straggle off in twos and threes that morning, their wages in their pockets, and perhaps some Cluain whisky for those especially favoured. I thought, as I watched that mist blot out the mountains, that if the weather turned cooler now, the malting would begin, and Callum would return to the distillery. And then I cursed myself for the vain wish that lay behind the thought.

But the thought of Callum would not be wiped out—never had been in all the weeks of the summer when I had grown into the world of Cluain. Had it actually begun, I wondered, on that first evening, the first time I had seen him there beneath the beeches below Ballochtorra. No, people of intelligence did not fall in love with the image of a man merely glimpsed. But was love ever intelligent—if I applied logic to my own madness, then all it was revealed as was just that—madness. But why had that moment of first sight remained so intensely with me—and now, when I thought of it, it could have been one of the times when he had ridden with Margaret Campbell, and had, that evening, watched her husband return home from a journey, and known that their freedom to meet must now be more restricted. I grew slightly sick at the thought. I heard again Morag's whispered words of the night before. "They do meet in the old bothy of his grandfather . . ." I did not believe it; they could not have established anything so permanent as a trysting place—nothing except the heather and the moors and deep rock shelters of the Ballochtorra crag. But as an animal will lick and probe its wound endlessly, feeling the hurt and yet not knowing how to stop, so did I. I had to know.

*　　*　　*

I lingered over the midday meal that day, drinking tea after my grandfather had gone back to the office. The itinerant workers had begun to shake off their night's revelry, and with a last hand-out of food from Cluain's kitchen, were starting back along the road to the bridge at Ballochtorra, and from there on to the next strath.

"The weather's turning against them, though," Morag remarked as she stacked dishes on the sideboard. "The next farmers may not be so fortunate as the Master." I noticed that Neil Smith had let Big Billy and his flock out from the pen by the warehouses; the gander was thoroughly enjoying harassing the strangers that he had been kept away from for so long. "Many were on their way very early, to try to get another day's work, at least."

"You were abroad early also, Morag."

She did not pause in her task of loading the tray—the tureen, the dishes, the knives and forks neatly and competently, without noise, as she did everything. "A sick child one of the women had, mistress. And Mistress Sinclair bade me take the little one some extra medicine before the family left. They were to go early, and Mistress Sinclair left it ready for me last night . . . I often do these errands for her. For all her cleverness with the herbs, she is still stiff with strangers. Once she knows which mixture to make, she has little to say to those she treats."

I nodded. It would be so. "It seems odd," I said, really for the sake of talk, "to see so many on the road. The strath will be quiet now they're leaving."

"Och," Morag tossed her head lightly as she lifted the tray, "there'll be enough coming and going for a while—as long as the shooting lasts. But when the snows come it is quiet enough. The gentry all run South then. Ballochtorra will be empty until the late spring. And Sir Gavin may come back alone, for Lady Campbell, they say, has made plans for the fashionable races—Ascot, is it?—and such things . . ." And with that she deftly balanced the tray on one hand, and pulled the door closed behind her, leaving me alone.

Leaving me to the disquiet of my thoughts, which could hardly now be borne, I took my plaid and went into the herb garden, and paced its walks—back and forth, back and forth. The tall thyme and the lavender nodded to me, but leaves were beginning to dry, and blow off the roses that climbed the wall. How quiet and deep the snow would lie on this garden. The white cat ran before me. Out here the cat seemed a kitten again; he scurried among the beds, and lay in wait to pounce on me, to grab with his paws for the swinging end of the plaid. I watched his pranks, and wondered how Mairi Sinclair could have used such an innocent creature to make him seem the instrument of the destruction of that silly white dress, the dress that seemed so far back in time now. What had she used?—the sharpened claws of a rabbit, or a bird? It might have deceived anyone who had not liked cats, had not known their ways. And there I paused. In my turns along the path I had seen that black figure seated in a chair by the kitchen range, Bible in hand, seemingly oblivious of my presence. It struck me that I had never seen her seated before; but she was human like us all, and must need rest. The harvest time had been gruelling for her, and she had tended more than one sick person among the workers. Morag sang by the scullery window as she washed the dishes. The cat made another playful dash for the plaid, and it occurred to me that no one could ever prove that it had been

239

Mairi Sinclair who had wreaked her dislike of me upon that white dress. But Mairi Sinclair knew cats and their ways, and suddenly it seemed too clumsy an effort for her. So I looked from that still black figure by the range, to the shining red hair of the singer by the scullery window. Morag did not like cats—so she said. But Morag said a great deal, and knew a great deal. She said she knew where Callum and Margaret met.

Suddenly I knew what I would do. I already wore my plaid, the new serge skirt sent from Morag's aunt, and the usual boots. I needed nothing else. I went out by the seldom-used door from the herb garden into the road, and then on to the stableyard. Both those watchers, the one by the kitchen range and the one by the scullery window must have heard the slam of the door. The song that had floated over the gentle rattle of the dishes stopped.

Ailis's big eyes greeted me as if she already had foreknowledge of our destination; if she had really known she would have thought me foolish. I slipped an ordinary saddle across her back, and hurried with the harness before John Farquharson could come to help me. If the track was as rough as Morag said, and there was the burn to cross near a waterfall, then I would need both feet in the stirrups.

Big Billy was quiet as I went by the warehouses. Perhaps he was worn out by the morning's exertions; perhaps he just knew that there was no longer any sport to be had from me.

III

It was as Morag had said. The track past Callum's cottage narrowed and went higher, skirting the edge of the burn, and weaving among boulders. The dry weather had dropped the level of the flow, but I could see how it would cascade when the floods of the spring thaws came, or a thunderstorm broke over the mountains. We went higher than I thought, and closer to Ben Cullen—

240

the terrain grew rougher and tighter, the glen narrowed almost to a gorge. The water spilled green on mossy rocks. It would be poor land up here when I did find the bothy poor, starved land that the cousin that Mairi Sinclair's father had willed it to would never have bothered with. The waterfall, when I came to it, was a gentle trickle, but it foamed into a deep pool. Stunted trees tried to meet each other across the burn; I saw the dark leaves of holly and the more tender leaves of laurel. The snow would lie here in the winter, but they would have shelter from the biting winds. I saw the way across, the fording place just below the pool, and if Ailis had not been what she was, and the water so low, I would not have liked to take that path; below it again was a sheer rock fall, and more boulders. But I turned her, and she led me across, calmly, quietly, and, as if she knew the way, she found the track on the other side. In the dry weather the ground had hardened, but this way was not unused. We emerged from the gorge at last, and out on to more open land—that is, free of trees, windswept, wild, and choked with gorse. It rose above my head, and if it had not been for the faintly defined track, I would never have found the place.

It was a tiny Highland "butt and ben"—the traditional two-roomed cottage, rough stoned, and the stones mortared with mud. The searing winds and rains up here had long ago taken most of the whitewashed plaster, and the gorse grew almost to the door. It was no longer land even fit for sheep to graze. I thought of Mairi Sinclair, as I sat quietly on Ailis and looked at it; she had been born here, and been a girl here, had walked this hard track all her young life. I remembered Morag's story of how she had been beaten by her father until the life almost left her. I thought of the last terrible downhill climb, over the ford by that deep pool, bearing the burden of her unborn child. Having made this journey, I now began to understand many things about Mairi Sinclair, gazing about at the grim, barren land, just looking at the place where she had grown from child to young woman, where she had been formed to the hardness of the granite. Hard and passionate, holding forever to whatever belief, whatever love, whatever hate.

I saw all the rest of it too, in those few minutes. I slipped from

Ailis's back, and led her to the second half of the ruined house—that with the gable end almost gone, and a quick roof of boughs and straw thrown over it to form a rough stable. It had been recently used—there were fresh droppings on the ground that the fastidious Callum would never allow to collect in depth, the fresh straw spread; there were two hitching rings fastened to the solid wall that would be the back of the fireplace in the other room; there was even a bag with feed in it. The space where the entry had been to this room from the other had been freshly blocked with stones, and plastered with mud. I left Ailis tied loosely there, and with a useless determination to see it all, I went to the door of the little house. That too, had been freshly mended, the rotten wood replaced, the lintel propped up, the catch was new, though there was no lock. Inside was emptiness—that is, if I could ever see emptiness in the place so imbued with the presence of those who had recently used it. The thatch was loose and rough enough, but sufficient to keep out the rain of the summer—and if it leaked in one place, they could move to another. The stone walls had been swept clean of dust and cobwebs, and newly whitewashed; the floor was the bare earth, but laid deep with clean straw. The old, tiny windows had been sealed so that no birds or rodents could enter and defile this place. I looked at it all with mute acceptance, wanting to close my eyes, and not being able to. I did not even have to touch the ash in the old fireplace. It was fresh and powdery, the smell of peat recently burned lay on everything. As if they were before my eyes I saw them there, Margaret and Callum, their hands upon each other, their white bodies on that clean straw. I saw the passion of Callum's face. "He on honey-dew hath fed, and drunk the milk of Paradise." The milk of Paradise. I turned and closed the door carefully behind me.

Afterwards I didn't remember how long I stood outside, registering the knowledge of what I had seen. There were no more dreams now, no more doubts. Whatever Margaret Campbell felt, I knew that for Callum to have gone this far, then he was gone very far indeed. The instinct I had had about him, that if I only waited he would be mine, had been totally wrong. Not for me would the earth floor be lovingly laid with a blanket of clean hay; not

for me would the peat fire burn. I took it in in a dazed, superficial kind of way; I realised vaguely that with time the hurt would
only be deeper. I stumbled towards the stable end with a kind of
idiot's half-seeing gait. With a rough pull I jerked Ailis's head out
of the feed bag, resenting her, somehow, for eating what I could not
taste.

"Greedy beast! Isn't there enough at Cluain for you!"

She looked at me with indignant eyes, and the slowness of her
walk seemed to mock my impatience. But her broad back received
me as willingly as always, and soon I found my arm about her neck,
and I leaned forward and lightly kissed her between the ears.
"No—I understand. There's not enough at Cluain for me, either."

At an ordinary time I would have noticed it sooner. But we were
down at the ford below the waterfall before I was fully aware of
the tremble through all her limbs; the leisurely pace had become
something more, a dragging, leaden pull—one leg deliberately placed
after the other, and she seemed to wait upon each step, as if not
trusting herself to make another. When we reached the ford she
would not descend to the waterline; she tossed her head in a
violent denial, almost the last energy she seemed to have left. Then
I slipped down from her back, and stroked her head, wondering
how I had not noticed before the sweat beginning to stand out
darkly on her coat. "Ailis?—what is it?" The usually knowing,
intelligent eyes looked at me with dull incomprehension.

I led her with infinite care across the stones of the ford, my
ankles and skirt deep in the water. She did not want to come.
Something in that great spirit had become afraid, confused; the
pool looked so deep, and below the ford the rocks of the gorge
seemed more jagged.

But we were across, and the downward track faced us. I trembled
almost as much as Ailis did, but with a nervous energy and
desperation that were not in her. I dared not mount her again, nor
force the pace. The way was so rough that if once she slipped,
I doubted I would be able to raise her heavy little body. I took off
my plaid, folded it, and laid it along her back, the best kind of
blanket I could devise.

I prayed on the way down that I would see smoke rising from

Callum's chimney, hear Dougal barking in the yard. But the cottage was closed and silent as before, and beyond giving a couple of shouts as I drew near, I didn't waste any time there. Ailis followed me obediently; I had the feeling that if once we stopped she would lose the will to go on. Her eyes looked with a kind of dumb wonder when finally we reached the place where the track to Callum's cottage joined the road. She was not so far gone that she did not know this place, and the firm, level surface of the road that led back to Cluain. Momentarily she raised her head and looked at me. I encouraged her with a light whisper. "Soon home, Ailis. Home!" But the even surface of the road made the trembling wobble of her tough little legs all the more painfully obvious.

Several people came to the doors of their cottages as I passed. There were offers of help, offers to shelter Ailis in their own lean-to stables. But I knew that above all she needed the reassurance of her own place, and I kept her going. It would be time to lay her down in straw when she reached the familiarity of Cluain. A woman sent one of her sons with me, to walk the rest of the way. He put his strong young shoulder against Ailis's, so that now she was supported on both sides. At last we were past the warehouses and into the stableyard. I had sent the lad on ahead to warn John Farquharson, and the loose box was open, and ready, spread with fresh straw. He rushed forward to take off the saddle and harness.

"Easy, lass—easy," he murmured. And to me. "What has happened, mistress?"

I shook my head. "Just bed her down, please, John, and give her nothing. Not water—not anything, yet."

And then I ran, using all the pent-up need of the slowness of the journey back. I burst in at the kitchen door, and Mairi Sinclair looked up from her task of setting the dishes for the supper she and Morag ate at the big scrubbed table.

"Mistress Sinclair, will you come at once . . . please! It's Ailis. There's something terribly wrong with her!"

The dark eyes met mine, lingering only a moment. There was a kind of wonderful assurance in her calm. She nodded. "I will bring what may be needed."

There had been neither foreknowledge or surprise in that gaze.

244

It was the instinctive, experienced unpanicked reaction of the healer to a cry for help. It was from Morag the exclamation came—not of questioning, but a little yelp of pain as she placed her hand carelessly against a hot pan on the range. But by then I was already on my way out, and Mairi Sinclair was reaching for the keys to the herb room, and flinging her plaid about her shoulders.

For the first time since I had come to Cluain we moved together, in common purpose.

*   *   *

We sat there by the loose box through the night, Mairi Sinclair and I. At first she squatted by the pony, feeling her, looking into her mouth, opening the eyelids that wanted to close; she put her hand, and then her ear to Ailis's heart. She stayed there for a long time, saying nothing, just watching; she did not reach for anything from the basket of medicaments she had brought from the herb room. She raised her head only when the shadow of Angus Macdonald fell across her.

"I don't know what it is, Master. Never have I seen anything like it—such strange symptoms in an animal—one thing going against the other. The heart is too fast, and yet she is sluggish. It is beyond my knowledge to prescribe anything for her. I am afraid of what I do not know. You must send for the veterinarian, Master."

"What—have you lost your courage, Mistress Sinclair? You've saved animals that veterinarians have given up."

She was stubborn. "I give my medicines when I believe I know what I am giving them for. When I am ignorant, I say so. And I say I do not know what ails the animal. What I know is that you set great store by this one."

"My granddaughter sets great store by Ailis, Mistress Sinclair. I trust your skills. We will wait until morning before we send for the veterinarian. He will not come this evening, in any case, and if he's been at the bottle, it were better he did not come at all."

"You place a burden on me, Master."

He looked down at her, hardness in his face. "And when has

Cluain not placed its burdens on you, mistress? This is nothing new."

And then he left us.

I remember Morag brought us things to eat in a basket, and hot jugs of tea. My grandfather sent a flask of whisky, which Mairi Sinclair refused, but I did not. We sat on stools and as it grew dark a lantern was brought, and placed between us. On her last visit that night, Morag brought Mairi Sinclair her Bible, and she read it, the pages held low to the light. But I noticed, as time went on, that she almost ceased to read; her lips moved soundlessly over the words, reciting the endlessly familiar chapter and verse. She needed no lamplight.

There was nothing to do for Ailis except to give her the knowledge of our presence. There was little to see, except that from time to time she still trembled, and her eyes were closed, and she sweated under the blankets. Occasionally Mairi Sinclair would rise and kneel beside her, bending low to listen to the heart beat, rolling back the eyelids. Several times she returned to her stool and nodded to me. "She holds—she holds, yet." And when I went to pat the sweating, heavy little body, Ailis would faintly flicker an eyelid, and once she struggled to rise. Instantly, Mairi Sinclair was there beside me, and together we forced the pony back. When she was quiet again, I went and paced the dark stableyard to exercise some warmth back into my cold and cramped limbs. But Mairi Sinclair seemed to need no such thing. Once more, at the coldest time of the night, I sipped a quarter cup of whisky, expecting to find the woman's eyes upon me disapprovingly, but there was no reaction. With her plaid about her head she seemed the immemorial figure of the woman who watches by a bedside, waiting for the hours to decide on life or death. She must have sat in that fashion so many times in her life.

Once, across the glow of the lamp, I whispered to her. "Did you sit this way with William?"

She shook her head. "Your brother did not like me, mistress. It did not calm him to have me by his bed." She said it as if she had known for most of her life that there were some who did not like her, for whom her presence did no good. There was a stoic acceptance of that, as of other things. "It was Morag who sat with him, and fetched and carried. I thought it might help him a little to see a young face beside him. She was very attentive."

We said no more. I sat hunched upon my stool, a plaid and a blanket about me. And before dawn I must have nodded in sleep. I woke with Mairi Sinclair's hand upon my shoulder, her face bent close to mine. I felt a sudden start of fear. "Ailis . . . ?"

"It is past. She sleeps naturally. The heart beat is normal now. The sweat is over. Now I may go and prepare a little bran mash for her, and put a gentle sedative in it. She should rest easy through the day. And when that is done, I will send Morag to warm your bed, mistress. It is time you went to your own rest."

So I stayed alone with Ailis, sitting in the straw beside her, in those last minutes while Mairi Sinclair went back to the kitchen and her tasks. The sky was lightening rapidly. I heard footsteps in the yard, and hastily brushed away the tears that had come as a relief in the privacy of those moments. Neil Smith's red, unshaven face looked down at me.

"The little lass is all right, then?" he said. "You will have her for a long time yet, mistress. These wee ponies live to a terrible great age. Mistress Sinclair has made her right again."

"Mistress Sinclair refused to dose her . . ."

"Then you may be sure that was precisely what she should have done. Mistress Sinclair has strange powers . . . if she will not dose, then it is best left alone. Good morning to you, mistress."

I looked after his squat little figure, wondering why I should ever have disliked him. He and Big Billy were as much part of Cluain as its very walls. And his words came home: "You will have her for a long time yet . . ." Through the open door of the loose box I watched the light grow steadily, outlining the far distant rim of the Cairngorms. The hurt of Callum came flooding back with the sweetness of the relief that Ailis would live. And Neil Smith thought I would be with Ailis at Cluain for a long time, the pain and pleasure of its life mixed as it had been this night.

My grandfather came from his room as I climbed to the tower stairs. I had never seen him in the long flannel nightshirt, and the plaid used as a robe about his shoulders. Perhaps he had spent his own vigil by his bedroom window, watching the light in the stableyard. Perhaps he saw the traces of tears yet on my face, and the relief and the weariness there.

"It is not the last long night you will spend sleepless at Cluain, Kirsty. You learn, Gurrl. You learn."

IV

I came down to eat the midday meal after my grandfather had left. My eyelids still drooped with half-finished sleep; I felt curiously numb. I wanted to drift on the tide of my fatigue and not to think. The thoughts, the remembrances would only bring the probe and the pain again. But before I sat down to eat, I visited Ailis in her box. She was standing, steadily enough, and looking slightly aggrieved; I guessed that Mairi Sinclair had kept her on tight rations that morning, and she was hungry. I didn't dare feed her; just stroked her nose, and fended off John Farquharson's questions about what might have brought on Ailis's attack. I remembered all through the night that Mairi Sinclair had asked nothing except if I knew had Ailis been feeding on any wayside herbage, and to that I could truthfully answer that she had not. I knew the more lengthy questioning would come, and with it I might have to say where I had been. So long as Ailis had recovered, I felt disinclined to tell anyone, not my grandfather or Mairi Sinclair, about the journey up to the ruined bothy above the waterfall.

I did not linger in the stable. I had woken to the sound of steadily beating rain, the straight rain that comes with no wind, and will not move on with the clouds. The stableyard was full of puddles; no one was to be seen out about the distillery. Big Billy kept his flock within their pen. I shook off the Inverness cape I had worn to the stable in the kitchen hall, and regretted the splashes it left on Mairi Sinclair's scrubbed flagstone floor. It was the kind of day that mud gathered on one from nowhere.

Morag served me hot soup, and a beef stew kept warm on the range. It was already growing late; the afternoon seemed dark after the golden days of the harvest. I began to sense what the winter would be like.

As if she knew my thoughts, Morag nodded towards the window and the steady downpour. "Aye, mistress, I'm thinking we may have seen the end of the summer. It is well the barley is in the barns. The days will start to close in quickly now . . ." She took the empty soup bowl, and began to ladle out the stew. "There's not many will be stirring on a day like this."

As she set the plate before me I answered, just to show a kind of spirit I did not truly feel. "Oh, not many, I agree." I dug into the steaming meat. "But everyone is not deterred. I saw Lady Campbell out on her mare—down by the river. Wet through, I'd say. So you see, Morag, perhaps she is less inclined to party-going than you think. She and Sir Gavin must have come directly back from the gathering at Cawdor."

"Lady Campbell?" The lid of the stew dish clattered a little as she replaced it. "Lady Campbell—is that so, mistress? Well, she'll hardly have much company on a day like this. I'll leave the stew, shall I, mistress, if you should like some more? I've the vegetables to see to for supper . . ."

But when I carried the dishes through the kitchen into the scullery it was deserted. The carrots and cabbage were laid there ready for preparing. And Morag's plaid was gone from the line of hanging pegs in the kitchen passage.

*　　*　　*

Perhaps I dozed that afternoon by the fire. I remember I built it up, and took some needlework, which bored me, and settled before it. I wore my cashmere shawl and the red slippers. I would be waiting so when my grandfather came in.

It was odd that this once I should have missed his coming, when so many times I had seemed to know it before the figure on the pony even appeared along the road. But it was the thundering bang of the knocker at the front door which roused me. The piece

249

of sewing had slipped from my lap. I did not wait for Morag or Mairi Sinclair to attend it.

Callum was still mounted on his pony. He was bareheaded, and rain streamed down his face; the bedraggled, mud-caked setter tried to find what shelter he could within the doorway, his tail hanging and a whimper in his throat. I let my eyes slowly travel upwards to Callum's face. I had never seen anything so awful—like stone set in a death mask of suffering.

"The mare has broken a leg. She is up there screaming, and may drown. Have someone go up with a gun and put her at rest. John will know where it is—the place just below the waterfall on the way up to the old Sinclair croft. Up beyond my cottage. Tell them to shoot the mare, and leave her where she is. I will see to the rest."

I could say nothing. One hand held the reins, and with his other arm he supported the sodden burden. The tweed cape I had seen her wear to protect her from the rain as she had splashed along by the river early that afternoon was wrapped about her, covering her head and face. The hand-made boots, fitted to the delicate ankles, hung limply from the familiar cinnamon-tan riding habit; the cream-coloured lace on her petticoat was mud splattered and soaked. I remember the horror of standing there, watching the rain stream off the heels of those boots, the unheeding rain.

"Margaret . . ."

"Dead. I'm taking her to Ballochtorra."

He flicked the reins, and the pony moved off; the dog was close by, as always, but keeping far enough back to avoid the mud kicked up by the pony's hooves. The rain became an obliterating curtain. I seemed paralysed there in the doorway, with the rain dripping down on my head from the eaves. I opened my mouth. The sound that came was a weird low moan, much like the whimper in the throat of the dog.

Chapter 9

The tales drifted to us in the next two days, while the rain hung on the strath, not the streaming, heavy rain of the day Margaret had died, but gentler, sometimes no more than a light sheet of mist. They were not spoken of within the household of Cluain—it was Mairi Sinclair's son the stories concerned, and even Morag knew enough to keep silent about that. It was a very silent household. My grandfather spoke less even than usual; our chess games were concentrated and swift, and ended soon, and I found myself going earlier to the tower room, where Morag had already completed her tasks, and made no excuse to linger. There were no songs rising from the scullery window. Even, for those days, the flow of those who came to seek Mairi Sinclair's aid ceased, as if no one could quite face her with this new, terrible thing which must be borne, but not spoken of. And yet, calmly, the night that Callum had brought Margaret's body to the door, Mairi Sinclair set out in that drenching rain to deliver the first child of a young distillery worker's wife. No one knew at the cottage what had happened, and the talk was normal, at least as normal as it ever was in the presence of Cluain's housekeeper, whom the whole strath held in some awe. But she was gentle, and soothing, and efficient, bringing her own clean linens from Cluain, hanging a sheet soaked in a solution of carbolic at the doorway of the tiny room where the child was born. The grandmother complained that there was unnecessary washing of hands, and too much water to keep boiling. She was outraged that she was not allowed to handle the child or the mother without washing her own hands and wrapping her person in linen which Mairi Sinclair supplied. When the young wife screamed in the pains of labour, Mairi Sinclair gave her a mild infusion of henbane, and the woman was lulled, though still awake.

It was about dawn, they said, and the child had been born and bathed, and slept peacefully, before Callum Sinclair came to the door of the cottage. He refused to come inside, and Mairi Sinclair stood in the road in the rain to speak briefly with him. When she came back inside, they said, she seemed no different—but there never was any telling with Mairi Sinclair. She washed again, took more clean linen, and went to tend the mother. Then finally she gave the young woman a potion that would give her complete sleep, and rest her tired and wracked body; and very gently she moved the cradle where the eyes of the woman would fall on the baby when she woke. In the last moments before sleep, the moments of emotional weariness when the tension and pain are at last gone, the mother lifted her eyes once more to Mairi Sinclair. "I shall call him Callum . . ."

"No, do not call him Callum. You would be better with any other name." And she did not explain.

And in her usual fashion, before she left, she ordered the young father to see that the fire was kept up, but the window open, that his mother was not to smoke her pipe over the cradle of the baby, and everyone who touched the mother or the child must first wash their hands. She left a solution of carbolic.

He dared to grip her hand in thanks, and offer a black shawl which his wife had knitted as a gift against this time, knowing, as they all did, that Mairi Sinclair never accepted money. But she shook her head. "Your mother will find it warming this winter."

"Then let me walk with you back to Cluain." Mairi Sinclair had looked at him with eyes that he swore afterwards he could never forget. She lifted her face, and he saw an expression of pain that not even his wife's trials during the night had produced. "Thank you, I will go alone. It grows light. And what harm can come to me in this strath—now?"

*　　*　　*

I heard this story, and others, from John and from Neil Smith, and the others who moved about Cluain—the outside people who perhaps were hoping in turn to have my version of what Mairi Sinclair herself said, or thought—as if anyone could ever know that. The stories drifted down first from the servants at Ballochtorra, and were added to by those who lived along the road to Callum's cottage.

First there had been the shock of Callum bringing Margaret back to Ballochtorra. He had taken her to the stableyard, because he had to have help in getting down from the pony. But they said that he would not then relinquish her body until he had finally laid it upon her own bed, and he himself had taken a towel and dried that cold, wet face, and tried to smooth the hair. Then he had gone downstairs, to wait on Gavin. What had been said between the two men when finally Gavin had been found, had visited Margaret's room, and come to the library where Callum waited, no one ever heard, even those who had listened too closely. The tone of the men's voices had never risen above a murmur—that, I thought, itself was a deadly thing. That conversation had been ended by the sudden scream of Jamie, who had discovered what had happened to his mother before Gavin had had time to tell him. That scream must have rung in Callum's ears as he left Ballochtorra, riding back past Cluain in the darkness, gathering a lad from the stable, and another from a cottage along the way. With them he had gone to the place below the waterfall where Margaret's mare lay. John Farquharson had hours ago put the mare down with one of my grandfather's guns. He was waiting for Callum at his cottage, and had joined the three on the uphill trek. They had taken a field gate, and dragged the mare's body, lashed to it, down that impossible track, and there, not too far from Callum's cottage, they had dug a pit. It was hard work, and the rain poured down; the hole had inches of water in the bottom. Callum went to the cottage and

253

brought whisky for them, the young lads taking their share. But they said he himself did not drink. And when the hole was ready Callum dismissed them, saying he would do the rest himself. He had, he said, Gavin Campbell's permission to bury the mare. They did not dispute him.

This I heard, and was told, but the rest was my own, and shared with no one but Mairi Sinclair.

She came to me as I lingered over my tea at the breakfast table the next morning. Morag had cleared away all the rest of the dishes, poked the fire and laid more peat on it against the dampness of the day, and had retired, unusually silent. I stayed on, wondering how I would fill the hours of this day, and hoping they would be easier than the sleepless hours of the night before. Would I ride to Balloch-torra and see Gavin? I shrank from it. Would I just ride, and hope to weary myself to the point of sleep? But Ailis was not yet well enough. I felt the dry prickle of my eyelids, and longed for them to close, but they would not. I thought of the one person who had locked in her herb room that which could give me sleep, and give me a little surcease from the pain, and yet she was the one person I could not bring myself to ask it of.

But she came herself. She came quietly, and closed the door of the dining room behind her. Then she moved close to the table, so that her voice was very low when she spoke. I knew where she had been the whole of the night before—Morag had spoken at supper of her having been called to the delivery. The only words I had had from Morag that morning was that the mother was well, and the child strong and healthy, and that Mistress Sinclair had returned just before breakfast and had gone immediately to her tasks at the range. Now I looked at this woman, and wondered if the gauntness of her features was in part due to the many nights she must have spent so, without sleep, and returning at once to her usual tasks. The seamed and cracked hands all at once became a badge of honour.

"Mistress, may I speak with you?"

Involuntarily, I rose to my feet. The occasion seemed to demand it. "What is it, Mistress Sinclair?"

"I spoke with my son this morning, very early. He left this with me." She now lifted her hand and held out the leather pouch that I recognised as the one Callum used to carry the meat for Giorsal, ready against the time when the peregrine had failed to kill, and must be lured back to feed.

"Left it? He has gone? Where . . ."

"I did not ask. It is his own business. He will be back . . . naturally, he will come back." There was no need for her to say anything else; it seemed inevitable that there must be an Enquiry.

She fumbled with the pouch nervously, and I knew how she must have hated having to come to speak to me this way. "He asks of you, mistress . . ."

"Yes . . . ?" I knew I was too eager.

"He asks if you would have the goodness to go and feed the bird. He says the bird knows you, and will take food if you offer it. But you must be careful to wear the gauntlet—there is a second one for the right hand in the shed. And you must not take off the hood."

She put the pouch upon the table. "It should be fed every day until he returns. But you know this, too. There is no one else, I think, he could ask. No one knows the bird so well—now." We both thought of Margaret then, and both recognised the thought. I nodded, and looked away from her, so that she was spared any gesture of thanks. All I heard was the door closing again softly behind her. And then I went and touched the pouch. How well, how cruelly well, Callum knew me, his servant in all but the way I wanted to be.

*   *   *

The second I opened the door to the hut where Giorsal sat on her long perch she bated off—flying up on the jesses, and screaming at me. I stood very still by the doorway until she calmed down and found her position back on the perch again. It seemed miraculous that she did; if she had not, and had hung upside down on the jesses, I would have had to have taken her in my own hands and lifted her back. When she had ceased screaming, I talked softly to her; she seemed almost to know my voice, though I could hardly believe that. What did I say?—I used her name a great deal, but I know I

255

talked about Callum, about Callum and Margaret. I told her about
the baby being born the night before, about Margaret being dead of
a broken neck. Mostly I talked about what it is like to love when
it is not returned. What does one say to a hawk?—I told her that
loving like that was as if she herself could never fly again, as if her
beautiful wing feathers, stretching and spreading in confidence were
suddenly damaged, and she would plunge to earth. After a while, the
hooded head bobbed and nodded to the rhythm of my voice, and I
stepped nearer her, and took up the long feather Callum used to
stroke her with. I kept on talking as I stroked, and at last she stopped
pacing the length of the perch, and stood still, soothed and slightly
hypnotised.

Wearing Callum's gauntlet was like plunging myself into his being;
but it was necessary. I took out pieces of the cut-up meat. At first
Giorsal would not leave the perch, but pulled at the meat from her
stand there; at last hunger and her sense of confidence overcame the
reluctance. She stepped on to the glove, and perched there, tearing
away at the meat greedily, waiting impatiently until the next piece
was offered between my gloved fingers. It was almost more than my
strength to do this—to take the weight of the bird, and the fierce
tugging as she tore at her food. The hardest time came when I had
to offer her the breast of the grouse which was included in the bag—
hawks, I remembered Callum saying, had to have some feathers in
their diet for cleansing their stomachs. As often as I had watched
Callum feed her a plump pigeon on days when it was too windy
or wet to fly her, still I never expected to have to make the offering
myself. Once through the glove I felt the fierce sharpness of her beak,
and the terrible strength of her claws as she sought a tighter grip in
order to tear at the bird. Hooded, she seemed frustrated in the
business of preening and eating the bird, but I could not remove the
hood. She had been trained to eat hooded, and I dared not remove it
because I would never have the skill to get it back on. Callum, as
always, expected a great deal. Thankfully, at last she finished what
was in the bag. When no more food was forthcoming, she reluctantly
went back on the perch; I lowered my aching arm.

I was glad it still rained, and wondered, had it been fine, if
Callum would have expected me to attach the jesses to my own
fist and carry her to the block by the burn, so that she could

bathe and dry off. He would expect anything, I thought—anything but that I lose his falcon. No, I could not risk the block at all, even if Giorsal did without her bathing until Callum returned. I did not know the falconers knots. She could be gone in one swift rise, and hooded, dash herself to death against a tree or a rock. No, he could not have meant that. She must stay safely in the hut, and I must go every day to feed her, and clean the tray under the perch. She must stay safely in her calm, dull darkness, and Callum would come back, because, even more than Margaret, who had been his passion and his madness, he loved this bird.

When it was all over and the door to the hut closed, I leaned against it and found myself trembling with fatigue and fear. But I had held Callum's falcon upon my hand. The smallest welling of improbable pleasure and hope rose in me.

II

It still rained the next day, and when Margaret Campbell was buried those who attended manoeuvred awkwardly with umbrellas, and the slope of the kirkyard was slippery with mud as we made our way from the kirk to the open grave. It was just across the path from where Christina and William lay; it would be the next in the row of shiny marble stones bearing the Campbell name. During the service, at which Gavin had forbidden any music, and for the time he stood by the open grave, almost no one dared to look directly into his face. All the time, in the kirk and in the graveyard, he held Jamie tightly by the hand, even at that grim moment when he had to scatter the customary earth upon the coffin. There were no flowers, except those that Jamie himself carried, the September roses from the garden of Ballochtorra, all of them golden, Margaret's colour. He simply laid them by the side of the grave, ready to be put in place when the grave should be filled. It was then, for the first time, that he turned his face against his father's side, and wept. They hurried down the path to the waiting carriage.

And all the time Gavin did not look right or left, did not seem to see any of the hands of condolence outstretched to him. Neither he nor Jamie wore the customary black, nor were there black bands on hats or sleeves. He had refused to plume the horses of the hearse in black. There were reports of a terrible explosive scene between Gavin and James Ferguson at this lack of conformity to the ritual that death then demanded. Gavin had refused to see those who came to call at Ballochtorra, and James Ferguson had received them alone in the darkened drawing room. The day before Margaret was buried the talk was that Gavin had taken Jamie riding all day on the moors, and so had been absent when the carriage had arrived at Ballochtorra bearing the hereditary chief of his clan, the Thane of Cawdor, who had come to offer condolences. It seemed that even James Ferguson was not quite unshaken by this meeting. The scandal of Gavin's odd behaviour spread.

I watched those two, Gavin and Jamie, hurry down the path. They went immediately into the carriage, and so had to wait for the unhurrying James Ferguson to join them. It was he who lingered for the handshakes, who replied to the formal phrases. He seemed a curiously shrunken figure, the lines newly graven in the red puffiness of his face. He appeared more nervous than sorrowing, his tongue licking his lips. He tarried too long, and suddenly, to everyone's shock, Gavin slammed the door of the carriage, and ordered the coachman to start on. This left Ferguson to ride back in the second carriage with his solicitor. It was known that Gavin had issued no invitations to anyone to return to Ballochtorra with him. But James Ferguson flung them about him like seed; anyone of any consequence was welcome at Ballochtorra to eat and have a dram. He could not stop being James Ferguson.

"Let us away then, Kirsty," my grandfather murmured close to my ear. We tried to slip past the knot of people at the gate of the kirkyard, but James Ferguson had seen us.

"You'll come, Macdonald. You'll come to Ballochtorra."

"Not this day, Mr. Ferguson. My own hearth is close by. I have sent a message to the Master of Ballochtorra of my own and my granddaughter's sympathy. You have it also."

258

Ferguson turned oddly pale. He came very close to us and his words were intended for my grandfather only, but I heard them.

"Telegraph for Lachlan to come. I will be at Cluain tomorrow morning."

My grandfather frowned. "This is a strange time for you to be discussing business matters. It should wait . . ."

Ferguson licked his lips again. "The matter will not wait. It will not wait on anything now."

We were silent all the way back to Cluain, the depression of the kirkyard settled on us like the misty rain; it was not a full year yet since my grandfather had stood there by William's open grave. I shook off my wet coat and hung it in the kitchen passage before I went to the tower room to change into my slippers. The fire was laid, but not lighted. I was tired and cold. I had been up very early to collect the leather pouch which Mairi Sinclair had left ready in the pantry. The walk to Callum's cottage to feed Giorsal had been hard going in the soft ground. But she had greeted me this time almost without fuss, reacting at once to my voice, eagerly looking for the meat, eating her fill from the pieces held between my gloved fingers with greedy ferocity. I wondered how long she would bear with the silent boredom of the hut, how long she would listen to the cries of other birds about her before she began to scream for the freedom of her own flight, for the joy of her own kill, the function for which she had been created. I almost began to envy the simplicity of the instinct of creatures so sure of what they are intended to be. To have no doubts, no choices . . . But my father would have rejected such a doctrine, and have opted, always, for the freedom of the soul to bestow love, even to have it rejected, to suffer if one must. Anything, he would have said, than not to feel; and somehow he and Callum would have made strange agreement on this point. And, to grant her the last justice, so must Margaret Campbell.

*   *   *

My grandfather was waiting in the dining room for the midday meal, still wearing his Sunday clothes. He looked fidgety, and turned to me with an air of relief when I entered. "Well, then—have a dram. It will take the chill off."

I accepted it; but the chill of death was something even whisky couldn't touch, the chill of the look on Gavin's face, the shiver that had wracked me at the sight of the golden roses lying in the mud and rain. The Inverness paper had arrived. My grandfather did not try to keep it from me. There was a picture of Margaret, blurred, though nothing could really blur those lines of beauty. *Baronet's wife killed in fall from horse. Daughter of James Ferguson . . .* The item was small, and brief and discreet, mentioning that Gavin was the heir to the Marquis of Rossmuir, telling again the story the paper had so recently used of the visit of the Prince of Wales. It said nothing of the scandal or surmise that was already raging in the whole district, and reaching the London papers. How she had died, and where, and who had brought her back to her husband was not mentioned.

"There will be a Fatal Accident Enquiry," my grandfather said.

"Yes." I did not want to talk about it, but he persisted.

"The post-mortem certificate was that she died of a broken neck from the fall. That much is simple. But I hear that the police have been making enquiries. It seems probable that they will want an Enquiry before a sheriff . . . Callum Sinclair will have to appear."

"Yes." He spoke as if he had to be sure I was prepared. It would only become more ugly; they would make it more ugly. They would defile that mountain croft that Callum had kept so clean because he had loved Margaret—and they would defile it with words that must come from Callum's own lips.

Chapter 10

———◆◄●►◆———

The next day the clouds scudded past on the rising wind, and after the rain and the mist, I noticed, as I walked up to feed Giorsal, that some of the birches had turned golden, as their leaves shook dry of their moisture. An autumn look had come on the land. Sometimes the sun broke through, reaching into, and suddenly illuminating a deep fold in the mountains, outlining a ridge I had never noticed before. There seemed to be no more guns on the moors; the land was silent, save for the wind.

And when I came back to Cluain it was almost time for the midday meal, and John was rubbing down the Sunday Lad after the trip to Ballinaclash to fetch Samuel Lachlan; the door of the room he always used at Cluain was open, and, as I passed on the way to the tower room, I saw Morag making up the bed. They anticipated a long session with James Ferguson. And it was a trap from Ballochtorra that I saw tucked away at the side of the stables, out of view of the road. James Ferguson was already with them, then, and did not want his presence advertised to those who might pass.

And the usual procedure of James Ferguson leaving while my grandfather and Samuel Lachlan ate together was upset. As I was getting ready to go down to the meal Morag appeared in the doorway, with that silent way she had of suddenly being where one did not expect her.

261

"Excuse me, mistress. The Master is taking his meal with Mr. Lachlan and Mr. Ferguson, and there is business they have to discuss. Mistress Sinclair has sent me to tell you that there is a tray ready for you in the parlour."

"The parlour—but I could have eaten in the kitchen."

I was following Morag down the stairs, and she turned swiftly and shot a look back at me that seemed almost to pity my simplicity. "That would never do, mistress. Mistress Sinclair would never permit it—and the Master would not be pleased." And so I was put back in my place, perhaps an unnecessarily exalted place in Morag's eyes, but nevertheless, my place. And there was the big silver tray laid on the long table in the drawing room, immaculately set with a snowy linen cloth. I sat in one of the straight-back Jacobean chairs, and ate mechanically, aware that the walk had made me hungry, but that food, since that moment when Callum had appeared at the door with Margaret's body cradled in his arm, had seemed to have no taste. This room had a window that looked up the road towards Ballochtorra. I thought about Gavin and Jamie, and I thought about James Ferguson's presence at Cluain's table at this time. Something was stirring, and I would only know the nature of it when my grandfather chose to tell me. But it came to me then that, with Margaret dead, Gavin would not leave the strath. I suddenly knew how it would be. He would take no more money from James Ferguson. If Margaret's dowry reverted all to her father, or was placed in trust for her son, I knew that it would matter nothing to Gavin. If he had to walk out of Ballochtorra, with Jamie, and toss the keys to James Ferguson, he would do it. I thought of that poor bit of farmland, still undrained, that he had dreamed of that day with me. This might be the way the tenth baronet of Ballochtorra, and heir to the Marquis of Rossmuir, would choose to live, eccentric, and out of his time, but his own man at last, and his son his own.

The meeting between the three men continued all afternoon. Twice I saw Morag cross the yard to the office with the loaded tea tray, but finally, as the hour for supper drew near, I heard the trap from Ballochtorra being made ready. My grandfather and Samuel Lachlan accompanied Ferguson to the trap; there was still some talk among them, but no handshakes. Ferguson gave an odd backward glance as the trap drove off, but the two men were already deep in talk again, and didn't even seem to mark his going. There was late sunlight for the few moments it took them to cross the yard to the house; my grandfather's white mane of hair was silvered in it, and stood almost upright in the wind. I noticed then that little piles of leaves had collected in the corners of the usually immaculate yard.

Downstairs the two men gave me the sudden impression of old age at the end of a long day. They had almost finished their first whisky when I came in, and I thought that it had been mostly drunk in silence, as if each needed the respite. Samuel Lachlan's black clothes were greenish in the lengthening rays of sun that streamed in the window; he got to his feet momentarily, and adjusted his glasses on his nose, which, I suppose, was the only sign of pleasure he ever permitted himself. But he said to me what I might have said of him. "You look tired, Kirsty."

My grandfather answered for me. "Och, it's the harvest, and this damnable business at Ballochtorra. Well"—as if that disposed of the matter—"it is a drying wind. We need it after the rain." To back up his statement the window rattled suddenly in a sharpening gust.

They took their second dram more slowly, but my grandfather did not have his usual place in the settle before the fire. It was very uncharacteristic of him, the way he paced between the window and the sideboard, his glass left there, sipping each time he came back to it. There was a kind of frenetic mood upon him that I had never witnessed before; something either troubling or exciting him. I wished it were not so; I wished, too, for a respite, a time of peace. There was yet much to come—so much more. All that the Inverness paper had hinted was yet to come.

Finally, it was Samuel Lachlan who spoke. "Kirsty—there is something we have to say to you—"

My grandfather spun around from the window. "Not yet, Samuel. Not yet."

He blinked through his spectacles. "We agreed that she should know, Angus. We agreed."

"Very well. But let us have our dram, at least, man. We've earned our spell away from it—"

"Christina must know."

"A while yet, man—a while!"

Morag brought in the first serving dishes, and Samuel Lachlan hurried to take his place at the table. How he must look forward to Cluain's food after those meals sent round from the chophouse. But when the food was set before him, he seemed less interested. He ate slowly, and forgot to have gravy, forgot even, the endless salt he craved. He was so slow, in fact, that Morag put her head inside the door several times to see if we were ready for the next course.

At last he spoke, and my grandfather seemed content to let him do so.

"Kirsty—Ferguson is going broke."

"Going—" Then the door opened, and Morag appeared once more. This time she removed the meat dishes, and I went to the sideboard and served the apple tart that Samuel Lachlan loved. Morag closed the door, and he poured the cream with absent-minded lavishness.

"Going broke," he repeated.

I could hardly believe it; did people who had castles and yachts on the Clyde go broke? But James Ferguson was clever, a self-made man. He could surely never fall into some pit he had not seen before his feet.

"Why?"

"Stretched too thin. There must be two dozen distilleries that have extended him credit—for far too long. He has accepted orders from America, with some advance payment—orders for millions of gallons that he now can't fill. He has indulged in overproduction of his own patent grain whisky, storing it up, extending, advertising, sending his salesmen all around the world. And now the malt that he needs for his blends—from the cheapest to the best—is locked up in warehouses all over the Highlands, and he hasn't the money to buy out the stuff, or pay the Excise on it. Even if the distillers would extend credit still further, there's still the Excise, and Her Majesty's Excise doesn't give credit—and the tax is the largest part of the bill."

"But didn't he *know* this would happen?"

"He knew—and didn't pay much attention to it. There was a big loan being raised in the City—London. He won't admit so much, but the merchant bankers he was getting it from have done a more thorough investigation of the affairs of James Ferguson than he thought possible. The loan is now refused. He has creditors everywhere, and no cash. It will be, he now says, only a matter of days until the news of the refusal of the loan leaks out. He has been up and down the Highlands begging for more credit, begging for the distilleries to pay the Excise on what he takes from the warehouses, and once the whole picture is put together there will be a rush to sell by the shareholders. Once that starts, the share prices will drop to the bottom. If he ever had the chance of raising money by pledging his own shares, they themselves are about to be made almost worthless. *That* is why he will be broke."

"And he owes Cluain?"

My grandfather broke in. *"No* one owes Cluain. Not after the first twenty years did anyone ever get a penny's worth of credit from Cluain. I am not in business to store unpaid-for whisky in my warehouses. The buyers come, and they pay, literally, cash on the barrel. Even the great James Ferguson has had to pay. I store it for them, and they are free to take it after the legal minimum, and they pay the Excise."

"Then he has whisky paid for and stored with you. Why doesn't he use it?"

"He has none. Not a gallon. His has all been taken. In this last year he has drawn out every barrel he owned. Telling me, always, that his business with England and America was so good he had to make up his blends as young as he could, to meet the demand. But I had a suspicion all along that he was drawing so quickly on his stock here because it might have been the only whisky he had already paid for. Why—I've even had trouble getting him to return the casks . . ."

"Then if he owes Cluain nothing, why does he keep coming? What has all the talk—"

Again Morag was back, removing the tart plates, placing the cheese, leaving the tray with tea. She was as quiet and deft as always, but I thought it odd that she came so often. Usually the task of clearing was done by myself. For some reason Samuel Lachlan liked to be waited on by me—perhaps he enjoyed the change after the years of boys rushing over with his tray from the chophouse. Lachlan waited quietly, took his Cheddar made in Mairi Sinclair's dairy, and piled the butter on her brownish golden biscuits. His poor false teeth worked hard at the task. He even sipped his tea a little without talking any more. I resigned myself to wait. His former impatience to tell me whatever was to be told had evaporated. There was enough to think about, besides savouring the relief that Cluain was not touched by James Ferguson's madness. I had not known until that moment how much store I had placed in the independence of Cluain, its self-sufficiency. There was danger there, of course—the kind of dangerous pride that my grandfather exhibited, his satisfaction at being able to snap his fingers at the world, and owe no man. But he had worked for it—oh, yes, he had worked for it. And now James Ferguson stood helpless in the ruins of his own monumental pride. As if Lachlan read my thoughts he spoke suddenly.

"Ah, well, that is often the way of it when a man gets in deeper than he knows." At last he was finished with his cheese and his tea, and he stood and moved back to his place at the settle. At once my grandfather poured two more whiskies, and handed one to Lachlan. "Yes," Lachlan said, as if he had never stopped, "if one will build castles and restore churches, and have a private railroad carriage, and a house in Belgrave Square, then there must be something very solid behind it. I have followed his career with interest—" He rubbed his thin nose. "Yes, great interest. He was a wealthy enough man when his daughter married Campbell, but after that he would have had to be much more than merely wealthy to support the kind of things he did. But he had a name for making money, and he paid good dividends, and the shareholders came running. He built and he expanded. How much he speculated in other things one does not know. But I—well, I myself was never tempted to buy a single share of Ferguson's. No, not a single share." He recited all this carefully, as if again retelling to himself, and perhaps for my benefit, a lesson long ago learned. Lavish spending disturbed him greatly. And yet I could not hear a note of satisfaction in his recital. He did not rejoice in the downfall of James Ferguson. Any edifice that crumbled was another attack on the sacred idea of capital.

He sipped his whisky quietly, waiting for Morag to be done with the last of the dishes, and when she was gone, finally, the crumbs swept from the table, the tray removed, he resumed.

"Yes, Kirsty, there has been much talk. Very much talk. And I have myself travelled too much for my age in these past weeks, in the matter of James Ferguson. I do not like too much to commit myself to paper in making enquiries. Discretion, and a quiet talk over a dram, with nothing recorded, is the better way. I have been back and forth between Cameron's and Macquarie's, and both distilleries are very inconveniently located. But both are solid— very solid. Solid men of business in each of them, and each held by the family. They keep their books and do their business at the distilleries, and there are no castles. They keep good horses, but there are no thoroughbreds in their stables. The young men of the familes marry sensibly, and settle down in new houses built near the distillery. Their wives keep good tables, but there is no waste. They fatten their own pigs, and silk dresses are for Sundays only. Yes, they are solid."

I did not much like the sound of it. Where, in all the respectable mass, the great solidity, was there room for a falcon to spread her wings, to swoop, to soar, to stoop? Where would there have been a chance for a man like my grandfather to come from his poor Western Isle, and declare that on this piece of land he would make his kingdom? Was the day, then, of one's own private kingdom gone—was there no room, any more, to be free. No, I didn't like the sound of all these solid people.

"Then why does James Ferguson talk to you? He owes you no money. Why have you had to make these visits to Cameron's and Macquarie's on his behalf?"

"I did nothing on behalf of James Ferguson. I simply did not trust what the man was saying. He spoke for others, and he was in a state where he might have said anything—"

"But to what purpose?"

267

Now Samuel Lachlan gestured to my grandfather, as if deferring to him as Master of Cluain. "He proposes, Kirsty, that Cameron, and Macquarie, and Cluain should join together to take on the business of Ferguson's. If the three distillers announced that they were joining up with Ferguson, Distillers, then the rest of the world need never know how much he was giving up in order to have us come in. Cameron and Macquarie are bigger than Cluain—ours would be a minority share, but a biggish share. And for Ferguson it would be a face-saving action. It would stop a run—at least this is what we think—by the shareholders. James Ferguson would have a seat on the board, for the time being, but with little or no voting rights, it would be nominal. We have his word, and would have it in a private letter from him before we moved farther, that he would resign in about six months' time, giving ill health and his daughter's death as reasons. Face-saving only. His name would still remain. But Ferguson's would belong to Cameron, Macquarie, and Cluain."

I gasped in utter disbelief. "But Ferguson's is huge, isn't it? Would it . . . well, it would need a great deal of money to keep it going. Can Cluain . . . ?" I didn't dare ask the question of these two men.

Samuel Lachlan answered me. "It would be close. Yes, there's no doubt it would be close. But we would be getting Ferguson's at a rock-bottom price. We would have a great organisation for blending and distribution already made—yes, and the market lies that way, Kirsty, no matter how the malt men may despise the product. And as to Cluain's position in this . . . as I said, it would be tight. But do not think Cluain has no resources. They have been carefully built up, husbanded. Like Cameron's and Macquarie's, all our goods are not in the shop window. Your grandfather . . . well, Angus?"

"No, not in the shop window, but in good, fine whisky. We have a certain production run each year, Kirsty. So many hundred thousand gallons. For the last ten or so years I have undersold the production run. I have my own warehouse—just casks marked with numbers and the workers do not know which distillery they have been sold to. In fact, they are Cluain's own. Unsold. The finest twelve-year-old malt, the first of it just ready, and each year more and more added, and maturing. And out of the operating profits I have set aside the Excise tax. That, and a little more besides, is Cluain's capital. And then there is Samuel. He will come in with more capital, if I wish to move forward with the matter. But not one of us—not Cameron's, Macquarie's—will move without the other two. And if we don't move, Ferguson sees no prospect of making an arrangement with others—and has not the time for it. He will simply go bankrupt—that is, he will go bankrupt publicly. The other way he has a chance simply to disappear, to fade out. In the end, as far as money is concerned, it is the same. He is broke." My grandfather was not like Lachlan; he did not even try to keep the satisfaction out of his tone.

I pressed my hands together, and rocked forward, looking into the fire. "And a few weeks ago, he was telling me that he would buy Cluain any time you wanted to sell—the Prince's visit—the cost of it! And all the time he was waiting on a loan simply to stay in business."

"A kind of madness," Lachlan said. "It got to the point where he could not stop. James Ferguson has never been known to gamble at cards or horses, or anything else. But a gambler he is. He is so used to everything coming as he tosses the coin, that he is quite unable to stop it. He went on spending like a fool, when the coffers were empty. A dangerous man—dangerous to himself, and to everyone associated with him. He used shareholders' money for reasons other than business. If we do not proceed, he will be lucky if he is merely bankrupt. There could be a gaol sentence for misrepresentation."

I suddenly looked up, looked at my grandfather. "Then why —why, in God's name, are you even prepared to associate with him? Even if he is powerless, what is it you are looking for?"

"Looking for . . . ?"

I gestured to the room, the whole world of Cluain about me, and my voice rose. "Isn't this enough? What more could you want?"

"Och, I was afraid you would not understand. I thought you had more of a head for business than this. Understand me, Kirsty. This is a chance to own Ferguson's. To be a world name in whisky. To—"

"To be a fool!" I almost screamed the words at him. "Wasn't this what James Ferguson first dreamed? To be a world name in whisky. Well, he's that, and it's lying in ruins about him. He is so fevered he cannot even properly mourn the death of his only child. Ferguson's is his child. That, and his pride, are more to him than anything else. And you tell me—two old men"—it was cruel, and I saw my grandfather's face flush with anger and affront—"that this is what you are even tempted into. *Why?* You have a whole world here. No one can touch Cluain. No one may lay a finger upon it, except by your leave. You have a pile of gold stored up there in those warehouses, and you are going to gamble it just as James Ferguson would have done. You have been Master of Cluain since the day you first won the deed to it from the Campbells. Are you now going to *give* Cluain to some little group that goes under the name of *Ferguson?* You tell me there are young men in the Cameron and Macquarie families. Do you think they will let you have your own way completely? Will you be able to run Ferguson's the way you've run Cluain?—everything exactly as you want it? No compromise?—no letting down of standards? Your precious twelve-year-old will be thinned out to nothing to help out the pile of rotgut neutral spirits that James Ferguson has run off. The name of Cluain will mean nothing. It will be *Ferguson's!* Those young men—those solid young men —will be here, looking over your stock, selecting what they want, three-year-old, four-year-old. Breaking your heart. And because you will be tied to them, hand and foot, you will not be able to stand out against them. You will go with them, because you have to. And *why?* Forget Ferguson—why do you hand over your heritage to the Camerons and Macquaries? They will decide, whether you like it or not, that Cluain can expand—can produce more whisky, and still more. There will be more stills put in, and men to manage them. And Cameron and Macquarie men at that. And what will become of you . . . ? Where will the Master of Cluain be then?"

I thought he cringed a little, but his face was turned away from me. "And what else is there to do? Where else am I to turn? If William had lived—but he didn't. There is only you . . .

and you're a woman." Now he looked back at me, and his tone was nearly one of pleading. "It is mostly for your sake. You have said we are two old men, and that we are. What will you do when neither of us is here?"

"Are you saying Cluain will be mine? Are you saying that precisely?"

He paused. "It is no easy thing for a woman—especially a young woman—to run a business. It is not a woman's world. But there is a prospect . . . Well, there is one of the young Cameron men yet unmarried. Personable, Samuel says. Intelligent. He has travelled, Kirsty . . ." His tone grew more eager. "He has been in America, and places like Paris and Rome. He is very sharp in business, they say. He would make any young woman a fine husband. You could do much worse, Kirsty. And Cluain—"

"No!" My hands went to my mouth to try to keep down the words that came rushing. But I heard myself screaming, screaming as if I had been struck. "No! You must be mad! The two of you— mad old men! Do you think I could marry because it would fit in nicely with the whole plan. Tell me! Tell me if that was part of all your visting back and forth? Oh, God!—that is what happens to women in China! Do you think my father would have permitted such a thing—even thought of it?"

"It is not unknown," my grandfather said curtly. "Marriages are arranged on much worse terms than these." He was stiff and embar- rassed; the value of property was being questioned, and the value of Cluain being weighed against the capricious wishes of a young woman. I began to see what this madness was; if William had been here there would have been none of it. Two old men, I had said. It was true. They were two old men and between them they had only me with which to envisage the future—me, unmarried, without a child, without a son . . . "Cluain is no mean dowry, Gurrl."

"Dowry! Whoever asked for a dowry? And given on condition that I marry a good solid young man who has travelled, person- able, was what you said, wasn't it?—and no doubt wearing a good suit."

271

"There is something wrong with a good suit?" Samuel Lachlan chided me.

"No—nothing. But everything . . ." I closed my eyes and there was the vision of a man in a kilt growing frayed at the edge, and a sheepskin dark with rain. "No, nothing wrong with a good suit—but I cannot marry a good suit."

"You're hasty, lass. You need time to think."

"And is there time to think?" I flung back at him. "You tell me it is a matter of days before Ferguson's position will be known to the shareholders. And in a matter of days I am expected to say I will marry someone I've never seen—who has never seen me? Grandfather, did you set me down in the balance sheet of Cluain? I wonder what price I was valued at? Was my stock high or low?"

"It was never a precise condition . . . just a suggestion. The young Cameron had heard of you—from others, it seems. Husbands like that are not picked up for the asking. You would show good sense to consider—"

"I'm showing the best sense I've ever done in my life. You remember your mother, Christina? Did *she* marry where she was bidden? Did she found a family, and carry on after her husband was dead? Did she begin a distillery out of nothing, and lose it for no fault of her own? Would you say she lacked the courage of a man—or three men? Did she breed you—from a husband of her own choosing? I tell you I will not be part of the balance sheet. If you make your arrangement with Cameron's and Macquarie's, then do it. But count me no part of it. If I have to leave Cluain tomorrow, then I'll leave. I will not be sold as part of the furnishings. On these terms, I do not want it. I can't lose what I never had. You can't take it away from me."

"Truly spoken, mistress. Who would have supposed you had such fire in your guts?"

We all turned. As we had talked together the room had grown darker, and there was only the light from the peat logs to glow upon our faces. It had been sufficient; in these last minutes we had not really wanted to look at one another. But now we turned. Morag stood with a candle by the open door, and in silence she moved forward with her graceful gestures, and laid the candle down on the sideboard. Her cap was off. The red hair streamed in its wonderful abundance on her shoulders.

"How right you are, mistress, to know you cannot lose what was never yours."

For a moment longer my grandfather was shocked into silence. Then his voice rose with a growl of fury. "What do you think you're about, miss? What kind of business is this?"

"The business of Cluain, Master. The business of Callum Sinclair."

"And how so his business? And what do you know of it?"

"How would I not know of it? Do you think I am blind and deaf? Have I carried trays to you these past weeks in the office, have I served you here all day with Mr. James Ferguson, and not known what was discussed, what was going on? Because women wait on men, Master, it does not mean that they must be stupid. And I would have had to be deaf indeed not to have heard Mistress Kirsty's fine speech of what she would not do for you. Women continue to surprise you, do they not, Master?"

"Impertinence, miss! You get above yourself. Where is Mistress Sinclair? Does she not know how to keep order in her kitchen?"

"Mistress Sinclair has retired to her room, Master. She has had long nights recently, and has need of rest. But she does keep order in her kitchen. I have learned very much from Mistress Sinclair. At this moment I should be washing the dishes in the scullery. There are times, though, that the dishes must wait on other things, and Mistress Sinclair disobeyed. *She* does not own me, no more than you do."

My grandfather took a deep breath, as if struggling for patience. It would not have surprised me to see him rise and give Morag a smart clip on the ear. For a second he glanced at me, and then back to Morag. Did he think that some spirit of perverse madness had suddenly possessed all the females of Cluain. What had happened to his well-ordered world? Samuel Lachlan was leaning forward in astonished wonder.

"You are bold, miss, and you try my temper. What *have* you come to say—what is all this nonsense about women? And again,

273

what business is it of yours what we discuss here, or in the office? What business?"

"If you had listened, Master, you would have heard my answer. It is the business of Cluain. And the business of Cluain is Callum Sinclair's business. Must I say more, Master? Will you put right what should have been put right years ago, or will you have me force your conscience further? Will you open the book yourself, Master? I have waited for this time—for years I have waited. But there was always the grandson. And then he was dead, and there was this girl, your granddaughter. And there is also Callum Sinclair. Will you speak now, Master?"

In the candlelight my grandfather's face had turned a yellowish colour; it was not fury that he struggled to control now, but an emotion that threatened to make him incoherent. A garbled sound came from his throat. For an instant he clutched at his chest, as if in pain, and then his hand went back to grip the side of the settle. There was no queston now that he might rise to strike Morag. I did not think he was capable of moving.

At last his words came, in a kind of gasp.

"Kirsty—Kirsty, fetch Mistress Sinclair!"

I ran. He seemed to be ill—and yet it was more than that. I had forgotten to bring a candle—the light from the open door reached only halfway up the curve of the staircase. From there I groped and fumbled; in the passage at the top the faint light from the sky helped me. I counted the doors to reach Mairi Sinclair's and I pounded loudly to wake her.

"Mistress Sinclair—will you come? My grandfather asks for you to come!"

But she had not been asleep. Almost immediately she flung open the door, and I had a glimpse of a bare, stark room, without comfort. There was a fireplace, but she did not permit herself a fire. A candle burned on a small table, and a single, straight-backed chair was before it. The familiar black book lay open. She wore the same long white nightgown and the plaid in which I had seen her on my first night at Cluain. Her black, silver-streaked hair was loosed, straight, and as shining as Morag's.

"The Master is ill?"

274

"I—no, I don't think he's ill. But he asks you to come—at once."

Without a word she went to the table and picked up the candle. Shielding it against the draught of her movements she lighted me down the stairs. Then she stood with her plaid tightly drawn across her in the door of the dining room, unwilling to come farther.

"Come in, Mistress Sinclair. Sit down." She moved farther into the room, but she ignored my grandfather's motion towards a chair.

"There is something wrong?"

He gestured helplessly. "It concerns you."

"It concerns Cluain, Master," Morag interjected. "And it concerns Callum Sinclair." She stood exactly as she had been when I left, facing the two men with no sign of faltering in whatever she had come to do. I had never seen such beauty upon her—the apricot-stained skin, and the glowing eyes. In the deep quiet that attended her words she turned and went then to the table where the big Bible had its place. It had always seemed to me a part of the furnishings of the room, built like the walls themselves, immovable. But Morag lifted it, heavy even for her strong arms, and brought it to the exact centre of the dining table on my side, placing the brassbound edge precisely parallel to the line of the table.

Mairi Sinclair's face clenched in anger as she observed all this. She made an instinctive movement, which she checked, as if she too longed to strike Morag. "How do you *dare?*" she demanded of the girl. "No one touches that Book!"

"I dare because you do not dare, Mistress Sinclair. I would dare very much for the sake of Callum Sinclair."

"And what have you to do with my son? What has *this* to do with him?"

"I make your son my business, mistress, because that is the way I would have it. I must do for him what you have so far failed to do. Have you not waited, also, mistress? Or have the years made you fearful? Have you stayed silent all this time only to find now that you have no tongue in your head? Have you believed that Cluain must come to him because it is his due—his right? Did you trust the final decency of this old man?—his

275

honesty? Well, I have to tell you, mistress, that there is no honesty in him. He and Mr. Lachlan between them are settling the future of Cluain, and your son's name is not even mentioned."

Mairi Sinclair looked around at all of us slowly. "What the Master does is his own affair. It has nothing to do with my son."

Morag threw back her head with a gesture that set the candle flame flickering. "Fool! You are a fool! *This* is the time. If you do not speak now it will be gone forever. *Demand!* It is his!—and they are giving it away! You have allowed yourself to be a servant all your life. But you cannot let that happen to your son, cannot let him be so cheated. How can you have that Heaven you pray for if you have done so ill by your own flesh? I tell you, if Callum Sinclair were not from home I would have him here this moment, and then see if any of you would dare to pass him by! Well, Master, will you speak? Will you open that Book and let all here read, or shall I tell them what I have seen written?"

"Bitch!" he said. "Prying, deceitful little bitch! How have you read from that Book?"

"The keys, Master—the precious keys of Cluain. Always kept about your person, and yet trusted to Mistress Sinclair and then to myself because it never seemed to enter your head that I could be other than she. Do you not understand that what is locked must always rouse curiosity? While the mistress was alive it was never locked. Often in this room, when I was a wee girl, I can remember her opening it. In her failing years she read from it often. I learned some of my letters from that Book. She was very patient with me. I can remember her pointing out where the names of your two grandchildren were recorded. I saw your daughter's name—the day she was born, the day she married, the day she died. All written there. I could barely understand all those names, but I learned to read them—William and Christina. And then the mistress died, and the Book was locked. And never opened—never! You do not remember the times, Master, when you were ill, and you sent me to fetch a dram of whisky? And gave me the keys, to be returned to your bedside at once. Did you think I would not remember the brass key with the fancy end to it—I had thought it so beautiful when I was a wee girl, and the mistress had shown

276

me how cunningly it locked the big Book. Children do not forget secret things. I was fourteen years old when you first trusted me with the keys. No doubt you thought of me as just such another as Mairi Sinclair. But I am not. I saw the little brass key, and I opened the book, and I looked at the back where the names are written. I held the knowledge to myself, and I waited. Shall I speak now, Master. Is there need to?"

"No!" Mairi Sinclair gestured violently towards my grandfather. "What have you done? What wrong, foolish thing have you done! I said never—*never!*"

But he was shaking his head. "It was done long ago. The night my wife died and I sat down to record her death, I knew that since I could no longer hurt her, there was something else to be recorded. What I hoped for then, I do not know. I could see the names of my two grandchildren there—but they were far away in China, unknown, perhaps never to be known." Before he put his hand in his pocket to bring out the bunch of keys, I saw him again hold his chest. Then he extended the keys to me. There was infinite weariness in the gesture.

"Here, Kirsty. Open it and read for yourself. We need no more talk from this meddlesome piece here."

"Angus . . ." Lachlan said.

"It is done, Samuel. What has been will never be undone. Kirsty will open it."

I sat down where Morag had placed the Bible. The key was small but easily recognisable by its elaborate design. But the whole bunch was cumbersome, and I fumbled as I tried to insert the small key in the lock. As if she were performing any other service, Morag calmly lighted another candle, and brought it to the other side of the Bible. Then, with a turn, the locked clasp was free.

Morag could not restrain herself. She leaned across me. "There, at the end!" It was her hand that turned the printed pages until the plain ones were reached. "You see, it goes far back in the family. It is the Macdonald family Bible, not the Campbells." Her finger traced eagerly the history of a family, written in many hands, over many generations. "You see here, how it traces back to Ranald, younger son of John, First Lord of the Isles. The

277

mistress taught me it all—she was proud of it. How it goes, splitting and splitting, and it grows too wide and far-placed for any to keep account of. So it becomes just this family—the Master's own family of Macdonald, on Inishfare. It is all set out. Here—his great-grandfather, his grandfather, his own father, his brother—himself. When they were born, when they died. His daughter, born here at Cluain, and her death. Your brother's birth, in China, and your own, and then recorded last of all, long beyond its time, his own son, the date and birthplace . . . Cluain."

The last entry was in my grandfather's hand. *Callum Sinclair Macdonald*. And the date of birth given was nearly thirty years ago.

I took my hands slowly off the Book, and looked at my grandfather.

"It is true?"

He inclined his head. "It is true."

The sickness and the pain were almost beyond bearing. I clamped my lips together so that I would not cry out, but there was no controlling the cold trembling that took possession. I wanted to run from here, and yet my legs would not lift me from the chair. Where could I hide from the gaze of them all? I turned my head from side to side, shaking it like a bewildered animal. The truth of all that I had ever sensed between myself and Callum was now laid cruelly bare, the feeling of something forbidden and dark that had not, could not be, fully comprehended. A blood relationship so close, and yet when I had pulled him down against me in the heather, he had been the sum of all my desires. I had hunted and followed him through the strath all summer. He had tried to shake me away, and he had not succeeded. What perverse blackness had possessed me, like an evil, rank growth. Half-brother to my own mother, and yet I had longed for him as a lover, had schemed and planned for him as a husband. How twisted and perverted could natural desires grow?—and grow from innocence? I had told myself that I could outwait all other loves that possessed him, and I had endured even the knowledge of his love for Margaret. I had said I would be stronger than that knowledge, overlook it, forget it; I knew how to wait. Well, now I knew that

278

the waiting was over—and still it went on. The hunger was there, and must be denied. It would be forever. I had lost, not only my hope of love, but the very right to feel it. It must not be offered; it could never be accepted.

Dumbly I read again those words. *Callum Sinclair Macdonald.* There was no wiping them out. Why was I even surprised to see them? The truth, revealed now, was startlingly plain. Why had I not seen it? I had been blinded because Callum so much resembled Mairi Sinclair. But were not the eyes, and the skin and the hair as much my grandfather's—and William's, and my own? When I had looked in the mirror, why had I only seen William's face, never Callum's? The blindness of love was infinite.

I found the strength to get to my feet. I could even face them all, and when I looked around I wondered why I should have been so concerned only for myself. Others felt, and they suffered. The impact of those words was visible about me; in those moments Samuel Lachlan had risen and had come to look for himself, because, in fact, no one had actually spoken that name. Now he shuffled back to the settle, and he showed his trembling, as much as I.

For me, then, Samuel spoke. "Why did not you tell us, Angus? It would have made a difference."

"Would have." My grandfather looked about at us all. "Aye, it might have made a difference if it had been right at the start. But I was a coward then, and I let myself listen to Mairi Sinclair's words. She would have none of it. She would not have the scandal settle about my wife and daughter. I might never have known, even, that she was with child, if her father had not beaten her to the point where the whole strath knew of it, and knew why he had beaten her. She was bent on going away, but my wife insisted on taking in this young girl, and I had not the courage to say what was the truth. Mairi Sinclair threatened then that if I spoke to my wife she would go—she would be off to Glasgow, or someplace else, and get work there, and no one would ever hear of her again. Thinking what wrong I had already done her, did I have the right to bring more hardship on her and the child? At least they would be safe and sheltered at Cluain. Then all I

279

could hope for was that the child would be a girl. A girl would have been easier to provide for. But it was a son—my only son—and I could make no claim to him then. Cowardice denied me what I had most wanted in the world."

For a moment he leaned back and closed his eyes, and there was remembrance of times long past, but always lived with. "It happened because I stayed some nights up on the shielings in those years. I could afford less farm help then, and I used to take my turn up there to let one of the older ones come down to his family. Mairi Sinclair was there also. It is to my shame that I allowed myself to do what I did, but I feel no shame, and have never felt shame, in having loved her. It was the only time we were together—that one summer. Since she has been in this house she has lived alone. When my wife died, I asked her to marry me, and thus her son could, by adoption, become my own. But she would have none of it. Some rubbish about refusing to profit from her sin. As if it could be counted profit . . . So many years had passed. It would have been a marriage in name only, and she refused the falsehood of it, and I had to respect that. And as for sin . . . she was not guilty, that girl of long ago. Seventeen, she was, and innocent. Intelligent and knowing, far beyond her schooling. Long black hair . . . She said I had no rights in her life, or her son's. And I had not. The man who acts as I did, has no rights. He can ask, but he cannot demand."

Shakily, Samuel Lachlan motioned me with his glass. I went and poured another whisky for him and didn't care, nor did anyone seem to notice, how much I spilled.

"But your *son,* Angus! A son for Cluain. I remember . . . I remember the time your wife took Mairi Sinclair into Cluain and I did not think it wise. But your wife was a very determined—and a very soft woman. I remember the child being born. If I had known . . . It would have been better, Angus, if you had spoken. *I* could have done something! *I* could have persuaded Mairi Sinclair that she owed something to her son . . . This girl here—" His gesture towards Morag indicated distaste, but considerable respect. "This girl here is right. I question her motives, but she is right. There should be no settlement of Cluain's future without

280

telling Callum Sinclair this. He has rights . . . Perhaps no rights in law, but in nature."

"And nature has always been between us, Samuel. It was as if Callum's knowledge of me as a coward and an adulterer was there from the moment that his eyes were fully opened. He grew up in this house, but he could have been as far from me as my grandchildren in China. Do not forget, Samuel, that when my wife died, he was a grown lad already, and past my possessing. He would take nothing from me. Not the smallest gift. Not the least help. All he would take from me was knowledge, and he milked me of that, whatever I had to give. He took it all, as he took knowledge from everyone. He had all his mother's intelligence. He seemed his mother's son entirely. Independent, proud, stubborn—no, obstinate. Many times I believed he hated me, and perhaps that is the truth. But he never tried to hide it. There was no currying favour with the Master of Cluain. I could have made life easier for him as he grew up, but he did not choose the easy way. He learned all I had to teach him—the farm, the distillery. He already had his mother's way with animals and nature. And then there came the day he walked out of this strath and went to school in Edinburgh on money provided by his mother, and his own savings from wages. Neither he nor she would take a shilling beyond what they had earned—and doubly earned—in work for Cluain. Nor will he take it to this day. The privileges he seems to have are his by right and agreement. When I asked him to return to the distillery we both knew it must be on his terms. He takes no favours from me—expects none. Since he had rejected everything else I have offered, I have no reason to believe that if I told him the truth, offered him a share in Cluain, he would not throw it back in my face. You see, I know him—and I know myself. He would know that if I made such an offer it would not be because I loved him as a father should love a son, but because Cluain needed him. I have tried to love him—it is not in my heart. And once he knew, if there was revenge in his heart, he could have it simply by refusing Cluain. That would be the surest way . . ."

"And he would refuse it, Master. I know my son."

Could we have forgotten Mairi Sinclair just because she had

remained silent? She stood there, the dark eyes deepened in that half-light, tall and majestically straight, a compelling, handsome woman, and one did not wonder at the magnetic quality she would have possessed at seventeen, beautiful then, and with knowledge beyond her years, different from other girls as she was from other women now. I imagined her up on the shielings, staying apart from the others when the fires burned at night, and there was laughter among the young people, and banter she could not join. The last flush of the twilight on the mountain, and the Master of Cluain for her companion. Not the man we saw now, but a younger man by thirty years, still struggling to make Cluain what it was, still with dreams unrealised, still hungry with wants and hopes. And perhaps it had been the same way with the black-haired girl, the girl with gifts already apparent, and beauty, and the beginnings of wisdom in her face, the girl from a crofter's cottage, as fierce in her pride as in her poverty. Not a girl to flirt, nor beg, nor afterwards to tell, even though her life was almost beaten from her. Nor one to deny life to the child she carried. How could we have forgotten her, even for a few seconds?

"You should never have written that name, Master. If I had known it was written, the Book, even that sacred Book, would have been destroyed. Not even that—there are acids that would have burned the paper, leaving only a cypher for the prying eyes of scheming little girls—little girls who know only the face of what they see, not the heart of it. It should never have been written, Master."

He sighed. "I wrote it after my wife died, remember. Perhaps I wrote it in remorse, knowing that then the truth could not hurt her—but great-souled woman that she was, I think she could have borne the truth, and perhaps Callum would have been less perverse with her than me. Perhaps I had some notion of it as a last testament. If those unknown grandchildren could not be mine, then after my own death, the truth would be clear. I looked at that name again—Callum's name—on the day that I made the entry of William's death. But Callum and I were so far apart that he seemed no more to me than that other grandchild, still in China. And then she came . . ."

282

"Master, remember that it would have been a useless cruelty to have told the mistress. Remember that I swore to you the time when you forced from me the admission that it was your child I carried, that if ever you spoke to the mistress, then I would be gone from Cluain that same day, and so would the child. Could you have two women of your acknowledged loving under the one roof? Could you have expected me to stay? In the beginning it was a penance every time I had to meet the mistress' eyes, but I stayed because I wanted my child brought up here, not in some city tenement. What punishment I bore would have to be my own, not his. But he would not be your son. He was no one's son but mine.

"And yet, I have always thought that he knew. As he grew, the knowledge seemed to come to him, though it was never spoken by me. It is, as you say, Master, as if he were born knowing, and perversely used the knowledge to punish you—to withhold from you what we all knew you most wanted, your own son. If he never accepted any gift, it was because he could never bring himself to thank you for it. Callum could thank no one. It is a hard fault, Master, and one that I am cursed with. I can give no thanks, but neither can I accept thanks. I do what I can, what I see to be right, as the Lord gives me to see. When your grandson came—so easy he was, so charming, and you both going along together as if it were he, not Callum, who had been here all his life—I felt myself possessed of jealousy and greed. I wanted your thoughts only for Callum. I prayed very long over that, and I believed my soul was finally freed of it. Then your grandson died, and I felt as if a judgement had been made on both of us, to see your happiness so destroyed. But then this girl came to take his place, and I suffered my jealousy and greed once again. I fought it, and prayed, and I began to see that my son was never to profit from the wrong I had done. And I knew what wrong he was committing with that woman, Margaret Campbell. It was wrong —compounding wrong. It seemed to stem from me, as if I had given him the seed of evil. For what fault I am not yet free of, I can only pray for forgiveness."

"And I say *damn* your prayers for forgiveness, Mairi Sinclair!"

Morag cried it with the fierceness of pent-up anger. "You and this old man here—so concerned with your souls and your consciences! What of your son? Until you have told him, face to face, what his position is in this household, you have no right, between you, to be worrying about your salvation and your repentance. It has gone beyond that. Now it is a matter for Callum. Will you take from him his inheritance because your soul is troubled? And you, Master, will you now weakly slide along into some plan for joining with other distillers, and leave your own son out of it because long ago you had not the courage to acknowledge him? Do you not stand high enough in your own estimation now to be able to afford this gesture? Is the Master of Cluain so small a man that he cannot make others accept his son? Think on it, Master, because if you do not tell him, then most surely *I* will. And can any of you deny now what you have seen written there?"

"But he *knows!*" I had found my tongue at last. "He knows! Even if he has not heard it in words from his mother or my grandfather, he most certainly knows."

Morag turned on me. "You are sure of that?"

"Certain. And by the certain, sure way that a woman knows. I'll say it before all of you, because I am not—I cannot—be ashamed of it. If I could have had him, Callum Sinclair would have been my husband. *Yes*—I wanted him in that way. But he would not give himself to me, and he went his own way, and he followed another woman to the moment of her death. But even if he had not loved Margaret Campbell, he would never have been mine. I see it now—so clearly. But I could not before. He tried to tell me—he *tried*. Even if there was nothing to prove whose son he was, he sensed it, and he tried to stop me from loving him. As if he could! I went on, and I kept my hope. Now I know what held us apart, and there never was a hope at all."

I did not care that they all knew now the way I had loved Callum. Let them know the dangers they had run of a dark and forbidden love growing up; let them know how close I had come to the ultimate disaster. I remember how he had called back to me that day on the mountain; *"Forget this day, Kirsty. Forget it!"* His instinct had tried to save me; if he had known for certain he would have said it in words. But we were alike, Callum and I; we had both persisted in our loves against reason and against hope.

Now I went back deliberately and seated myself again in front of the Bible, reading once more the names—William's and my own, set down before Callum's, which should have preceded them.

"So there is something to be put right, Grandfather. I can see that so long as there was William, you still might have hoped for a legitimate heir for Cluain—but even so, justice would not have been done. I think you have made it too easy for yourself all these years since my grandmother died. When Callum was a child, his mother could speak for him, force conditions on you. But when Callum was grown, there was no excuse, before God, not to tell him the truth. He should have been given a share in Cluain—on whatever pretext you or he wanted to present to the world. Either that, or a chance of honestly refusing it. Of saying no to you! But you kept placing your hope in William, and pushing aside an old shame. How can either of you speak for Callum now? —most especially *now,* when my brother no longer gives you even the faintest reason to hold off. When William died, Grandfather, your last excuse died with him. There is more shame to you now that you talk of bringing in Camerons and Macquaries and even of marrying me off to one of them—and your own son is left out."

"He will refuse. He will take nothing from me."

"Then let me hear it from Callum himself! Let us all hear it. Do we need Morag to do this task for us? I will tell him myself if you do not. I will tell him, and then I will leave Cluain. Because I *have* loved him. Do you understand love, Grandfather? I doubt that you do. This was a wrong love, a wrong and twisted thing. I could not stay here, and see him day after day, and have the knowledge of it fester in me. But before I go, I will tell him—I swear it! And I will not see Cluain parcelled off without his consent. If he wants to let it go, then let him say so. But in all that you are now deciding for Cluain, remember that the Camerons and the Macquaries will not stand still after your death. They will chip away at what Cluain is, at what you have built up. It is how these things always go, no matter what promises are made, what contracts are signed. You *must* know for the Camerons and the Macquaries you have one great counterweight. Dear God, in Callum Sinclair you have a *man!*"

Then I could stand it no longer. I put my face in my hands, and prayed that I would not weep here and now for all that I had lost, and for all that I was throwing after it. Callum could never be mine—never. And now I had said that Cluain would not be mine. I felt the awful bleakness of it. There was nothing left to love.

"Is there some whisky in this house? I have need of a dram or two. I have just come from Edinburgh . . . and from Balloch-torra."

Callum's voice. My head flew up, and my spirits seemed to bound with pleasure; and then came the dull remembrance. He stood in the doorway of the kitchen passage, his body slumped against the frame, with the look of exhaustion upon him. He had never seemed more like his mother. His eyes seemed sunken with sleeplessness; I wondered if he had thought to take any food at all since Margaret had died; his face and lips were pinched and white. There was silence as he advanced into the room, and took, un-invited, a chair at the table. The movement seemed to release us all from a kind of spell. My own chair scraped back as I rushed to the decanter, to be there before Morag. But she already had her hand on it, and I banged it loudly against the glass as I pulled it from her.

"*I* will pour," I said. I had had enough of Morag. She was right in her demand for justice for Callum, but she did it with no sense of disinterest. I wondered why I had never seen ambition before in those bright, knowing eyes, the ever-present willingness to help, the thirst for knowledge. For a young girl in this quiet, slow strath she knew so much, and she had kept her most important knowledge to herself until it could be made to serve herself. I wanted no more of her.

I poured a large glass of whisky, and spilled a little water into it. I placed it on the table before Callum. He took it slowly, and drank a little, and then set it down.

"You need some food," I said. "Morag will bring you something."

"Morag will bring nothing. She will stay where she is. And I need no food."

He took another drink. "I wonder what Cluain is coming to? I have come in and stabled the pony, and no one has heard me. Not a dog barks. Big Billy's flock do not open their mouths. A man can be too well known to a household. You're all so full of your own concerns, you have ears for nothing. I've been standing there near half an hour. Not hiding—just standing there where any of you could have seen me if you cared to look. It made too interesting hearing to interrupt. It isn't often a man gets a chance to hear the truth about himself—good and bad. Mostly, it seemed to be bad."

"If you'd had the decency to declare yourself . . ." my grandfather began.

Callum's weary gesture of dismissal silenced him. "Do you want to talk *now* about decency, Mr. Macdonald?" He looked around us all. "Well, between you, you've left almost nothing unsaid. I've never heard such a lot of pious prattling in my life . . . no, I'm sorry." He turned himself sideways and reached for my hand, pulling me down into the chair next to him. "I'm sorry, Kirsty. That wasn't for you. I'm sorry about everything. For me, this summer has been the whole climax of my life—it has been . . . *everything*. For you, it has been hell. The kind of hell that I live in now. Yes, I did try to stop it, but how can you tell someone not to love? I didn't want you hurt, but I didn't understand how deep it went with you. Forgive me for not allowing you the feelings I had myself for Margaret. I did you an injustice. If I had guessed that it was more than a light fancy, I would have said more. I would have stopped it. Because I knew that I would leave Cluain when Margaret went, at the end of the summer. Oh"—he gestured with the glass—"I knew I would not be with her. I wouldn't have followed her to London like a love-sick boy, though that's what I was. And I could not wait here to be a summer diversion for her again next year. I was not completely blind, even if I was in love. I did not blame her—she never fully knew what she was to me. But I knew I could not endure it here without her. I would go away, and in time you, Kirsty, would love someone else, and no

287

damage would be done. How stupid it sounds now—no damage would be done. But that was what I thought. If I had dreamed it could hurt you so, nothing would have stopped me speaking."

"You knew then—about my grandfather?"

"My father." We could have been speaking alone together in that room. Suddenly all the barriers were down. The first free and unconstrained speech we had ever had, and it took place before an audience. It didn't matter. All the pretence was gone, the striving. The love was still there. Like the name written in the Book, it could not be wiped out, even with the acid of my pain; but it had undergone a strange transmutation. I looked at Callum with other eyes, but not less loving eyes.

"My father. Yes, I knew—or guessed. Not that anything ever was said, and I didn't suspect that he could be capable of the kind of sentiment that would cause him to write my name where he did. Perhaps we had a chance, and lost it—long ago. But only between two people related as closely as we are could the kind of feelings we had exist. I could not have been so involved with someone not close to me. I would simply not have cared. It seems I can only love or hate. Most of the time I thought I hated him—overbearing, arrogant, too full of himself and Cluain. And then at times I knew great pity for him, growing old alone, sitting here at nights alone, going to his bed alone. If my mother thinks she has saved her soul by refusing to marry him, then she should look into her heart for a little Christian charity towards him. For all she says of praying, she has not forgiven him—or herself. She had her own revenge, my mother, and called it penance. All these years, however she tries to deny it, she must have believed Cluain would be for me. Who else was there? We quarreled, the old man and I, and still he had to call me back. I was glad when William came. I was released. The old man had company, and hope. And I was free. I was no longer possessed by a future which might be dictated for me. I neither had to accept or refuse Cluain. Then everything changed again when William died—and Margaret came to me. It all changed so suddenly that my head spun with trying to comprehend. I lived in a haze of joy so

288

long as I had Margaret, and I was so blind to what you felt. I knew it was going to hurt like death when it came to an end. And like death it is. I'm sorry, Kirsty. I would never have let it be this way for you if I hadn't been so wrapped in my own joys and woes."

The exhausted face looked at me with a kindliness I had never experienced before. Suddenly I put my hand on his, as it lay on the table, just gently put it on his, not gripping. It might have been William I touched.

"We will both survive," I said. "One does not die so easily. I will leave Cluain, and you will stay, because you must. But we will both survive."

"I will not stay at Cluain," he answered. "Not for anything. Not for this old man, or anything he can give me. I gather there is some talk of a merger with Camerons and Macquaries—well, I will not stay for *that* either. There is nothing anyone can give me now. So it is *you* who must stay, Kirsty. You who will have to battle out Cluain's future. They will try to arrange a marriage. But take nothing you do not want yourself—accept no one and nothing in which there is not willingness and love. Once you have known love, you will either seek it again, or live without it. You will not take what pretends to be love—not for money, or convenience, nor for the sake of peace. You and I, Kirsty—we are not made for peace, it seems. It is not a family inheritance."

Samuel Lachlan could contain himself no longer. His glasses came off, and his glass tipped wildly, so that the whisky spilled on his trousers.

"Do you mean, Sinclair—Callum—that you will not stay at Cluain? That you refuse, should Mr.—your father—offer? That you would not stay and take over—when the time comes, of course."

Callum seemed not to hear him. He was looking at me very directly, a way he had not looked almost since the first time we had encountered each other, a look that searched my face, with tenderness, with compassion. Then I felt his hand, which had rested under mine, quietly, slowly, fold over, until it encompassed

289

mine, held it, gathered it to him, for what comfort it would offer. "I'm sorry, Kirsty," he said again. "I'm leaving you an uneasy future. Cluain is no gift, but a burden. I'm sorry."

It was only then he looked beyond me to the two men. "No—I am not staying. My years of service to Cluain are ended. We cannot unmake the past—my father and I. It is too late, for both of us. We cannot stop being what we are, and what we are will not live together. So go on and make what plans you must. I will not be part of them. I will be going as soon as you can find a man to replace me."

"You are certain?" my grandfather said. He looked at Callum and his face twisted with bitterness. The pretence was gone from between them also. It must be almost impossible for Angus Macdonald to comprehend that Callum could be willingly leaving behind a chance to be Master of Cluain, even though, to this moment, he himself had not formally offered it. He looked very old, the lines of age unnaturally harsh. I thought that for thirty years he must have carried at the back of his mind, the thought of Callum, perhaps unconsciously believing, that if every other plan failed there was the ultimate heir to Cluain. And now thirty years was gone, and so was Callum. He was left with me.

"It turns to ashes," he said. "A man works all his life . . . for what? You and I, Samuel, what have we laboured for?"

The other man looked more bewildered than ever. All around him, the forces on which he had based his life, the sanctity of hard work, the sacredness of capital, of possessions, was being challenged. Before him were two young people, and in these last minutes he had heard each of us refuse what had taken Angus Macdonald and himself a lifetime to build. He shook his head, mute.

"Well, then, Callum Sinclair, let us not detain you," my grandfather said. "I am still capable of a day's work in the distillery. We are about to begin malting, and I have a fair knowledge of how it's done. I have not yet lost my eye and nose for good whisky. Let us not keep you a day longer than needs be. If Cluain does not satisfy you, then let us not hold you here against your will. Another man will be found. There are many who would be glad to come to Cluain. Do not trouble yourself that we shall

290

not continue to make good whisky without your help." It was the final dismissal.

Mairi Sinclair made only one sign of protest. Her hand went out suddenly in a gesture, as if she would have kept Callum seated there, as if she would have kept him forever. Then slowly it fell again to her side. She also was losing Callum. For her also the years at Cluain without him stretched ahead.

Almost at the same instant as her hand fell, the real protest came from Morag. "Callum—you are *mad!* You cannot do this thing! You cannot throw away such a prize. Think of it!—*Cluain!* Is it not everything a man could want? A fine house, a fine farm— a famous distillery. Look at those two old men!—you have only to nod your head, even now, and it is yours. Do not believe what he says about going. He would have you—and gladly. He is pushed —he *needs* you. Och, you have lost your senses over this dead woman. In time—in a very little time, you will come to yourself, and find what you have thrown away. You will find that she did not matter. Frivolous, light-minded creature she was. You will wonder how you could ever have given time or thought to her. She was not worth more than her looks."

Callum turned slowly towards her. After her struggle with me over the decanter, Morag had retreated to the kitchen passage door, almost beyond the candlelight, where Callum had stood, as if she would remain unnoticed, and not be sent away.

"And what is it to you, Morag, how I choose to give my time, where I choose to give my love? I gave both—gladly. Never mind what Margaret was. She gave me things no woman has ever given me. Her death has not taken them away. They remain forever."

"Then you are doubly a fool! Your sense is in your loins, not in your head. You ask what it is to me? My life—that is what it is! Since you came back here, since I was fifteen, I have waited for you, Callum Sinclair. I have waited, and learned to do and be everything that a wife for a man like you should be. Do you think there have not been others after me?—and I have withheld myself until you would one day see me. Yes, *see* me! If I had had the clothes of Margaret Campbell, and the soft hands, and rode a mare

291

like hers, would you not have noticed me sooner? My hands are rough, but my face is not, nor my body. I could have given you anything she could—and loyalty as well. There has never been anyone else for me but you, Callum. I cannot *stand* to see you throw away Cluain. I have counted on you—and it. It was to be your future. And mine. Even Angus Macdonald must see this. Together, you and I, Callum—we could make a whole generation to succeed at Cluain. Children . . . sons. I could give you *everything*—and Cluain what it most needs. No, you cannot throw it away. I will not let you! It is too much if what I have done is for nothing."

"And what have you done, Morag?"

She was silent for a time. I stared at her, fascinated. She was like a creature suddenly broken from a shell; the red lips were full and passionate; there was now no winning smile, but the wilful stance of a woman in the full spate of her needs and desires, someone who sees the fruits of a long toil about to be snatched from her. She was so different from the faded, resigned old-age acceptance of Samuel Lachlan and my grandfather. There was no acceptance in Morag; she was fighting.

"What have I done?" she repeated, at last. "I have loved you, Callum Sinclair. *That* is what I have done. I have loved you lawfully, keeping myself for you. It had not been like the love of that woman, Margaret Campbell, who sought to pass an idle summer, and bewitched you out of your senses. She who lost a lover when Master William died, and looked about for the one to take his place. No, my love has not been like that, nor like the love of this girl here, who has loved where she should not have done—well, it is not her fault, but she is foolish, and was love-sick, and would not listen to me when I tried to tell her that you were not for her. I have loved you the way a woman should, ready to do anything for you, to be anything. And I have waited. So you see, you cannot leave Cluain. You cannot leave me."

Callum drank from his glass again. "How old are you, Morag?"

She drew herself to her full height. "Old enough. Nearly eighteen."

He shook his head. "It's a sad waste, Morag. You think I haven't seen you? I have. I have seen you about my mother's kitchen, and

292

I have seen no woman, but a child with a scheming heart. There is no innocence in you, Morag. You talk of Margaret Campbell —but what did you know of her? It is the evil minds of those like you who make her seem sullied and corrupt. She was not that. She was never capable of a calculated gesture. She was simple—even guileless, no matter what the world says of her. She never stopped to consider that friendship with a man, laughter, enjoyment, could lead to love. And when love came, she took it gladly, whole-heartedly. You do not understand that kind of love. You never could. You don't know what love is, Morag. You have waited, and planned. Planned for what?—I don't know. So far as I'm concerned, it's all wasted. Turn your talents elsewhere. I will leave."

"I have said Callum Sinclair," Angus Macdonald broke in, "that we have no need of you here." How cold and tired his voice had grown; I sensed the anger of his rejection taking hold.

"I will go," Callum replied, "as soon as I am permitted to go. There may be legal procedures which require me to stay some time yet."

"An Enquiry?" My grandfather said it with contempt. "And what will that be but a formality? Because the sheriff is a friend of the Campbells he will gloss it over. But of course you will have to describe what happened, since you were with her. However carefully you choose your words, the whole countryside will know what you were about. The relationship between you and Margaret Campbell was already a scandal. You could hardly claim you were in attendance on her as a groom."

"I will never pretend I was anyone's groom! But there will be more than a polite glossing over of her death. The reason for her death is quite clear. She broke her neck when the mare stumbled on the rocks below the waterfall, and pitched her down on her head. She did not live beyond that second. But there was more than that. It was not a normal fall the mare took. I was riding after Margaret and I saw it clearly. The mare did not slip— she staggered. And at a bad place. I had noticed there was something wrong and I called to Margaret to dismount. But she seldom paid heed to advice like that. She went ahead, crossing the ford, and it was there the mare's legs suddenly folded under her, and she and Margaret together fell down on the rocks below."

"The mare was ill?" My grandfather leaned forward. "It is not like Ballochtorra to send an unfit animal out from its stables."

"The mare was well enough when she went out. I told you I have just come from Ballochtorra. I have spoken to Gavin Campbell, as I had to do before, to get his permission to act in the first place. Before the mare was buried, up there by my cottage, I removed her stomach. Then I took it to a pathologist in Edinburgh—a friend I made when I was at school. I did not tell him the full circumstances. He trusted that I would make the right use of the information he gave me. And the law will probably be about my neck for taking things into my own hands. But I wasn't absolutely certain. If I had been wrong, there would only have been more gossip and speculation, and Margaret's son would have suffered all the more—without need. If I had waited to call the constable from Grantown, and all the rest, the countryside would have been ringing with the news. And perhaps I had been wrong. I hoped I had been wrong. But I wasn't."

"What did the man find, then?"

"Hemlock—more than a trace of digitalis—foxglove. Henbane—hyoscyamine. The mare had taken enough hemlock to have eventually killed her. She had eaten while we—while Margaret and I were in the cottage. That staggering walk was the beginning of the vertigo that comes from the drug—so the pathologist tells me."

His voice had faltered as he recalled the details of the scene. He leaned back and sipped again from his whisky. "There was a feedbag with oats there. I had made a rough little stable of the second half of the croft—just to shelter the animals from the weather, perhaps to shelter them from prying eyes if anyone came that way. But people never went up that track except to purpose—the gorse up there is above head high, and they would only come looking for a strayed sheep. I never saw any—so that is unlikely. But also I never left any feed there. Why should I? I did not want to advertise our presence—the use of the place more than I had to. But the feed bag was there that day, when I tied up the mare and my pony. Margaret had dismounted and gone into the cottage.

I did not say anything to her about the feed bag. I thought it was some kind of cruel hint from someone who knew we met there, and who wanted to make an ugly joke. Nothing we did there was ugly—and I did not want to make it seem so to Margaret. But I can never forgive myself for not taking the feed bag beyond reach of the mare. There is no doubt she ate from it."

"Och, what nonsense," Morag cried. "You are making a big and tragic event because your fancy woman has been killed, and you want to make someone else suffer for it. The countryside is filled with hemlock in the wild places. Where it is not cut it will sprout and grow wild and big. Every child knows that."

Mairi Sinclair intervened. "Hemlock is a rank, evil-smelling plant—repellent. Only hungry animals would graze on it. Horses from the Ballochtorra stable would never touch such a thing in its wild state. As to the henbane—I do not know. It was in the oats. It would have been a potent dose."

"How do you know it was in the oats?"

"I know. I know the mare could never have grazed on enough of it to make such a concentration in the stomach to kill her. Mice may die of nibbling at hemlock—not horses. It was not a natural fall she had. Was she dead when John went to shoot her?"

Callum shook his head. "She was not. But she was not screaming and struggling as an animal would who is in great pain from a broken leg. The drugs would have been having their full effect by then. John told me she was lying very still, and she hardly opened her eyes when he came near her. I asked him to say nothing, and he agreed. *He* trusted me, too. I thought of the oats myself, and I went up at first light the next morning to bring the bag down. But it wasn't there. I have no proof that the mare got the hemlock from the oats—or the henbane or digitalis, or belladonna. What I have to know—and I may never know—is who it was who knew that Margaret and I met there. If it was meant simply as a warning—the warning of some narrow-minded zealot that the wages of sin is death, then it succeeded. But it was meant for the mare—and now Margaret is dead! God, if only she had dismounted when I called to her! If she had never crossed the ford . . ." He wiped his hand across his forehead. "The Enquiry may reveal nothing but these facts—and I cannot produce the bag of oats. But I will not leave the strath until I know every single person who knew that Margaret and I met there. I *will* know!"

"I knew," I said. "I knew—and I went there the day before Margaret died."

Callum shook his head in disbelief. "Kirsty!—*you* couldn't."

"I did not. I told you I knew. I went there. Even with all I had seen, even after the night of the Prince's ball, I still did not quite believe. But then I saw the cottage—how could I not believe it then? The feed bag was there, and in the few minutes I stood at the door of the cottage Ailis got to it. She did not have time to take very much. She lived."

"How did you know, Kirsty?—about the croft?"

"Morag."

She did not flinch under all our eyes. She stood erect, blazing with anger and passion.

"Yes, I knew. And so did half the strath."

"But you told *me* about it the night the harvest feast was spread, Morag. You told me where to go, and what to look for. And very early the next morning, just at first light, you left Cluain. I saw you. Later you told me you had gone with something Mistress Sinclair had given you for a sick child of one of the workers."

Mairi Sinclair's words were sharp and dry. "I did not send her."

Morag's head went up farther. "And so—what if she did not send me? What business was it of yours to enquire? I have no life of my own? Is Callum Sinclair the only one who may go to meet a lover if he chooses?"

Callum leaned both arms on the table, and put his chin in one hand, rubbing it wearily. He did not look at Morag any longer. "And what is all this you have said about keeping yourself for me?" He sighed, and I thought he would rather not have gone on. "Morag—Morag, don't lie! There was or there was not a sick child. There was or there was not a lover to meet?"

When Morag made no attempt to answer, I spoke. "She meant it for me. She dangled the knowledge of the croft before me that night like bait, and she went with the feed bag the next morning, knowing that I could not resist seeing the evidence for myself.

To those like Morag, I must seem such a fool—but who in love is not foolish? I went, as she guessed I would. There was nothing so obvious as poison for *me*—but something to tempt Ailis. Who knew what could have happened? Everyone knows that Ailis will eat anything presented to her, for as long as it's there. She could have fallen anywhere along that track—most of the glen is narrow and steep, and boulders most of the way—some of it dangerous to a rider like myself. A fall—perhaps a night in the open. Ailis too drugged to get back to Cluain. Perhaps dead. Perhaps myself hurt, and with luck, some rain. Who knows that I would not have followed on the way William went? It took three days and two nights to find him."

"What has this to do with Margaret?" Callum demanded sharply. He forced himself upright in the chair.

"Yes . . . what?" I was asking it of myself, remembering, trying to recall each moment of the day that Callum had hammered on the door, and Margaret's slackly hanging boots had dripped rain, almost in my face.

"I remember I got up very late that day—the day Margaret died. We had been up all night in the stable with Ailis—Mistress Sinclair and myself. And as I was getting dressed I saw Margaret riding along by the river. It was a surprise to see her—Morag had told me she and Gavin were at Cawdor, and were going on to some other place. It was such a terrible day—the rain pouring down. I guessed where she was going. And just to show Morag that I did not care as much as she supposed—what a stupid pretence that was—I told her I had seen Margaret out riding. Morag hurried with my meal, I remember, and talked about having vegetables to prepare. But when I went out into the scullery, she wasn't there."

"What are you saying, Kirsty?" Callum said impatiently. "Make yourself plain, for God's sake!"

"I'm *trying!*" I snapped back at him. I was weary of it all myself. "I think it is coming plain." I looked at Morag. "It was meant for me, wasn't it, Morag—for Ailis? Margaret didn't matter, not that much. Callum could never have married her, and she would be gone soon. But I was here—and in your mind, I stood in the way of Callum having Cluain. Did you rush up the mountain that afternoon I told you I had seen Margaret out riding?—knowing as well as I did where she would be going on an afternoon like that? Did you go to get the feed bag before her mare or Callum's pony could get to it. You had not expected anyone there so soon—she was supposed to be away at Cawdor. And it was too late. Margaret and Callum were there before you, and Margaret's mare had eaten the oats. And Margaret fell with the mare."

"You are *accusing* me! You have not the slightest proof!"

"No—I haven't. But are you as clever at getting the keys to Mistress Sinclair's herb room as you were in getting the key to the Bible. It would have had to be a strong, prepared dose of hemlock—the juice only, to mix with the oats. And a little digitalis, just to make sure?—a little henbane."

"So, it's hemlock from Mistress Sinclair's room now, is it? Then why should it not have been Mistress Sinclair who put the bag of oats there? Why should it be me? Did she not have reason to dislike Margaret Campbell, who had led her son into what she calls the paths of unrighteousness? Does she not have the skill to mix such a compound—and the keys to the herb room are hers, not mine."

"It was a very unskilful mix, the pathologist said. Too strong to be normal—that is, if the mare had grazed on it," Callum answered. "Surely my mother knows better how to administer a poison if she is determined to do it. It does not fit."

"Nothing fits," Samuel Lachlan said. "It is a tangle of supposition. And what, Kirsty, do you mean by Morag intending you to follow William?"

"It was thought, wasn't it, that William had a good chance to live when he was found and brought back after the shooting accident? He was young—strong. He had the best attention—and the will to live?"

My grandfather half-rose from his seat. *"What* are you saying? My grandson had every care. Nothing was spared."

"No—nothing. A surgeon from Inverness to remove the bullet, even a doctor from Edinburgh, a renowned nurse and herbalist to bring down the fever, to bring him back to health. But he died.

I think . . . I think he died because Morag knew how to get the keys of the herb room. She had a little knowledge, picked up from Mistress Sinclair—enough to be dangerous. And William's name came before Callum's in the Bible—as mine does. No—I don't think it possible she could have planned the accident with the gun. It doesn't seem possible. But she knew her opportunity when it came. Remember, Mairi Sinclair did not actually do much nursing of William. She prepared the food, and gave the medicine the doctors ordered, and her own remedies as well. But it was Morag who fetched and carried to him, who sat up there with him in the tower room. Mistress Sinclair herself told me that William did not like to have her by him. I think Morag added enough to those brews and medicines to turn the balance—a little of this, a little of that—to confuse the doctors and Mistress Sinclair. All of it deadly if given in too strong a dosage. Enough to defeat William's struggle for life."

A wild laugh broke from Morag. "You are joking! You make these mad accusations against me, but there is not the least proof. Is all this come from the fact that one little pony was ill—and recovered?—and Margaret Campbell's mare had eaten from a poisonous plant? It is all fancy—all this about Ailis and Margaret Campbell's mare. All about Master William's death. Your grief and your thwarted love has sent your imagination reeling. I would have a care if I were you. Accusations like these must have a proof, and I will not sit still under them."

"There is proof. The proof that Callum had brought, serious enough for him to offer it at the Enquiry."

"*That* is no proof against me! I have already said that it would far more likely have been Mistress Sinclair who did that. That is what most will say. As for your brother . . . Do you know more than the doctors? Were you here when he died?"

"I only have what proof he sent me. I did not come to Cluain uninvited just to have a roof over my head. Something unnatural had happened to my brother. Something not explained. God knows, it was slight enough, the proof he gave—but perhaps all that a man who felt he was dying had strength to provide. Something that

299

would not be discovered and destroyed. It was sent to me in China. It was that which brought me to Cluain."

Now I had risked everything. The meaning of those words of William's would never be plain. Had they been the last fevered thought of Margaret, of her terrible, though strangely innocent power to wreck and destroy? Or had they literally meant what they had tried to say, and as strength had waned, been left unfinished? Who could ever know what had been in William's mind. And I was challenging Morag with them.

"There *is* no proof—no proof!"

"It exists, Morag. It exists. But I had to come to Cluain to be certain. I had to find out many things I could not have known."

"None exists!" Her tone rose close to panic. "I made sure. There was no writing—nothing."

"You made sure, Morag? Why did you have to make sure of anything, if there was nothing to hide? It is there in writing—but something you couldn't read, and not in a letter, which you might have suspected and destroyed. The words are written in Mandarin characters on a scroll—a scroll with the drawing of a bird on a bare branch. You will remember that. You packed and sent that scroll to me in China. *You* brought me to Cluain."

Now my grandfather got to his feet. He walked towards Morag with slow steps, the heaviness of his body menacing. But she did not shrink from him.

"*My* grandson. I entrusted him to you. Was there murder done so that you could secure Cluain for the man you wanted to marry?"

"Murder, is it?" Morag tossed her head. "Better ask that of Mairi Sinclair! I don't know what proof your granddaughter imagines she has, but there is nothing to it, or why would she have waited this long time to bring it out? Oh, no, Master, I shall not be so easy. You may make your accusations until the breath has left your body, and I shall deny them. And I will point to Mairi Sinclair, who had equal, and more chance than I, to do any mischief that might have been done."

The slight flaring of panic had left her; her confidence grew with her argument. "After all, who am I? I merely do what I am told at Cluain. I carry out Mistress Sinclair's instructions. I don't

300

care what is written or not written on a heathen scroll. There will be no proof that *I* have done wrong. All I have confessed to is opening the Bible and knowing what it contained. That—and the crime of loving Callum Sinclair."

"You confessed, before us all, that you made sure there was no proof of anything amiss before you packed William's belongings," Callum said. "There is more than fancy in what Kirsty is saying."

Morag looked directly at me. "Does that writing name my name? Does it?"

I could only shake my head. "It names no name."

"There? *Now* bring your proof. Shout it to the whole country. A fine business it will make. Will they dig up your grandson's body from the kirkyard, Master, to see if it contains poisons? How will you like that? Your name and the Campbell name—if Callum goes on with his nonsense—linked in the courts by a servant girl who is accused of causing two deaths. Or will it be Mairi Sinclair who is finally accused?—she who will then become known as your one-time lover? It will be a fine scandal to take into your declining years—and it will not change anything—not as you wish it changed. It will not bring your grandson back—"

Samuel Lachlan interrupted her, speaking directly to me. "The nature of this proof you say you have, Kirsty? It is not definite? Has William made an accusation?—of some specific thing—named some specific person?"

"No. Morag is right. There is only a fragment . . . obviously written when he was in a high fever, to judge by the characters. There is no name—no crime that a court of law could fasten on to. That is why I have not spoken of it. I hoped to find out for myself—to be a little more sure. But in the cold light of day there is still so little. The pathologist's report that Callum brought back— but no bag of oats to go with it. There is William's scroll with his few words splashed on it. *'She has killed . . .'* is what he wrote, and even what he wrote is open to question. Even my father's translator was not quite sure . . ."

I stopped, because Samuel Lachlan was shaking his head. "It will not do." He rubbed his nose pensively. "If ever there was enough evidence assembled to bring either of these women to

301

trial—and I doubt that—you know what the verdict would be. *Not Proven.* The Not Proven verdict is uniquely Scotland's law. The question would forever remain, no matter how sure *we* are that Mairi Sinclair could not have done such a thing. But there is also little proof that this girl here *did* do it. Unless you can find a witness who saw her on the way to, or at the cottage that day, you will achieve nothing. And then, what did she do, but cause harm to a horse? The matter of William is more delicate still. Two doctors attended him, and neither suspected foul play. Doctors are notoriously conservative in these matters. They do not like their judgements questioned. You would find it difficult to get an exhumation order on the strength of those few words William wrote. Were they dated?—were they signed?"

"No."

He shook his head again. "It will hardly stand up. I doubt that any of it would get past a Court of Enquiry. And do you want it to? Do you want it, Angus?"

"I want—" Callum cut in. Samuel Lachlan silenced him with a lift of his hand.

"You, Angus. You have everything to consider before you make a move. The reputation of Mistress Sinclair. The good name of Cluain. The scandal that must attach to such a hearing, when a name like Lady Cambell's is involved. You would have every newspaper in England with its representative here. If once the accusation is made publicly—if even the present facts are brought out, you will never know a moment's peace again."

"You are suggesting," Callum said, "that the whole thing be ignored. For the sake of hushing up a scandal!"

"Are you seeking vengeance, Callum—or justice?" Lachlan said. "Consider your own mother, and her position in this. Justice is an abstract thing—but vengeance can become a monster that turns and consumes itself. The dead will not come back. The living will suffer, and, even so, the guilty may go unpunished. Think well about it. Perhaps it would be the better part of justice if your friend in Edinburgh were told that the mare had indeed grazed on poisonous herbage . . ."

"Then you mean me to stand up at an Enquiry and say that

302

before my eyes the mare stumbled at the middle of the ford, and pitched them both down. *That* is what you want me to say?— and you call yourself a man of the law."

"That much would be the truth. And it is because I am a man of the law that I count myself also a man of sense. It is revenge that is senseless, Callum. You have lost your . . ." He stumbled over the difficult words, ". . . the woman you love. Your natural instinct is to hit back. Think of those you will have to injure with that action—and this girl, *if* she is guilty, I think—yes, I think this girl would go free. Her kind do. She would make a most impressive witness in the hands of a good advocate. Juries are impressionable. Set her beside your mother—I beg your pardon, Mistress Sinclair, but this must be said. Your mother will be spoken of as the one-time lover of Angus Macdonald. Set this girl beside the story of your liaison with Lady Campbell. Beside those facts, this girl will appear as innocent as a babe. I know juries, Callum. They judge—but they do not always give justice."

"I will face what I must," Mairi Sinclair said. "Do not consider me in this. Blessed are they who hunger and thirst after justice, for they—"

"It is the Bible that is abstract here, not justice," Callum said to her. "For God's sake—I *must* consider you, since you've never considered yourself."

Morag stepped away from my grandfather, and paused in the doorway. She raised both her arms until her hands rested on the doorframe. Her confidence was supreme. "Well, then, I will leave you to your considerations. And let us hope that you will hear the sense of what Mr. Lachlan has said. For believe me, I will make it hard on all of you. I will be just as Mr. Lachlan says I will be—I will be that and more. And you will all rue the day you raised a voice against me." Then her contempt got the better of her control. "You are fools—all of you! But you, Callum—you are the greatest fool of all. You did not see what was before your eyes. You would not stoop to pick up what was under your hand. There was Cluain, which you could have demanded as a right. And there was me, whom you could have had for the asking. And what did you choose? Your wilful, prideful ways. Cluain was thrown away because it would have meant a few years of putting up with that old man there. I was not good enough for you—you preferred that foolish woman who could give you nothing but her body. You did not see me beneath your feet, for gazing up at the sky. Like that hawk you fly. Well, your pride is like that bird's, and you look too high. But you will fall to the ground, as she must, some day. Oh, you will fall. Believe me, you will fall."

Then she lowered her arms, and very gently closed the door behind her.

When she was gone, Mairi Sinclair moved, almost mechanically, to build up the fire. In silence we all watched her poke the embers and lay on more peat and wood. Then she went to where the Bible still lay open; she closed it with great care, locked it, and then she took the bunch of keys to my grandfather.

"The keys, Master."

It was as if she were indicating that the ritual of Cluain would continue, must continue. It was more enduring than the present storms. Then she went back to her place at the end of the table, and waited.

Callum turned and said quietly to me, "Kirsty . . . Kirsty, you have come all the way from China for this . . . for *this*."

I stretched out my hand to him and once again touched him. It was not the touch of desire, but of knowing, of loving and knowing the love returned. It was not now desire; I knew I had his trust.

"Yes, for this. And worth it—for *this*."

How does one mark the end of one relationship, and enter another? With no further words, Callum and I did in those moments. They were the last moments of grace we had.

My grandfather went slowly back to his place on the settle. For long minutes he stared into the fire. "That is your true opinion, Samuel—that we should leave things be. Not attempt to prosecute the girl . . ."

"It is."

He sighed. "William is gone. Better leave him in peace." The sigh was like a faint echo of the wind outside, a gusting, moaning sound. "Perhaps it might be the better thing to leave ourselves whatever peace we may yet be permitted. Perhaps better to forget

304

it all. Forget Ferguson, forget Camerons and Macquaries. Perhaps Kirsty is right. Expansion is just to become another Ferguson. Perhaps peace is what we need. There are not so many years of Cluain left to me. We will try to hold on to our senses—and perhaps to gain our peace. Honour—honour I let slip from me many years ago. I could have had a son. I have no son . . ." His great eyebrows hooked together as he looked at Callum. "That is so, is it not? I have no son?" It was the final question.

Callum got to his feet, and went to the decanter and poured for himself. He drank at one gulp. "That is so, Mr. Macdonald. You have no son. I will go, when I am permitted to. I must. I will live only so long as I can live freely—come freely, go freely. My falcon is mine only so long as she chooses to be. The day she chooses to go on the wind, to fly on, and never return, then she is mine no longer. We live together on those terms. *I* can live no other way. And when I fall, I will fall hard, as Morag said. I know it—I accept it. I can be no permanent part of Cluain. That burden must fall on Kirsty."

He replaced his glass. "And now, Mr. Macdonald, I am going up to my cottage. I will wait to hear from you. It is *you* who must go to Gavin Campbell and give him your reasons for proceeding or not proceeding with this thing. I have told him what I know. And whatever you say, whatever your arguments, it must ultimately be he who decides in the matter. If he says I am to tell the whole story at the Enquiry, then I will. And all of us must bear the consequences. If you want to preserve this peace you suddenly crave, for once Cluain will have to make common cause with Ballochtorra. It rests with him—and with you. Good night, Mr. Macdonald."

When he reached the door he turned and looked at me. "Good night, Kirsty. Good night!" The way he spoke, it might just as well have been good-bye.

He still hesitated in the doorway, as though there was something he had still to say. Then the door of the kitchen passage crashed open, and banged against the wall. The wind of it swept through the room, and sent the candle flickering wildly.

Neil Smith, red-faced and frantic, glared in upon us. "Is it deaf you all are? Are you so gone in your drink ye cannot hear or see?

Get out of here and get the place roused. Can you not hear the screams of the horses? The stable's afire!"

I suppose we all cried or shouted something in that first second; I knew only my own word. "Ailis . . . !"

II

We should have heard the horses—except that their screams seemed almost part of the wind, the howl of its gusts. The tumult of our hearts inside that room had been too great to allow other sounds, perhaps we had, as Neil Smith said, been too far gone— but not in drink. He had seen, he shouted back to us as we ran through the kitchen passage, the glow from the window of his cottage. And the high garden wall had kept the same sight from us.

"Never mind water—the horses first," Callum shouted. He seemed to have taken charge; my grandfather was momentarily bewildered. "And you, Kirsty, run up to Farquharson's cottage and rouse them out. Have them send the lads on to the other cottages. We need every man here."

As he raced to help Neil Smith open up the doors of the loose boxes, I caught at his arm. He checked impatiently. "Ailis first," I said. "Ailis."

"Very well—Ailis!"

And then my grandfather came to life. He rushed to join the two men, and for a moment I stood and watched, wondering if it could be done. And what had I asked Callum—his own pony was probably tethered in one of the empty stalls. But we were fortunate in Cluain's stables. Built of stone, like the distillery and warehouses, with slate roof, and all the loose boxes opening into the yard, instead of two rows of stalls into a central passage, as it would have been in a bigger stable. It was the hay that was the danger; the hay was alight in the lofts above, stray wisps were blowing in the wind, and pieces falling among the bedding straw of the fear-maddened horses.

Most of the animals were untethered, but it needed skill to get them to back away out of the boxes when a rain of fired hay seemed to fall between them and the freedom of the yard. But one or two, those of uncertain temper, were tethered, and someone would have to go past those lunging heels and take the halter and turn and lead them out. In the last instant before I started running I saw Callum pull off his coat. Ailis, sensible creature that she was, was already free, and retreating into the kindly darkness beyond the roaring threat. Then I saw Callum plunge past the heels of the worst of the huge Clydesdales, the one called Trumpeter, and fling his coat over the crazed animal's eyes. The fight was on. I didn't look any more. A single blow from one of those enormously powerful legs, and Callum would not live.

I saw something else, though, as I ran. Morag stood alone in the middle of the stableyard, just where the tidal edge of the light from the blaze fell upon her. She stood quite still, calm in the midst of the clatter of the hooves of the freed horses, and the calls of the men, wrapped in her plaid against the wind, watching as if it were some interesting spectacle, but none of her business. Perhaps it wasn't—now. She glanced at me as I ran past her, but she made no attempt to move; no attempt either to leave or to take some action to help. I knew it was useless to urge her.

Before I reached John Farquharson's cottage the door had opened, and he was out, still buttoning his trousers over his nightshirt. "I've already sent the two lads up the road, mistress," he called to me. "I've told them that *everyone* is to come. We'll get the horses out all right, but the building will be hard to save. The pump is ready in the cooperage—but we'll have to get the line down to the river . . ." His words trailed off as he ran past me. From the doorway his wife called. "I'm dressing, mistress. The lads will bring whatever women can leave their bairns. It must not touch the distillery, mistress."

It was all of them, it was the whole world of Cluain, their jobs, their families, their loyalties. And as I turned to follow John back, I glanced upwards, and the first lights were beginning to come on at Ballochtorra. There would be more men on the way. As I came back within the shelter of the walls of the farthest warehouse I could already hear, distinguishable among all the clamour, Big Billy's honk of alarm and indignation; but he was well away from it, separated by the width of the road, and Neil Smith would never forget him and his flock. And there, in the darkness which was already beginning to be lightened by the glow of the fire, I felt a nudge on the shoulder, a nuzzle rub along my cheek. "Ailis . . . is this as close as you'll come? Well, stay then, good girl. And don't wander too far off." I did not attempt to tether her to any of the posts or gates; she would feel more easy that way and I did not have to worry that she would stray far from Cluain. "There'll be horses to look for all over the strath tomorrow . . ."

And there would be. I counted the open doors of the loose boxes, saw the horror of the inferno in the hay, above in the lofts and on the floor. There was a series of ominous explosive sounds, like the retorts of a gun, as individual slates cracked in the heat. But I could see no sign of a horse still left within those fiery shells. I thought they were all clear, and most of them had disappeared into the friendly darkness. Some would have jumped fences they had never thought to try before, some would stay by the roadside, a safe distance from the fire, some we would have to search the hills for, and some, too panic-stricken, would injure themselves, and have to be put down. There, in the midst of the small crowd of men that had now reached the yard from the cottages, and the growing number of women joining them, I knew the first real moment of fear. There had not been time until now to take in the full implication of what yet could happen. And I cursed the wind that blew, and brought the heat of the flames to my face.

*　　*　　*

By the time the pump and hose line to the river was hooked up, the men had arrived from Ballochtorra. The stable hands, coachmen, and gardeners went to work as if they knew what they were doing; the indoor servants were almost more hindrance than help, and I could hear my grandfather cursing one or two of them. It was a big, wheeled hand pump, kept for such emergencies, and like every- thing else at Cluain, old, but in good repair. The river was in full spate after the rains, so we did not, after the pump was ready, lack water. What was needed was the pressure and the energy to raise it the height to the buildings themselves, high enough to wet down the roofs of the house and the distillery. I suddenly knew then the good reasoning behind the placing of the warehouses on the other side of the road. Distance now was everything. It worked for and against us. The distance to the river, which protected the house and distillery when the river was in flood, seemed now impossibly far to pump the water, the distance for the jet of water to reach the tower room of the house was too great. But distance from the other buildings protected the warehouses. All the men took turns at the pump, while the others rested; the hay in the loft of the stables was now consumed, but the timbers were on fire. One of the faces I saw rushing by me in the now smoky haze that overhung us, intent on making his way down to the river, was Gavin Campbell. He didn't see me, and I didn't try to detain him. I stood for a moment with Samuel Lachlan, who leaned, trembling, against the garden wall. I tried to comfort him; he just kept shaking his head. "Such a loss!— such a loss! All the horses saved though . . . Sinclair had to fight with those two brutes . . . Angus is doing too much. He's too old . . . too old. *I'm* too old. There should be another pump . . . Angus should have had another pump."

"There wouldn't be men to work it," I said.

"Another pump," he insisted. "Oh, I'm too old." And he was. His frail body still shook from the exertion of that first effort to open up the stables and free the horses, shook from excitement and fear. At last I managed to persuade him to give up his post at the garden wall, and come around into the road outside the house. There, incongruously, he was ensconced in a chair from the drawing room. The small group of women who had come from the distillery cottages, and some of the younger maids from Ballochtorra, come to watch the spectacle, had been organised by Mairi Sinclair, who was now wearing a black coat over her nightgown. Methodically, she was overseeing the removal of the most valuable pieces of the furniture from the ground floor of the house. It was no small task. The great hall table had to be left—it would have needed eight men to lift it. And so also the sideboard from the dining room. I myself brought out the Bible, and set it down on a settle placed opposite Samuel Lachlan. "Watch it now, Mr. Lachlan—and should I go and start bringing the ledgers and files from the distillery office?—no, I can't. My grandfather has the keys."

"The distillery! The distillery will not take fire—not the distillery!" He was imploring.

"A precaution, only . . ."

"A precaution, oh, yes."

"Since you are here, Mr. Lachlan," Mairi Sinclair broke in, "would it trouble you to place your eye on these things. That light-minded lot down from Ballochtorra might take a fancy to one or two." She had loaded the settle with silver trays, and tea pots and jugs and tongs. There, under the settle, were the fire-dogs with the Cawdor crest. My grandfather's chess set was laid beside them.

"Yes, mistress—yes," Samuel Lachlan replied. I had never heard such meekness from him. The stable was smoking now, smoke that even the wind did not immediately clear; smoke full of menace, because no one could see the swift lick of flame that might still curve about a timber. While I stood there, and Samuel Lachlan huddled in his chair, a stream of water from the hose, meant to be directed toward the roof of the house, fell short of it, and reached over the garden wall, and onto me. I staggered for a moment; it did not touch the old man. Suddenly, now that the flames were gone, and the heat no longer there, I was drenched and cold. Then, leaving Samuel Lachlan, I walked around the corner of the garden wall. The smouldering building was hard to see—the wind drove the smoke into my eyes, and they watered. I shivered in my wet dress.

"They all were got out, Kirsty." Callum's voice beside me. I looked up. "Ailis was first. But I haven't seen her."

"Ailis is all right. She is taking care of herself. She always does."

One side of his face was horribly swollen; even though it was darkened by soot, I could see the distortion. And there was blood, already caked and dried, at the hairline above his left eye.

"You've been hurt!"

"No. I was slammed into a post getting one of the Clydesdales out. But no horse perished, Kirsty. That's what matters. Your grandfather will have to build new stables, but his heart will not be broken. If we stand by till the wind has dropped, and keep the pressure on the hose up, the distillery and the house are safe. We can just hope—or pray, as Mr. Lachlan seems to be doing—that no spark takes hold on the distillery. Every piece of wood there is saturated by forty years of alcohol."

"How did the fire begin?"

"Time enough to ask that when we know we have it beaten. Everything will wait on that."

"Callum . . . ?"

He had already turned away from me, answering some call from the midst of the men. There was some trouble with the hose; my grandfather was ordering it to be extended, but to make the coupling, the pressure would have to be reduced.

"Callum . . ." He was gone. His figure melded into the group about the hose. I didn't even know what I had meant to say to him. It was part of the chaos of that whole scene—I saw and knew only parts of it, fragments, my impressions scattered like the burning hay in the wind, like the distraught horses dispersed over the countryside. Then I pulled myself up. I was standing and staring, but doing nothing, less useful than Samuel Lachlan, who at least guarded part of Cluain's treasures. So then I went into the house and placed myself under Mairi Sinclair's direction. She nodded to me, as if she knew my helplessness. "Go to your grandmother's room, and bring whatever you can that seems valuable—take one of the trays to carry on. I have cleared the silver from the pantry. If you see anyone upstairs in the house who is not the wife or child of one of the Cluain workers, order them out, or we shall have small items missing when we come to count."

"It won't spread to the house," I said, even as I went off to obey her. "They just have to watch the stable now, and keep wetting it down."

She answered me with my own word: "Precautions . . ."

So I went to my grandmother's room, and began passing out to the waiting arms and aprons and trays of the Cluain women and children the precious things that Mairi Sinclair had stored away there, all the softening touches that the rest of the house lacked, the mirrors, the pictures, the little ornaments, the rolled-up rugs. These

311

last were carried down between two of the strongest women who offered themselves. The little girls were given the ornaments to carry, one at a time, carefully, down the stairs. I grew weary of it, because, looking from the window, it all seemed unnecessary. The fire was not out completely, but it was controlled, and there was nothing very combustible left to feed it. They would have to keep watch on it all night, and when daylight came, to start cutting away at the smoking timbers.

"Shall we start to take down the books, Mistress Kirsty?" one of the women asked me. I looked at the two bookcases there, crowded with volumes, and decided against it. There was a sudden sound of china shattering on the staircase, and the instant, nervous giggling. Well, it was inevitable that some things would be broken, and everyone was not familiar with those strange stairs, curving, and without a rail. It occurred to me then, when I thought about the books, to go down and ask Mairi Sinclair if she had removed her own herb and medicine books from the herb room. How one missed Morag in all this; her quickness and intelligence would have been worth the strength of six of these women.

I went and spoke to Mairi Sinclair about clearing the herb room. She shook her head. "Not unless it is necessary. After what has been said tonight, do you think I want to unlock that door?"

"But your books—your own records! They are more valuable than anything that's upstairs."

"Perhaps it would have been better for us all if they had never been. But go, mistress, and stay with Mr. Lachlan. I will try to bring a hot drink soon. He does not seem well. One of the women will come with me to the kitchen and make tea to pass out. The men need something now. I will tell the others to go—they are getting careless. A vase has been broken, and the leg of a chair damaged. The frame of a mirror chipped . . ." She grieved over a mirror, she who never looked into one. I did as she said, and went to stay with Samuel Lachlan. Before I went I brought from the passage the Inverness cape for him. He accepted it about his shoulders without comment. He sat, bemused, amidst the great jumble of what had been taken from the house—china, chairs, bedding, silver, like a strange old spider in the middle of a fantastic web of collections.

Who would have thought that the bare starkness of Cluain had contained so many riches?

I stood with him for a while, talking about anything that came to mind, but he hardly seemed to hear me. He was muttering under his breath, his own litany of incantations about carelessness and waste, of bad stewardship. "But it's only the stables, Mr. Lachlan," I said impatiently. "We have been lucky it was no more."

"Waste!" was the only reply I got. I went to the corner of the wall. Here the wind blew straight at me, and the smoke was carried with it. Ironically, now that the hay no longer blazed, it had been necessary to bring lanterns so that the men could see to move about. Clouds were scudding before the wind, blotting out the light that might have helped them, but too swiftly, I thought, to bring rain. Rain would have helped us, and yet made the operation more difficult. Down at the river they would be standing in mud. I wondered where Gavin Campbell was. I wondered if I should go and ask my grandfather about taking the books from the distillery office. I didn't know where he was—or Callum. I started for the thickest group of men standing before the ruin of the stable.

Halfway across the yard I heard Neil Smith's voice—his tone carrying all the agony of a man who sees his life's trust betrayed before his eyes.

"God Almighty! Look, Macdonald!—look! The back end of the warehouses!"

I was amongst those who crowded to the road to look along it, and there, in the warehouse farthest from the yard and the distillery, was the terrible glow. The iron bars across the high, small windows were outlined against it.

*   *   *

I was one of the ones near to Neil Smith as we gathered closer to the warehouses. The main doors were flung open wide—I think it was he and I together who rushed to free Big Billy and his flock from the pen close to those doors. In the first minutes the big gander went about biting every leg he found available, unwilling to believe that he and all his family were not the personal objectives of the holocaust.

It had become a holocaust. There is no way that water can fight spirits once they are alight. Useless to get up the extra length of hose, useless to urge the men at the river to pump. Water was only the means of diluting the stream of fire, perhaps spreading it farther. It already flowed, the deadly stream released by the explosion of casks soaked for long years in sherry and whisky; it ignited the columns and beams already impregnated by contact with the saturated casks. And all the doors—the doors big enough to allow for the passage of the distillery drays, had been opened right through to the end, where the fire had begun. With the wind blowing, it created a natural funnel for the flames, a lateral chimney by which fire fed on fire.

I witnessed the anguish of Neil Smith as he came out of his cottage, after the geese had been released. I remember the grip of his hand, biting into my arm, the old broken nails still having the power to hurt. "God help me! I didn't think to take the warehouse keys with me when I went running to the house first. Someone had been in and taken them from the board. Look at the doors— standing wide open to the world! It's the end of me!" Then he looked up realising at last whose arm he clutched. "It's the end of Cluain, lass!"

My grandfather directed the added lengths of hose to be run along the road at the side of the warehouses, and the water to be played upon the roof—but there was nothing he could do about what was happening inside. The small jet of water was futile against the force of energy set alight within. There was one great explosion in the end warehouse, and suddenly, through the ventilation holes at floor level, the stream of fire flowed. It followed the drainage channels, and finally reached the place where the burn flowed beside the buildings. It caught. The burn itself was afire, fed by the endless stream of alcohol from inside the warehouse. It was a sight I could not wholly believe in, even though I saw it myself. The burn ran with fire, and where it was channeled under the road, at the little bridge, there was a weird gap of blackness between the two fiercely burning streams. It ran on down to the river, finally to be diluted by that much greater torrent, to nothingness.

For a moment, close to my ear, I heard Callum's shout. The roar of the flames was already greater than anything the stable fire had produced. "It's still in the end warehouse. The doors have to be shut. It's the only hope we have to save anything. If I can close the doors we have a chance to soak them with enough water to stop the spread to the rest. Go and tell your grandfather to bring the hoses up through the warehouses. I'll try to close the doors one by one."

He was gone, escaping my clutching hands, escaping my cries. Neil Smith and I stood and watched as he ran through the open main door of the warehouses, the stacked casks high on each side making his figure even smaller and smaller. Did we see it—did we actually see it—or was it fantasy? In that last second before he reached the end doors—those massive doors that had to be swung and closed against the force of the heat and energy generated within that inferno, the draught that sucked the fire in upon itself and stoked it—did Neil Smith and I see that figure for a second?—that slender figure with fiery hair, the momentary dark figure silhouetted against the blaze, the figure of a young woman, who only began to run as the fire raced to engulf her? Was it she whom Callum also saw? What else could have made him rush within the raging territory of the last warehouse, beyond the door that might have meant safety. We never really knew—Neil Smith and I. What we thought we saw was Callum's running figure, and then the shape that might have been Morag, suddenly outlined, helplessly caught, the sleepwalker awakened too late from sleep. They did not meet, those two figures—I would swear to it. Before Callum reached the last doors, the end warehouse, feeding totally upon itself, erupted. The whole mass went in one explosion of blazing alcohol. An enormous fire ball shot up, devouring support columns, beams, and roof. The air all around was sucked towards the dreadful centre. Slates crashed in upon the burning casks, the ventilation holes choked, so that the liquid spilled back upon itself, finding other ways to run, into the forward warehouses. The door to the last warehouse was engulfed before Callum could reach it. And after that, there was no distinguishing one part from another. It raced like the wind, explosion upon explosion, the slates raining down on the men who stood dumbfounded in the road at the side of the building, helpless, speechless. All I could feel was the tightening grip of Neil Smith's fingers upon my arm. No smoke now, but fire consuming fire, raging, pouring, as fuel was added to unquenchable fuel.

"Callum . . . !"

It seemed so few minutes before it was consumed. The whole stored wealth of Cluain disappeared before our eyes, and in the midst of it was the man who might have been its future wealth. We never even had a glimpse of Callum again.

My grandfather went on. I don't know from what source he gathered his strength, but he did. He saw forty years consumed in minutes, but he still had the energy to direct the men to bring the hose back to the distillery and wet it down. The distillery before the house. Then the house was again soaked, stone walls and roof, a fairly hurried operation because they had to return to the distillery, which was much more vulnerable. The sparks from the warehouse flew upwards, and I stood rooted, dreading to see the first glow from within the distillery. But with a fire so hot, there was very little left of the warehouses—it was quick, and powerful and sure. It flared and died almost as rapidly. And my grandfather continued to direct the whole operation to safeguard the distillery as though he were unmoved by the holocaust which consumed his life and his work, and by the cries of Neil Smith, who watched his neat cottage, attached to the warehouse, also disappear.

It wasn't until I told my grandfather—when the fire in the warehouse seemed to fold in upon itself, when the burn ceased to run with fire—that Callum had gone into the warehouse, and was dead, that he turned aside. Without an order to any other man to take over, he abruptly turned aside. He went back into the house, into the dining room, Samuel Lachlan grabbing unavailingly at him. We stood there, still, unspeaking, and my grandfather kept his back turned to the windows, so that even the enormous, dying glow of the warehouses was just, for his eyes, a reflection on the walls.

*　　*　　*

We moved some chairs back in, Mairi Sinclair and I, and she poked some life into the peat turfs, and laid some fresh. I remember forcing my grandfather down into a chair, keeping his back carefully to the garden, so that he might not watch the glow that still lighted the sky. Gavin Campbell came; I don't think he said anything, just took my grandfather's hand for a moment. My grandfather didn't seem to notice his presence. I helped Mairi Sinclair bring bread and ham from the kitchen, and we served it on the thick kitchen crockery. She seemed now not to care for the good china stacked up outside in the road, or Cluain's silver. I also helped her carry out food for the men standing about in the stableyard, still pumping water on the distillery. There were plenty of women about in the kitchen would have done the task just as well, but it seemed right that if my grandfather was not there, I should appear.

Then I came back to the dining room, and began to pour whisky into glasses that one of the women had brought in from the road. I passed it round, and to Neil Smith, who still stood in the doorway, halfway between our group and the men in the yard. He really belonged nowhere, and his world was just as much finished as ours.

"Grandfather," I said, "I have sent whisky with the food to the men. It grows cold, and they must still keep wetting down the distillery."

He looked at me with dulled eyes. "Aye—that's right. Don't spare it, Kirsty. I have a few casks in the cellar—Excise paid, mind you, Neil Smith." He rose to his feet and went to pour more whisky from the decanter. "No, let us not spare it this night. We might as well drink the best—here, Samuel, your glass." The old man was rocking in his chair, sipping at the whisky, and keeping up a continual little moaning sound, that might be his substitute for weeping. "And you, Campbell, you drink Cluain's whisky this night, and savour it. Because when these few casks are done, there will be no more for a long time. And tell Callum . . . Tell Callum Sinclair . . . My God!— Callum . . ."

Now he stopped. His back was towards us as he stood at the sideboard. The action was so slow that I actually saw the glass slipping in his hand, and his desperate fight to hold onto it, and himself. Then it fell to the ground and smashed. He held himself upright, hands pressed on the edge of the sideboard, for a few seconds longer, then that burly body crashed down, and one hand lay among the broken glass and the spilled liquid of his life.

Chapter 11

Two days later Angus Macdonald was buried in the plot between his wife and his mother Christina. Next to Christina was William's grave and beside that was the grave of Callum Sinclair.

Mairi Sinclair had protested. "You cannot. It is not right, now."

"If it is not right now, it shall never be. Is it not now time we all laid down our pride and our fears, and admitted to the truth? I intend Callum to lie beside William, and close to his father. And his headstone will be marked Callum Sinclair Macdonald—as my grandfather wrote it in the Bible. It is long ago time that all who care to know, should know. He is dead—shall we bury him in some corner of the kirkyard? He must lie with his family. Do you dare to say no?"

If she wept, I could not tell it. She was as silent and withdrawn as ever. How silent the whole house was. Samuel Lachlan sat in his chair by the fire; how frail he seemed after the bulk of my grandfather; how deep was the quiet without Morag's voice to break it. I made journeys to feed Giorsal, and she was becoming tamer to my hand. I had John shoot me a rabbit or a pigeon for her each day. I stood in the shed with Giorsal, stroking her with the feather, as Callum had done, and it was there I did my weeping alone, where no one could see, or hear. Cluain in these days had need of a calm presence. I could no more afford to indulge grief than Mairi Sinclair.

Gavin sent the Ballochtorra landau for the journey to the kirk-yard; it had to be borrowed, since the Cluain trap had gone in the stable fire. But the Sunday Lad had been found, and it was he who was between the shafts, not one of Ballochtorra's horses. Gavin came with the carriage to Cluain to escort us to the kirk, and to take Samuel Lachlan. Again there was the confrontation between myself and Mairi Sinclair when I insisted that she break the habit of a life-time, and ride beside me.

"We are burying your son, and my grandfather this day, Mistress Sinclair, in the same family grave—marking them with the same name. Will you have me pass you on the road as you walk to your son's funeral? A time of change has come at Cluain. It is as well to recognise it."

"Yes, a time of change. It is as well to recognise it. I will be pack-ing my things tomorrow, mistress. I would be grateful if you could keep my books for a little time until I have found a place to take them. Of my other belongings, there is little enough."

"Your books will stay at Cluain forever—as you will, Mistress Sinclair. I think your grief has turned your senses."

"I cannot stay where I am not wanted. *You* cannot want me here. I take no charity . . ."

"None is offered. Cluain has need of both of us, and well you know it. It is unthinkable that you should leave. I do not offer you charity—or ease. Cluain will use both of us hard. It will make its demands, as it always has done. You do not exist away from Cluain. As my grandfather could not—nor Callum. We have lost very much. Let us not lose more than we need."

All she did was nod, and turn away. But when the Ballochtorra carriage arrived I found her waiting in the hall, wearing, as always, the plaid about her head. We did not speak all the way to the kirk-yard, nor back again, but she rode beside me.

Those two burials were hard. The anchor of Cluain was gone, and, almost, its hope. I wondered where I would turn now. With my hand on his arm, more to support him than anything else, I felt Samuel Lachlan tremble. And then I looked across Callum's open grave at Gavin's face, and remembered that beyond the crowd that surrounded us now, just across the path, Margaret lay. The grass had not even started to sprout on that grave; and she lay so close to two men who had loved her. And Gavin's eyes met mine, then; we both seemed to know what the other thought, and the thought was the same.

*   *   *

Gavin escorted us back to Cluain, and Samuel Lachlan, as though he dreaded the thought of the empty, quiet house, asked him to come in.

"Angus was more than ten years younger than me," Samuel Lachlan said. "I had not thought to be the one left."

And then he picked up the Inverness paper, which had arrived while we were gone. There was a picture of the remains of the warehouse at Cluain, and an article about the fire which I did not even want to read. But the main headline was reserved for something else. PANIC RUSH TO SELL SHARES. FERGUSON'S BANKRUPT?

He held it towards Gavin. "What do you make of this?"

"What am I to make of it? I'm sorry for James Ferguson. I'm not sorry for myself and my son."

"You mean you're *glad?*" Samuel was dumbfounded; how could anyone not mourn the fall of a capitalist's kingdom?

"I think it may be my son's salvation. Ferguson can make no claim on him now. There is nothing for Ferguson money to buy. And Ferguson does not understand any other relationship, so he will leave my son alone. Jamie will be what I am—that is, a poor man. I think he will be no worse for it."

"But—Ballochtorra . . . ?"

"Ballochtorra cannot be run without money. The servants have had their notice—I gave them that the day my wife was buried, before I knew about Ferguson's difficulties. I suppose, if Ferguson goes into liquidation, the receiver might justly claim the contents of Ballochtorra—the horses and all the rest of it. But the title to the house and lands has to stay with me. If it's possible to find a buyer, I'll try to sell the house. The land, such as it is, must be kept for Jamie. There will be no gamekeepers, of course. But the grouse moors are there, and will stay, even though they might not provide a worthy day's shooting for a prince. They could be rented perhaps . . . We'll see."

"And you?" Samuel was so shaken by the events of the last days that his reserve and probity seemed to have dropped from him. I had not thought him capable of asking such questions of someone who was almost a stranger to him.

Gavin took the tea I poured, and munched on the ham sandwich as if he suddenly found himself hungry. "We'll do as I've always wanted to. There's a little money—I'll borrow the rest—and I'll drain the only piece of Ballochtorra land that's worth trying to do anything with. It could raise a crop or two—it *could* make pasture. We would not be hungry, Jamie and I. And the gatehouse will soon be empty."

"The gatehouse!" Samuel Lachlan was thunderstruck. "And you are the heir to the Marquis of Rossmuir!"

Gavin actually laughed. I heard the sound with pleasure; it broke the silence of mourning in this house, a sound that would help to bury the past.

"And the present Marquis of Rossmuir wishes he had some place as comfortable, no doubt. Though I can't speak for the old gentleman; I've never met him. But it will do very well for Jamie and me . . . until we can sell the house, or find a tenant. And then the money will build us a small house on the land I want to farm. I know the place where I want to build. It is out of sight of Ballochtorra—which is no great loss. Jamie will fish the river, and we will be able to keep a gun or two. I've always noticed that small houses are warmer than big ones . . . We will manage, Jamie and me. And he will not go to school in England. It is the one piece of news that has made him happy since his mother died. He will have a pony—not the thoroughbred he has now. A garron—one of the kind we breed around here. Far safer—far tougher. What he really longs for, of course, is that I should buy Ailis for him."

"I will never sell Ailis."

"You suppose I don't know that? But let him dream. In time he will love his own pony—and he will love it better for having to take care of it himself. So you see, Mr. Lachlan, that Ferguson's going bankrupt is a bad blow for James Ferguson, but I cannot think it is wholly a disaster for his grandson."

"But . . . but he will be an *earl!*"

Again Gavin laughed. Why did the sound affect me so much? It was like the spring of hope, of new life. He saw no adversity before him, or Jamie. I sipped my tea and thought of his remark about small houses, and how he and Margaret had lost each other in the vastness of Ballochtorra.

"Yes, an earl. I must try to explain it to him soon. That poor old man can't live much longer. They say he is pitifully weak, and can hardly see or hear. So Jamie will be an earl. I think his grandfather has given him the impression that a coronet will appear like magic— a real coronet. But children forget easily. If he can fish his river, and ride his pony on his own moors, I think the coronet may not matter so much. I'm sorry his grandfather will think it is such a come-down for his only grandchild. But James Ferguson will never see it any other way. Without money and power, he is a ruined man in every respect. If I give my life to it, I will see that Jamie does not become that kind of man."

Then he took his hat and went. I saw him motion to the coachman to give up the reins, and he himself took them. The sullen look on the man's face indicated that he had had his notice along with the others, and thought also that Sir Gavin had indeed come down in the world, and had no business to appear so cheerful about it.

"I will send John tomorrow with the landau," I called to him. "He can walk the Sunday Lad back."

"Use it as long as you like. Fergusons can't begrudge you that little favour. I don't think the Receiver will be in by tomorrow."

I went back to Samuel Lachlan at the fire, and suddenly the house was silent and empty again. I fought, in a moment's panic, against the depression that started to come over me, the loneliness, the sense that now the fight was just beginning. And I had need of Gavin's laugh, his cheer, the sense of courage he imparted. But I had to go back to the old man by the fire, and try to give him what I had hardly begun to scrape together for myself.

"Extraordinary!" Samuel muttered. "I do believe he means it!"

"Means what?"

"He really doesn't care about the money. Imagine having to do without Ferguson's money, and not caring!"

"It's possible some men are like that. Like Callum—who didn't want Cluain. *He* would have parted with what he loved rather than be a James Ferguson. It's possible, Mr. Lachlan . . . it's possible."

He shook his head. "I don't understand it. Give me some whisky, Kirsty. The kirkyard was cold . . ."

And he warmed his bones before the fire, and on Cluain's whisky, remembering, perhaps, what my grandfather had said—that when those few casks were empty, there would be no more until Cluain's next distilling came of age. At that moment, I had no idea when that might be.

II

Even after they combed the wreckage of the warehouses there was nothing found that even suggested the body of Morag Macpherson. "But I saw her," Neil Smith kept saying. He repeated it again and again, to the Excise officers who came to investigate the fire, and to the police. "I saw her there, right at the end, in the last warehouse where the fire started. And that was a laid fire—the doors opened all through like that. Deliberately set. Well, Mistress Howard here will tell you the same thing. She stood beside me—"

I had to tell them that I could not swear that we had seen Morag Macpherson in those seconds—something that appeared to be the figure of a woman outlined against the inferno behind her. The blaze had been so intense it had almost seemed to sear the eyes. Callum, I knew, had never reached her—if she had been there.

"If she had been there," one Exciseman said, "we would have found the remains. No one could have escaped from where you thought you saw her. And if it is arson . . ."

"It *was* arson! Do I go leaving my warehouses open to who wishes to walk inside? Is it for this I have built my reputation

324

in the service? I tell you that girl started the blaze in the stables as a distraction—and then she waited her chance to start the fire that really destroyed Cluain." Neil Smith was indignant and shamed.

And afterwards, when he had walked off up the road to the cottage of one of the workers where he was temporarily lodged, the Exciseman turned to me. "Well, we all knew it was past time for Neil Smith to retire—but he *had* built a fine reputation in the service, and it being so quiet up here, and he never leaving the place—no family, no distractions, and never touched a dram in his life. But to go and leave the keys . . . no matter *what* was taking place outside the cottage. If the sky had been falling on him, he should have thought of his keys first. It will go badly with him, Miss Howard. He cannot expect to stay in the service now."

"He will stay at Cluain, however," I said. "No one could imagine him leaving."

"You will build again, then?" The man was looking at me with frank curiosity. "You will go into production?"

"Why not?" I answered. "There is a distillery, isn't there? The men haven't lost their skills overnight because of a fire! We will find warehousing."

"It will have to be adequate, Miss Howard. Bonded is bonded. It must be secure, and with accommodation for Excise officers. It isn't like the old days, you know, when Mr. Macdonald first set up. They say that in those days he had a fence and a shotgun. That sort of thing won't do now."

"It will be done exactly as it should," I retorted. "Cluain has never been in trouble with the Excise, has it? It has never been short on quantities? Well—that is how it will go on."

And the Exciseman, staring at me, was wondering how it was to be done, just as I was. But he said no more about it. It was my business. No doubt the word would run through the whole Excise service that Angus Macdonald's granddaughter was just as tough and irascible as the old man, that he would not be dead while she lived. But I was not Angus Macdonald, and this was not the Cluain of forty years ago, a simpler, more trusting world, where things could begin small, and be permitted to grow.

The distillery waited—but that was all. Its product had to be stored and guarded, it had to be serviced. There was so much, and it had to come from me.

But once I could bring myself to look beyond the fearful ruins of the warehouses, I was calmed. The world of Cluain was still here, damaged, but essentially the same. The sleek cattle grazed the river meadows, the barley was safely stored. This was no dubious heritage Angus Macdonald had left in my hands.

And as I went back to eat dinner with Samuel Lachlan after that interview with the Excisemen and the police, I pondered the fate of Morag. Had we really seen her, Neil Smith and I? Was it a trick of the fire?—unnatural shadows thrown for a few seconds only that had deceived us? No young body had been found crushed and charred in the wreckage. It was not possible she had found some other way out. There was no other way. I imagined her, as calmly as she had stood in the stableyard watching the race to bring the horses out, then going, in the midst of the incoherent pattern of that first fire, into Neil Smith's cottage, taking the keys, and making her way right back to the very end of the warehouses—the place hardest to reach with the hose, the place where it would last be noticed. And there setting the first small blaze, which she knew would take hold. And then as calmly opening wide and hooking back each set of doors as she returned through the building, leaving the front door itself open to the wind. And then, with the same unhurried calm, replacing the keys on Neil Smith's rack—for that was where they had been when he had thought to look—just before the fire took his cottage. He still held the keys to the blackened, roofless ruin.

And where was Morag now? Had she just walked as far as Grantown and taken the first train from there in the early morning? —before news of the fire had come, before anyone thought to look for a young girl? With a plaid half over her face, she would not be in any way remarkable. I thought of her, and the future. She would go, probably to Glasgow, and lose herself in its teeming warrens until the search and enquiries about her would die away. She could turn her hand to so many things, could Morag, and her tongue and wit would not betray the background of Cluain.

But Morag did not care for crowded places. In time she would go off—Canada or Australia. Clever as she was, and knowing her own worth, she would not give herself to anyone who asked; when it came to marriage, Morag would choose well. She was beautiful, and young, and clever. And how her heart must have been filled with rage and hate to do what she had done. It was formidable to think of that lovely face, its skin flushing apricot in excitement and passion, the shining red curls—and the kind of inner madness of greed and cunning it had masked. She had dreamed of being Mistress of Cluain, of having Callum. And yet, had I not dreamed the same dream? How different were we? It was a sobering, humbling thought.

I shivered in the September wind as I scurried across the yard from the distillery office; light drops of rain blew into my face. No, I did not think Morag Macpherson had died in the fire. Somewhere she went on, planning, under another name, a future just as great as she had sought here at Cluain. And, being Morag, I thought it was very probable that she would find it.

III

I faced Samuel Lachlan with the facts as we sat before the fire that night.

"Mr. Lachlan, I have told all the workers that they will stay on. I have told them that we might have to miss a season's production, and that they might have to turn their hands to anything that comes—building labourers, farm workers, anything that Cluain needs. But they need not leave their cottages, and their wages will be the same as if they worked in the distillery and the warehouses. I cannot let them go . . . they will be needed, more than needed, when we are back to full production."

"And where will you get the money?"

"You will lend it to me, Mr. Lachlan."

327

"On what surety?"

"Cluain."

"I charge a high interest rate. What would I do with Cluain if you fail?"

"If I fail you will own a fine farm—and distillery buildings. You will own the assets of Cluain."

"The assets of Cluain would not pay me back what you need to start again. The insurance will cover what you will owe to the blenders whose whisky was stored in the warehouses, but Cluain's wealth rested in those barrels of unsold spirits which Angus Macdonald held for himself. Have you any idea how much money you are asking for?"

"No—I thought you would tell me."

"You expect me to be broker and banker at the same time? You ask a lot, young woman."

"Yes, I ask a lot. My grandfather asked a lot of you the day he walked into your office in Inverness and asked you to take his case for no payment, but the justice on which it rested. And then he borrowed from you to make his beginning. Was he really asking for *less,* in those days, than I am asking for now?"

"But he was . . . well, he was Angus Macdonald."

"And I am Angus Macdonald's granddaughter. You're going to say that a woman cannot run a distillery? Have any tried? Have any failed? Yes—I know, my great-grandmother failed, but she was on a poor little island out in the Hebrides. There was no Cluain for her."

"If you were married . . ."

"If I were married I might be married to some fool who would spend your money foolishly. Men have failed also, Mr. Lachlan. Fergusons is now in the hands of the Receiver. A year ago, would you have said it could happen?"

"I told you I watched Ferguson closely. I heard the stories of him. And I never bought a penny share of his stock."

"Would you buy *my* stock? Would you buy the stock and seed of Angus Macdonald? That is all I have to persuade you with. I am ignorant, yes—I'm too well aware of that. So have others been, and they have learned. Look at me, Mr. Lachlan. Do you see any of Angus Macdonald in me? The men will stay with me, and I will learn—from you and from them. There are all those ledgers in my grandfather's office from which I will learn. I expect long days—and nights—of work. I welcome them. You will see no grand living here, Mr. Lachlan. And no silk, even for Sundays. What do you say, Mr. Lachlan?"

"It is a risk. A huge risk. And what is in it for me? I am old. I may be dead before you sell your first cask."

"That too is a risk, Mr. Lachlan. And what is in it for you? —am I presumptuous if I say that in it for you is the right to sit where you now sit, at Cluain's fireside—the right to guide Cluain, as you have done for forty years. You can always go back to your rooms in Inverness, Mr. Lachlan—and I've no doubt I could go and find buyers. There would be buyers, I haven't any doubt, for a fine farm, and a distillery in good working order, with skilled distillery hands ready. Oh, I think there are plenty who would take it off my hands. Let us start with the Macquaries and the Camerons. *They* know the value of Cluain—even just as a name, a reputation. Yes, I think I could sell it all. And then you and I, Mr. Lachlan, we both would have lost it. I would have some money in my pocket, instead of debts. And you would avoid a big risk. But what would we lose, both of us?"

"You will be cheated. Men will try to cheat you because you are a woman."

"Let them try! They'll not do it a second time. Do you forget what I learned in China? There, I knew by exactly how much each was *allowed* to cheat. It is quite a skill, Mr. Lachlan. Not learned in an accountant's office. And, yes, I will make mistakes with the farm—but I will listen to advice. Has no man ever left his crops too late?—or a storm come before they were ready? Well, these are the problems my grandfather fought, and I would want to try to fight. It would be easier if I did not. I would have money, and some comfort, and no doubt, in time, a husband who liked the bit of money I brought with me. And you would still have *your* money, safely invested wherever it is invested. Or we both can have Cluain. Which, Mr. Lachlan—which?"

"You press me very hard, woman. Very hard."

"I am Angus Macdonald's granddaughter, Mr. Lachlan. Would you expect anything else?"

"Yes, you are Angus Macdonald's granddaughter. And that is where I will put my money."

I went and got him a whisky. "It is your own private reserve now, Mr. Lachlan. For as long as Cluain's whisky lasts, it is for you alone. For ourselves, for the first years, we will make do with an inferior product. You will live—you will live to drink these last casks, and by that time the first of Cluain's new distilling will be fit for drinking. You are like Ailis. You will live to be a terrible great age—at Cluain."

"Ah—" He shrugged off the words. "There will be little enough time for me to be at Cluain. Do you realise, Kirsty, how I will have to work to get this money to lend you? I must be back to Inverness tomorrow to draw up the papers. Everything must be in order. I will be back next week . . ."

And every week, I thought, so long as he lived. And he must be ever welcome at Cluain's fireside—however old, however irritable. Angus Macdonald's granddaughter must always make sure of that.

Chapter 12

It was early the next morning when I rode up to Callum's cottage on Ailis. It was the first time she had been ridden since her illness; there was the bouncy freshness of a young pony in her step, but, as always, no trace of skittishness. It was a grey morning, chill, with a light wind. I held my plaid closely about me, glad to leave behind the yard of Cluain, where the smell of the charred timbers and the earth soaked with spirits still hung, despite the wind. Ailis did not hesitate as I turned her head up the track that led to Callum's cottage; if she thought at all of the fearful journey when she had last come down here, she did not show it. I carried a pigeon, shot by John that morning, in the pouch. Giorsal would not eat any but fresh-killed meat.

I checked Ailis before we crossed the burn to the cottage, looking at the scene, thinking that already, in the few days it had been untenanted, it seemed to wear an air of desolation. There were leaves gathering before the door of the cottage, and against the walls; in a few weeks weeds would grow there. If there were not regular fires kept up in the range, the damp would begin to creep in, and as the winter snows began to drift down from the heights, the field mice would find an entry, and settle, and the rooks nest in the chimney. I could not bear the thought of it falling into ruin—like that other cottage up there, where Mairi

Sinclair had grown up. I wondered, sitting there on Ailis, if Neil Smith would come up here to live. He would no longer be with the Excise, but he would stay at Cluain, I knew. He could have Callum's pony for the trek up and down to Cluain—I was sure Mairi Sinclair would agree to that. I looked about me. It was so lonely here, in this little clearing by the burn, the silence so complete. I wondered if Neil Smith would mind the loneliness, he who had always lived so close to the centre of Cluain's life. Would he want to bring Big Billy and the flock with him? And where would we make a pool for them?—the burn was too swift and too narrow. And I realised, as I sat there, looking at the place that had been Callum's own, and would be forever that way in my heart, that the practical, everyday problems of Cluain were already impinging. What I had promised Samuel Lachlan last night must be carried out. There could be no waste at Cluain. To think of it inhabited by any other than Callum was like pressing on a raw wound, but some arrangement must be made. I pictured it as I knew it—the books stacked haphazardly on the shelves, the untidy roll-top desk. I would ask Mairi Sinclair to come up here and select that which she did not wish to leave to another. For myself, I did not think I could ever enter that door again.

I put Ailis in the empty stable. Giorsal greeted me with a harsh cry, and ran up and down on the perch. She had ceased bating off at my arrival. It signalled food to her, and she welcomed me, welcomed, also, the release from the boredom of sitting on her perch. She was growing very restless. It was too many days since she had sat in her block, too many since she had bathed and preened herself. She danced up and down the perch in greedy anticipation. She spread her wings for me, as if to remind me that she had them, that flight was being denied her. I slipped on the gauntlet, and took the first piece of pigeon out of the bag. Without hesitation, she stepped on to my fist, and began to pull with a claw and beak at the piece of bird I held between my fingers. It was strange how quickly I had become used to handling the pieces of pigeon, watching her pull a few feathers away, and then swallow the rest. It offended me now no more than seeing the uncooked meat in the pantry at Cluain. This was Giorsal's natural food; with it, she stayed healthy.

But she would not finish the whole pigeon. I kept extending the pieces to her between my gloved fingers, but finally she moved back on to the perch, and took up again the restless pacing, up and down, up and down. Even when I stroked her with the feather she was not appeased. She looked towards me and uttered her strange cry.

"Come now, Giorsal. It is time."

First of all I removed the hood; it would be easier here where she was on the perch, and I had both hands free for the task. I could not hope to match Callum's dexterity with his teeth and one hand. When the hood came off I left her alone for a few minutes, talking all the time to her though, while her eyes grew accustomed even to this amount of dim light after the long darkness. I sweated with nervousness as I released the jesses from the swivel, and twined them through my fingers, trying to remember how Callum had done it. She did not at once realise what had happened, and I had to entice her with a piece of fresh-cut carcass meat to move forward from the perch on to my fist. Then, as she pulled and tugged at the meat, I took my first steps backwards, away from the perch. She stopped in surprise. I saw her wings begin to flex up, and wondered what I would do if she bated off my hand, and would not return, finally hanging head downwards, and swinging from the jesses. She would sense, of course, that I was frightened. A timid, uncertain handler was an invitation to trouble from a hawk. Desperately, I did not want to botch these next few minutes. If she did not completely trust me, if I had not learned enough from watching Callum's calm, sure handling of her, there would be trouble and danger for her before I got her into the open. If she spread her wings here and tried to escape me, she could damage their tips, and perhaps be hampered in flight. If the hood were back on her she would be calm, but with either course I would have difficulties.

I opened the door very slowly, so that she did not see too much of the sky at once. But the light streamed on her, the pupils of those big eyes contracted in response to it. Again she raised

333

her wings, and I felt a powerful tug on my fist. But we were safely past the doorjamb, and in the open. Here her wings could stretch, and she might attempt a flight, but with no harm, except for the possibility of pulling me off balance.

But she was wonderfully quiet, just raising her head to the sky, seeing her world again, sensing it, smelling it. I swear that she took her time to look around the clearing, and up beyond it, where the folds of the mountains could be seen. She felt she would soon be among it all again, but she was in no hurry. In all my nervousness I also paused; Callum had shown me one of the noblest sights seen by man, the flight of the falcon. And now I looked at that wonderful, proud head as it slowly turned, and I was grateful. No span of time, no dimming of memory, would ever take this from me.

The next was the hardest, and the most dangerous—dangerous for Giorsal. If I bungled it, she would be dead in a very short time, and she would be a trapped and maimed creature for whatever time she did live; she would die miserably, tangled in a tree or thicket.

So I took the piece of fresh grouse meat, shot illegally on Ballochtorra's moors that morning, the piece I had saved for this moment. I put it between the thumb and first finger of my left hand, where Giorsal sat; I twitched it a little, to make her notice it. Her eyes were full of her world, and her crop was full already, but the scent reached her, and she began to pull daintily at it, as if it were something to play with. While she was absorbed, I reached into the bag with my right hand, and groped about for the scissors. They were small, with blunted end, but a sharp cutting edge, borrowed from Mairi Sinclair who used them for preparing dressings. I had explained what I needed them for, and she had shaken her head, even as she tried to sharpen them still more. "I doubt they'll cut through. They are not meant for leather."

"I will have to try. I don't know how to manage any other way."

But they cut; Callum had kept the leather oiled and supple. First the bewits that held the bells—a little tinkling sound as the

334

one attached to the left leg hit the ground. The second was difficult, because it was on the leg with which Giorsal was gripping the meat. But finally I had manoeuvred the scissors between her leg and the leather, and cut through. The second bell hit the ground, and rolled among some stones. She ceased eating on hearing the noise. She stayed for a long minute, looking down and around her. Then she turned to the meat again. This time I went to the upraised leg first; if I could cut the jess off that without alarming her, the task was almost done. She stopped eating again, and looked around at me, cocking her head, and swivelling to try to understand this strange new thing that was happening. But I had reached in clean and near to the leg, and the whole jess fell away. The second one was simple. Giorsal was still holding up her leg, with claws extended, seeing its odd nakedness, without bell or jess, when I reached and cut near the second leg, the one with which she gripped my fist.

"Good-bye, Giorsal . . ." I lifted my arm with the motion I had seen Callum use when he cast her off. She lifted her wings, and momentarily hovered, the wings brushing my face, as if she did not quite know what to do with this freedom. Where were the long streamers which had been her shadow from her first year of life —where was the sound of the bells? But finally the sense of joy gained in her, and she was up, rising quite slowly, trying her wings. She circled the clearing a few times, as though making up her mind in which direction she would first fly. There would be no need for her to hunt today. She would soar, and float and stoop, making mock passes at the birds of passage, pretending, playing. Then she would bathe, and preen, and dry. And tomorrow, when she felt hunger, she would kill, and she would be on her own, and free.

But in case she did not kill, I would come back for three days and leave fresh pigeon for her here in the clearing, on the block. She would not so soon forget where her shelter was, where she had returned each time from hunting with Callum. By then, she would either have adapted to the wild state, or she would have failed, and she would die. But better to die out here, in the country she loved, in her own element, than live her days, hooded, in a darkened shed, on a perch. No one but Callum could have cared for her properly; none would now try.

She rose a little higher above the trees of the clearing, above the high rocks behind it, as if to take her bearings, to remind herself of the lay of her territory. She hovered a little there, and all at once she came down. Just in time, as she came at me, I raised the gloved hand. There she clung, perhaps three seconds, perhaps five, wings still outstretched, her black eyes boring into mine. And then she was off, swift and high this time, higher and higher, up and off along the wind, tearing down the strath towards the crag of Ballochtorra, where she had been born.

I dropped my hand. She was gone—that most beautiful of birds in flight, that graceful, swooping creature, that shadow of death to the other birds of the strath—she was gone. But she had returned, once, for those magical seconds, to my hand, bestowing the gift of her freedom upon me. I knew then, fully, the joy Callum had had in her. I was truly melded with him, for just this one time.

This, rather than his burial, was our real parting. "Good-bye."

I picked up the cut jesses, the bewits, the little tinkling Indian bells. I couldn't make myself go into the cottage to leave them, so I put them in the pouch. They would go back to Cluain with me. They would join William's scroll in the leather trunk that had come from China—one which I would seldom open.

It was then his figure came from the shadow of the trees near the burn. He did not look at all like Callum, and yet an odd resemblance was there in his figure, his bearing. I had not seemed to notice before how tall he was. He wore the green Cawdor kilt and stockings, a hazy green tweed jacket that seemed to fade into his background. But there was the blond hair, streaked lighter in parts, from going without a hat, and the strangely brilliant blue eyes. No, Gavin did not look like Callum, except in the familiarity of the way he moved about this terrain, the long easy stride of the hill walker, the economy of movement, the quietness.

"She paid you the supreme compliment, didn't she, Kirsty?— Callum's peregrine—to come back to your hand."

"I have been feeding her . . ."

"That is not everything. I held my breath when she came back. No jesses—no bells. A free creature."

"She had to be free. There is no one else who could manage her. And it is right that she be free. Callum could never bear to be tied. I know I did what he wanted."

"You did it magnificently."

"I was frightened. I was afraid I would bungle it. If the jesses had stayed on, she would have tangled in some tree, and probably hung head down until she died. I could never have forgiven myself for that."

"But you did it—and she is free." He moved closer. I noticed now his pony tethered on the other side of the burn. "I called at Cluain, and Mairi Sinclair told me you had come up here. It is unlike her to part with such information. She keeps such a close mouth, always."

I drew off the glove, and I couldn't help the sigh that came. Was it fatigue after the strain of the effort, the fear?—was it the sadness in the knowledge that both Giorsal and Callum were finally gone?

"None of us is unchanged by these last days, Gavin. Perhaps she had kept a close mouth all these years because of Callum. Now everyone knows he was my grandfather's son. There is less reason for silence at Cluain now—and yet, how silent it is. How unnervingly silent! So quiet that I hear a kind of creaking inside of me. I wonder if it is fear, or loneliness—or what. There is so much to do. And so much I know I did not do in the past, so much I misjudged. Will I do it again?"

He put his hand on my shoulder. "Hush, Kirsty, hush . . . Weep when you must, but do not weep for anything you have done."

"I loved him—I loved Callum. And I should not have."

"No love is ever wasted—or lost. *I* have to keep telling myself that too. *I* have to keep asking myself where I misjudged, where I failed her. But Callum loved you, Kirsty. As his falcon did—in the way that a creature, a near-wild creature, sometimes does. The falcon came back to your hand, Kirsty. Never forget it. It was as if Callum, in the only way he could, was back with you —for that instant. No one should forget such things. And no love should ever be forgotten, no matter what went wrong. It is precious —beyond price."

His tone was soft as he went on. "How does that falconer's rule go . . . something about an eagle for an emperor, a falcon for a queen . . ."

"A king," I corrected him.

"A falcon for a queen, Kirsty. And a queen you are—this territory is yours, just as surely as it is the falcon's. There are those who in nature are noble—you, and the falcon. Not made for mean or small things. They only know great joys and loves—great griefs. When they fly, they fly high and sure and swift. When they fall, they don't stumble, they crash. If they should fall, it is the end— and they accept it. You and the falcon, Kirsty. I can never forget that sight . . ."

I brought Ailis from the stable, and Gavin and I started down the track. It was wild and lovely, as were the high moors and the deeply shadowed glens, and I would miss them. But the girl who had ridden Ailis through all the valley this summer was gone; she had vanished with the fire, and the flight of the falcon. What woman would come to take her place I was not quite sure; a woman of affairs, who would run Cluain as I had promised it would be run, a woman who must now grow larger in spirit, in heart, so that there was not only room for Callum, and William, and—yes, Angus Macdonald—but for the others who would come to join them.

I looked back at Gavin. "Tell Jamie I have a gift for him."

"What is it?"

"I am giving him Ailis."

I was glad he made no protest. Instead he came forward and our two ponies stood side by side. "Ailis will be the most precious thing Jamie will ever possess." Then his hand sought mine—momentarily, a touch only. "And me, Kirsty—will there ever be anything for me?"

I looked, not at Gavin, but upwards, my eyes reaching up, searching for Giorsal; but I got no sight of her. I turned and looked back. The clouds had lifted higher with the wind, and on the highest, farthest fold of the Cairngorms that I could see, what had fallen as rain in the valley the night before, up there lay in a glistening white band, the first snow of the coming winter.

"Who knows? Perhaps in time . . . in time . . ."

Epilogue

So it was that the lands of Cluain and Ballochtorra were joined again through Gavin and myself. That old man, dying so slowly in Edinburgh finally lost his hold on life, and when King Edward VII was crowned, it was I, not Margaret, who had the right to be seated in Westminster Abbey and wear a marchioness' coronet. But Gavin and I were not there; Gavin had never formally taken his seat in the House of Lords, and we had no notion to spend the money for the extravagance of the robes, and the cost of the journey. Nervously, Samuel Lachlan suggested to Gavin that he might be permitted to pay, but we did not even consider it. There was endless building going on at Cluain, and the debt to repay. There seemed not even time for such a trip, even if we allowed Samuel Lachlan to pay. I think he was disappointed; he had looked forward to the gossip we would bring back. We celebrated Coronation Day in 1902 with a picnic on the moors, in a place, not high and lonely, but easily accessible to the road. We went there by trap, because Samuel Lachlan could not walk far, and because I was expecting my first child. Only Jamie talked about his memories of the time when the Prince, who was now the King, had visited Ballochtorra.

But as the children came, Jamie still retained his special place with me—as much loved as they, perhaps even more. He was my link back, through Margaret, to William and to Callum. He had always been a child of grace, and he grew into a beautiful young man. We gave him the tower room at Cluain; I have moved from it into my grandmother's room after Angus Macdonald's death. I wanted no more of the sweeping view of the strath, up to Ballochtorra, down to the river. I think Gavin himself was not unhappy that the other wing of Cluain cut off the sight of Ballochtorra. We both lived with our own ghosts, Gavin and I.

The buildings of Cluain continued, never stopping, never quite ready, it seemed, to take the new season's production of whisky. Two Excisemen and their families came to take the place of Neil Smith, because we were growing so fast. With the loan only half paid off, Gavin and I contracted another one for a second distillery building, with four pots stills. This meant extra warehousing. "Have a care, Kirsty. You will become like James Ferguson," Samuel Lachlan said. But he advanced the money, and we continued to repay him, and to pay the interest. And he continued to come to Cluain, more and more frequently, living on to a great age, as I had predicted. He lived to drink up his own special reserve casks of Cluain's whisky, and the new distilling was a very respectable age before he tasted it. He enjoyed it all, I thought, in his own odd way —the ceaseless activity, the difficulties, the small triumphs. He seemed to enjoy seeing Gavin and I together at Cluain. It was not as peaceful a place as it had been. Young children are noisy, and need room to play, and more servants. Samuel Lachlan didn't seem to mind. They played about him like puppies, and I never forgot the day, not long after I married, when he came to Cluain dressed in heathery tweed, because Jamie had teased him by saying that only rooks went on the moors in black suits. Samuel Lachlan never went very far on the moors, nor for very long, but he loved Jamie. And Jamie seemed to give back that love, unself-consciously. Samuel Lachlan came into the golden age of his life, with Cluain, and love and companionship.

Mairi Sinclair remained at Cluain, but she mellowed only slightly with the years, always retaining that awesome dignity and her own austere habits, even as Cluain changed about her, becoming a hard-used, slightly untidy household of books and pictures, music and flowers. But as my children struggled to stand and take their first steps, I noticed it was her skirt they would reach for, her hand they would clutch, as readily as mine. They grew up respecting her, but without fear of her. In unguarded moments, when I saw her eyes upon each of them, it seemed to me that the anguished hunger of her expression was gone. I came to believe that she, too, lived those years with more happiness than she had ever known.

Jamie finally went to school, protestingly, in Edinburgh, and it was at Edinburgh University he got his degree in science. Samuel Lachlan wanted to pay for him to go to Cambridge, and Jamie had refused. "Edinburgh's best," he said, with youthful chauvinism, "and besides, Cambridge is too far from home." He surprised everyone then, with his degree in his hand, by saying that he wanted to stay on at Cluain and work in the distillery. Samuel Lachlan was doubtful. "It looks well to have an earl's name on the letterhead— but we already have a marquis! Can an earl *work* in the distillery?"

"I'm a chemist," Jamie said, and he went to work. And the distillery workers never called him anything but Master Jamie. "Scotch whisky is becoming *the* world's drink, Mr. Lachlan," he had said, so earnestly, as if we were just discovering the brew. "I want to be in whisky." He worked his full hours in the distillery, and in his spare time he roamed the strath with the pony Samuel Lachlan had given him after Ailis had died, and he fished the river, and hunted the moors. He learned to play the organ from Gavin, competently enough, but without his father's distinction. Samuel Lachlan paid for the organ repairs, when they became necessary. Samuel used to go to listen to Jamie's organ lessons with Gavin, and then began to stay to hear Gavin play. It came late to him in life, that discovery of music.

And then Jamie was killed in the Somme offensive in 1916, and there was a grave in Flanders for him, and only a memorial tablet to mark his name in the kirk at Ballochtorra.

After Jamie's death Samuel Lachlan failed quickly. He loved my children, but he loved none as he had loved Jamie. "I am too old," he said, as he had said when my grandfather had died. "I am too old still to be living, and Jamie was too young to die." Watching the grieving of that old man was worse than Gavin's sadness. I urged him to give up the rooms he clung to in Inverness, his symbol of independence, and come to Cluain. He agreed, after argument, but he did not very long survive Jamie. It was strange

343

to hear his will read, made out so carefully in his lawyer's language. Gavin and I had worked so hard to repay the debt, and the interest—but that was according to Samuel Lachlan's principles, and that was what I had promised. His will, the latest one made directly after Jamie was killed, left his entire estate to me. He was buried in the kirkyard of Ballochtorra, and another granite headstone rose there.

No one ever bought Ballochtorra, though the moors were rented each year for the shooting. Gavin made no attempt to keep it in repair. "Shall I beggar my children to keep up a front that no one needs?" he answered Samuel Lachlan's criticisms of a building falling into ruin. "It started as a small fortress-castle. The rest is James Ferguson's creation. Why should I try to preserve *that?*"

Gavin had had his own satisfaction in the reclamation of the river meadows beyond the bend of Ballochtorra—meadows where cattle as sleek as any Cluain had ever had now grazed.

So the terraced garden of Ballochtorra blurred over with weeds, and young saplings took hold. The putty in the windows dried out, and the panes fell and crashed; the roof began to let in the snow and rain. The ivy crept in. The rooks nested in all the crannies of its crenelated towers, their raucous cries a part of our lives. Almost every Sunday I walked with Gavin and our children through the kirkyard of Ballochtorra, and I saw the granite headstones, and every spring, when the snows thawed, I went to cut the long grass on those graves, and let the wild flowers reach to the light. And every spring I looked for falcons bringing food to an eyrie on the crag of Ballochtorra. I cherished the thought that Giorsal had found a mate, and had made her nest up there somewhere on the rock shelves near where she had been born; I made myself believe that her descendants came back there to mate and to nest. Sometimes I did see the high, hovering speck of a falcon. And I never forgot that overpowering moment of wonder when one of that kind, a peregrine named Giorsal, had clung, willingly, to my outstretched hand. Gavin was right; one does not forget.

And we did not beggar our children; we did not keep up a front. Perhaps we learned, at last, the true meaning of the Cawdor motto—*BE MINDFUL.*